Praise for

SUE MARGOLIS'S NOVELS

Forget Me Knot

"Light and quippy, Margolis's newest is perfectly agreeable."
—*Publishers Weekly*

"A perfect beach read, with a warm heroine."
—Parkersburg *News and Sentinel*

"Amusing...the story line is fun and breezy....This is a fun inane frolic...fans of Sue Margolis will relish the cast's antics."
—www.genregoroundreviews.com

"A wonderful glimpse into British life with humor and a unique sense of style...the characters are vivid and as varied as you can get...as the characters work out their lives, it's great fun to sit back and watch as they bumble through painful situations with humor...If you're looking for a light hearted romance with original characters and lots of fun, look no further...This is one British author that I'm glad made it across the pond and I will definitely be looking for more of her books."
—NightOwlRomance.com

Gucci Gucci Coo

"A wickedly prescient novel...Likeable characters and a clever concept make this silly confection a guilty pleasure."
—*USA Today*

"It's Margolis' voice that separates *Gucci Gucci Coo* from other entries in the fast-growing chick-and-baby-lit category....Her language...is fresh and original....*Gucci Gucci Coo* is a fast, fun read. . . . This is a great book for any smart girl who has ever had to attend a baby shower." —*Chicago Sun-Times*

"This popular British author keeps turning out fun and witty novels that readers will grab off the shelves. . . . Though her previous books have drawn many *Bridget Jones* comparisons, her writing may become the new standard for the chick-lit genre."
—*Booklist*

"If you liked any of Sophie Kinsella's *Shopaholic* books or Allison Pearson's *I Don't Know How She Does It*, you'll like this British take on pregnancy and motherhood. . . . It's a fun, entertaining read and a book you'll pass on to friends."
—Mamarant.blogs.com

"You'll laugh out loud at Ruby's humorous escapes . . . and relate to her many misgivings about her life and where it's going. Ms. Margolis' trademark witty, bright writing style shines through in *Gucci Gucci Coo*. Fun!" —*Fresh Fiction*

"The absurd, good-humored mystery and a colorful array of secondary characters sets this bit of chick lit a notch higher than your typical girl-meets-doctor." —*Publishers Weekly*

"This humorous, personable tale has an added touch of mystery which makes for a fun and enjoyable read. . . . Don't miss *Gucci Gucci Coo*. It's the perfect book for the summer!"
—*Romance Reviews Today*

Original Cyn

"Hilarious . . . Margolis' silly puns alone are worth the price of the book. Another laugh-out-loud funny, occasionally clever, and perfectly polished charmer."
—California *Central Contra Costa Times*

"Delightful . . . Fans will appreciate this look at a lack of ethics in the work place."   —*The Midwest Book Review*

"Has something for everyone—humor, good dialogue, hot love scenes, and lots of dilemmas."   —*Rendezvous*

"A perfect lunch-time book or, better yet, a book for those days at the beach."   —*Romance Reviews Today*

Breakfast at Stephanie's

"With Stephanie, Margolis has produced yet another jazzy cousin to Bridget Jones."   —*Publishers Weekly*

"A heartwarming, character-driven tale . . . a hilariously funny story."   —*Romance Reviews Today*

"A comic, breezy winner from popular and sexy Margolis."   —*Booklist*

"Rife with female frivolity, punchy one-liners, and sex."   —*Kirkus Reviews*

"An engaging tale."   —*Pittsburgh Post-Gazette*

Apocalipstick

"Sexy British romp . . . Margolis's characters have a candor and self-deprecation that lead to furiously funny moments. . . . A riotous, ribald escapade sure to leave readers chuckling to the very end of this saucy adventure."   —*USA Today*

"Quick in pace and often very funny."   —*Kirkus Reviews*

"Margolis combines light-hearted suspense with sharp English wit. . . . Entertaining read."   —*Booklist*

Perfect Blend

ALSO BY SUE MARGOLIS

Neurotica

Spin Cycle

Apocalipstick

Breakfast at Stephanie's

Original Cyn

Gucci Gucci Coo

Forget Me Knot

Perfect Blend

a novel

Sue Margolis

BANTAM BOOKS TRADE PAPERBACKS

New York

A Bantam Books Trade Paperback Original

Copyright © 2010 by Sue Margolis
All rights reserved.

Published in the United States by Bantam Books,
an imprint of The Random House Publishing Group,
a division of Random House, Inc., New York.

BANTAM BOOKS and the rooster colophon are registered
trademarks of Random House, Inc.

LIBRARY OF CONGRESS CATALOGING-IN-PUBLICATION DATA
Margolis, Sue.
Perfect blend : a novel / Sue Margolis.
p. cm.
ISBN 978-0-385-33901-8
I. Single-mothers—Fiction.   I. Title.
PR6063.A635P47 2010
823'.914—dc22   2010008288

Printed in the United States of America

www.bantamdell.com

2 4 6 8 9 7 5 3 1

To Greg, Jack, Don, and Jackie
(House, Bauer, Draper, and Nurse),
who kept me company on all those rainy afternoons
when I played hooky from writing.

Perfect Blend

Chapter 1

AMY WAS ABOUT to slide her front-door key into the lock when her date, the knee-tremblingly sexy, not to mention witty and amusing, Duncan, whom she'd been seeing for three weeks and who had just treated her to seared marinated loin of Scottish venison, celeriac remoulade, toasted hazelnuts, and Parmesan tuile at Le Caprice, drew her toward him, gently cupped her face in his hands, and began kissing her.

It occurred to her that somebody might see, but it was past eleven, and except for Perry Mason summing up at some volume inside old Mr. Fletcher's apartment down the hall, there was nobody about. Amy made no attempt to pull away. As things got steamier in the kissing department, she was in no doubt that her first night with Duncan was going to be perfect. She'd certainly planned it carefully enough. Charlie, her six-year-old, was safely tucked up at his grandmother's. There was Moët in the fridge, fresh linen on the bed, and Space NK jasmine candles on the nightstand.

By now they were giving off enough energy to heat a small town. "Let's move this party inside," he whispered. Just then, Amy's mobile started ringing in her bag.

"Ignore it." Duncan pulled her jacket off her shoulder and began planting kisses across her collarbone. "This time of night is way past the cutoff for calls."

"I'm sorry," she said between soft cries of delight, "but I

really have to take it. It could be Mum. There might be something wrong with Charlie."

He gave a shrug and leaned against the wall, arms folded.

Had she glanced at the number on the screen, she would have seen that it wasn't her mother calling but her best friend, Bel.

"Hi, hon, it's me. Sorry to phone so late, but…"

"Look," Amy whispered, sliding her key into the lock, "this really isn't a good time."

"Oh, God, it was your big date tonight. I totally forgot. So are you and Dan in the middle of things?"

"Duncan. His name's Duncan."

"Sorry. 'Course it is. So are you?"

"Are we what?"

"In the middle of things?"

"Sort of." Amy turned the key, but it refused to budge. Duncan saw that she was struggling and took the key from her. He started jiggling it in the lock but couldn't make it turn either. "I think you need a new lock."

"There's a knack," Amy said.

"Look, I wouldn't have bothered you," Bel continued, "but I'm frantic because I've got the attention-this-vehicle-is-reversing audition tomorrow." Bel was an actress slash automated announcement artist, although she would be the first to admit that she hadn't had any proper acting work in over a year. Bel's most notable work—automated announcement–wise— was her "Mind the gap" heard at all London Tube stations where there was a space between the train and the platform edge. Then there was her highly acclaimed "Power on, select valid mode," which had been taken up by vacuum cleaner manufacturers in nearly every English-speaking country in the world.

"It's only one line," Bel said, "but I can't get the emphasis right. I need your help." As a strict method actress trained in the Stanislavski school, Bel was always looking for her motivation or analyzing the emotional authenticity of a part. In Amy's opinion, this would have been fine if she had been playing Phèdre or Ophelia, but surely such detailed introspection wasn't necessary to deliver lines like "At the rotary, take the third exit." There were people who thought Bel was a pretentious ham. Amy, who had known her since first grade, knew her needless overanalysis was due to a deep-seated fear of failure that had begun at school.

"Okay," Bel continued. "Should it be: Attention, this vehicle *is* reversing...Attention, this vehicle is *reversing*...or...*Attention*, this vehicle is *reversing?*"

"I dunno," Amy said. "What about putting the emphasis on all the words? I mean, it's meant to be a warning."

"You think? What, like a shouted exclamation: *Attention! This vehicle is reversing!*"

The volume of Bel's voice, not to say its pitch, caused Amy to wince. "Yeah, something like that."

"Hmm, that could work," Bel said. "So you think that's better than *Attention*, this vehicle is *reversing*, which I have to admit was my personal favorite."

"I'm not sure. Look, Bel, you'll have to work it out. I really have to go...That's it, Duncan. Harder, harder, jiggle it a bit more. Yep, we're almost there."

"Omigod," Bel said. "I'm thinking that you and I have seriously crossed a boundary here."

"Behave." Amy giggled. "Duncan is trying to open the door to my flat, that's all. The lock's jammed again. Listen, I really do have to go..."

"Okay, speak soon. Love you."

"Love you, too. And good luck with the audition."

Smiling and shaking her head, Amy put her phone back in her bag. She apologized to Duncan for the interruption and explained about Bel being a struggling actress with a heart of pure gold but one who was prone to frequent outbreaks of anxiety-driven neediness.

"It's fine. Forget it," he said, his attention still focused on the lock, which was refusing to budge.

"Here, let me," she said. "I'm used to it."

He stepped aside.

"The trick," she explained, "is to pull the key out ever...so...slightly and then turn...There! Dunnit!" The door swung open.

"You know, I happen to find technically competent women incredibly sexy."

"That's nothing," she said coyly, starting to stroke his cheek. "Charlie will tell you that I'm a whiz with Legos, and I do say so myself that I make the best Play-Doh green eggs and ham in the business."

That made him laugh, and they started kissing again. Barely losing mouth contact, they managed to get into the flat, close the door, and take off their jackets. Finally, Amy kicked off her slingbacks and took his hand. "The bedroom's this way," she whispered.

They had taken no more than a couple of paces when the weird vocals started up in the living room. The door was closed, but they could clearly make out two voices, one male and one female, engaged in soft, perfectly synchronized atonal chanting: "J-lo's bay-gel. Jay-lo's bay-gel. Jay-lo's bay-gel." At least that was what it sounded like to Amy.

Since she recognized the voices, there was no gasp of fear. Instead, her eyebrows knitted in confusion. "What is going on?" Then came the flush of embarrassment.

Duncan seemed mildly amused. "This must be a first: burglars with a sideline in Transcendental Meditation."

"J-lo's bay-gel. Jay-lo's bay-gel. Jay-lo's bay-gel."

Amy managed a thin smile. "I'm really sorry about this. It's my mum and her new boyfriend, Trevor. He's a shaman. They're supposed to be looking after Charlie at her place and taking him to school tomorrow. I can't imagine what they're doing back here."

"What's a shaman?"

"A sort of spiritual healer. I don't know much about it, but they're very in touch with nature, apparently. And they chant a lot."

"Fascinating." Duncan couldn't have sounded less fascinated.

Suddenly, the voices stopped. They were replaced by light rhythmic drumming. After a few seconds Trevor started chanting again. "I'malobster. I'malobster. I'malobster."

Now Amy's mum, Val, joined in: "I'malobster. I'malobster. I'malobster."

AMY OPENED the living room door. Val and Trevor were sitting on her sea grass rug, legs crossed, eyes closed. Val was holding a drum—rather like a tambourine—which she was beating with a wooden stick. Trevor's arms were at his sides, elbows bent at right angles, thumb and middle finger touching.

Trevor was tall and gangly but not unattractive for a man in his sixties—even with the ponytail. He was wearing his usual getup of loose-fitting burlap shirt over baggy cotton trousers. His feet were bare. Around his neck was a Native American turquoise choker with an arrowhead pendant. Amy could understand why her mother found him cool and interesting. While most of the retired men in Val's circle spent their days on the golf course, Trevor went on astral journeys.

Val had known Trevor for a couple of years, ever since she'd started working with him at the local tax office. With his ponytail, he wasn't your average-looking civil servant. Val was intrigued from the get-go. The attraction was mutual, but Val had always been adamant that they'd start dating only after she left Amy's father. Trevor finally declared his love for Val— shortly before his retirement—at a disclosure of tax avoidance schemes seminar in Hartlepool. A couple of months later, he moved in with her.

Val, plumpish, barely five-four in her heels, was still in her work clothes: black pin-striped trouser suit, crisp white shirt. Her patent courts were lying beside her on the rug. Amy had never seen two people who professed to be a couple look less like one.

"Mum, is everything all right? What are you and Trevor doing here?"

Trevor didn't react to Amy's voice. Val, on the other hand, opened her eyes and looked up. "Ooh, I didn't hear you come in. You made me jump. Trevor persuaded me to do some shamanic chanting with him. It's really soothing. I must have been more relaxed than I thought. Don't worry, I made sure that one ear was listening for Charlie."

"But Mum, what are you doing here? And is Trevor all right? He looks like he's in some kind of a trance."

"He's fine. Best not disturb him," Val said with an almost maternal smile. "He's just set off on one of his astral journeys. He won't be gone long. A quick confab with Spirit and he'll be back . . . Anyway, we're here because we had a bit of a domestic crisis at my place. I had water pouring through my kitchen ceiling. Trevor went up into the loft and discovered the tank had burst. We've got no light or water, plus we're not sure if the ceiling's safe. There's plaster all over the place, and it's still coming down. In the end we thought it best to bring Charlie back here. He's sound asleep. Hasn't been a moment's trouble." Val began lifting herself up off the floor, letting out a heartfelt oomph as she went. "I did text you to let you know what was going on."

"Don't worry," Amy said, bending down to pick up the drum and stick, which she handed to her mother. "My phone was in my bag. I didn't hear it. I'm glad you brought Charlie back. Probably the best thing." A beat. Then: "Mum, this is Duncan."

"Hello, Duncan," Val said, giving her daughter a "this one is gorgeous" grin. She shook his hand and said how pleased she was to meet him. Afterward she slipped on her shoes and sat herself down on the leather sofa. "So, Duncan," she said, moving a scatter cushion into the small of her back, "Amy tells me you're an electrician. You know, with this burst tank and water going into the electrics, I could really do with somebody to give the wiring the once-over after the plumber's been. Maybe I could give you a call. What's your hourly rate?"

To his credit, Duncan didn't take offense. A smile hovered on his lips as he started to speak. He had barely uttered a syllable before Amy, cheeks burning, waded in. "Mum, I explained to you the other day that Duncan is a lecturer in electronics at Imperial College."

Val considered this for a moment. "Oh...right. So he doesn't do wiring, then?"

"No," Amy said.

"That's a shame." Her face, which had fallen a second before, suddenly brightened. She turned back to Duncan. "But surely you don't get to be a lecturer in electronics without knowing the basics. And what with the credit crunch, maybe you'd appreciate a bit of freelance work. I'm happy to pay cash." She tapped the side of her nose. "No questions asked."

Amy didn't know where to put herself.

"That's very kind of you," Duncan said to Val, "but to be honest, household electrics isn't my field. You really need a skilled electrician."

"Well, if you're absolutely sure you can't do it. Such a pity. You seem so nice and trustworthy." Val picked her handbag up from the coffee table. "And you don't look anything like I'd imagine an electronics lecturer to look like. No horn-rimmed specs held together with Scotch tape. No ancient woolly full of holes."

Amy watched her mother as she finished taking in Duncan's trendy suit with drainpipe trousers and skinny necktie. "Now, then, don't worry, you two; Trevor and I won't hang around. We'll be out of your way in a tick." She gave Amy a knowing wink. "Trevor and I had a lovely evening. We watched X Factor, and since then he's been seeing to my *prana*."

Duncan seemed unsure where to look. Amy wanted the

floor to swallow her and deposit her somewhere in the vicinity of the earth's core.

"Ooh, no, it's nothing like that!" Val said, suddenly hooting with laughter. "Good Lord no. *Prana* is energy. Trevor has been working on my energy levels."

At that point, Trevor surfaced. He was apparently back from his astral travels. He took a moment or two to come to.

"Hi, Trevor," Amy said, brightly. "You with us?"

He sprang to his feet. "I'm so sorry. You must think me terribly rude. It's just that when you find yourself rising above body consciousness, it's so hard to get back."

"Ooh, I know," Val said, giggling. "Happens to me all the time."

Trevor laughed. "You may mock, but one day I will get you on that astral plane and you'll see what I mean."

"Well, only if I get to go business class." Val chuckled. "I'm not slumming it in coach."

At that point Amy broke in and introduced him to Duncan. For reasons that Amy suspected had more to do with politeness than with interest, Duncan seemed keen to engage Trevor in conversation about shamanism.

"Ah, well, you see," Trevor said, lowering himself onto the sofa and picking up a sock, "the principal function of a shamanic practitioner is to invite the healing process." His tone was gently avuncular, but there was no mistaking his passion. "We call this sacred midwifery. Then, using voice, sound, rattle, or drum rhythm, archetypes arise from the universal unconscious, transforming the splintered psyche into a consistent whole. These tonal substances work their alchemy within the corporeal entity, anointing it with sound—"

"Come on, now," Val said, gently chiding Trevor, who was slipping his feet into leather sandals. "Fascinating as we find it, these two have got better things to do than listen to you going on about your sacred midwifery. I really think we should be off."

"Mum, you and Trevor don't have to go. Not if you don't have any light or hot water. You can sleep here on the sofa bed."

Amy caught Duncan's look of alarm and then his instant relief as Val said she wanted to be at home in case her kitchen ceiling collapsed.

"Right, then," Val said, putting the drum and stick into her outsize patent tote. "We'll be off."

Amy watched Trevor pick Val's jacket up from the sofa and help her on with it. She couldn't remember her father doing that for her mother. Phil was a lot of things, but gallant wasn't one of them—at least not where Val was concerned.

"What a gentleman," Val said, touching Trevor's face. Her expression was one of pure pleasure and delight.

Their goodbyes and nice to have met yous said, Val and Trevor finally took their leave.

A few moments later, Amy was flopping down on the sofa beside Duncan. "I am so sorry about all that."

"Forget it," Duncan said, moving toward her.

"Mum means well, but occasionally she is inclined to get hold of the wrong end of the stick." She paused. "I really ought to go and check on Charlie."

"Hey, come on. What about me? Your mum said he's fast asleep." The next moment he was kissing her on the lips. Amy felt herself gearing up to a full-on make-out session when a little voice piped up.

"Mum, why are you kissing vat man?"

Charlie, eyes heavy with sleep, his two middle fingers in his mouth, his blankie trailing on the floor, was standing in front of them. He began scratching idly under his pajama top.

"Charlie Walker," Amy said, her tone half-scolding, half-soothing. "You should be fast asleep. You've got school tomorrow."

Charlie removed his fingers from his mouth. "I know, but why are you kissing vat man?"

"Charlie, this is Duncan. He's a friend of mine."

"Hi, Charlie," Duncan, said, offering him a smile.

Charlie said hello and turned back to his mother. "Ben at school is my friend, but I don't kiss him."

"I know, but it's different between men and women friends. Now, then, I think it's time we got you back to bed...Say good night to Duncan."

"But I don't want to go to bed."

"'Night-night, Charlie," Duncan said, a slight edge to his voice.

Amy scooped up her protesting son and carried him to his room. She lowered him onto the bed and brought the Spiderman duvet up to his chin. "Now shut those eyes. It's time to sleep."

"My stomach hurts."

"Oh, Charlie, come on...this is just delaying tactics."

"It does hurt. Honest."

"Tell you what, give it five minutes. I'm sure it's just a bit of gas."

He nodded. "I think I've godda fart. Yeah! Great big stinky fart." She left him giggling and blowing raspberries under the duvet.

Amy returned to the living room. "Sorry. The sound of Mum and Trevor leaving must have woken him."

"Hey, you don't have to keep apologizing." Duncan held out his hand and pulled her gently onto the sofa. "Now, where were we?" He pushed down the shoulder of her emerald satin dress and began planting kisses on the tops of her breasts. She let out a gasp of delight. Then his mouth went to hers. She parted her lips, felt his tongue probing hard in her mouth.

"Mum."

Amy and Duncan sprang apart.

"I've puked all over my Spiderman cover. I said my stomach hurt. You didn't believe me. And now I've puked."

Amy saw Duncan take in Charlie's vomit-spattered pajamas and grimace.

By then she was kneeling in front of her son. "Oh, darling,

I am so sorry. You were right and I was wrong." She felt his forehead, but his temperature seemed normal. In a moment, she would double-check it by taking it with the thermometer. "Come on, let's get you out of these sicky PJs." She glanced at Duncan, who by then was standing at the bookcase, going through Amy's CD collection. This was clearly taking his mind off the barfy PJs.

It took the best part of half an hour to hose Charlie down, change his bed linen, load the washing machine, and get out of him that he had been sick not because he was ill but because earlier in the evening, while his grandmother and Trevor were watching TV, he had stolen a packet of sweets from the kitchen cupboard and gone back to his bedroom, where he had demolished the lot.

Amy finally settled him down by reading to him from his *Book of Nonsense Poems.* His favorite was "The Dong with the Luminous Nose," which he insisted on her reading three times. She tucked him in, and for the second time she returned to the living room. She sat down beside Duncan.

"I'm sor—"

"Hey, come on. This isn't your fault." He put an arm around Amy's shoulders. "We just need to think about Charlie and work out some kind of a plan."

"Plan?"

"Yes. I think when two people are at the beginning of a relationship, they need to focus on each other." His fingers were trailing over her cleavage. "You know, like now . . . So why don't you think about farming Charlie out on the weekends? Then I can stay here or you can come to my place, and we won't be interrupted. You've got loads of friends, and then there's your mum and Trevor the shaman. I'm sure you won't be stuck for people willing to take him."

Amy couldn't believe what she was hearing. "I'm sure I won't," she said with a faux brightness that was lost on him.

"Brilliant. We could put them all on a rotation."

"Good idea. Then everybody would know where they were."

"Precisely. So on the weekends we put him in Kiddie Kennels, and in the school holidays there are all these camps he can go to."

"Gosh, how utterly fabulous. I need hardly ever see him, and you get it on whenever you want."

Duncan seemed genuinely nonplussed. "What? No. You've got it wrong. I'm talking about us, not just me."

"I don't think so." Amy removed Duncan's hand from her cleavage and edged away from him. "Look, I agree with you that when a couple are at the beginning of a relationship, they do need to make time to get to know each other. That can take some organizing when one of them has a young child, but the point you seemed to have missed or maybe I haven't made sufficiently clear is that Charlie is my first priority. You need to understand that he and I come as a package. Anybody who wants me has to want Charlie, too. Yes, I have a baby-sitter and my mum is happy to have him for the odd weekend, but he will never ever be *farmed* out. There will be no kennels and no camps."

Duncan responded to her speech with a shrug. "Okay, it's your choice, but if you ask me, you're in danger of turning him into a spoiled brat."

"I wasn't asking you. And while we're on the subject of brats, it takes one to know one. Now I think you should leave." She paused. "For good."

"You're finishing with me? But I really thought we had something going."

"So did I."

"Okay, if that's how you want it." He headed for the door. After a few paces, he turned around. "Look, it really seems a shame to let this go. I really like you. Maybe we could meet up for the odd shag."

"What? I don't believe I'm hearing this. Duncan, just go."

"Why don't you just think about it? I mean, it could suit you, too. You can't get that many offers with a kid in tow."

"Bloody hell! Will you please leave?"

Another shrug. He turned to go. A moment later she heard the front door close.

AMY WAS too angry to get upset. She was furious with Duncan for being such a jerk, but she was even more furious with herself. She couldn't believe that she'd gotten him so wrong, that her asshole antennae had failed her so completely. On the other hand, maybe she had ignored what they had been telling her. Maybe she had been so bowled over by this charming, handsome, sexy guy that she'd chosen to overlook things she didn't want to see—like how on the odd occasion when she mentioned Charlie in conversation, he always changed the subject.

She wandered into Charlie's room and looked down at her sleeping child. His middle two fingers were back in his mouth. He had come into the world sucking those fingers.

Bel and her mother had been with her throughout the ten-hour labor, holding her hand, feeding her crushed ice cubes, urging her like a Greek chorus to breathe and push and then to stop pushing and start panting instead. Her dad had preferred to pace outside. Finally, the midwife placed Charlie in her arms. Her mother and Bel both started to blubber. Her dad called him a "smashing little chap" and a "real bruiser." Amy just gazed at her perfect son. As the process of falling in love with him began, she wondered, as she had during her pregnancy, if it was an act of supreme selfishness to bring a child into the world with only an anonymous sperm donor for a father.

Months turned into years, and he never complained that he had to play soccer in the park with his sissy mum—or occasionally his granddad, who tended to get a bit puffed these days—while the other boys were kicking around with their dads. Even the boys in Charlie's class whose parents were divorced had fathers on the scene who one day would teach their sons about hard drives and electric drills and how to oil a cricket bat.

Back when she was planning to get pregnant, Amy had convinced herself that she could be both mother and father to her child. After all, millions of women brought up children alone and did a great job of it. But as Charlie grew from toddler to boy, she found herself wishing he had a dad.

Of course Amy didn't date men purely to find a father for her son. She wanted somebody for herself. In her twenties, she'd fallen in love twice—with men who had loved her back but weren't ready to commit. The others—the ones who were ready to commit—she hadn't wanted.

Since having Charlie, she'd been on plenty of dates. Once or twice it had even looked as if she was on the brink of a relationship, but even the most decent guys struggled with the thought of taking on a child that wasn't theirs. On the other hand, not one of them had suggested farming him out or putting him in kennels.

She bent down, picked up Charlie's blankie, which had fallen on the floor, and tucked it under the duvet beside him.

Chapter 2

"WEBBED FEET?" AMY raised her voice, partly to be heard over the whiz-rattle of the industrial coffee grinder and partly to register her astonishment. "You're planning to end it with Maddy because she has ever so slightly webbed feet?"

"And hands," Brian said. "Don't forget the hands. I can't believe you haven't noticed. We went out to eat last night, and each time she reached into the bread basket, all I could see was this opaque webbing at the base of her fingers. It was like having dinner with a duck-billed platypus."

Brian Potter, runner-up Barista of the Year, 2009, and owner-manager of Café Mozart, which brackets London and the South East, turned off the coffee grinder, opened the lid, and inhaled. "Whoa!...Get a load of that aroma." He took out a scoop of coffee and held it under Amy's nose. "You should be getting a smoky top note with just a hint of caramel."

"Um, very nice." She had been working for Brian and receiving his expert tutelage for almost a year but still didn't know her Indonesian Kopi Luwak from her Jamaica Blue Mountain. If she was honest, she drank coffee out of habit or to be sociable and could pretty much take it or leave it.

"Nice? That's it? That's the best you can come up with? Amy, this new roast is magnificent. It is the Bentley of beans, the Cristal of coffees."

She decided to stop him before he got to the Saint Laurent of stimulants.

"I cannot believe you dumped Maddy," she said, pulling the cellophane sleeve off a newly delivered tray of croissants and pastries that were still warm from the oven. "She's pretty. She's bright, and judging from the couple of times I've spoken to her, she seems to be crazy about you."

Brian shrugged. "I know. You don't have to tell me." He began spooning the dark roast into what Amy now knew to refer to as the portafilter and not "the metal basket thingy." "But I can't get beyond the webbing. Last night I stayed over at her place for the first time, and in the middle of things she asked me to suck her toes. I totally freaked out."

"So what did you do?"

"I didn't know what to do," he said. "I just lay there, frozen. In the end I told her I thought she had a plantar wart."

"Good thinking, Batman. That must have gone down well."

"Actually, she didn't take it too badly."

The portafilter was now full. Meticulously, Brian leveled off the ground coffee with his index finger. First north to south. Then east to west. This was called "grooming the dose."

The "dose" was made from a bean called Crema Crema Crema, a newly created Arabica grown high in the mountains of Indonesia ("The higher the growth, the harder the bean, the better the roast" was Brian's mantra). It had been developed to produce the ultimate crema, one that contained the perfect balance of vegetable oils, proteins, and sugars and that trapped the coffee aroma better than the crema of any other bean. Recent articles in the trade magazines had been steeped in superlatives. In the United States and Europe, newspaper lifestyle pages had eventually picked up on the "Crème de la Crema" story. There was now a two-month waiting list on both sides of the pond. That included Hollywood A-listers, many of whom, according to the tabloids, were furious at having to line up along with everybody else willing to pay eighty bucks for a pound of coffee. Even at that price, it was selling by the ton.

Brian's order for Crema Crema Crema finally had arrived a

few weeks earlier, but he refused to sell it in Café Mozart until he had "fully familiarized" himself with the bean. This meant that each day after closing time he would stay on at the café for a few hours, determined to turn the coffee into the best possible espresso. The following morning he would furnish Amy with a comprehensive update on his progress. Sometimes he reported that the grind was a bit off and it was a slow pour. Occasionally he got the brew pressure wrong. Amy listened and tried to show interest but didn't pretend to understand the technical details. Finally, this morning, Brian announced that no more experimentation was required. Crema Crema Crema espresso was ready for its debut at Café Mozart. At seven quid a cup, not everybody was going to order it. Brian was relying on his small band of coffee aficionados, the dozen or so customers who shared his passion for the bean and had encouraged him to order it.

Amy, who was now transferring the pastries onto a large stainless-steel platter, paused for a moment.

"While we're on the subject of dumping people, I gave Duncan the heave-ho."

"You're kidding. You really had the hots for him."

She brought him up to speed on the previous night's events. "He actually used the word 'kennels.' I couldn't believe it. Hearing him talk about Charlie that way... it was awful."

Brian grimaced. "What a piece of work. You're well rid of him."

"I know, but..." Her voice trailed off.

"Come on, Ames, there *is* somebody out there for you. I promise. You just have to hang in there." Amy's boss, who had also been her friend for fifteen years, abandoned the espresso machine to give her a hug.

"Bri," she said when they'd finished hugging.

"What?"

"You know, sometimes I wonder if I did the right thing, bringing Charlie into the world the way I did."

"You knew it was never going to be ideal, but what choice did you have?"

"I could have taken my chances."

By that she meant that she could have gambled on not starting menopause at thirty-two as her mother had. Val hadn't been too troubled by her early menopause, an event that her doctors had told her was rare but by no means unheard of. By then she had Victoria and Amy and wasn't planning any more children. Val's sister, Penelope, who had started her menopause even earlier, at thirty, wasn't so lucky. She didn't marry until her late twenties, and by the time she started trying for children, it was too late. Her husband divorced her a few years later and went on to father four children. Auntie Pen fell into a deep depression and never recovered.

The image of a sobbing Auntie Pen being comforted by Val after her husband had walked out never left Amy.

By the time she reached her teens, she was absolutely certain that she wanted to become a mother one day. By her midtwenties, the pressure was on to fall in love, marry, and get pregnant. Victoria, who was five years older, didn't share her sister's anxiety. After leaving Oxford with a first in economics, she'd walked into a job at the treasury. Determined that one day she would rise to permanent undersecretary, she lived and breathed her job and hadn't the remotest interest in having children.

At twenty-nine and with another commitmentphobe on the way out, Amy made an appointment with a fertility specialist. He confirmed what her mother had told her, that because of her family history there was a good chance she, too, might go into early menopause. Since Amy had pretty much known this for years, she'd had time to come to terms with it. Val, on the other hand, shed a few tears and said how guilty she felt about this being her legacy to her daughters.

The specialist said there were two options. Amy could freeze some of her eggs or get pregnant while she still could. Freezing her eggs made the most sense, but she was petrified that something might go wrong. What if the eggs deteriorated for some reason? Suppose the lab where they were being stored burned down and her eggs were destroyed? In the end she decided to get pregnant. She supposed she should have frozen some eggs as a backup, in case she wanted a second child, but she couldn't think beyond this first pregnancy.

She and Bel spent weeks going through sperm donor catalogues looking for the perfect father. "Ooh, what about this one?" Bel would pipe up as if she were in Mac choosing a new shade of lippy. "He sounds megabright. Ph.D. in engineering. Member of Mensa. School spelling bee champion. Hobbies include Sudoku, cryptic crosswords, and trying to solve the Riemann zeta math hypothesis."

"I'm picturing a science nerd with one of those Amish beards with no mustache who probably has advanced Asperger's...Next."

In the end, Amy must have read a hundred profiles. Nobody seemed to possess the genes she wanted for her child. There were the sports jocks (big heads), the wannabe literary novelists (even bigger heads), the trainee corporate lawyers (money heads). The more profiles she read and rejected, the more frustrated she became. She didn't want to be choosing sperm donors from catalogues. What she wanted was to meet a man, fall in love, set up a home, and in time make babies the way normal people did. She didn't want to select her child's father on the basis of his health records, vital statistics, and CV. But that was all she had.

In the end she chose a six-foot blond, blue-eyed, rock music— and comedy-loving marathon runner who was studying for a Ph.D. in political science. She guessed he seemed to tick all the boxes. He was tall and athletic, which meant he was healthy. According to his medical notes, his family had no history of inherited diseases. He was pursuing a Ph.D., which meant he was smart. It was in political science, which meant he thought about the world and had views on how it was run. Of course he could be a fascist Holocaust denier, but that was the chance she took. She hoped that since he was into rock music and comedy, he was pretty gregarious. On the other hand, he could be a sad loner who lived with his parents and spent his free time in his childhood bedroom playing air guitar and watching *Mork & Mindy* reruns. There was so little to go on. It was impossible to *know* this person. What sort of mother didn't know her child's father? There were times when what she was planning seemed like the height of irresponsibility. Maybe she was being selfish, putting her need to be a mother over her child's right to have a father—or at the very least to know his identity. What emotional problems was she storing up for him or her? She'd often heard it argued that people didn't have the God-given right to a child. Maybe they didn't.

Whatever the rights or wrongs, her mind was made up. She was being driven by her body, her biology, her hormones. She needed to parent a child.

Her mum and dad supported her decision but fretted about how she was going to manage as a single parent.

On the day of the insemination, Bel came to the clinic with her. The whole thing was over in a few minutes. Bel suggested to the male doctor that the least he could do was offer Amy a cigarette. He rolled his eyes—but not without humor. He'd clearly heard it a thousand times before. As Amy lay on the bed with her legs raised "to help the sperm along," the first twinge of excitement hit her. "Omigod, Bel. Do you realize that I might have just made a baby?"

She had. Forty-two weeks later, Charles Alfred Walker came into the world, sucking the middle fingers on his left hand. By the time he was three, he was asking Amy why he didn't have a father.

When Amy explained about the mummy's "baby-making egg" getting mixed with the daddy's "baby-making seed" he was clearly confused.

"But I don't have a daddy."

"I know, poppet. That's because the daddy is usually the

mummy's husband. I don't have a husband. Instead, a very good and kind man gave me his baby-making seeds and they helped to make you."

"So I do have a daddy."

"Yes, but not one who is part of our family."

"Why didn't he want to be part of our family? Were you nasty to him?"

"Oh, no, darling. I wasn't nasty, and nor was he. Like I said, the man who helped make you was a very kind man. He gave away his seed to help me become a mummy, but he has his own family."

"Will he ever come and visit?"

"No, darling. He won't."

"But I want to show him my drawings. He wouldn't have to stay. He could go home again. I wouldn't mind."

Hearing him say this always reduced her to tears. Then she would kneel down and hug him. "I know you wouldn't, sweetie, but seed-giver daddies don't visit. That's just the way it is."

During those conversations Charlie became thoughtful and sad, but only for a few minutes. Being six, he was easily distracted. Amy knew this wouldn't last. The day would come when he would turn on her and blame her for not providing him with a proper father.

BACK IN the café, Brian was kissing Amy's forehead. "Okay, here's an idea. How's about we make one of those pacts where we agree to marry if we're still single at forty? I mean, you're a beautiful woman. I could do a lot worse."

She gave his arm a playful slap. "Idiot. You'd run a mile if I said yes, and you only suggested it because you know full well I never would."

He turned down the corners of his mouth and pretended to be hurt. Then he grabbed a pain au chocolat off the tray and bit off a massive chunk.

Although Amy had worked at Café Mozart only since

Charlie had started school, she'd known Brian since university. They'd both majored in English at Sussex and had shared a grotty student house with three others in Brighton just off Lewes Road. One night during the first term, finding themselves alone in the house, they'd gotten drunk and ended up naked on the sofa. Despite being young, good-looking, and horny as hell, their activities fell short of penetration. It wasn't simply that Brian had been too pissed to rise to the occasion. Deep down, they both knew that although they clicked personalitywise, there was no real sexual chemistry between them and that they were destined to become friends rather than lovers.

Amy's thoughts returned to Maddy. "You know, Bri, you can't go on like this. You've dumped four women in as many months. Each time it's the same story. One minute you're telling the world you've found the love of your life; the next you're ending it because she has a mole or big nostrils."

"I know," Brian said, clearly exasperated by his own behavior. "You think I don't get it? I mean, it's not like I'm exactly God's gift." He ran his hand over what had lately become a noticeable gut.

"Oh, behave," Amy chided gently. "You are a great-looking bloke. You just need to lay off the pain au chocolat and spend some money on yourself, that's all."

At that point they both joined in with what had become a familiar chorus: "All my money goes back into the business."

If Brian found it hard to understand what women saw in him, Amy didn't. Despite plumping up ever so slightly, he could still pass for a decade younger than his thirty-six years. His round fresh face, brown puppy dog eyes, and hamster nest hair made him appear boyish and vulnerable. There was a certain type of woman who loved to mother him.

Brian adored being adored. He made no secret of it. These days he was in therapy, and he had come to understand that his neediness was tied up with his parents' deaths. They had been killed in a car crash when he was thirteen. Brian's father had been driving them to their accountant's office in Greenwich. They had been called in for urgent talks about their printing business, which was about to go bust. Friends and relatives suggested that they committed suicide, but the police reports ruled that out. Their deaths had been an accident. Brian received a decent insurance payout but no inheritance.

He admitted to Amy that his parents' screwing up their business and failing to provide for him had left him angry but determined to succeed.

Amy suspected that it was the loss of his mother that had affected him the most. Even though he was now a grown man, in some ways he was still a boy looking for his lost mother. It occurred to Amy that this might be one of the reasons his sartorial choices hadn't changed as he'd gotten older and he still dressed like a grungy teenager. Today, for example, he was wearing his usual uniform of low-slung jeans, tatty Converse with fluorescent green laces, and a zip-up hoodie over a Vandelay Industries T-shirt. Years after the series had ended, Brian remained a *Seinfeld* nut and had all the shows on DVD. One of a handful of people in Britain who had taken to the series, he had spent the whole of 1997 tagging "giddy-up" to the end of his sentences and perfecting Kramer's style, skidding to a stop at room entrances and demonstrating his moves to his baffled friends.

Some women loved Brian's style. Lucy—two girlfriends ago (continuous eyebrow)—confessed how much she loved smelling Brian's hair and running her fingers through it. In Amy's opinion—not that she had shared it with Brian for fear of upsetting him—his sweet-scented thicket needed thinning and layering by somebody other than Jack Dash of Tooting Broadway (police informant slash coiffeur), who charged clients a tenner for a cut and finish. When she looked at Brian's locks, it was clear that Jack always got called away on police informant business before actually finishing his hair.

Having unpacked and arranged all the pastries on platters,

Amy began slicing one of the lemon drizzle cakes. She swallowed as her taste buds responded to the citrus aroma. At the other end of the counter, Brian had just picked up another coffee-making apparatus: the tamper. This was a metal disk with a red-painted handle. Amy watched him press down on the coffee in the portafilter. Thirty pounds was the requisite pressure. He had practiced this maneuver so many times that she would have put money on it being precisely the correct pressure. Apparently, tamping eliminated any "voids in the coffee bed." Amy had learned that there was a debate among baristas about whether to tap the side of the portafilter between tamps. Some believed it had the beneficial effect of dislodging a few coffee grains that may have gotten stuck to the sides. Brian, on the other hand, believed tapping could break the seal between the coffee and the portafilter. He was an impassioned nontapper and made no apology for it.

Ever since Amy had known Brian, he'd been a man of enthusiasms and passions. While other students were merely "in to" Karl Marx, Brian became totally immersed. Late into the night, Pink Floyd blasting from his room, he read and reread *Das Kapital* and *The Communist Manifesto.* He could quote lengthy sections with the zeal of a Bible-bashing evangelist. " 'Capital,' " he would proclaim to his housemates, who were usually sprawled out in the living room watching daytime soaps, " 'is dead labor, which, vampirelike, lives only by sucking living labor, and lives the more the more labor it sucks.' It's so simple. I can't believe I never saw it before." When he failed to get his friends' attention beyond "Shuddup, *Quincy's* just getting to a good bit," he would stomp off, muttering, "Lackeys of the bourgeoisie," as he went.

In the third year, the didgeridoo arrived. Brian had spent the previous summer backpacking in Australia and claimed that the three-foot-long wind instrument made from the hollowed-out wood of a eucalyptus tree had been conferred upon him by an aged, leather-skinned Aboriginal wise man whose family had used it for generations to summon up the healing spirit of the Light Dreaming Man. It wasn't until years later that Brian confessed to having bought it at the airport gift shop.

Not only was he overcome with the desire to play the instrument, he wanted to play it like an Aboriginal. Among other things, this meant perfecting "circular breathing," which enabled him to make a continuous sound without giving any indication of having taken a breath. Brian went to great lengths to find books on didgeridoo playing and spent his last year at university, when he should have been studying for his finals, honing his skills. The low blasts could be heard from the street. Passersby must have thought somebody was keeping a farting hippopotamus in the house. Brian always ignored his housemates' pleas to pipe down. They got back at him by regularly going into Brian's room when he was out and confiscating the didgeridoo. On his return, he would be reduced to hunting for it under beds and on top of kitchen units like a truculent five-year-old who'd been punished for vrooming his toy cars too loudly.

"My shrink says I have intimacy issues," Brian continued now, alluding to his decision to dump Maddy. He reached for another pastry. Amy attempted to slap his hand, but he dodged her and grabbed a prune Danish. "She reckons that my parents dying when I was so young means that I'm reluctant to get close to women in case they abandon me. Instead of hanging around to see what happens, I find an excuse to end it before they leave me."

"But your gran brought you up after you lost your mum and dad. She never abandoned you."

"No, not until she died last year." He took a bite of the Danish and started chewing. "As an adult it's really hard telling people that you're pissed off with your poor, sick old gran for dying, but I was furious with her."

Amy nodded. "I can understand that," she said gently. "So that would explain why your problem with women began so recently." She paused. "Okay, how about this for an idea? Now that you know what's causing you to end relationships before they even start, maybe you should try going on a few more dates with Maddy and see if you can get over these feelings."

Brian swallowed. "That's what my shrink said."

"I think she's right."

"But they're such powerful feelings. Do you really think it's possible to overcome them?"

"Who knows? But I think you should at least give it a try."

He wrinkled his face and shoved what remained of the pastry into his mouth. "I dunno..."

"Oh, come on. You're being asked to spend a few more hours in the woman's company. Nobody's suggesting you marry her."

He shrugged. "Okay. Why not? I'll give it a try. I'll carry on seeing Maddy and see how I feel in a couple of weeks."

"Great. You won't regret this."

"I wish I had your confidence," he said, latching the portafilter onto the espresso machine and switching on the pump. After a few seconds, dark viscous droplets of coffee were falling into two tiny cups.

"Just look at it...the color of a monk's robe."

Now he was examining the crema and smiling with approval. It appeared that the hallmark of a great espresso was as it should be: a light golden foam. He cut through it with a spoon, and it immediately came back together. He handed Amy one of the white porcelain espresso cups, optimum storage temperature forty degrees Celsius. "Taste that," he said, triumph in his voice. "What do you think? Tell me honestly."

She took a sip. "Um, well, it's definitely very coffee-flavored."

"Omigod, eight months under my impeccable tutelage and the woman still has the palate of a plankton. How am I ever going to make a barista out of you?" He brought his cup to his lips and closed his eyes. Amy watched as he swirled the liquid around in his mouth before swallowing. "Full, velvety, smooth texture, slightly acidic. No bitter aftertaste...a flavor that lingers. Truly magnificent."

Given the choice, Amy would always choose hot chocolate over coffee. To her, the bitterness of coffee didn't compare to the sweet, heady aroma of really good hot chocolate.

Sometimes, on a damp, slate-sky winter's afternoon, when it was too cold and miserable to go out, she would make hot chocolate for herself and Charlie. First she would melt the very best unsweetened dark chocolate with a couple of tablespoons of water so that it didn't stick to the pan. When it was thick and glistening, she added full-fat milk and sugar. The smooth, chocolaty brew was so thick, you could almost stand a spoon up in it. Then came the bit Charlie loved best—the spraying of the whipped cream. Now that he was old enough and had the strength in his fingers to press down on the aerosol squirter, Amy let him do it on his own. They would both collapse with laughter as he inevitably lost control and the cream spurted over him, over her, over the worktop—over everything except the hot chocolate.

After she'd wiped Charlie down, the two of them would curl up on the sofa with their mugs and a large bowl of marshmallows and watch *Toy Story* or *Chicken Run*.

UNTIL AMY came to work for Brian, he had always refused to serve hot chocolate. He looked down his nose at any beverage that came in instant, powdered form. He even had no time for the fuller-flavored, less sweet upmarket brands of hot chocolate. On the other hand, parents kept asking for it on behalf of their children, particularly in winter. So, one morning when things were quiet, Amy went out and bought a couple of bars of her favorite French chocolate. "Okay," she said to Brian after she'd performed her magic and turned it into a thick, velvety brew, "try this. We are talking ninety percent cocoa solids here." After the ritual inhaling and mouth swirling, Brian was forced to admit it wasn't half-bad.

Amy even persuaded him to add whipped cream (he insisted on it being nonaerosol) and sprinkles and call it Bambinocino. The kids adored it, and so did their parents. To make it more sophisticated for the adults, Amy stirred in freshly ground cinnamon and nutmeg.

As a result of Brian's supreme effort and dedication—not to say obsession with producing the perfect espresso—people flocked to Café Mozart. Proud as he was, he freely admitted that running a neighborhood café was his plan B and that it didn't come close to fulfilling his ultimate dream.

Brian's plan A was to open a trendy, upmarket coffeehouse in Soho. He'd first attempted this at the beginning of 2009, but even in a recession, leases in central London cost a fortune. Brian still had a few thousand left from the insurance payout he'd received after his parents died. The bulk of it had gone to pay for his private education and university. Brian's gran had also left him some money in her will, a little over fifteen thousand pounds. There was no money tied up in her house because it had always been rented. The inheritance, together with his own nest egg, meant Brian could finally give up his job in logistics—which had never been a match for his talents—and set up his own business. Had the economy been booming, he would have sunk all his money into his dream, but since there was a good chance the project could go belly up, he needed to keep some money back as a buffer.

In the well-to-do inner London suburbs south of the river, commercial property still didn't come cheap, but it was just about affordable. So it was that in June 2009, Brian pitched his tent in Richmansworth, aka Nappy Valley, an urban village full of thrusting young bankers and lawyers (their thrust apparently undiminished even in these troubled times), their skinny blond, Ugg-booted wives, and their gorgeous straight-toothed, glossy-haired children.

Compromising on location meant Brian was forced to do

the same thing when it came to branding. Café Mozart wasn't a proper coffeehouse. That is to say, it didn't resemble those hard-core London coffeehouses the likes of which Brian dreamed of presiding over, where funky, edgily coiffed Japanese baristas dressed in black presented customers with a cup of espresso on a little wooden tray with a glass of water to freshen the palate and, for afterward, an exquisite froufrou pastry so tiny that it was almost invisible. A family neighborhood—even a discerning one like Richmansworth—couldn't have sustained such a niche business. Instead, Café Mozart was a traditional café-boulangerie that served the best breads, pastries, and coffee for miles around.

But as Brian was always telling Amy, he hadn't given up on his dream. Because it was the only decent coffee and cake place in the neighborhood and because it was in a great position, only a few hundred yards from the Tube station, Café Mozart was weathering the recession rather well. When the business had made enough money, Brian planned to leave it in the hands of a manager while he set up his new, intimidatingly trendy coffee-house in Soho or maybe somewhere in the East End.

"Wow, I can see it all," Amy would tease him. "A glass and steel twenty-first-century salon, nameless save for your signature elegantly carved at the bottom of the heavy, rough-hewn wooden door, filled with writers, artists, and intellectuals composing haikus on their MacBooks while engaging one another in earnest discourse about the state of the planet."

"You may mock," Brian said, smiling and wagging his finger, "but when Potter's Coffeehouses take off in London, Manchester, and Edinburgh, you will be laughing on the other side of your face."

Amy could hear the certainty, the familiar determination in his voice, and decided he might well be right.

CAFÉ MOZART was part of a row of Victorian shops that overlooked the common. Like the rest, it had an ornate fascia, which had been immaculately restored and painted. It was sandwiched between the organic butcher—catering to a clientele that even in a recession thought nothing of spending the best part of a hundred pounds on a piece of sirloin—and a gift shop specializing in Cath Kidston flowery wellies, Alessi kettles and juicers, and cashmere cardigans for newborns at seventy quid a pop.

The café had been there since the eighties. Since then, the place had been bought and sold maybe half a dozen times, but nobody had ever changed the name. This was probably because it was such a well-known local landmark that changing it was considered bad for business. Brian had seen no reason to break with the tradition.

Decorationwise, he had done very little to the place beyond giving the interior a lick of white paint and installing a fancy-schmancy espresso maker.

Brian was less than keen on the interior. The last people to own Café Mozart had run it as an organic vegetarian restaurant and had decorated it in a way that reflected their wholemeal lentil ethos. He summed up the stripped wooden floors, pews, and pine dressers in one word: "hummusy." It was all a million miles from his ultimate steel and glass fantasy. Whereas Brian couldn't wait until he had enough money to update the interior, Amy, to her surprise, found that she rather liked it. For Amy, interiors weren't so much a hobby as a passion. She was always fantasizing about how she would redesign and decorate her flat if only she could afford it. Her style, like Brian's, veered toward high-tech minimalism, but every instinct told her that that wasn't right for Café Mozart. This wasn't Soho. This was a family neighborhood, and people were looking for a place that was warm and inviting. In Amy's opinion, the old wood gave the café precisely that feel. She loved the mellow yellow stripped and polished floorboards, the original white marble fireplace. She saw character in the scratched and dented stainless-steel counter that ran down one side of the room. She particularly liked the mix of old wooden tables, pews, and chairs, not one of which matched. "At least people don't feel intimidated coming in here," she'd said to Brian. And it was true. From half past eight in the morning until five when they closed, the place was buzzing.

Amy would get to work around eight, having dropped Charlie off with Ruby, the child minder. Ruby would take him to school, along with the six-month-old baby girl she looked after and her own children—twins who were the same age as Charlie and in his class. Ruby was an amply bosomed earth mother type who treated Charlie like one of her own. Even though Charlie adored her and loved playing with Ed and Flora, Amy hated not being able to take him to school in the morning and pick him up at the end of the day.

But she had no choice. The only way she could support herself and Charlie was by working.

Now that Charlie was at school full time, she could have gone back into PR and earned a great deal more than what Brian was paying her, but she was adamant that she wanted a job that meant she would be home each day by half past five. That way she got to spend a full two hours with Charlie before bedtime. A couple of hours wasn't much, but if she'd taken a job in PR similar to the one she'd had before she'd left the business, she would hardly have seen Charlie at all.

As a senior PR executive at Dunstan Healey Fogg, one of the country's top public relations firms, Amy had earned a six-figure salary, plus a commission on the new accounts she brought in. For that she put in ten-hour days and attended after-work dinners, launches, and events, one or even two of which happened most nights. Even on the weekends she was going to parties and networking in an attempt to land juicy accounts. It wasn't unusual for her to get home from an awards do at midnight on a Friday and be on a flight to Nice first thing the next morning. A few hours later she and a hundred other guests would be sipping Cristal on some oligarch's yacht that looked like it had been interiored by Paris Hilton and Liberace's ghost. The following day, having charmed the pants off a dozen CEOs, she and her BlackBerry would be on a flight home, ready to start the whole process again on Monday morning.

When she was a teenager, Amy's plan had always been to get her degree and then find a job with a charity. When she and her sister were growing up, their parents had always impressed upon them the importance of "giving something back." Amy's mum did her bit by volunteering a couple of afternoons a week at a local charity shop and gave it up only when she started working full time. Even now, one Saturday a month, her dad stood outside Marks & Spencer on the High Street and shook a Save the Children Fund charity box. Amy couldn't remember a time when she wasn't aware of Third World poverty and hunger.

When she and Brian were students and he was going through his Marxist phase, she frequently would accuse him of ignoring the fact that many of the people dying from hunger and dirty water lived under so-called Marxist regimes. That was a red flag to Brian's Marxist bull. Suffice it to say that he didn't take kindly to her analysis.

After graduating, Amy started looking for a job, but it seemed that money was tight and few of the big charities were taking on new staff. She applied for anything that came up, only to be told over and over that there were twenty applicants for every job and most of them had previous experience, even though none was required. She didn't get a single interview.

Then a friend from uni who had a job in PR told her that Dunstan Healey Fogg was looking for a junior account executive. The job appealed to Amy because the company had several charities on its books, for which they acted pro bono. At her interview it had been made clear that if she was offered a job with DHF, they would allow her to assist with some of those accounts. Two years after starting work with the company, that still hadn't happened. When she asked why, her bosses said that since she was showing huge promise, they weren't about to waste her talents on accounts that generated no revenue.

Instead they used her talents to counsel apparently happily married male celebs who had been caught in bed with a couple of rubber-clad rent boys with pink ostrich feathers sticking out of their G-strings on how to handle the media. When she wasn't doing that, she was planning the launch of another Hollywood A-lister's insipid new fragrance or exercise DVD.

She often thought about leaving, but it was hard. It wasn't the money, although she had to admit to her shame that she had grown accustomed to expensive haircuts and being able to buy a pair of shoes or a bag simply because it took her fancy. The real reason she found it difficult to leave was that she was very good at her job and enjoyed the praise that came with that. What was more, the job involved writing, and that was something she had come to love.

Until she came to DHF, Amy had no idea how good a writer she was. While she was at Sussex, she'd penned several pieces for the student newspaper on famine and the need to abolish Third World debt. After each piece appeared, students and tutors alike complimented her on her clear thinking and well-constructed arguments, but nobody mentioned the actual writing. Then, when she started work at DHF and hard-nosed journalists who usually made a point of binning press releases on receipt began seeking her out at press launches to congratulate her on her witty, attention-grabbing missives, it occurred to her that she might have a flair for writing.

She also had a flair for coming up with wacky, offbeat ideas for media campaigns and launches. Amy's "blue-sky thinking" was legendary at DHF. Pretty soon, she was rising through the company at a rate her bosses all agreed was extraordinary.

Then DHF got into financial difficulties. One of the directors started taking out huge loans, which he used to invest heavily in the stock market. That wouldn't have been a problem had he not used his shareholdings in DHF as security. No sooner had he been sacked than three of the fledgling companies he'd backed went bust. This meant that the bosses at DHF were forced to honor their former partner's bank loans to the tune of several million pounds. It was inevitable that redundancies would be made. Since Amy was one of their most highly favored employees, they held on to her as long as they could, but in the end she was just too expensive and they had to let her go.

What the directors at DHF never knew was that Amy, while by no means delighted to have been sacked, wasn't quite as devastated as she might have been. Her substantial payoff combined with her savings meant she could put her plan into operation. She could have a baby.

She moved to a cheaper part of town and bought a ground-floor garden flat in a Victorian house. At the same time she started cutting back on expensive clothes and luxuries. By doing this, she had gotten by for over six years.

By the time Charlie started school, she had set her heart on becoming a journalist. Time and again she wished she had gone into the profession straight from university, but back then she'd had no idea that she could write.

If she hadn't been so set on getting pregnant, she would have tried breaking into journalism after leaving DHF. Back then it wouldn't have been so hard because she still had all her media contacts. In the last half dozen years they had disappeared. The journalists she once knew had moved on or lost their jobs in the recession. There was nobody to schmooze over lunch and ask if he'd put in a good word for her with his features editor.

She realized that without contacts it would be well-nigh impossible to get her foot on the journalistic ladder. On the other hand, she had nothing to lose by trying.

After Charlie started school, she spent the first few months scouring the local papers for stories that might interest the nationals. She followed up articles on dodgy time-share deals and

Spanish property developers conning people by selling them nonexistent apartments on the Costa Brava. She wrote a piece about debt collectors terrorizing the ill and the elderly, who it often turned out weren't even in debt. This piece had been based on her elderly neighbor Mr. Fletcher, who had spent months trying to convince British Gas that he didn't owe a preposterous two thousand pounds for three months' worth of gas. Despite letters going back and forth from poor old Mr. Fletcher to British Gas, the company had "sold" the debt to a firm of debt collectors, and he was now being pursued and threatened by, as he put it, "shaven-headed yobs built like brick shithouses." The fear had taken its toll, and he was taking pills for his nerves.

The Mr. Fletcher story almost made it. *The Daily Mail* even sent a photographer to take his picture. Then a weather girl Amy had never heard of gave birth to quads, and Mr. Fletcher was forgotten.

She carried on pitching ideas. Some editors replied to her e-mails. Most didn't. The ones who did usually said she was thinking along the right lines. The only reason they weren't using the piece was that they had covered the story a few weeks earlier. Then Amy would feel stupid and kick herself for not keeping herself up to speed with what was appearing in the papers. Occasionally they paid her for a tip or idea but refused to let her write the piece. *The Daily Mirror*, for example, loved her idea for a feature on the pros and cons of breast-feeding but insisted it be written by some woman who had recently given birth on *Big Brother*.

Occasionally, when she submitted an on-spec piece, an editor would get back to her to say how well written it was. This at least made her feel she hadn't lost her touch writingwise. Then came the "but." "But families living on the breadline is so boring." "But the whole antifur thing just is so 2001."

She was earning nothing and her savings were dwindling, as was the romantic image she had of herself as a freelance journalist who spent school hours penning meaningful pieces on social injustice.

When Brian mentioned that one of his staff had just left and asked if she fancied coming to work for him, she practically bit his hand off. The hours were perfect, the traveling time was minimal, and with what remained of her savings she could just about manage on the money Brian was paying. She decided that she would continue bashing away at the journalism in her spare time.

ZELMA ALWAYS got in at the same time as Amy. Their first job was to unpack and put out all the pastries, cakes, and breads, which were delivered fresh every morning from Konditorei Wiener, along with thick, rich deli-style pizzas and savory French tarts. Next they would start filling baguettes and ciabbatas. Ripe fig and Gorgonzola was Amy's favorite filling, closely followed by farmhouse pâté and cornichons.

Each morning until eleven, pots of homemade jam, marmalade, honey, and organic butter were left out on the counter so that customers could help themselves. Since the café was self-service and there was no hot food to prepare, the three of them could cope. Brian was the full-time barista, but when things were quiet, he would happily pitch in with Amy and Zelma, serving food, clearing tables, and loading the dishwasher.

BY NOW Amy had finished slicing the lemon drizzle cake and had turned her attention to the richly frosted carrot cake.

"Where's Zelma?" she said to Brian. She had just looked at her watch and seen it was a quarter past eight. "Not like her to be late."

Brian didn't seem too bothered. "Her bus probably got stuck in traffic."

Mrs. Zelma Cohen had been with Brian virtually since Café

Mozart had opened. A Help the Aged representative had been visiting small businesses in the area, trying to persuade them to take on retirees. Brian didn't hesitate. The café had been open a few weeks, and he'd taken on two gap-year students to help run it. It turned out that both of them preferred sleeping to showing up for work and were clearly aiming at a gap life. Having decided to let the students go, he found himself warming to the idea of employing somebody older and reliable who possessed a decent work ethic.

Since a true lady never revealed her age, Zelma kept hers strictly to herself, but Amy and Brian agreed she had to be seventy. A tiny, birdlike woman, slightly stooped, she would arrive every morning dressed to the nines. Anybody passing her on the street would have said she was off to take morning coffee at the Savoy. Her honey-gold bouffant 'do was always immaculately frosted. Clotheswise, she favored Chanel-style suits with tiny jackets and pencil skirts, the kind that once had demanded a pillbox hat to set them off. The soft knitted, round-necked jackets were edged in braid and had chunky gold buttons on the breast pocket and down the front. They did up courtesy of tiny chains. Underneath she always wore one of her trademark chiffon blouses with a pussycat bow. She accessorized the suits with good patent shoes and matching, roomy handbags. Her lips were always precisely the same shade as her nails, which were painted every week by "a wonderful girl who comes to the house."

Since the sixties and until she retired a few years ago, Zelma had worked in the same Marble Arch dress shop—Maison Sandrine in Seymour Place. With a faraway look in her eyes, she never tired of telling Amy how she had "met them all, darling: Lauren Bacall, Grace Kelly, Judy Garland—even the chief rabbi's wife...the one we had decades ago, not the one we've got now. Now, she was a real lady...a bit saggy on top, but she looked a knockout once we got her into a decent bra."

Zelma had no need to work. Her late husband, "My Sidney, God rest his soul," had left her well provided for, but Zelma was bored at home. She missed "going to business." "It would be different if I'd been able to have children," she would say, looking soulful. "Then there would be grandchildren to visit and spoil, but it wasn't to be."

She had been perfectly honest with Brian about how she knew next to nothing about the catering industry, but Zelma turned out to be a quick learner, not to mention a great saleswoman.

When a customer—usually a young woman—ordered a skinny cappuccino and nothing else, Zelma would step in. "Excuse me, miss," she would pipe up from behind the counter. "If you don't mind me saying so, you look like you could do with a little something inside you." Only Zelma—because she was old and motherly and utterly charming—could get away with this.

The woman wasn't allowed to take her coffee and sit down until Zelma had taken her on a tour of all the wonderful bready comestibles on offer. "Now, then, what about one of these cream cheese bagels, maybe? I tell you, these aren't your usual supermarket bagels. Oh, no. These are the old-fashioned traditional bagels. We have them brought in every morning from Golders Green. I call them the real McOy-veh!" At this point she would pause for laughter, but none ever came because Café Mozart, being south of the river, wasn't exactly overrun with Jewish customers. "You'll have one? Good girl. With a slice of smoked salmon, maybe? You need your fish oils. It's brain food... Yes? Excellent. Now, then, let me show you our coffee and walnut cake. I tell you, darling...this...this is to die for. Melts in the mouth. It's like angels dancing on your taste buds. You'll have a slice? Wonderful. A slip of a girl like you can afford to put on a few pounds. What are you, a size six?"

And she wasn't even on commission.

BY NOW Zelma was forty minutes late. Brian and Amy were starting to get worried. "Two years she's worked here," Brian said, "and she's never been late. She's such a stickler for punctuality." He paused. "God, what if something's happened to her? I mean, she's not getting any younger."

Just then there was a tap on the door. They could both see Zelma's agitated outline through the frosted glass. Brian went to open the door.

"Darling, I am so sorry I'm late," Zelma gasped, barely able to catch her breath. "I've run all the way from the corner." She paused for a moment, hand clamped to her chest, before stepping inside. "I tried phoning your mobile, but you weren't picking up. I can't bear letting people down. Not when they're relying on me."

Brian said his phone was probably on silent. "Zelma, it's okay. Take it easy. You haven't let me down. You're only a few minutes late."

"No, I'm not. I should have been here forty-three minutes ago. You should have opened up by now, and I've made you late. You're losing money because of me."

Brian told her not to be so daft, and Amy took her arm and led her to a chair. "Now sit down and tell us what happened," she said.

Zelma lowered herself onto the chair. "Bus strike."

Amy and Brian both looked out the window at the stream of buses passing by.

"No, there isn't," Brian said. "There are plenty of buses."

"I know. I know. You don't understand. When I woke up this morning, I turned on the wireless, and the announcer said there's a one-day bus strike, so I decided—since I don't live near the Tube—that I couldn't get to work. I thought about phoning for a cab, but I didn't bother because I assumed they'd all be booked solid. Anyway, after breakfast I pottered about for half an hour or so. When I went back upstairs to get dressed, the radio was still on, and this time there was a different announcer talking about this bus strike. I started listening because I was waiting for *Thought for the Day* to come on—they've got Rabbi Goldman from my synagogue on all week—when the announcer says the strike is in . . . Warsaw. I was listening to the World Service instead of Radio 4. I don't know how it could have happened. I'm so sorry. I wasted all that time messing around at home when I should have been on my way here."

Amy and Brian immediately started hooting with laughter and agreed that it was one of the funniest stories they'd heard in ages.

Zelma seemed perplexed. "But Monsieur Etienne at Sandrine's would have sacked me for something like that. Back in the sixties, us shop girls used to have to clock in, and if we were more than five minutes late, that was it. You were out on your ear."

"Well, this is not Sandrine's and I am not Monsieur Etienne. You are totally forgiven. Now, how about a cup of something before you get started."

Zelma said she'd have a milky tea—coffee gave her palpitations—but if it was all the same to Brian, she'd prefer to get started straightaway. With that she took off her pink tweed suit jacket and pulled her neatly folded overall out of her bag. "So," she said to Amy as she slid an arm into the sleeve of her overall. "How did it go last night with that new man of yours?"

Amy explained. Zelma sighed and patted Amy's hand and told her not to worry, as there was plenty more kasha in the knish. Amy laughed and said she didn't have the foggiest what that meant but she got the picture.

Zelma patted her hand. "Every lid has a pot," she said before calling out to Brian, who was in the kitchen. "So, darling, how you getting on with Maddy?

"Not so good."

She exhaled heavily. "So what is it this time? A big nose? Bandy legs?"

"Webbed feet," Brian came back.

Zelma gave an exasperated shake of her head and turned to Amy. "I'm telling you, that boy needs to find a new head doctor, because the one he's seeing isn't doing him any favors."

. . .

TEN MINUTES after opening, Café Mozart was filling up fast. It was the same every morning: foggy-headed folks on their way to work queuing for large, double-shot espressos to bring them around. The men would also take a croissant or pain au chocolat to go. The women might have an organic smoothie or, if Zelma had worked her magic on them, a slice of buttered wholemeal toast. A few people would sit down with their coffee and grab one of the newspapers off the rack. Café Mozart provided *The Times, The Guardian, The Independent,* and *The International Herald Tribune.*

Mega-earning alpha mummies with four children under eight, a house refurb, and a UN peace deal on the go would dash in, their Burberry cashmere coats flying. Somehow they managed to order coffee and search through their purses for the right change while conducting frantic conversations on their mobile phones, usually with the nanny. "Look, Tracy, I've just this second realized that I've forgotten the going-home bags for Oscar's birthday party tomorrow. Be a darling and pop into John Lewis and pick up thirty Nintendo games. Get whatever you think the kids are into. I'll send a courier over to you with my charge card."

THERE WERE a fair number of Café Mozart regulars. First there were the authors, journalists, and other media types who worked from home and came in after the early-morning rush with their MacBooks and sat sweating over articles and TV proposals. Several took a real interest in the coffee. They were lavish in their praise of Brian's espresso and often broke off from what they were doing to ask him about the provenance of this or that blend. Like him they referred to "complex" noses and "astringent, lingering" aftertastes.

Amy couldn't help noticing how the journalists—inevitably

on a deadline—stabbed the keys on their laptops far too hard and kept looking at their watches, after which they always muttered "fuck" or "bollocks." She could almost feel their adrenaline and couldn't help feeling jealous. She'd approached a couple of them for advice about breaking into journalism, but each time the message was the same: With the recession, freelancers were struggling across the board. Payments were lower now than they had been ten years ago. A couple of them were kind enough to give her the names of people she could speak to about doing the odd shift. She e-mailed and left voice mail messages, but nobody got back to her.

OF COURSE, it was the mothers who kept Café Mozart going. Without Richmansworth's stay-at-home mummies, Brian couldn't have survived. They arrived each morning, after the school run, in small posses. Some would be minus children, having deposited their entire brood at the school gates. Others were accompanied by babies and toddlers. The toddlers always made a dash for the play area in the corner, which Amy had created and filled with books, puzzles, paper, and crayons. Part of the wall had even been covered in blackboard. Brian had needed a good deal of persuading to give up a table for six and turn over the space to children, but he didn't regret it. The play area had proved so popular that the mothers stayed longer and spent more money.

As the women chatted and fed pastries to their squawking offspring, they rearranged the furniture to make room for more mothers, nannies, and their buggies. Pretty soon—courtesy of the buggies, tricycles, and dolls' prams—it was practically impossible for Amy and Zelma to squeeze between the tables. They had to wait until everybody was gone before clearing all the coffee mugs, plates of half-eaten croissants, and plastic water and fruit smoothie bottles—not to mention the bits of baby detritus that got left behind: beakers, feeding bottles, dummies, barf-covered muslins.

The mothers and babies were gone by just after eleven. Then Brian would put something soothing on the DVD player—Greig, maybe, or Tchaikovsky. Cue the arrival of arty media types. There was another rush at lunchtime, followed by a brief lull. Then, just after half past three, the mothers were back. This time, though, they were accompanied not only by babies and toddlers but by their irritable school-age children in desperate need of a sugar fix in the form of hot chocolate and a piece of cake.

It was then that Amy missed Charlie even though she knew that at that very minute he was probably blissfully happy watching Nickelodeon with Ned and Flora and stuffing his face with Ruby's homemade brownies.

AMY KNEW most of the mothers by sight and often got to chatting with them while she was taking orders or clearing tables. To look at, Richmansworth mothers weren't much different from the women she'd made friends with since moving to Debtford. They tended to be the type of nicely brought up English girls who had been taught that it was vulgar to flaunt one's money. To that end they wore the same Gap jeans, T-shirts, and Converse sneakers as Debtford mothers. It took a second glance to spot the clues to their wealth: a Tiffany diamond heart necklace here, a Burberry tote there, a Joseph cashmere poncho, albeit bobbly and covered in baby barf. Their hair might be in need of a wash and scragged back into a ponytail, but a closer look confirmed that the blond highlights were subtle and expensive-looking. Their Ugg boots were always genuine and never cheap imitations.

Their conversation was another clue. They chatted about summer holidays, which were taken in rented villas in Brittany or Tuscany. They skied at Easter. Their vehicle of choice was a seven-seater SUV. They all knew these vehicles used too much fuel and discharged filth, but hello—how else were they going to get the whole family plus luggage down to the Devon manor house they were renting for the school holidays? They attempted to make up for their yeti-sized carbon footprint by using organic cotton shopping bags that declared "I Am Not a Plastic Bag."

In Amy's part of South London, there wasn't much money and Tiffany was just a girl's name. Anyone conducting a social survey outside Charlie's school would have found young single mums living on state benefits, unemployed dads, and young professional couples, many of them working in lower-paid public sector jobs such as nursing and social work. There was also a smattering of Labor MPs who took the view that if one represented the working classes in Parliament, one should live among them.

If you discounted the hippie-dippy women with their waist-length graying hair and children called Windsong and Patchouli who had fried their placentas with onions after giving birth and never went anywhere without their Rescue Remedy and Gingko biloba, on the whole Debtford folk were down-to-earth types who holidayed under canvas or in rented RVs and served spaghetti Bolognese and bottles of Tesco £3.99 Sauvignon at their dinner parties.

It wasn't just money that separated Debtford women from their Richmansworth neighbors. In Debtford nobody criticized a working mother for leaving her children with a baby-sitter or at a nursery. It was assumed that she needed to work to pay the bills. By the same token, nobody accused women who chose to stay at home of not fulfilling their potential or letting down the sisterhood.

It wasn't like that in Richmansworth. There, as in many other middle- and upper-middle-class areas, stay-at-home mothers and working alpha mothers were practically at war.

A stay-at-home mummy—role model: Angelina Jolie, motto: "The best academy, a mother's knee"—believed that by being permanently available, she was raising well-adjusted children who would blossom into delightful, angst-free adolescents and emotionally stable adults. So she devoted her time to finger painting and making low-sugar wholemeal cupcakes with her brood. She fed them a careful balance of carbs, protein, and vitamins. She was also a firm believer that small children shouldn't become overburdened by too many after-kindergarten activities. Her kids were encouraged to pursue destressing pastimes such as kiddie yoga, Kindermusik, and tending the plants at the Tots Herb Garden.

An alpha mummy—role model: the former prime minister's wife, Cherie Blair (lawyer, author, mother of four), motto: "In it to win it"—believed that by combining motherhood with a high-flying career, she was achieving the goals that her teachers and university tutors had set down for her. Moreover, she was proving to the next generation that it was possible for women to have it all. "Discipline" and "determination" were her watchwords. The first thing an alpha mummy did after giving birth was phone her CEO. These days she was on the treadmill by six, making shopping lists at half past, and on the phone to the Shanghai office by seven, checking the Far East markets. These mothers lived to work. Their offspring—twin boys being coached for Eton, a pretty girl with a part in the new *Harry Potter* film—were simply another project, to be managed and organized with the same steely efficiency and determination that they used to pull off a takeover or merger.

Because an alpha mummy believed that free time was wasted time, her children were made to fill their after-school hours with mind-improving activities. The nanny was constantly ferrying them between Mandarin, chess club, and Suzuki violin.

Amy assumed that apart from school functions, alpha mothers and stay-at-home mothers rarely met. Their paths certainly didn't cross at Café Mozart since the alpha mothers were already at their desks by the time the stay-at-home mothers arrived. Their mutual loathing was, of course, well known. God forbid the two groups should ever lock horns. Amy imagined naked mud wrestling with briefcases and breast pumps flying.

Of course, it went without saying that jealousy was

responsible for the groups hating each other. Amy would have put money on there being nights when both sets of women cried themselves to sleep, each craving what the rival group had. She had no doubt that despite the day and night nannies, the gardener and the housekeeper, life for alpha mothers wasn't as remotely glamorous as it was thought to be. Alpha mothers knew that "having it all" came at a price. That price was permanent exhaustion, and guilt about abandoning their children.

Amy suspected that the SAHMs cried because they were bored. After another day spent attempting to soothe cracked nipples and tantrumming toddlers, they surely craved the intellectual stimulation that work provided.

She knew from listening in on their conversations that many SAHMs felt they had let themselves down by abandoning careers that as women they'd often had to fight for. These women had hung on for as long as they could before getting pregnant. Now they were knocking on forty. If they stayed at home until their babies started secondary school, they would be fifty—far too late to pick up their careers.

Amy had no intention of waiting until she was fifty. She was aware of how important it was to break into journalism now, before it was too late. And if she freelanced, she would have the luxury of being able to work from home and set her own hours.

By a quarter to twelve, there was only a handful of customers left in the café. Things would stay quiet for twenty minutes or so. Amy was in the kitchen, wiping down surfaces. Zelma was next to her, loading the dishwasher. She held up the bottle of detergent. It was almost empty. Amy said she would nip out and get some more.

"You sure, darling?"

"Positive. I need to pick up something for supper, anyway."

Amy pulled on her jacket and took her purse out of her bag. As she walked through the café, she noticed that Brian was sitting at one of the tables with a chap in a fashionably crumpled linen suit. They were having an intense discussion about Crema Crema Crema. There was much sipping and swirling and uttering of superlatives. Amy decided that Brian wouldn't thank her for interrupting him to ask if she could have some petty cash to pay for the dishwasher detergent. She would pay for it, and he could refund the money later.

The early summer breeze felt warm on her face. Underneath the car fumes, there was a hint of freshly mown grass. She turned her head toward the common and saw a chap in his shirtsleeves driving one of those sit-on motor mowers. She watched him for a few moments phut-phutting over the grass while mothers and dog walkers called out to their charges to keep out of the way. Aware that she was squinting in the bright light, she thought about going back for her sunglasses, but she couldn't be bothered. Instead, she set off down the road. She paused at the posh organic butcher and looked in the window. She had a hankering for lamb chops. Then she saw the price and moved on. They would be far cheaper at the supermarket. On the other hand, there was a deli a few doors down. Maybe she would get a couple of portions of lasagne. That and beef casserole were Charlie's favorites. She smiled as she remembered the first time she had offered her son dumplings with his casserole and he had refused them on the grounds that it was cruel to the ducks. Months later, she was still having to reassure him that baby ducks weren't called dumplings.

She decided she would pick up the dishwasher detergent and call in at the deli on the way back. As she set off again, it occurred to her that she hadn't spoken to her dad in days. She really ought to give him a call and see how he was doing.

Even though it had been months since her parents' breakup, Amy still found herself moved to tears when she thought about it. Ashamed as she was to admit it, she was upset mainly for selfish reasons. Despite her being a grown-up, her "child within" felt bereft. As a couple, Phil and Val had always been strong and united. With a few exceptions, which had had more to do with Victoria's upbringing than with hers, they had been great parents. They had always been her soft place to fall. Of course, as individuals they would always be there for her, but it wasn't the same somehow.

Val had left Phil on the grounds that he never really spoke to her, took her out, or told her he loved her. According to Val, he was interested only in the business, his newspaper, and watching football. "One of the things that attracted me to your dad," Val told Amy shortly after the split, "was the way he cared about all the injustice in the world, but in the end he didn't care about the person closest to him."

Val had always owned a tiny terraced cottage in Clapham. She used to live there before she married. Until recently she had rented it out, but when her last set of tenants moved out in January, she moved in.

The other day when Amy went to visit Val, she'd heard her on the phone to her best friend, Stella. Apparently, prior to her leaving Phil, they hadn't had sex in months. "And when we did do it, there was never any foreplay. It was a case of brace yourself, Val, I'm coming in." Amy had cringed and hotfooted it into the kitchen to make Charlie's lunch.

There was no doubt in Amy's mind that her father had treated Val badly. In recent years, she couldn't remember her parents having a proper conversation. She was aware that Val tried to engage Phil in discussions about things she'd read about or heard on the news, but mostly—probably because he considered her interests trivial—he just grunted from behind his paper. Their conversation rarely went beyond Val asking him what he wanted to eat, which of them was going to phone the bloke about the guttering, or whether those briefs and socks strewn on the bedroom floor were destined for the wash or another wearing. Amy couldn't help thinking that if she'd been Val, she'd have walked out, too. But Phil was still her dad. She loved him to bits. He'd always taken a massive interest in her life—without interfering—and wanted to know her news.

They had proper conversations. Whenever she walked into the living room, he would immediately put down his paper or turn off the TV. His face would light up at seeing her. If she had a problem, he made time to listen. He was exactly the same with Victoria. It always upset Amy to think she had such a good relationship with her dad while he neglected Val, but if her mother was jealous, she never said a word.

Now that he was on his own, Phil was pretty much living on takeaway curries and KFC. The last time Amy visited, they'd sat in the kitchen. The area by the back door was covered in empty beer and wine bottles. Amy asked him if he missed Val. "I've been missing her for years," he said, desperate sadness in his voice. "Ever since she went back to work when you and Victoria were teenagers. From then on, she became so independent, always out with her friends from her book club. She didn't need me anymore. I know I treated her badly. I admit that and I'm sorry, but I just couldn't get over this feeling that I was superfluous to her requirements."

"That's ridiculous," Amy said, trying to be gentle. "Of course she needed you. She wanted a companion, somebody to talk to and make a fuss about her, tell her she was still beautiful, show her he loved her."

"Well, she's certainly got that now." He took out a boil-in-the-bag kipper and dropped it into a pan of water.

AMY TOOK her phone out of her jacket pocket and tried Phil's mobile. When there was no answer, she tried the office. Phil Walker owned a builders' merchant. As a young man, he'd had no plans to go into the family business. Instead, he went to university, studied sociology because it was trendy, and planned a career working with deprived inner-city children. Then his father had a heart attack and died. It was the mid-1970s and the country was in recession, with most of the population on a three-day working week. Even though the business was struggling, Phil didn't have the heart to wind it up and sack the staff, who had been loyal for decades. He took it over, sat tight, and prayed.

Back then it was a small business on the outskirts of a pretty Surrey village. In the early eighties the village expanded. It began to draw soap stars, C-list TV presenters, soccer players, and their wannabe model actress wives—all of them in urgent need of bricks, cement, and mock Grecian pillars for their new McMansions. The word on the new gated developments was that Walker's was the place to go. Phil was earning several times what he would have made as a social worker, and by then he and Val had a huge mortgage. (For some reason, maybe because even then she saw it as a potential bolt-hole, Val refused to sell the Clapham cottage.) It was too late to follow his dream. He was never going to "make a difference." He relieved his guilt by giving up a Saturday morning once a month to rattle a collecting box in the High Street. It wasn't much, but by then things were so busy at work, he was putting in twelve-hour days. It was the best he could do.

"Hello-Walker's-Chantelle-speakin'-how-may-I-help-hew?" Another ditzy, singsong temp on reception.

"Oh, hi, this is Amy, Mr. Walker's daughter. Is my dad there?"

"Can I ask with what it's in connection with?"

"Excuse me?"

"Can I ask with what it's in connection with?"

"I'm his daughter, Amy. That's the connection."

"Oh-right-I-see. Bear with me. Trying to connect you." Cue "Greensleeves." "Sorree, Mr. Walker isn't at his desk at present. Can I be of help to yourself?"

Suddenly Phil came on the line. "Hello?"

"Oh, you are there. It's me, Ames. Nothing important. I was just ringing for a chat and to see how you are."

"I'm fine. Really good. Listen, sweetheart, it's sweet of you to phone, but I haven't got time to talk. I'm on my way out and

I'm running late for an important meeting. I'll speak to you later. Love you."

The phone went dead. That was odd. Her dad never had meetings. His accountant came twice a year to go over the books, and that was about it. She'd temped at Walker's often enough during her university vacations to know that his day involved e-mailing or phoning suppliers. When he wasn't doing that, he was dealing with builders who came in; ordered fifty kilos of cement or bricks; trashed the Prime Minister, the state of the economy, or the latest Russian oligarch to acquire a newspaper or soccer team; paid cash; and left. Where could he possibly be going? Still, he sounded remarkably chipper. That made a change.

Tesco was just off the main drag, opposite the Tube station. A few doors down was the old Odeon cinema, its elegant geometric Art Deco facade faded and flaking. Having been closed for years, the building was being redeveloped. It was covered in scaffolding, which butted out onto the pavement. This meant that pedestrians were forced into a narrow covered walkway in the road. As Amy stopped to let through a woman pushing a twin buggy, she noticed a sign attached to the scaffolding. It was the familiar brown and cream coffee bean logo that caught her eye. BEAN MACHINE COMING SOON, the sign read. What? This was the first she'd heard of it, and she was certain Brian knew nothing about it. He would be up in arms if he did.

Amy wasn't just shocked. She was mystified. Everybody knew that the old Odeon building was being developed as office space. The town council had sent the plans to all the local businesspeople and invited them to raise objections. As far as she knew, there had been none and the plans had been approved. This had happened months ago. Contracts would have been signed with the office developers. How on earth had Bean Machine been able to claim the space? Amy could only assume that the original developers had pulled out, leaving Bean Machine free to march in and make the council a financial offer it couldn't refuse.

However it had come about, the imminent arrival of Bean Machine was the worst possible news. Amy was no doom-monger, but there was a recession on. Café Mozart was doing okay because the coffee and food were so good. But it wasn't cheap. She had no idea how the café would fare, faced with competition from a corporate coffee giant whose prices were so much lower.

By now the woman pushing the buggy had gone by. Amy emerged from the scaffolding tunnel. As she reached the entrance to the old cinema, she slowed down. The building was massive, she thought. Way too big for a coffee shop. It made no sense.

Just then she noticed a man about her own age standing in the doorway, his gray suit accessorized by a yellow hard hat. He was carrying a clipboard and jotting down notes. Amy went up to him. "Excuse me, I'm sorry to bother you," she said, happening to notice that he was writing on paper with a Bean Machine letterhead. "But is Bean Machine really opening here—in this building?"

He looked up at her. "Yes. Underneath the new offices."

So Bean Machine was sharing the space. That made sense. "Bloody hell," Amy murmured. Talk about the perfect spot. Not only would Bean Machine cater to all the office employees upstairs, its position opposite the station meant it would grab all the commuters. Brian would lose all his early-morning trade. And since the mighty Bean Machine could afford to undercut Brian's prices by miles, it would probably steal most of his other trade, too.

Amy asked, "Do you happen to know when Bean Machine is due to open?"

"A few weeks. The moment the builders move out, the shop fitters move in."

"I see. As soon as that."

She must have looked troubled because the chap asked her if she was all right.

"Yes, I'm fine." She offered him a meek smile and carried on toward Tesco.

She bought the dishwasher detergent, but in her rush to get back to Café Mozart, she completely forgot about picking up lasagne from the deli.

In the end, she decided to wait until the lunchtime rush was over before telling Brian about Bean Machine.

By half past two the place was empty. Brian was standing behind the counter, talking on his mobile. He was trying to get through to the biscotti people to find out why the weekly order hadn't arrived. Zelma was sweeping the floor. She never did it when customers were around because she felt that it put them off their coffee and cake.

Amy hovered, waiting for Brian to finish his call. Eventually he flipped down the lid on his phone.

"Bri, have you got a minute? I need to talk to you."

"Sounds ominous," he said, shoving the phone into his jeans pocket.

When she'd finished telling him, he seemed confused more than anything.

"But I've had no letter from the council. If another coffee shop were opening so close, I might well have the right to raise a formal objection. Are you absolutely sure about this?"

Zelma, who had been eavesdropping, came across and said he should get on to the "authorities" and demand to speak to the "head one."

"Look," Amy said, "the guy I spoke to was from Bean Machine. Surely he should know. And there was a bloomin' great sign up."

Brian ran his hand through his thicket of hair. "Bean Machine is a huge multinational. They can undercut us by at least twenty or even thirty percent. We're fucked."

"Excuse your French," Zelma said, "but why don't you just undercut them?"

"I can't afford to," Brian came back. "I only buy the best

fair-trade organic beans. They don't come cheap. My profit margin is as low as I can get it."

"Look, darling, if it would help, I have a few thousand I could lend you. Then you could bring down your prices."

Brian managed a smile. "Thanks, Zelma. I really appreciate the offer, but it would take more than a few thousand quid to compete with Bean Machine."

"But an organic, ethically sourced product matters to some people," Amy piped up, desperate to say something reassuring, even if she didn't really believe it. "We might lose a few customers, but the rest will stay loyal, I'm sure. And our food is fantastic. Have you ever tasted a Bean Machine cheese food and Marmite panini?"

"Come on, Amy, get real. There's a recession on. People are only interested in the bottom line." He rubbed his hand over his chin. "God... and it's opposite the Tube. We'll lose all our early-morning trade. That's it. It's over. I may as well sell out now. Bloody hell, I'm going under, just like my parents did."

"Brian, you are not your parents. Believe it or not, going bankrupt is not genetically inherited. Look, I admit things don't look great, but you have to stop panicking. Something will work out. Why don't you phone the council and check if you have the right to appeal?"

The next moment he was back on his mobile, dialing information to get the number of the council's planning department. While he waited to be connected, he disappeared into the kitchen. Five minutes later he was back.

"They said that everybody has been informed that the ground floor of the old cinema is being given over to Bean Machine. I never got the letter. Not that it matters because the council's position is that even in a small neighborhood like this, there is enough trade to go around." He paused. "So... short of Bean Machine pulling out of this deal, we are stuffed."

"Nonsense," Zelma declared. "You mustn't even think of giving up. I mean, what would have happened if the hemorrhoid people had stopped at Preparation G?"

"Or...or...Chanel had stopped at No. 4?" Amy added.

Brian wasn't about to be jollied along. He looked as if he might burst into tears. "God would never let me be successful. He'd kill me first. He'd never let me be happy."

"That sounds vaguely familiar," Amy said. "It's a famous quote, isn't it? Who said it? I bet it was Nietzsche or one of those other miserablist philosophers."

"Nope. George Costanza."

Chapter 3

MICHELANGELO WAS SUFFERING from wet bottom. Amy had spotted his soggy rear last week and taken him to the vet. He had prescribed antibiotics, but they weren't working. Michelangelo's condition was getting worse. A few moments ago, when she went into Charlie's room to check on him, the hamster "in a half shell" was lying curled up in a ball, barely moving. Amy had read up on wet bottom. Left untreated or if antibiotics were ineffective, it was pretty much fatal. There was no hope. In a few days Michelangelo would be a goner.

She decided to transfer the cage to her bedroom. She didn't want Charlie waking up one morning to find Michelangelo stiff as a board. As she walked down the hall, she wondered how to break the news that his ninja hamster was at death's door. He'd asked her a few months ago what "dying" meant, and she'd told him what her mother had told her when she was little—that dying happened to very old or sick people and it meant they went to a special place called heaven to be looked after by God. Of course, then he asked her who God was. "Oh...kay...well...God is good and kind and looks after all the people and creatures on the earth."

"You mean like Mr. Incredible?"

"Yeah...a bit like Mr. Incredible."

Charlie had finished his supper—in the end they'd had take-out pizza—and was sitting at the kitchen table drawing, his crayons spilled out in front of him. In an effort to assuage her guilt—this was their second takeout in less than a week—Amy brought the fruit bowl over and offered him a nectarine.

Charlie shook his head. "Bucket!"

Bucket was their code name for sweets. It had started last Christmas. One of Val's more modest presents to Charlie had been a load of mini chocolate bars that came in a small plastic bucket.

"Listen," Amy said, "you threw up last night because you ate too many sweets. You had pizza for supper. Your body needs a rest from junk. Now, how about I slice you up a pear and a banana?"

"K." He wasn't pleased, but he didn't try to argue.

She went to fetch a plate and a knife. When she came back, she sat down at the table opposite her son and began peeling the pear. "Poppet, there's something I need to tell you."

He looked up from his drawing—an impressive purple shark with a fiendish green eye and red teeth.

"It's about Michelangelo. I'm not sure those tablets the vet gave us are working."

Charlie nodded. "Is he going to die?"

She reached out and put her hand on her son's. "I think he might."

"K."

"That's very sad, isn't it?" He didn't say anything. She kept her hand on his and waited for the tears. But none came. Instead, there was just a shrug.

"He's boring," he said, taking his hand out from under his mother's. "All he does is go around on his wheel. You can't play with him." He went back to his drawing and added a huge fang. She sat watching him color in the fang, unsure whether she was relieved or disturbed by his reaction.

"Well, anyway," she pressed on, "I want you to know that if Michelangelo dies, he won't be in pain anymore and he'll go to hamster heaven. He'll be with all the other hamsters, who will help God look after him. And maybe we could bury him under the apple tree in the garden. Perhaps you could make up a special prayer."

"Mum?" He was still coloring in the fang.

"What, darling?"

"When Michelangelo dies, can we get a snake?" He was looking at her now, his eyes darting with excitement.

Amy shivered. She'd had a thing about snakes ever since she was a child and a neighbor's pet python escaped. One night she overheard her parents discussing how it might find its way into the sewers. Twenty-five years later, there were still times when she was sitting on the toilet and found herself thinking about the never-recovered Spike and how even after all these years the gaping-jawed creature could have found his way to Debtford and be lurking in the waste pipe, poised to rise up into the toilet pan. "What? No. I'm not having a snake in the house."

"Oh, please. Tom in my class says you can get these small ones that eat real live mice and stuff. He knows 'cos his brother's got one."

"Charlie, we are not getting a snake and particularly not one that gets fed live food. That is disgusting."

"Okay, what about one that eats dead food?"

"No, not even one that eats dead food. Maybe we should think about terrapins."

"Bor-ring." He paused. "So is that man from last night coming to our house again?"

Ah, so Duncan was playing on his mind. She wasn't surprised. Seeing her kissing him last night must have stirred up all kinds of emotions. She needed to reassure her son that he was still number one in her life.

"Actually, I won't be seeing him again. We're not going to be friends anymore."

"Why?"

"It's complicated."

"Why?"

"Okay, I decided I didn't really like him, after all."

"I don't like Katie Miller anymore. She's in my class, and she smells. All girls smell. Did Duncan smell?"

She thought about her response. "You know what," she said, her face breaking into a grin, "he sort of did smell."

"Of poo?"

"Well, not exactly..."

"Pooey Duncan!" Charlie squealed with laughter.

She waited for him to stop. "Charlie, do you want to talk about how it felt when you saw me kissing Duncan? I know it must have seemed a bit weird, but I just want you to know how much I love you and how important you are and how I will always be here."

"Can I watch my *Shrek* DVD?"

Amy blinked. "Sure. So there's nothing troubling you? There's nothing you want to talk about?"

"Just the snake. Maybe we could go and see one in the pet shop. Please?"

"Charlie, I've explained to you that we're not having a snake."

"You are so mean."

"Oh, and I've moved Michelangelo into my room so that I can keep an eye on him in the night."

"K."

With that he jumped down from the chair and stomped off into the living room.

"IT'S LIKE he can't wait for Michelangelo to die," Amy said to Bel a couple of hours later, "so that we can get a snake." Bel had popped around, bearing Sauvignon and Sonic Sour Cream Doritos to celebrate landing the "attention this vehicle is reversing" gig. Her high spirits didn't last long, though. After a couple of glasses of wine, she became positively maudlin and started bemoaning the fact that she hadn't had a "proper" acting job in months, not since she'd played Third Crone in *Macbeth*. "I just don't know where my life's going. Maybe I should accept that I'm never going to hit the big time and get a real job."

"Like what?" Bel wasn't the type who could cope with having a boss. She had "authority" issues and could be lippy to people who tried to give her orders. Plus, her London bus red hair and piercings—ears, nose, and navel—and her current penchant for superskinny drainpipes and four-inch platforms meant she couldn't exactly walk into a job in the average HR department.

"I suppose I could always move to the country and open a post office. I love the outdoors."

"Since when?" Amy said. "For you the outdoors is the bit you have to pass through to get from your place to the nearest Mac concession."

"Maybe I should change my image," she said, looking down at her nails, which were coated in black polish. "You know, lose the hair color. Develop a more sophisticated look. Or maybe I should think about changing agents."

In the end, they both agreed she should carry on as she was and hope that her big break would come sooner rather than later.

Bemoaning over, they spent the next ten or fifteen minutes discussing Brian and Bean Machine. Finally they got around to Charlie and the snake. "And he wants to watch it eat live mice," Amy continued. "You could practically see his mouth watering. Meet my son, the six-year-old psychopath." She picked the wine bottle up from the kitchen table and topped up their glasses.

Bel started laughing. "Oh, come on, you've read the child development books. All six-year-olds are psychopaths."

"Yeah, I know," Amy said. "They haven't yet developed the imagination to appreciate suffering in others."

"Of course it's worse in boys. My brother Gavin was still pulling the wings off flies when he was sixteen."

They decided to take their drinks into the living room, as it would be more comfortable. As they passed Charlie's room, they could hear his gentle snoring. Bel insisted on taking a peek at her favorite (and only) godson, whom she hadn't seen in all of three days. The two women stood at the end of Charlie's bed. His fringe was damp with sweat and stuck to his forehead. As usual, his blankie was on the floor. Amy picked it up and put it next to him in the bed and went to open the window a crack.

"Aw, look at him," Bel whispered. "That cute little face has barely changed since the day he was born. And look how he still sucks those same two fingers."

Charlie loved Bel because she possessed a childish, playful streak. When they bounced together on the garden trampoline, there was so much whooping and squealing that it was hard to tell which of them was enjoying it more. Bel could sit on the floor with him for hours building Legos and get really enthused about what they were building. When she read to him, the actor in her created voices that charmed and transported him.

Bel often said how she couldn't wait to become a mum. Her problem was finding the right man. She tried to deny it, but her friends all agreed that she wasn't the world's best picker.

They sat on the white IKEA sofa, which—courtesy of Charlie clambering over it in his sneakers all the time—was considerably less white than it had been three months ago when Amy bought it.

Amy put her wineglass to her lips. "Omigod, I cannot believe I haven't told you my big news. What with all the Bean Machine stuff, I actually managed to forget...I dumped Duncan."

"What? But when I rang last night, you seemed to be going at it like a pair of stoats. What happened?"

Amy explained.

"He wanted to farm Charlie out every weekend, just so's he could get laid? What a piece of work." Bel gave a shudder. Then she took her friend's hand and gave it a squeeze. "Ames, I'm so sorry. This is really crappy—just when you thought you'd found a decent bloke...but you have to hang in there. Your time will come."

Amy gave a doubtful smile. "That's what Brian said."

"Well, he's right...What pisses me off most about this whole Duncan thing is the way men can be so selfish and not see anything wrong with it." She took a glug of wine.

"So you'll be wanting to put your boyfriend's dirty laundry in my machine, then," Amy said, grinning at her clever and insightful segue. But Bel failed to pick up on it.

"Yeah, do you mind? My machine's on the blink again. I'm waiting for the bloke to come and fix it."

As well as bringing wine and Doritos, Bel had lugged around two carrier bags of washing. Mark, whom she had been seeing for a couple of months, apparently saw nothing wrong in dumping his laundry on his girlfriend. Bel owned a washing machine, he didn't. QED. When Amy suggested to Bel that Mark take his smelly socks and underwear to the Laundromat, she made excuses about his crazy work schedule and how the poor soul simply didn't have time. She used the same excuse to justify schlepping across town to his place most nights and cooking for him.

Bel often talked about how much she enjoyed "looking after" Mark. She would come over and plan dinner menus or try to convince Amy that ironing a man's shirts and underwear was a gesture of love and affection. As she listened, Amy started to feel as if she'd slipped through a gap in the space-time continuum. She half expected Bel to morph into one of the stiff-skirted, chain-smoking wives in *Mad Men* and start discussing Tupperware and Avon ladies.

Amy's silence must have betrayed her thoughts.

"Look," Bel was saying, "I am not some surrendered girlfriend, okay? I like doing things for him, that's all."

Amy held up her hands in defense. "I never said a word."

If appearances were anything to go by, Bel couldn't have looked less like a surrendered girlfriend. As well as the London bus red, chin-length bob and the nose and ear studs, she was wearing chunky ethnic bangles and rings on every finger. At five-ten, with her huge emerald eyes and elfin face, she could carry it off the same way she could carry off the drainpipe jeans and orange patent platforms.

It wasn't just her looks that made her appear anything but put upon. Bel was one of the most independent and spirited women Amy knew. She allowed nobody to control her or put her down—except her boyfriends.

Raised by her parents in Leeds, she'd left home when she was sixteen. Her father had started hitting the bottle and Bel's mother. He'd been doing both on and off for years. For years Bel had been begging her mother to leave him, and she had always dithered. When her mother finally refused, Bel decided she'd had enough. She couldn't stand around watching her mother getting beaten black and blue. If she tried to intervene, her father turned on her. Gavin, her brother, wasn't able to help as he'd already left home. Bel came to London with a few hundred pounds in savings in her pocket—enough to get her some crappy digs off the Great North Road. A few months later, she applied to drama school and was accepted. She temped or worked in pubs to support herself.

Amy met her when she came to temp at Dunstan Healey Fogg. By then Amy had already been made redundant and was working out her notice. They got to talking a few times at the water cooler and hit it off. She loved Bel's sense of style, her humor, and the fact that she could be impulsive. One morning she decided to get her head shaved. By the end of her lunch hour it was done. Since Dunstan Healey Fogg prided itself on its cutting-edge image—something that Amy had never quite been able to live up to—nobody batted an eyelid. Another time, she dragged Amy to a vintage dress shop in Islington and persuaded her to buy a purple Marilyn Monroe tea dress and glitzy sunburst orange cocktail ring. "Omigod, with your boobs and tiny waist, it's perfect."

When Amy was in her teens, she was hugely conscious of her 34 double-D bust and ample rear. She tried to diet them away with little success. When she lost weight, it was always on her legs or face. It was only when she started university and blokes began hitting on her and girls confessed how much they coveted Amy's boobs and hips that she stopped trying to diet away her curves. Eventually, she came to love them. She especially liked her breasts, which one boyfriend at uni described as "the most magnificent jugs" on the planet.

One day, Bel got a phone call at work. Her mother had been rushed to the hospital. She had a ruptured spleen. Amy found out later that this had come—surprise, surprise—courtesy of Bel's drunk of a father. For some reason Bel felt able to confide in Amy, and throughout that summer Amy listened and offered her support. Bel's mum recovered and was finally persuaded to press charges against her husband, and eventually he went to prison. As Bel's family crisis subsided, the two young women started going to clubs and gigs and having fun. Slowly, their relationship turned from counselor-patient to a proper even-handed friendship.

Mark—known by everyone apart from Bel as Jurassic Mark because of his Neanderthal attitudes toward women—was a great big muscle-bound Aussie, a himbo fitness trainer with a man tan and a jaw that looked like it had been chiseled by the bloke who'd carved the presidents on Mount Rushmore. He called Bel "babe" and introduced himself with lines like "G'day, I'm Mark. I can bench a hundred and sixty K." He bought her flowers, perfume, and sexy underwear. She cooked him lasagne from scratch, ironed his track suits, and on one occasion even cleaned and waxed his vintage midnight-blue Jaguar with cream upholstery.

Back in the kitchen, Bel pulled her baggy green "boyfriend" cardigan around her. "Okay, you're right. You're always right. I hate it when you're right."

"Right about what? I still haven't said anything."

"I know, but you've said it before. Look, I know Mark's a sexist control freak, but here's the thing." She took another mouthful of wine. "God help me for saying this, but I think a bit of me enjoys being controlled and dominated by men. I think it has to do with seeing how my dad treated my mother."

"I think you might be right."

"Sometimes I think about leaving Mark, but then we make love and... what can I say? That man controls me like I'm some racing car, engine all revved up to go, but he holds me back. He has this way of bringing me to the brink of an orgasm and then taking his foot off the throttle and holding me there. I just lie there gasping and pleading, and then finally... when he's ready... Oh... my... God. I'm addicted. I just don't know how to wean myself off him. I wake up planning to ignore all his calls and go cold turkey, then by the evening I'm in bed with him and back in horny heaven. In that postcoital glow he asks me to collect his dry cleaning or trim his nose hair and I'm helpless to resist."

Just then the door buzzer rang. Amy frowned a question. She went over to the intercom. "Hi, it's me." It was Brian. She buzzed him in and went back into the living room. "It's Bri— probably wants a shoulder to cry on."

"I'm not surprised."

"Go easy on him tonight," Amy said. "He's a bit fragile. Don't start winding him up."

"What do you mean, 'don't start winding him up'? I never wind him up. He's always the one that starts it."

They heard the front door close. Brian plodded into the living room, looking pretty forlorn. His sweatshirt hood was up. Amy noticed that it was covered in raindrops. "Starting to chuck it down out there," he said by way of general greeting. Soon his eyes were fixed on Bel. His expression began to change. A smile hovered on his lips. "I see you've come as a traffic light." He was clearly referring to her red hair and green cardigan combo.

Bel didn't miss a beat. "And you've come as a mugger."

Brian pulled off his wet hood. Bel's eyes went straight to his hair. "Ooh, and the ferret family rang. They want their nest back." She was on a roll and, judging by her grin, delighted to be beating him.

"Well, the pedestrian crossing rang, and it wants you back."

"Okay, kids," Amy butted in. "Enough. If you don't stop scrapping, I'm going to turn this car around and neither of you will get ice cream."

"But he started it," Bel protested, doing an excellent imitation of a whining seven-year-old. "He called me a traffic light."

Amy had often thought slash hoped that Bel and Brian's mutual teasing disguised a sexual tension between them, but in the half dozen or so years they'd known each other, nothing—at least nothing that she knew of—had happened between them. Amy couldn't help being disappointed. She was a romantic and would have liked nothing better than for her two best friends to fall in love.

They were both creative, arty types with a left of center worldview. They were surely perfect for each other. When she put this to Brian, he said it wasn't that he didn't find Bel attractive. It was just that there was no way he would get into a relationship with a woman as self-obsessed as she was. When Amy asked Bel if there was any way she could see herself falling for Brian, her response wasn't dissimilar. "Look, don't get me wrong, I like Brian a lot and he is cute—there's no getting away from it—but he's so bloody neurotic. I mean, this thing he has with women and their physical appearance. What is that about? He'd drive me mad."

These days, Amy had come to accept that Brian and Bel would always connect as competing, teasing siblings rather than lovers.

"I'm sorry," Brian said to Bel. "I'm in a lousy mood, that's all. I had no right to take it out on you."

"You're forgiven," Bel said with a wave of her hand.

Amy offered them a maternal smile. "That's better. Now play nicely, you two."

"Have you really got ice cream?" Brian asked Amy.

She said she thought she had some rocky road in the freezer.

"Ah, rocky road. How appropriate." Brian gave a bitter laugh.

Bel took this as her cue to commiserate with him about Bean Machine. "God," she said as Amy disappeared into the kitchen to take the ice cream out of the freezer, "these people think they can just march in wherever they want and destroy small businesses. It's appalling. There should be some legislation, something to protect people like you."

"I know, but there isn't. Short of a miracle, I'm stuffed." He flopped into Amy's battered brown leather armchair.

"Yeah, well, I'm going to be stuffed, too, if I don't get some proper acting work soon."

"Does that mean you're running out of money?" There was real concern in his voice.

"No, I just got another electronic voice job. I'm just looking at my career as a whole, that's all. You know, wondering where I'm going..."

"So you're not facing potential bankruptcy and ruin, then?"

"Well...no."

"No bailiffs about to knock on the door."

"No."

"So, all in all, your life's looking pretty fine and dandy."

By now Amy had come back into the living room, having left the ice cream to thaw. "And there are no bailiffs about to knock on your door, either," she said to Brian, her tone gently scolding. "I know the Bean Machine thing is pretty scary and we're all worried, but have you allowed yourself to consider just for one moment that you might actually survive?"

"Yeah, and Boy George might actually be straight." He let out a long breath. "Anyway, believe it or not, I didn't come around to talk about the Bean Machine thing. Something else has happened."

"Oh, God, what now?" Amy said, lowering herself onto the sofa next to Bel.

"It's Maddy."

"What about her?"

"She just dumped me."

"She dumped *you?*"

"Yep. Can you believe it? She's the one with the webbed feet, and she dumped me."

"Maddy?" Bel piped up. "Who's she? Why does nobody keep me in the loop? I thought you were still seeing Emma with the tail and the hairy back. You know, if you could get all these women together, you could set up a tent and start charging admission."

Brian managed a good-humored eye roll.

Amy made the point that in a way Maddy ending it was good news. "I mean, you'd pretty much decided it wasn't going to work out between you."

"I know," Brian said, "but I wanted to be the one to end it. I never, ever allow myself to get dumped. That's my whole emotional MO—rejecting women before they can reject me— you know that."

Amy asked if Maddy had given him a reason for ending it. He took a deep breath. "She says I have moobs."

"Moobs?" Amy repeated.

"You know... man boobs," Bel volunteered.

"Yeah, yeah... I know what moobs are. I was just processing, that's all."

"Anyway, she says she finds them a turnoff. I went home, but I was too scared to look in the mirror, so I thought I'd come here. Amy, I want you to tell me honestly, do I have man breasts?"

With that, he stood up, took off his sweatshirt, and lifted his T-shirt to his chin. Amy wasn't about to hurt her best friend's feelings by telling him he had moobs, but Bel—who hadn't even been invited to give her opinion—wasn't so squeamish. She stood in front of him, eyes level with his chest, squinting.

"Okay, turn to the side," she said, making a twirling motion with her finger. He was clearly embarrassed, but he turned.

"Hmm. Well, there's definitely a bit of abdominal swelling going on. You planning an epidural or a natural birth?"

"Look, I know about the gut, okay? I need to diet and get back to the gym, but please tell me I don't have breasts."

"There's nothing," Bel said. "Not really."

"What does 'not really' mean?"

"It's nothing. Honestly."

"No, 'not really' means there's something."

"Okay, maybe there's just the teensiest budding, but you can hardly see it."

"She's right," Amy said. "It's barely noticeable."

"Budding? I have budding? What am I, a pubescent girl?" He fell back into the armchair. "Oh, God, I'm repulsive."

Bel told him to stop dramatizing. "Of course you're not repulsive. You've put on a couple pounds, that's all. It's no big deal. You'll lose it in no time."

Brian pulled down his T-shirt, and Amy went to fetch another wineglass.

"I agree," she said as she poured him some wine, "It's nothing to worry about. When blokes put on weight, it often goes to their stomach and chest. Did you see those pictures of Jack Nicholson on the beach the other day? Massive malumbas."

"The man has to be over seventy," Brian said, wobbling his right chest with his hand. "I'm still in my prime." He paused as a thought occurred. "But what if it's hormonal? They say that with so many women on the pill, the water supply's getting contaminated with estrogen."

"I'm no expert," Amy said, "but I'd say the chances of you developing female secondary sexual characteristics from the water supply are pretty minimal, but if you're worried, you should go to the doctor."

He nodded and said he thought he would, just to be certain he didn't have a hormone imbalance.

"And if you are turning into a woman," Bel said, going over to put an arm around him, "I've got this slinky little black shift that would look just great on you. If we did your hair, got you some pearls and some long gloves, you could have a real Audrey Hepburn thing going on."

"Gee, thanks."

"Amy! Quick! Get him off me. He's giving me an Indian burn."

Chapter 4

THE FOLLOWING DAY, Charlie's school was closed. The local council was holding elections, and the building was being used as a polling station. Charlie had been due to spend the day at Ruby's, but at half past seven she'd phoned to say she had woken up with a blinding migraine and the twins were going to her mother's. "I'd ask Mum to have Charlie, too, but she's getting on, and I'm not sure she'd cope with three of them tearing about her tiny flat."

Amy completely understood and wouldn't have dreamed of imposing on Ruby's mum, but it did leave her in a bind. There was no point phoning Val or asking Charlie's friends' mums to see if one of them could have him because they all worked. There was only one viable plan B: Victoria. She had two children, Delilah, known as Lila, who was nine, and Arthur, who was seven. Lila would be at school, but Arthur was at home getting over a stomach bug. The boys got on well, although Arthur, who was a tall, hefty lad, was apt to throw his weight around, not that Victoria ever acknowledged it.

Victoria had spent years devoted to her career, declaring that she didn't have a maternal bone in her body and that if she went through early menopause like her mother had, so be it. Then she met, fell in love with, and married Gorgeous Simon—he of the patrician jaw, Grecian curls, and megabucks salary courtesy of a top City law firm, where he was a partner.

They hadn't been back from their honeymoon (Bora Bora) for more than five minutes when, with much fanfare, they announced that they were pregnant.

Before that, there had been a glorious white wedding on the river at Henley, paid for by Simon's parents, who were loaded. Victoria, who along with her brains possessed a hand-span waist, hazel eyes that were perfect almonds, and auburn tresses that looked like they belonged in a Herbal Essences commercial, wore an understated slinky satin gown trimmed at the shoulders with drop crystals. As they posed for photographs— Victoria with her hair and eyes, Gorgeous Simon dashing in his top hat and tails—grandmas and aunties oohed and aahed and said what a handsome couple they made.

Amy was matron of honor. She wore an off-the-shoulder peach crinoline confection chosen by Victoria. Her sister claimed to adore it and said how perfect it was for Amy's figure. Amy believed her until the best man got up to deliver the traditional bridesmaid toast and assured her that one day she would rebuild Tara. Of course everybody hooted. Amy's girlfriends told her not to get upset since everybody knew it was the bride's prerogative to ensure that she wasn't outshone by her bridesmaid even if the bridesmaid was her sister.

Victoria's pregnancy at the age of thirty-one clearly indicated that she wasn't heading toward the early menopause Val had experienced. Amy was encouraged by this, but she knew that she still could have inherited her mother's predisposition. At the age of twenty-six she had every right to be fretting about her own fertility.

Nobody could believe the change that came over Victoria. Her pregnancy took over her life. She gave up work at once in order to "be there for my fetus." She spent nine months reading child-care books, playing Beethoven to her unborn child, and going to birthing, breast-feeding, and child-rearing courses.

She embraced pregnancy—and subsequently motherhood— in much the same way she had embraced her studies at school and university. For her, coping with pregnancy and child care wasn't about instinct, natural impulses, and doing what felt right; they were subjects to be conquered and mastered. Child-birth and parenting were tests, and she had to graduate with honors. What was more, the rest of the world had to be made aware of her successes and triumphs so that they would look up to her and admire her—maybe even love her.

It had occurred to Amy that as a child Victoria had received so much praise when she did well at school, she had grown up believing that all love was dependent on her success. That would explain why she threw herself into her studies and then into her job. Now she was doing the same with motherhood. Victoria was a self-appointed mother superior, eager to bestow upon other mothers the benefit of her knowledge and wisdom. She lived under the impression that she was respected and ad-mired. Amy suspected that the truth was different. It occurred to her that the moment Victoria appeared in the school play-ground, women cried out: "Omigod, duck, everyone. Here she comes."

Since having Charlie, Amy had come across several mothers superior like Victoria. For them, motherhood was nothing less than rhapsodic. Mothers superior would never admit that being stuck at home on a wet afternoon building Lego towers with a toddler who immediately demolished them and then demanded they be rebuilt was a chore. In their view, the mistake other mothers made was failing to see the experience as a truly mean-ingful step on junior's epic journey toward learning to play and interact with significant others. It was something to be cele-brated, not endured.

They were never sleep-deprived because they were slaves to Gina Ford's *Contented Little Baby Book*. They knew that looking after infants was all about routine and letting a newborn know who was boss.

A mother superior produced babies who slept through the night from age two weeks. They also napped twice a day: from ten until twelve and from two to four. That way she had time to lobby for a position on the board of governors at the school her three older children attended, help paint the scenery for the end-of-term play, and do her pelvic floor exercises.

AMY'S RELATIONSHIP with Victoria had never been easy. For a start, Victoria was five years older, which meant that for a long time she was physically bigger than Amy and able to push her around.

At school, Victoria did well in everything. If there was an academic prize to be won, she waltzed off with it. The upshot was that she turned into a bossy know-it-all who believed she was right about everything and couldn't be challenged. Her parents and teachers should have addressed her arrogance and reined her in, but they never did.

One of Victoria's favorite sports was crowing over her sister and calling her stupid. Of course she was savvy enough to do this well out of parental earshot. Despite her sister's bullying, Amy did well at school, but unlike Victoria, she wasn't Oxbridge material. She left Sussex with a perfectly respectable two-one. Of course Victoria left Oxford with a first.

By the time Amy reached her teenage years, her confidence had grown and she refused to let her sister put her down. Amy learned to fight back, and there were often huge rows. Back then she was unaware that she was jealous of her sister. She saw herself as a helpless victim, eager to love Victoria if only she would stop being such a bully. It was only in the last couple of years that Amy had begun to acknowledge her resentment and admit—to herself at least—that there were times when she teased and goaded her older sister.

As the sisters turned from teenagers to women, the slanging matches continued. They were usually followed by months of bad feeling. These days, their parents having separated, Amy decided that there was enough family friction around and made a particular effort to get along with Victoria. It was by no means easy, though, and there were still times when Amy could have throttled her and happily served the time.

"Of course I'll have Charlie," Victoria cooed down the phone. "We haven't seen him for ages. And Arthur's not infectious anymore. I'm sending him back to school tomorrow."

"That's fantastic. Victoria, you're a total lifesaver." On the rare occasions she felt close to her sister, like now, Amy still got the urge to call her Vics or Tory—the way she had when they were kids—but Victoria had put a stop to that years ago on the grounds that both sounded common. On the other hand, it wasn't common for Delilah to be known as Lila. Amy had given up trying to fathom her sister's logic.

"I know how hard it is for you working mums to find child care. I'm so lucky that Simon earns enough for me to stay at home. I can't imagine not being there for Lila and Arthur."

From the moment Amy got pregnant, Victoria had made it clear that she disapproved of her sister choosing to become a lone parent. Even now she took every opportunity to remind Amy that she was failing Charlie by not providing him with a father. As a rule, Amy wasn't afraid of standing her ground on the subject, but since Victoria had agreed to mind Charlie, she wasn't about to debate the issue and risk turning it into an argument.

"I'll take them to the park," Victoria went on. "Then I'll give them lunch. I've made a shepherd's pie. I'm sure Charlie will appreciate some home cooking for once."

Amy let that go, too.

"Sounds great. Honestly, I really do appreciate it."

"And then in the afternoon I've organized a nature trail and treasure hunt for the local play group." She helped out at Little Rascals a couple of mornings a week. "Of course the boys will be older than the other children, but I'm sure they'll enjoy it. And I know you and Charlie don't get out much, what with you being at work all the time."

"Wow, you've organized a nature trail *and* a treasure hunt," Amy singsonged, though how she managed it through clenched teeth, she had no idea. She felt an overpowering need to change the subject. She asked Victoria if she'd gotten around to baking anything for Lila's school fete, which she knew was being held on Sunday. Ask a silly question. "Actually," Victoria began, "I've made Sleeping Beauty's castle, which they're raffling. I was up until midnight, icing it. And if that wasn't enough, I had to finish her wood nymph costume for the ballet school's latest production. Strictly *entre nous,* a couple of the speckled frogs aren't going to look brilliant. Some of the mums are just sticking half Ping-Pong balls onto green hooded tops and leaving it at that. I ask you."

Amy saw no point in saying that in her opinion sticking half Ping-Pong balls onto a hooded top seemed a rather inventive way of making a frog costume and that she for one was going to make a note of it.

They agreed that Amy should take Charlie with her to Café Mozart and Victoria would pick him up after she'd dropped Lila at school.

CHARLIE LOVED being taken to the café. Brian made him Bambinocino and, if they weren't too busy, brought the Connect 4 over from the play area and challenged him to a game. He always let Charlie win. Brian was Charlie's godfather, and like Bel, he took the responsibility pretty seriously. Not only did he baby-sit from time to time, there had been outings to the zoo, the science museum, and the children's theater in Wimbledon. For Charlie's last birthday, Brian had taken him to the circus. Charlie still talked about the trapeze artists and the clowns who had buckets of water poured over them, only the water turned out to be glitter.

Zelma always fed Charlie chocolate cake, which he loved. He was less keen when she pinched his cheek and told him that she could just eat him.

This morning, he seemed happy enough to sit drawing at one of the tables. He was working on what was turning out to be a magnificent gorilla swinging from a tree.

"It's like the great big huge one we saw at the zoo," he said to Brian, who was standing beside him, admiring his work.

"I can see that," Brian said, picking up Charlie's empty Bambinocino mug. He turned to Amy, who was clearing the next-door table. "That gorilla is fantastic. I've said it before: That son of yours has got a real gift."

"I know," Amy said, glowing. "His teacher has noticed, too. I've no idea where he gets it from. Certainly not from me. And artistic ability wasn't on his father's list of talents."

"Would you like the gorilla when I've finished?" Charlie asked Brian.

"You betcha," Brian said, ruffling Charlie's hair. "I'll take it home and stick it on my fridge. That way I'll get to look at it all the time."

With that, Brian made his way over to the front door, unlocked it, and turned the CLOSED sign to OPEN.

By the time he returned to the counter and started filling the coffee grinder with beans, the smile he had managed to turn on for Charlie had vanished. "What's to become of me?" he said to Amy. "A bankrupt in a man bra."

"You mean a Bro," Amy corrected, giggling.

"Bro?"

"Yeah. Come on, you're the *Seinfeld* nut. You must remember the episode where George's dad invents the man bra. He considers calling it the Mansiere but rejects it in favor of the Bro."

"Oh, yeah." Charlie nodded without a hint of amusement.

"We could always bind you up," Zelma volunteered, coming from the kitchen carrying a stack of clean plates. "It's what the flapper girls did in the twenties to make their busts flat."

"Why doesn't that make me feel better?"

"Oh, come on, Brian," Zelma said, putting the plates down on the counter, "I'm only trying to lighten the atmosphere. Amy's right. You need to go on a diet, that's all."

"I'm too stressed to diet." With that he shoved a cheese Danish in his mouth.

Amy put her hand on his shoulder. "We will get through this Bean Machine thing, you know. And I'll be here as long as you need me. I'm not going anywhere."

"Me, neither," Zelma said.

"Really? What about when I can't afford to pay you anymore?"

Zelma shrugged. "I don't work here for the money. You know that."

"Anyway," Amy said, "it won't come to that." But she knew it might.

THIS MORNING, no sooner had the commuters left than a gossiping gaggle of blond, hair-flicking American girls appeared, their perfect teeth and noses accessorized with Dolce & Gabbana totes and pastel-colored Juicy Couture sweatpants. St. Agatha's, the snooty private school up the road, was always organizing foreign exchange visits. A couple of months ago it had been loud pushy Italian teenagers for whom the concept of queuing was clearly anathema coming in for their morning espresso. Amy assumed that the Americans were the latest arrivals. As she wiped tables and gathered up dirty crocks, she couldn't help overhearing their conversation.

"He so totally said that to her." A girl with hot pink lips was addressing the entire group.

"No way," somebody gasped.

"Way."

"So I like totally paused."

"Ditto."

"Piers is such a jerkoff."

"Duh."

At that point Zelma appeared. She had come to relieve Amy of some of the dirty mugs and plates. "Can you understand a word they're saying?" she muttered to Amy. "And what's a jerkoff when it's at home?"

Amy grinned and said she'd explain later.

As usual, Brian was on barista duty. "So what can I get you?" he said to the girls.

"I think all the Briddish guys we've met are jerkoffs," Hot Lips pronounced, ignoring him. "They all have zits and crappy teeth. Like, don't they have dermatologists and orthodontists in this country?"

"So what will it be?" Brian persisted. He wasn't in the best of moods to start with. By now he was becoming increasingly thin of lip.

"And what about nail bars? Yesterday I'm out after school with this girl Arabella, and I'm like, 'where can I get a manicure?' And she's all like, 'Well, you could try this place in Fulham where my mom goes.' So I call, and they want fifty dollars for a French manicure. I'm like.... yeah, as if."

"And you can't get Tylenol in the drugstore. It's like being in Spain or Italy or one of those other loser countries."

"And lesbians are like soo big over here," pronounced a girl with chunky headphones draped around her neck. "I'm not kidding. Have you noticed all these cars with red L's stuck to the trunk? I guess it's like some kind of lesbian rights group."

Amy, who had been finding it hard not to laugh, almost choked when she heard the last remark. Brian, on the other hand, seemed to be experiencing total body clench. "Actually, the L doesn't stand for 'lesbian,'" he broke in, "it stands for 'learner,' as in learner driver."

Hot Lips turned on her friend. "Doofus."

Headphones shrugged. "Hey, how was I to know?"

"Ignore her," Hot Lips said to Brian. "She thinks Minnesota's a soft drink."

"Screw you," said Headphones.

"What is more," Brian continued, "we do have Tylenol, but over here it's called Panadol."

"It is? So how come you guys changed the name? That is such a lame thing to do. And what is it with the Brits and all these dumb-ass names that nobody can pronounce like Lee-i-cester Square and that other place—Mary-lee-bone?"

Amy could swear Brian's nostrils were flaring.

"That would be 'Lester' Square and 'Mar'leb'n.' For your information, we Brits consider these dumb-ass names to be part of our heritage."

"Whaddever."

Brian took a deep breath and offered the girls a rictus smile. "So now that's settled, what can I get you?"

"Okay," Hot Lips said, "I'll take a vente mocha with one shot, caramel sauce on the top and bottom, no whip, light on the ice, and seven pumps of peppermint syrup."

Then the girl who'd called Piers a jerkoff piped up: "And I'd like an iced single vente, nine pumps peppermint, caramel sauce top and bottom, light ice, no whip. Mocha. Goddit?'

Brian didn't move. Even at the best of times, he had a thing about American customers and their lists of demands and preferences. "What are the milk choices?" "I'd like four shots—two regular, two decaf. No, make that two regular, two half caf." Brian gave in to these demands so long as, in his opinion, they didn't cross the line and adulterate the coffee. Right now Brian's line had been well and truly crossed. In fact, the line was so far away, he couldn't even see it.

The girls were beginning to look uneasy at Brian's lack of springing into action. "So, er, like, have you goddit?"

"Actually, no," Brian replied with a smile. "I 'like' haven't goddit.'" He cleared his throat, clearly preparing to climb onto his high horse. "You may or may not have noticed that this is a coffee shop, not a confectioner's. We do not serve coffee with caramel sauce, whip, or any kind of flavorings, peppermint or otherwise. The nearest Starbucks is a couple of miles down the road. The 65 bus will drop you right outside."

Somebody muttered "Well, lah-di-dah," at which point the girls burst into a fit of giggles and headed for the door. "See, I told you all Briddish guys were jerkoffs."

Out the window, Amy could see one of them flagging down a black cab. She looked at her watch: "They'll never make it to Starbucks and back before lessons start." Brian said that bearing in mind the extortionate fees these brats' daddies were paying St. Agatha's, their teachers would probably be more than happy to hold up lessons until they got there.

THE FIRST group of mothers arrived at nine thirty on the dot. They came in roaring with laughter. One of them was saying how she and her husband were so exhausted from all the sleepless nights with the new baby that they hadn't had sex in months. "It's like Belgium," she said. "Always there, but we never go." As the laughter subsided, somebody said she was so behind with the laundry that she'd spent the last three days in the same panties. Then a woman confessed that she had just given in to a tantrumming child who was refusing to eat breakfast by providing him with a packet of Monster Munch. The women were sitting down, grabbing more chairs and pushing tables together, when Victoria walked in with Arthur. Amy gave both of them a hello wave from behind the counter. Arthur noticed Charlie, who was now busy building Legos in the play area, and ran over to join him. No sooner had he disappeared than Victoria, who didn't live in the neighborhood, spotted somebody she knew among the Monster Munch women.

Amy watched as Victoria didn't so much greet as accost the woman. "Claire!" she boomed, squeezing her way past chairs and buggies to get to her. "How wonderful to see you."

AMY LOOKED at Claire, who was trying to placate an irritable toddler while breast-feeding her newborn. She couldn't work out if it was the stress of dealing with her offspring or seeing Victoria that caused Claire to return the salutation with rather less gusto.

Amy didn't know Claire, but they had gotten to chatting a few times in the café. She mostly came in with other mummy friends, but toward the end of her pregnancy she'd started coming in alone when the café was quiet. She would bring a book and tell Amy how her mother had agreed to have child number one for a few hours each day and that she was making the most of it before the "onslaught" of the new baby. Usually Amy left Claire to her novel, but occasionally they got to chatting and ended up exchanging pregnancy and baby stories.

Claire had given birth a couple of weeks ago. Amy knew that her husband had taken time off work and that her mother had come to help out for a few days, but she was going it alone now and looked worn out. Her eyes were puffy. Her hair looked like it could do with a wash. She'd clearly thrown on the first thing she could find—Gap jeans with seriously frayed bottoms and a pair of Havaianas flip-flops. Amy couldn't help noticing that her T-shirt had two tiny wet patches at the nipple area.

By then Victoria had reached Claire, her eyes fixed on the woman's postchildbirth muffin top, which was pretty evident even under her T-shirt. As Amy watched the grimace form on her sister's face, she prayed that Victoria's opening remarks wouldn't concern the importance of postnatal abdominal exercises. But in the end her sister opted for congratulations rather than humiliation.

"Well done, you," Victoria gushed. "What did you get?"

As usual, the gleaming-haired Victoria looked like she'd stepped out of the Yummy Mummy catalogue. She was wearing a knee-length A-line floral skirt. She'd set this off with a short denim jacket, silver sandals, and an "I Am Not a Plastic Bag" canvas eco bag.

"A little girl. Phoebe."

"How lovely. And just ignore the people who tell you that Phoebe's become really common since *Friends*." Victoria peered at the suckling infant, "Oh, look at her. Isn't she adorable? I wouldn't worry about that cradle cap and the milk spots on her face—they'll clear up in no time. Of course, if the cradle cap gets worse, you'll need some shampoo with salicylic acid. Works wonders...So, how was the birth? I'm dying to hear all the gory details."

"Actually, it was pretty traumatic. I had a twenty-hour labor. In the end I was so exhausted that I had a cesarean."

"Oh, but you mustn't feel too guilty. Not everybody's got the stamina for natural childbirth. I was so fortunate—two water births and not even the teensiest tear. Of course I did massage my perineum every day with olive oil. I'm sure that helped."

By now the rest of the Monster Munch mummies, who didn't know Victoria, were exchanging who-the-hell-is-this-stuck-up-bitch glances. But not one of them had come to Claire's rescue. This was typical. Nobody ever stood up to Victoria. Amy felt she should step in, but Brian had just gone to the bank, leaving her and Zelma with a queue of customers.

"And how has Ben taken to the baby?" Victoria continued, offering Claire's eldest a smile. This morphed into a look of mild disgust when she noticed him attempting to brush croissant crumbs off the front of his sweatshirt with jammy fingers.

"Oh, he's become a bit noisy and attention-seeking," Claire said, rummaging in her bag, presumably for a tissue.

Of course, Victoria magically produced a baby wipe in an instant and began cleaning Ben's fingers. "There, isn't that better?" she said when she was done. "We mustn't let Mummy go out without her wipes in future, must we?"

"My godda poop!" Ben announced.

Claire leaned down and smiled. "Okay, darling. I'll take you to the loo."

"Oops. My did a yukky fart."

"Gosh, do you let Ben say 'fart'? You are brave. I never let mine say it. The thing is with children and rude words, you just never know where it'll end. Have you read Helga Klein on the subject?"

More looks and eye rolling from the other mummies.

"Pee-nis. Peenis. My godda penis...Look."

Claire turned beetroot. "Omigod! Ben! No! Put it away at once..."

"Peee for pee-nis. My mummy's got a ba-gina."

"Ben, for Chrissake, stop waving it around."

One of the women touched Claire's arm and told her not to worry; this kind of behavior was perfectly normal from a toddler whose nose had been put out of joint by the arrival of a new baby.

"I can't say I agree," Victoria said. "His behavior seems rather disturbing, if you ask me. If it's of any help, I met this amazing child therapist at dinner the other night. I'm sure he'd be glad—"

"That's really kind of you, but I think we can manage."

By then Claire looked as if she might burst into tears. It was clear from their expressions that the other mothers really felt for her, but nobody seemed prepared to tell Victoria to shove it.

Amy couldn't listen to any more. Aware of how nasty Victoria was being and how vulnerable newly delivered mothers were, she felt compelled to go over and defend Claire.

"Sorry," she said to Zelma. "My sister has got her claws stuck into that poor woman. I've got to go over there."

"Go," Zelma said, shooing her. "I can manage." Zelma knew what Victoria was like. They had met only once, but Victoria had made her mark by regaling Zelma with an account of a documentary she had watched on assisted suicide for the elderly.

Having said hello to Claire, Amy greeted Victoria with a double kiss. "I had no idea you two knew each other," Amy said to Claire.

Claire explained that a few months ago she and Victoria had taken an art history class together. Amy got the impression she wanted to know what Amy's relationship was to Victoria, but before Amy could enlighten her, Victoria was off again.

"So, how's Phoebe sleeping?" Victoria demanded.

Amy didn't give Claire a chance to reply. "Didn't you tell me she was sleeping through?"

"I did? She is? Oh, yes...yes. She most definitely is. No problem at all. Sleeps from ten until six every night."

"Isn't that fantastic?" Amy said. "How many newborns do that?"

Victoria wasn't about to be outdone. "Oh, I always insisted that Arthur stay in his crib until half past seven. I simply left him to cry. I refused to be manipulated by a newborn. He soon got the message. I think that's why he's such an easy, well-balanced child now. He's been in the play area over there with his cousin for ten minutes now. Not a peep. He interacts so well with his peers."

At that point, one of the Monster Munch mothers broke in. "Is he by any chance the little boy in the red T-shirt?"

"Yes, why?

"Well, I think it might be worth you taking a look. I'm not sure he's interacting quite as well as he might."

Victoria craned her neck to look for her son. "Omigod! No! Arthur...put down the swizzle stick. You'll put Charlie's eye out."

This time, the looks exchanged by the other mummies were more than a little smug.

Amy could by now see what was happening. "Charlie, come here!" She began squeezing between the tables in an effort to reach the boys. Where had Arthur found a swizzle stick? Not here. Brian's customers stirred their coffee with Sheffield stainless steel, not balsa wood.

"Arthur," Victoria cried again, following her sister, "I said put the stick down! He picked it up in the park yesterday. I thought he'd left it there. He must have hidden it in his pocket. Stoppit! You can't go around stabbing children just because they won't hand over their toys."

By now Charlie, who was several pounds lighter and a couple of inches shorter than his burly older cousin, was running toward the door. Arthur was giving chase: a four-foot, cherub-faced hooligan wielding a swizzle stick blade. Before Victoria or Amy—or anybody else, for that matter—had a chance to reach Charlie and Arthur, a thirty-something chap in a suit came into the café and almost tripped over them. He seemed to realize immediately what was going on. As Arthur closed in on Charlie, his arm raised in preparation to stab his cousin some-where about the face, the chap bent down to child height and gently prized the stick from him. "Er, not a good idea, young man," he said. His voice was kind, but it was clear he meant business. Arthur suddenly looked sheepish. A moment later, both mothers were on the scene. "Arfur hurt me," Charlie wailed to his mother, pointing out a scratch that went across two of his fingers. "'Cos I wouldn't give him my Lego man." He was clutching what remained of the model in his other hand.

"Well, that's not very nice, is it?" Amy took his fingers and began blowing on them. It was what she always did when he hurt himself. She called it "magic air," and it seemed to take the pain away.

"Oh, it's nothing," Victoria said, peering at Charlie's wound. "I'm sure Arthur didn't mean it."

"He did mean it," Charlie bellowed with red-faced defi-ance. "He did."

Arthur responded by burying his face in his mother's skirt.

"Actually, I'd be inclined to agree." It was the man who'd separated the two boys. He was still holding the swizzle stick. Amy found herself staring at him. She was sure she recognized him, but try as she might, she couldn't place him.

"What do you mean?" Victoria snapped.

"I mean that your son gave every impression that he was about to hurt this child if he didn't hand over the Lego man."

"Don't be ridiculous. He was playing, that's all." By now, Arthur was burrowing sullenly into Victoria's skirt and she was rubbing his back.

"You call it playing. I call it terrorizing," the man said.

"I'll have you know that my son is academically gifted. He needs constant stimulation. He gets cranky occasionally, but that's just a symptom of his frustration with the world."

Amy rolled her eyes. Victoria always fell back on the tormented genius argument to excuse her son's bad behavior.

"Academically gifted or not," the chap persisted, "he's a bully, and it strikes me that you are perfectly happy to indulge him."

Victoria stood in front of him, blinking and sputtering. People so rarely stood up to her that when they did, the shock left her lost for words.

"How dare you?" she managed eventually. Then she turned on Amy. "The trouble with Charlie is that he doesn't have a father. He has no male role model, nobody to show him how to stand up for himself. He needs to toughen up."

"My being a single parent has got nothing to do with this," Amy said, doing her best to keep calm. "And you know it. Arthur has been naughty. All kids are naughty. When it happens, you have to accept it and deal with it."

Victoria's face was scarlet with fury and embarrassment. Not only had she been defeated, she had been defeated in public, and the public was finding it hard to conceal its fascination. All the women in the restaurant had interrupted their conversations to listen to the fracas. By now the place was silent. Even the children had picked up on the atmosphere and were quiet.

Victoria's response was to move away from the engrossed onlookers. Not that there was anywhere to go. She headed toward a quietish corner near the loo. Amy took Charlie's hand and followed her. The pair watched as Victoria turned on Arthur, her voice an angry whisper. "I told you to put that filthy stick down when we were in the park. Why did you disobey me? Now, then, say sorry to Charlie."

This was typical of Victoria, defending Arthur in public and scolding him in private. Arthur blinked at her as if to say: "Hang on…inconsistent parenting. A second ago you said I was a troubled genius and that none of this was my fault." The poor child was clearly confused. He buried his head again and refused to move.

"It's okay," Amy said to her sister. "I think Arthur's had enough. Let's leave it now."

At that moment, Victoria's expression changed. She looked at Amy, accusing her. "You didn't give the boys sweets while they were playing, did you? I know you let Charlie have rubbish with food coloring, but Arthur's sensitive system can't tolerate chemicals."

"No, I didn't. Anyway, I've been with you most of the time. And for your information, Charlie isn't allowed food coloring, either."

Victoria prized her son off her knees and turned him to face his cousin. "Okay, apologize to Charlie or it's the naughty step for you when we get home, and I was going to take you both out for ice cream after the nature trail."

The bit about the ice cream hit home. "Sorry," Arthur mumbled.

"Louder, please."

"Sorry!"

"That's better. Now give Charlie a hug and we can go."

Arthur shuffled over to Charlie and hugged him.

The embrace over, Amy asked Charlie if he was happy to go to Arthur's house. He nodded, but without much enthusiasm. That worried Amy, and she almost suggested that he spend the day at the café, but she knew that he would only get bored and irritable. Since having Charlie she'd learned that kids fought, made up, and didn't bear grudges.

Victoria was still looking tight-lipped.

"You okay?" Amy said in a low voice so that the boys couldn't hear.

"Of course I'm okay. Why shouldn't I be?"

"It's not easy," Amy said, "having somebody tell you that your child's a bully."

Victoria shrugged. "I'm really not interested in other people's opinions. I'm his mother. I know the truth, and that's all that matters…Arthur is a very special child." With that she took a deep breath and arranged her face into a smile. "Right, boys. Are we ready to go?"

They were on the point of leaving when Victoria turned to Amy. "Oh, by the way," she said, "I have huge news."

"What?"

"Dad's got a girlfriend."

"What? You're kidding. How do you know?"

"That ditzy new receptionist of his let it slip. She seemed to think I knew."

"So Dad doesn't know we know?"

"Correct"

"Does Mum know?"

"Not sure. Best not say anything. Anyway"—she stiffened—"suffice it to say that Simon and I most definitely do not approve."

"Why? What's wrong with her?"

"Mum…Charlie did a smelly fart." Arthur was in fits of giggles, as was Charlie. Like so many males, they had bonded over fart gas. In a few years they'd be setting fire to them.

"What have I told you about saying that word?" Victoria turned back to Amy. "Look, I've got to go. I'll explain when you and Charlie come over on Saturday."

"We're coming over?"

"Yes, didn't Mum tell you? The en suite bathroom is finished at long last, and I'm desperate to show it off. Come for lunch. Nothing fancy, just potluck."

Amy was making her way back to the counter, when Claire stopped her. Phoebe was asleep in her sling. Ben was at his mother's side, his T-shirt covered in more croissant crumbs. "We're off now," Claire said, "but I just wanted to thank you so much for sticking up for me back there. God, I loathe that woman—may her ovaries shrivel and die. Sorry, I know she's a friend of yours, but—"

"Actually," Amy said, "Victoria is my sister."

Claire's face turned scarlet. "Oh, God. I had no idea."

"Don't worry." Amy smiled. "I know Victoria can be a pain in the backside, and I apologize. All I'd say in her defense is that she has one or two underlying emotional issues."

"One or two?"

Amy giggled. "Okay, several. Not that I'm excusing her."

"Say no more," Claire said. "I totally understand. And thanks again."

"Wass ovries?" Ben piped up. He seemed to have forgotten all about going to the loo.

"I'll explain when we get home, darling." Claire took his hand and said goodbye to Amy, and they made their way to the door.

Seeing that nobody was serving the chap who had rescued Charlie, Amy darted over to him and apologized for keeping him waiting.

"No problem. I'm not in a rush."

Nice smile, she thought.

She was about to thank him for getting between Arthur and Charlie, but he got in first.

"Look, I'm really sorry if I went too far back there. Maybe I was a bit hard on that woman, but I really felt for your little boy."

"Don't worry. I really appreciate what you did. Actually, Arthur is Charlie's cousin. He can be a bit of a handful."

"So that woman is your sister?"

Amy nodded. "She's pretty intimidating. Not many people have the courage to stand up to her."

"Well, you seem to manage okay." His eyes were fixed on hers. She could swear the man was flirting with her. "By the way, I'm Sam Draper."

"Amy Walker," she said, holding out her hand, which he took. His handshake was firm and warm.

They exchanged "Pleased-to-meet-you"s. "So you're raising Charlie alone?" he said. "Can't be easy."

"It's better now he's at school, but I admit it was a bit hairy when he was a baby—night after night without sleep. I don't think I quite knew what I was letting myself in for."

"My sister's got twins. Neither of them slept as babies. I'd go around there, and she and my brother-in-law would be virtually on their knees with exhaustion."

Amy said she couldn't imagine having twins even with a husband on hand to help. "So, Sam, what can I get you?"

He ordered an English breakfast tea to go. She found herself staring at him again. She could swear that she knew him from somewhere ... only he looked different somehow.

He was clearly having the same thoughts about her. "Your face seems familiar," he said. "I'm sure we've met."

"I know. I was thinking the same thing." She placed a tea bag into a cardboard cup and filled it with boiling water from the dispenser.

He stood thinking. "Goddit. You came up to me the other day and asked when Bean Machine was opening."

"Of course. You were wearing a hard hat—that's why I've been struggling to recognize you."

"You seemed to be in a real hurry," he said.

"I was. I had to get back to tell my boss that your company was about to put him out of business." Amy was rarely hostile toward people even if she had good reason, but the thought of Brian going under after all his hard work made her angry.

"I'm sorry?"

"Have you any idea what you're doing to this business?"

"Me?"

"Well, you and the rest of Bean Machine. The moment you open, Café Mozart will be forced to shut down. There's no way we can compete with your prices."

"I understand, but ..."

"You know what? Actually, you don't understand." Her heart was pounding with adrenaline. She was starting to get really worked up. "You don't understand at all. My boss is a close friend who has invested all his savings in this business, and you are about to ruin him."

"That's awful."

"Thanks for caring," she said, her voice heavy with sarcasm. "He's put so much work into building up this place. The coffee is the best for miles around. Our bread and cakes come from one of the finest bakeries in London. What are you going to give people? Marmite and cheese food bloody paninis, that's what."

"People like Marmite and cheese paninis."

"Name me one."

He shrugged. "Me. I love the meaty, savory taste."

She wasn't quite sure where to take her argument from there, so she decided to change tack. "Bean Machine is all about homogenized café culture," she said getting onto her high horse. "It doesn't matter which branch you go into. The art on the walls, the music, the furniture—it's all the same. Bean Machine is about the blandizing of the coffee shop. Café Mozart isn't like that. This place is original—a one-off, and we offer great quality—"

"I know, but the thing is—"

"And I haven't gotten to the most important part. You claim to be a fair-trade company, but everything you hear about Bean Machine indicates that you exploit coffee growers. Your profits are huge. You make billions every year. Why can't you pay these poor people who work for you a basic living wage?"

"Look, if you'd just calm down for a moment—"

"Please don't patronize me. Why should I calm down? What your company is doing is reprehensible. And another thing…"

"What?"

"Bean Machine coffee is lousy. It's weak and bitter."

"I agree."

"What?"

"I agree."

"What do you mean, you agree? How can you possibly agree?"

"Easy. I don't work for Bean Machine, at least not directly."

"Of course you work for them. You were inspecting the building, and I saw a Bean Machine letterhead attached to your clipboard."

"I was inspecting the building because I am the architect responsible for the renovation work. The reason I had a Bean Machine letterhead was that they'd written to me requesting some last-minute design changes."

"I see." Her face was flushed with embarrassment. She grappled for something to say. "Well...you could always refuse to do business with unethical companies."

"I could also refuse to buy products from countries with dubious human rights records."

"What's wrong with that?" she said, pouring milk into the tea.

"Okay, name me one country that hasn't been criticized for human rights violations."

"I dunno. Norway?" She reached for a plastic cup lid.

"So I take it that everything you buy—all your clothes, household goods, and electronic equipment—is homegrown in Norway."

"No, of course not." She handed him his tea. He thanked her and returned to his theme.

"That's because even if Norway made all that stuff, nobody could afford to buy it. Like the rest of us, you buy cheap Chinese imports, and while hating yourself for doing it, you turn a blind eye to their human rights record." With that he handed her the exact change.

Sam was right. When she shopped, she did pay more attention to price than to human rights. He had backed her into a corner and won. She had no choice but to swallow her pride and concede the point. She also owed him an apology for accusing him of being part of Bean Machine and being so shrill and aggressive. She was about to say her sorries, when Zelma appeared.

"What?" she said to Sam. "You're not having anything to eat? A strapping chap like you needs a snack midmorning. It'll keep your blood sugar up—stop you getting irritable. Now, then, what can I interest you in? A pâté and cornichon baguette, maybe? Tell you what, I could fry you some bacon and make you a bacon and egg ciabatta."

In the end he took a slice of ginger cake. There was no opportunity for Amy to say anything because Zelma kept fussing and clucking around him, trying to sell him a nice smoked salmon bagel to go with it.

As he was leaving, he and Amy exchanged awkward good-byes.

"Gorgeous-looking young man," Zelma whispered. "What on earth were you arguing with him about?"

Amy explained. "I can't believe I made such a fool of myself. I'm such an idiot, jumping to conclusions and losing my temper."

"Look, we're all on edge about this Bean Machine thing. You were thinking of Brian, that's all. In your shoes I would have done the same thing. Don't be so hard on yourself. He seemed like such a lovely chap, though. Those brown eyes are like two pots of chocolate pudding."

"Actually, they're not brown."

"They're not?"

"No. They're dark gray—almost charcoal."

"You sure?"

"Positive."

Chapter 5

DESPITE VICTORIA'S INSISTENCE that Saturday lunch would be a "potluck, take us as you find us" affair, it turned out to be a sumptuous, meticulously planned three-course feast consisting of onion tart, roast beef, and baguette and butter pudding. Simon greeted everybody in freshly pressed chinos, John Lobb brogues, and a Ralph Lauren shirt. Victoria made her entrance in a baby blue Agnes B shift and had a go at Simon for wearing suede brogues with chinos.

Amy turned up in 501s and flip-flops, bearing a bottle of Chardonnay. Simon thanked her profusely for her contribution, but when they sat down to eat, it was nowhere to be seen. Instead, there were two bottles of vintage Châteauneuf-du-Pape on the table. Val and Trevor hadn't risked dressing down. Val was in a navy Jaeger shirtwaister. Trevor had opted for boho chic: a loose-fitting linen jacket with a mandarin collar over his usual baggy trousers. Trevor presented Victoria with a bottle of his homemade rose-hip liqueur.

"Fabulous," she said, unable to hide her look of disdain. It was as if the Duchess of Kent had just been handed a corn dog.

Val came loaded with Bendicks Bittermints (By Appointment to Her Majesty the Queen), a supermarket coffee and walnut cake, plus drawing books, crayons, and Cadbury Creme Eggs for the children. Victoria accepted her mother's gifts with good grace, but later on Amy overheard her in the kitchen sounding off to Simon about the way her mother practically force-fed the children sugar and how they would all collapse in diabetic comas before the day was out.

While the grown-ups enjoyed prelunch drinks and nibbles in the living room, Victoria insisted that her children perform their party pieces. Lila needed no persuading. A pretty child who had inherited her mother's auburn hair and supreme self-confidence, she sat down at the piano and bashed out Scott Joplin with the aplomb of somebody twice her age.

Arthur was less obliging. He was tired and hungry after his morning swimming class and had no interest in reciting Edward Lear. He demonstrated this by throwing himself on the sofa and burying his head in one of the cushions. His mother wasn't to be defeated. First she tried sweet-talking him. Next came the begging. Then she got cross and refused to take no for an answer. Arthur's muffled voice kept telling her to go away. By then Val and Amy were exchanging uneasy looks.

Finally Simon stepped in. "Victoria, stop bullying the child. He's made it clear he's not in the mood."

"I'm not bullying him," she retorted.

"Yes, you are. You bully everybody. Including me. Now just give it a rest."

Victoria opened her mouth to speak and closed it again. This happened two or three more times, making her look like a goldfish. Finally she was able to form a sentence. "For your information, this is not bullying. It is what's known as parental encouragement. Not that you'd know much about that."

"Excuse me?" Simon was too well mannered to raise his voice in public, but he was clearly seething.

"It's true. You work all hours. You're never here."

"I work to pay for all this. I don't notice you going out and getting a job."

"The children are my job."

At that point they both seemed to realize that this was

neither the time nor the place to air their grievances. For a few moments nobody spoke.

Val seemed to be groping for something to say. She cleared her throat. "Duncan seemed very nice," she trilled to Amy. "Very good-looking."

"Actually, we decided not to see each other anymore."

"Why on earth not? He's handsome and clever."

Amy hesitated. She wasn't about to reveal what had happened between them, at least not in front of Charlie. "I know, but I could tell we weren't right."

"You know what your problem is?" Victoria piped up. "You're too fussy. If you're not careful, you'll end up old, miserable, and alone."

Amy thanked her for the vote of confidence.

"I don't know about anybody else," Val said, her expression overly jolly, "but I'm starving. Why don't we all move into the dining room."

"Good idea," Trevor said, rubbing his hands together. His relief was palpable. Until now, he'd given every impression of not knowing quite where to put himself.

For some reason, Arthur chose that moment to take his face out of the cushion and announce that he was prepared to perform, after all. He stood on the sofa and proceeded to recite—word perfect—the first two verses of "The Owl and the Pussycat." Val managed to focus on Arthur, smiling and urging him on while at the same time cuddling Charlie on her lap. After everybody had applauded Arthur, Val asked Charlie if he had a poem he would like to recite.

Amy knew this was her mother's way of making sure Charlie was included, but he wasn't used to performing in front of people and she suspected he might get shy and embarrassed.

"Mum, best leave it. Charlie's never—"

"Wass recite?" Charlie broke in.

"Say aloud, dummy." It was Lila. She was sitting in an armchair, legs draped over one arm like a truculent teenager.

"Lila!" Simon was glaring at his daughter. "How dare you speak to Charlie like that? Apologize at once."

"You don't have to shout at her," Victoria came at him.

"Sorree," Lila said to Charlie, rolling her eyes. "Look, if you've got nothing to recite, then do your elbow thing. You haven't done it in ages, and it scares Grandma."

"Don't you dare!" Val said to Charlie. "You know I can't bear to look."

"Akshully, I do have something," Charlie announced, not without pride. "It's a song."

"You have?" Amy said, assuming it was something he'd learned at school.

Charlie nodded.

"Okay, darling, off you go," Val said, lifting him off her lap and onto the floor. "Deep breath..."

Charlie puffed out his chest. There was a long pause, followed by a little voice: "Like a vir-ir-ir-irgin, touched for the very first time. Like a vir-ir-ir-irgin..."

Amy slapped her hand to her mouth. The other adults immediately got the giggles—all except Victoria, who looked like she was sucking on a lemon.

"Charlie, darling," Victoria said through a rictus smile, "I think that's enough." She turned on Amy. "Do you really think that is the kind of music a six-year-old should be exposed to?"

"It comes right at the end of the *Shrek* movie," Amy said. "It's his favorite film. I'm not going to stop him from watching it because of one song."

"I know what a virgin is," Lila piped up.

Victoria winced.

"Omigod," Simon groaned.

"It's when you don't have a boyfriend...like Auntie Amy."

"Lila!" It was Simon again.

Amy reached out and touched her brother-in-law's arm. "Leave it," she whispered. "Let's just go and eat."

• • •

VICTORIA DISHED up while Amy served. Val took charge of the children, mopping up juice spillages and urging them to "eat up" and "sit nicely." Meanwhile, Simon asked Trevor about shamanism and listened far too intently in that patronizing, "you are the most important person in the room" kind of way so typical of posh Oxbridge types. Trevor seemed wise to the tactic, though, and niftily turned the conversation to cricket—England was about to beat Australia in the Ashes.

At one point Arthur started pinching Charlie, and Val told him to "stop that at once or you won't get any pudding." Despite Arthur having turned red with guilt, Victoria turned on her mother, accusing her of not investigating what had gone on and insisting that Arthur wouldn't have pinched Charlie without provocation. Val was by no means a shrinking violet, but she found her daughter's bossy domineering manner hard to deal with and like most people rarely stood up to her. Today was no exception. She made no attempt to come back at Victoria. Trevor looked at Val. Seeing her distress, he put down his knife and fork and opened his mouth to speak. Val instantly grabbed his arm and shook her head at him. Amy watched as Trevor stood down. He was a gentle soul, but it was clear that he wasn't finding it easy to watch Val being attacked and undermined.

Meanwhile, Simon turned on Victoria. "Actually, I was watching the boys, and Charlie did nothing to provoke Arthur. You had no right to attack Val. She was only trying to help."

Victoria had the decency to say sorry to her mother, but her tone was less than heartfelt. "I just don't see why Arthur always gets the blame for everything."

"He gets the blame," Simon retorted, "because nine times out of ten he's in the bloody wrong." Simon looked at his son. "Now say sorry to Charlie or you will go to your room." Arthur mumbled an apology. Only Amy heard Lila call her brother a wuss.

Val said the baguette and butter pudding should be ready. "Why don't I get it out of the oven."

Trevor said he would help her dish up. As they left the room, Amy heard her mother thanking Trevor for being prepared to take on Victoria. "Phil would never have spoken up for me," she said. It was true. Phil's confidence and sharp wit meant he never had any trouble telling his daughter to get back in her box and stop being such a madam. He couldn't understand why Val found it hard to challenge her older daughter and had little sympathy for her.

"I held my tongue once because you asked me to," Trevor said. "Don't expect me to do it again."

Amy looked on as her mother gave Trevor's arm a squeeze.

SIMON OPENED "a rather special dessert wine." As the adults knocked it back along with Victoria's sumptuous baguette and butter pudding, the atmosphere lifted.

After lunch Simon and Trevor watched the children while the women went upstairs so that Victoria could show off her much ballyhooed en suite bathroom.

Amy sat on the dark mahogany toilet lid, desperate to undo the top button of her jeans. She'd eaten far too much.

"I have to admit that I did hover over the bidet," Victoria said, nodding toward the piece of newly installed reproduction nineteenth-century sanitaryware. "I know they're terribly petit bourgeois, but I was won over by this article I read in *The Times*, which said the French have the lowest rate of yeast infection in the world."

Val said she was suddenly picturing Nicolas Sarkozy striding to a bidet and tending to his undercarriage. Amy started laughing. Victoria stiffened. A moment later she was pointing out the hand-painted rosebuds decorating the rim of the bidet. Val said she thought they were ever so sweet. Soon she was turning her attention to the lavatory with its overhead cistern and long chain. "Ooh, look. There are tiny rosebuds on the chain handle, too."

"And around the inside of the bath." Victoria beamed. She went over to the rolltop iron bath with its claw feet. This had been positioned bang in the middle of the steeple-ceilinged bathroom. "The suite is a limited edition reproduction of one they had installed at Sandringham for Edward VII."

"Must have cost a fortune," Val said, stroking one of the chunky brass bath taps.

Victoria gave a self-conscious flick of her impossibly shiny auburn hair. "Well, Simon is a senior partner now."

Val seemed to be summoning up the courage to speak. "Darling," she said eventually, "I don't want to interfere, and feel free to tell me to mind my own business, but is everything all right between you and Simon?"

"Of course," Victoria retorted. "Why on earth shouldn't it be?"

"C'mon, take it easy," Amy said to her sister, careful to keep her voice steady and soothing. "Mum was only asking." Then she heard herself say, "Why can't you ever give her a break?"

Victoria turned on her. "Amy, do not start. I said I was sorry for the way I overreacted downstairs."

"I'm not starting. All I said was—"

"Come on, your sister has apologized," Val said to Amy. "I know she didn't mean what she said. Now, let that be an end to it."

"Fine," Amy said, cross with her sister for snapping at Val and frustrated with Val for always wanting to keep the peace. Amy turned back to her sister. "So you and Simon really are okay?"

"I admit we've been a bit tetchy lately, but it doesn't mean anything."

Amy wasn't convinced. "I'd say you were a bit more than tetchy. You both seemed pretty rattled down there."

"God, will the two of you get off my case? Simon's been working all hours these past few months. I've had builders crawling all over the place ever since we moved in, and it's finally gotten to me. We need a break, that's all, and then we'll be fine."

"Of course you will," Val said. Whether she meant it or was merely eager to placate her daughter, Amy couldn't tell.

"By the way," Val said to both daughters, "I bit the bullet and phoned your father." Emotions had been so fraught since the split that they hadn't spoken other than to discuss finances and whether they should formalize the separation by getting divorced. So far they hadn't come to a decision on the matter. "We actually managed to have a reasonably civilized conversation."

"Good for you, Mum," Amy said. "One of you had to make the first move. So are you two planning on being friends now?"

"I think things might be heading that way." Val smiled. "By the way, has he told you about his floozy?" She was chuckling.

"I wasn't sure if you knew," Victoria said.

Amy was frowning. "His *floozy?*"

"Calls herself an 'erotic poetess,' if you please. Now I've heard everything. Still, if she floats his boat, who am I to object?" Just then they heard a child crying, and Val said she would go downstairs to check on how Simon and Trevor were managing.

"What on earth is an erotic poetess?" Amy said after her mother had gone.

"It's bloody disgusting, that's what it is," Victoria hissed. "The woman writes rhyming porn and reads it out in public. People actually pay to hear her."

"Porn poetry evenings?" Amy laughed. "Gawd, I wonder what sort of stuff she writes." She paused, waiting for the muse to strike her: "Okay, I've got it. 'Oh, Jemima, your vagina is like an ocean liner/Let me anchor my tanker between your thighs in Sri Lanka.'"

"How can a vagina be like an ocean liner?" Victoria was

actually giggling. They were sharing a moment, their first in months, years even.

"I dunno. It was the best I could come up with at short notice."

"Anyway, I'm not happy."

"Maybe not, but this is Dad's business, and it has nothing to do with you or any of us. If Mum isn't bothered, why should you be?"

"I'll tell you why—because our father has turned into a middle-aged pervert. What sort of example is he setting for Arthur, Lila, and Charlie? Their grandfather is dating a prostitute."

"Oh, come on. The woman might be a bit strange, but you know Dad as well as I do. It's preposterous to even suggest that Dad is dating a hooker."

"Fine," Victoria retorted. "Have it your own way, but has it occurred to you, even for a second, that we might not know Dad as well as we think we do?"

"No, it hasn't."

Victoria looked like she might be about to burst into tears. "Do you mind telling me why we can't just be a normal family?"

Amy put her arm around her, and to her surprise, Victoria didn't resist. "What's normal?" Amy said.

"Not this—our mother dating some weirdo healer. Our father seeing this…this porn peddler. What will people think?"

"Who cares what people think?"

"I do. People's opinions matter to me. We have to put a stop to this relationship. If we let it continue, Dad will become a laughingstock."

"No," Amy said. "This is Dad's life. No matter how much you disapprove, you cannot possibly interfere."

"What about Mum's life? What will her friends say?"

"Mum has the kind of friends who won't give two hoots. You've got this thing totally out of proportion. There is no way that our father is involved in anything sleazy. And even if he were, Mum is separated from him. How could his behavior reflect on her?"

Victoria shrugged. "Okay, you might be right about Mum, but it is still going to reflect on me and my children." She pulled away from Amy and began rubbing a fingernail over some imagined imperfection on the bath surface.

"Victoria, are you all right?" Amy said tenderly. "You sure there's nothing else you want to talk about?"

Victoria looked up, clearly irritated. "I've told you. I'm fine. Now *please* let it drop."

AS SOON as they got home, Amy went to check on Michelangelo. He was curled up in a corner of his cage, barely breathing. The next morning, to her astonishment, he was still hanging on. His impending demise reminded Amy of how her parents had dealt with her grandfather's death. She must have been seven or eight when one day they announced that Grandpa Ted had unexpectedly and in his sleep moved to Eastbourne. She accepted it without question. A few weeks later Victoria took enormous delight in telling her sister the truth. For months Amy had nightmares about her parents dying.

Just before ten, Victoria was on the phone to say that she and Simon were meeting some friends for lunch and would love Charlie to join them. Victoria was making a real effort to be friends, Amy thought. It occurred to her that the sadness and distress they'd both felt when their parents separated might in some strange way end up uniting them.

"We're going to Soho House," Victoria said, pausing for effect. Amy's heart sank. This wasn't entirely a hand-of-friendship call. It was also about Victoria needing to impress. Amy didn't say anything. She wanted to let her sister know that she could take Soho House in her stride. "Simon joined a few months ago," she persisted. "Last time we went, Jude Law was at the next table."

Amy called out to Charlie, who was sprawled on the living room floor doing a jigsaw and eating toasted crumpets, and asked him if he would like to go out to lunch with his cousins. He demanded to know what was on offer if he didn't go out with Lila and Arthur. Amy couldn't help being mildly irritated that her son saw her as the entertainment committee. She told him that they were going to IKEA to buy a desk and a chest of drawers for his room. For Charlie it was a no-brainer. He was adamant that he wanted to help choose his furniture.

Victoria said she was sure that Charlie would prefer Soho House to traipsing around IKEA. At that point Amy could hear Lila shrieking in the background.

"Yay, Charlie's going to IKEA. Can Arthur and me go, too, and have Swedish meatballs and fries in the restaurant?" She could hear Victoria singing the praises of Soho House fish cakes, but judging by the commotion, the children had made up their minds. In the end Victoria insisted that her two come to Soho House. Amy could hear them sobbing and calling her a big fat poo.

Amy had arranged to go to IKEA with Bel, who wanted to buy a new bed. The two of them had agreed to split the cost of hiring a van.

Bel arrived half an hour late with Jurassic Mark in tow. He was thickset and muscle-bound and smelled overpoweringly of Fahrenheit. His green-and-white-striped rugby shirt, collar turned up, was set off by a surf necklace made of carved wooden beads. On his feet he wore Ugg duck boots. "Sorry we're late," he said, ending the sentence as if it were a question, the way all Aussies did and more Brits were starting to. He stopped to fingerfluff his hair in Amy's hall mirror. "Still, you have to admit I'm worth waiting for. I got up today and thought God gave and He just kept on giving." He leered at Amy's cleavage for a few beats before placing his hand on Bel's right buttock and squeezing. "Right, babe?"

"Right," Bel said, removing Mark's hand and shooting Amy an apologetic look. "Actually, the reason we're late is that

I've just started this biog of Coco Chanel and I'm totally hooked."

"Yeah, and I was updating my Facebook status." Mark piped up. "Came up with something really witty, though." Another audible question mark and then; " 'Congratulations. If you're reading this, you survived my cull.' "

Usually this would have been Bel's cue to offer up girlie giggles and extol Mark's comic genius. Instead her face formed a pained expression. "Very funny," she said in a deadpan voice.

Mark winked at Amy and cocked his head toward Bel. "The little lady's just pissed off that she didn't come up with it."

"Yeah, that'd be it," Bel said.

"You know, babe, I don't find uppity Sheilas much of a turn-on."

"Is that right?"

Amy blinked. Bel never ever spoke to Mark like this. Was it possible she had finally woken up and smelled the slime?

Before Amy had a chance to give her verdict on Mark's Facebook update, he was off again. "So, Amy, any chance of a glass of the amber fluid?"

"Yeah, I think I've got a carton of apple juice somewhere."

Mark turned to Bel. "You know, she's quite witty—for a Sheila."

"Why, thank you," Amy simpered.

"My pleasure." He was gazing at her cleavage again.

"Mark, if you've got something to say, please address it to my face and not my breasts."

"Mark, for Chrissake," Bel hissed.

"Aw, come on—fair go. A bloke can look, can't he? I mean, by anybody's standards that is a bit of a bloomin' rack Amy's got there."

Amy decided that nothing she could say would make an impression on Mark. Bel just looked weary and fed up.

Mark seemed to sense that he was making himself unpopular. "You know what?" he said to Bel, "I think I'll go and sit in the pub and have a few cold ones. Then this afternoon I might go to the football game."

"But what about IKEA?" Bel said. "You promised you'd help us load all the stuff into the van."

"You're big girls, particularly our Amy here. You can manage. I'll see to you later, babe. And don't forget to pick up some pizza on your way through. I'll have a quattro stagioni with extra olives, anchovies, cheese. And get them to drizzle some of that chili oil on top. You always forget that."

"Right." Bel couldn't have sounded less enthusiastic.

"And pick up a few beers, too. I'd get them myself, but I benched a hundred and twenty K yesterday and the old back's really crook."

"'Course it is," Bel muttered.

AS IT turned out, the van had room only for three passengers and there wouldn't have been space for Mark. They decided that Bel should drive. Charlie sat in the middle with his headphones on, listening to *Charlie and the Chocolate Factory*. Amy sat beside him, her arm across his shoulders.

"I've finally had it," Bel said, attempting to pull away and stalling the engine. "I'm ending it." She turned the ignition again. "The man is a misogynist jerk." She rammed the gear shift into first. Despite the grinding sound, the van started to move.

"Hang on. A few days ago you were adamant about how you loved doing things for Mark and that you couldn't leave him because the sex was so fantastic. Then there was the bit about how you liked to be controlled by men. What happened?"

"Okay, I know you'll think I'm mad, but the other night I'd had a couple of glasses of wine and I ended up phoning that shrink on Capital Radio, Dr. Beverly."

"You're kidding."

"Nope. I said I thought I was addicted to controlling men

and that when I was with them I had this total personality transplant and became subservient and compliant. She told me that if I didn't give up on toxic guys, I could end up with one that beat me. That seriously scared me. She made me realize that I confuse love with control and that, like I thought, it has to do with the way my dad treated my mum."

"She's totally spot on, but this is an addiction. It's going to be hard to break."

"Tell me about it," Bel said. "And that's not taking the sex into account. Sleeping with Mark is like shooting up some class A drug. And it's not like I can half dump him and gradually wean myself off him. If I finish with him, I have to go cold turkey." She slowed down to negotiate a roundabout.

"You know you've done brilliantly to get to this point. There were times when I thought the penny would never drop."

"You can stop fretting. I'm sorry I took so long, but it has dropped—well and truly."

"And I'm here if you need me . . ."

"I know and thanks for the offer, but I think I'll invest in a vibrator if it's all the same to you."

They both laughed.

"By the way, talking of sex, my father is seeing—get this— an erotic poetess."

"An erotic poetess? What does she do, make them have sex in iambic pentameter?"

That made Amy giggle. "Victoria thinks she's a hooker."

"Your dad and a hooker? That's the most ridiculous thing I've ever heard. She'll just be some giddy middle-aged hippie."

"That's what I said."

At that point Charlie took off his headphones and piped up, wanting to know if they were there yet.

Amy said it was going to be at least another half hour. She produced a juice box and a packet of Hula Hoops from her bag. The Hula Hoops were a rare treat. His eyes lit up, and he started making a puppy dog panting sound.

"You'd think I never fed him," Amy said, watching him tear

into the packet. A moment later he was chomping away, ear-buds back in place.

"Once I've finished with Mark," Bel said, "I will need to be very careful about the men I choose to go out with. I have to find blokes who aren't sexist control freaks."

"There's always Brian. He's definitely not a sexist control freak."

"Going out with Brian would be a nightmare."

"Do you really think so?"

"Come on, we been over this before. You know it would. Our relationship is based on mutual piss taking and competitiveness. We're like brother and sister. Plus his obsessions would drive me mad."

Bel sounded pretty adamant. And she was right that this was old ground. Amy decided there wasn't much point pursuing the subject.

"Oh, I didn't tell you what happened in the café yesterday," Amy said. She told Bel about Arthur bullying Charlie and how this chap Sam Draper had come to his rescue. "He even had a go at Victoria for condoning Arthur's behavior."

"No. God, not many people take on your sister and live to tell the tale."

"It was the first time in years I'd seen her completely lost for words."

Bel chuckled. "Wish I'd been there."

"Anyhow, then I got chatting with this Sam and managed to make a complete fool of myself."

"How?"

She recounted their conversation. "I just assumed he worked for Bean Machine. You should have seen me. Talk about getting on my high horse. I was so unpleasant and aggressive. I don't know what got into me."

"You were just angry on Brian's behalf and you told this guy what you thought of him."

"Yeah, but when I found out he didn't work directly for Bean Machine, I had a go at him for having anything to do with unethical companies that exploit Third World workers. Then we got into this whole debate about buying goods from countries with dodgy human rights records."

"I don't get it," Bel said. "Why are you so bothered about your behavior? You were upset. You lost your temper. It happens."

Amy shrugged. "I dunno. I just hate giving people the wrong impression. Now he's gone away thinking I'm this bad-tempered, argumentative bitch."

"So what? Who cares? Unless, of course, you fancy him."

"Don't be daft."

"I'm not being daft. A fight can be a bit like dancing—you know, a vertical expression of a horizontal desire."

Amy became thoughtful. "You could be right. He did have rather nice eyes. Sort of midgray verging on charcoal, with these golden highlights."

"Hello. If you can describe his eyes in this much detail after one meeting, you are definitely smitten."

Amy felt herself blush. "Look, finding somebody attractive doesn't amount to being smitten. I don't even know the man."

"Maybe not, but you're smitten."

"Stop it. I'm not smitten."

"Oh, yes, you are," Bel singsonged.

"I am not."

"Are, are, are, and are."

"Behave," Amy said, giggling. "So how do you intend to wean yourself off sex with Mark?"

Bel shrugged. "Dunno. I'm going to have to find some other activity to take its place."

"Like what? Crochet?"

They both laughed.

"Don't worry," Bel said. "Something will turn up."

IKEA WAS mobbed as usual. As the three of them worked their way past the room settings and frazzled couples doing battle with their irritable, noncompliant offspring, Bel wondered if the company ever ran out of Swedish names for the furniture. "And how do they decide on the names in the first place? Do they have meetings? Take votes? Or does somebody just look at a shelving unit and decide it looks like a Knut or an Ingvar?"

Amy chose a chest of drawers called Toborg and a desk called Stig, both of which met with Charlie's approval because they were painted blue and red, his favorite colors.

Bel found two beds that she liked but couldn't choose between them. After half an hour of bouncing, hemming and hawing, and Charlie demanding to be fed, she gave up and said she would come back another time. Amy said this was daft because they'd laid out for the van, but Bel said there was no point making a decision if she wasn't sure.

Once they'd loaded the van with the chest of drawers and desk, they went to the restaurant and devoured Swedish meatballs and fries. Before they left, Amy bought a jumbo bag of chocolate Dime bars, most of which they demolished on the way home.

Back home, the women carted Stig and Toborg out of the van and into Charlie's room. Amy hated building IKEA flat packs because she could never understand the instructions, but Bel, who had never done it before and kept asking "How hard could it be?" insisted on having a try. "Maybe this is just the kind of activity I need to take my mind off sex with Mark."

Amy put the kettle on and set Charlie up at the kitchen table with his poster paints. Afterward she went to check on Michelangelo. Still no change. She was wondering whether to take him to the vet in the morning so that he could be put out of his misery when she heard swearing coming from Charlie's room. It was Bel, fulminating about the inadequacy of the building instructions.

"I told you so," Amy said as she handed Bel a mug of tea. Bel was sitting cross-legged on the floor in a sea of nuts, screws, and drawer knobs. The instruction sheet was spread out in front of her.

Bel sipped some tea and carried on studying the sheet. "Hang on," she said eventually. "These instructions aren't for a Toborg, they're for a shelving unit called Ingmar."

"You're kidding," Amy said, running her fingers through her hair. "God, now we're going to have to pack it all up and go back."

"Unless..." Bel said, grinning in a way that suggested she'd had a brain wave to end all brain waves.

"What?"

"Okay, I've got this Swedish neighbor called Margit. Anyway, we got chatting the other day, and she happened to mention that one of her friends has moved in a few streets from you."

"So?"

"Duh, he's Swedish. What if I go around there and ask if he would mind helping us build Charlie's desk and chest of drawers?"

"What? That's outrageous. You cannot possibly knock on some strange person's door and ask if they'd mind dropping everything to come and help us build flat pack furniture. Plus you're assuming that because this bloke is Swedish, he will automatically know how to do it."

"But he will." Bel had started laughing. "Swedes are practically born in flat packs. Plus Margit says he's totally gorgeous. This would be an excuse to get a good look at him. I'm going to phone her and get his address."

"Don't you dare!" She tried to grab Bel's phone, but she was too late. Bel was already on her feet, dialing her neighbor's number. She listened as Bel told Margit her plan. A few moments later Bel had the address. "Margit says he's all on his own today and would probably love to come over. I'm going around there."

"But what will you say? How will you put it? I'm going red just thinking about it. It's such cheek."

"Stop being a wuss. Leave it to me." Bel headed for the door.

"Whatever you do," Amy called out after her, "please don't

mention the bit about all Swedes being born in flat packs. He might not take it very well."

"Ooh, you think?"

Twenty minutes later, Bel was back. Accompanying her was a six-foot-six, blond-haired, blue-eyed Viking hunk.

"Amy, I'd like you to meet Ulf." Bel was looking up at him, her false eyelashes fluttering nineteen to the dozen. Amy couldn't help thinking that any minute now drool would start running down her chin. "Ulf has very kindly agreed to help us build Charlie's furniture."

Amy got up off the floor, where she had been gathering up screws and nuts. "Hello, Ulf," she said, extending her hand toward him. "This is so kind of you. But surely you've got better things to do on a Sunday afternoon than build furniture for strange women."

"Oh, no. It is not a problem. I am more than happy to help." Like most Scandinavians, he spoke perfect, albeit rather formal, English in a constantly changing tone that suggested melody rather than speech. "I have just finished my shift at the hospital. It will be soothing to do some practical activity."

"Ulf's a neurosurgeon," Bel announced. "That means he operates on people's brains. Isn't that just awesome?"

Amy agreed that it was truly awesome.

"He actually drills into skulls." She turned to Ulf again. "How do you do that?"

Cue matinee idol smile: "With a very steady hand."

"And that's not all. He even finds time to work at a homeless shelter."

Amy let out an inadequate "Wow." Under normal circumstances she would have been more than eager to show an interest in Ulf's work, but right now it felt like Bel was showing enough interest for both of them.

Ulf colored. "It's not much, only twice a month. So far I have only been once."

"You're too modest," Bel said. "It's wonderful what you're

doing. Most people don't give a stuff about the poor and needy."

"Now, then," Bel said to Ulf, "what can we get you? Some herrings, maybe? Sourdough? Gravlax? Lingonberry jam? Brill?"

"Yes, I have a fridge full of herrings and brill," Amy chirruped, shooting Bel a "what planet are you on" look.

"Coffee would be great," Ulf said.

"Coming up," Amy said. "Bel, maybe you'd like to help me?"

Bel followed Amy into the kitchen. "I have found it," she squealed. "I have found it."

"Found what?" Amy said.

"The activity I was looking for. I'm going to get over Mark by getting under Ulf. He's sensitive and caring... I've found the new type of man I was looking for." She started to giggle. "You could say that I've finally turned over a new Ulf."

"My God, Bel, you only decided to dump Mark five minutes ago. What about taking some time to lick your wounds?"

"I've licked them already... God, I am so in lust." She slapped her hand to her chest.

"Great. So what are you planning to tell Mark? I seem to remember you're due over there later with pizza and beer."

"Bugger. Okay, I'll phone him. I'll tell him I'm ill. I'll say I've got some kind of sudden-onset skin fungus. That'll put him off for a bit and give me time to think about how I'm going to dump him. Now let's make that coffee. I want to get back to King Canuty."

ULF FINISHED the desk and chest of drawers in a couple of hours. It would have been sooner, but Charlie running in and out demanding to help slowed him down.

Everybody agreed—especially Charlie, who was thrilled to bits with his new desk—that Ulf had done a perfect job building Stig and Toborg. Amy wanted to say thank you and suggested she buy everybody Chinese. Ulf seemed up for it, but it was clear that Bel had other plans. "Ulf," she purred, "why don't you and I go back to your place? And if you're very good, I'll let you explore my cerebral cortex."

In the end they stayed for Chinese and left together just after eight.

After they'd gone, Amy went to run Charlie's bath. While it was filling up, she went to check on Michelangelo. She found him rigid and lifeless. She broke the news to Charlie as gently as she could but wasn't really surprised when he showed a complete lack of interest. "We'll bury his body in the ground," she persisted, "and that will help fertilize the soil and nourish new life."

"Mum, please, please can we get a snake?"

"Charlie, for the last time, we are not getting a snake. Now, are you going to come into the garden after your bath and help me bury Michelangelo?"

He gave a vigorous shake of his head.

Apart from a paper towel holder, Amy couldn't find anything to bury the poor animal in. She didn't possess a shoe box, and anyway, that would have been too big. She had loads of takeout containers, but they were the plastic kind that would delay Michelangelo's decomposition. He needed to be buried in cardboard. She looked in the recycling container, which lived just outside the kitchen door. It was empty save for a jumbo-sized Tampax box. She grimaced. She couldn't even contemplate burying Michelangelo in a tampon box. He might be only a hamster, but he was still one of God's creatures. How did that song go? "All God's critters got a place in the choir..." No, Michelangelo deserved some respect. On the other hand, she was bereft of ideas. It would be unthinkable to put him out with the rubbish. That left her with the Tampax option. Would it really be so terrible? After all, he was a dead rodent. He was hardly going to know the difference.

She hemmed and hawed a bit longer, before wrapping the furry corpse in several sheets of Bounty and placing it in the Tampax box. Afterward she dug a hole under the greengage tree in the garden and committed Michelangelo's body to the ground. As she covered his Tampax coffin with soil, she found herself humming "All Things Bright and Beautiful" and wondering if Charlie could be a psychopath, after all.

Chapter 6

THE NEXT MORNING, Charlie hardly spoke as he sat eating his Coco Pops.

Amy asked him if he was okay.

"Has Michelangelo arrived at heaven yet?" he asked by way of reply.

"Oh, I would think so," Amy said. "By now the hamster angels will probably be showing him around. I bet you anything they've got this amazing hamster wheel and some great tunnels for him to explore." She took an apple and a small bunch of grapes from the fruit bowl and placed them in Charlie's Incredibles lunch box, alongside the tuna sandwich and organic low-fat, no-salt potato chips. Charlie was less than keen on the healthy potato chips, and most mornings he pleaded for Hula Hoops or Quavers. Amy saw no reason not to give him the occasional treat, but since his school had a policy of confiscating junk food, it was the approved option or nothing.

"So, how did he get there?" Charlie persisted.

"To heaven? I'm not sure. What do you think?"

Charlie became thoughtful. "I think he went by plane or maybe in a space rocket."

With that, Charlie ran to get his crayons and some paper. Soon he was drawing a smiley Michelangelo looking out of the window of a rocket. Brilliant red, orange, and yellow flames were bursting from the engine. A boy and a woman were waving him goodbye from the ground. "That's me and you," Charlie explained. "We're happy that he's not ill anymore, but we're sad, too, 'cos we won't see him again."

Amy felt her eyes filling up. If she was honest, she had had no real doubts last night as she buried Michelangelo that Charlie was anything other than a regular kid, in possession of all the normal human emotions. Nevertheless, it was comforting to have it confirmed. "Come here and give me a hug," she said. Charlie jumped down from his chair and ran over to his mother. "Love you," she said, squeezing and kissing him.

"Yuk, I've got your lick on my face." He pulled a face and began rubbing his cheek.

AMY HAD just gotten off the bus and was making her way to the café when she got a text from Brian. He was going to be late because he had a doctor's appointment.

GETTING MOOBS CHECKED OUT. SORRY, ONLY APPT THEY HAD LEFT. HOPE U 2 CN MANAGE.

The early-morning rush was never easy, but she knew she and Zelma would just about cope.

It helped that when they walked in they would find the place sparkling and immaculate. On Saturday and Sunday, the café was run by two catering students, Otto and Fidel. The leather-trousered, nipple-pierced duo ran the place with such flair, panache, and efficiency that even Brian was in awe. On top of that they were both hygiene freaks. Every Monday morning Brian, Amy, and Zelma arrived to find the floors scrubbed, the loos smelling of jasmine, and the kitchen without a speck of grease. Brian thought his standards were pretty high, but these guys were in a different league. Heaven only knew what time they left on Sunday night.

The plan was that when Brian left to set up his cutting-edge coffeehouse in Soho or the East End, Otto and Fidel would manage Café Mozart full-time.

Today there were fresh flowers on the counter and all the tables.

Amy took charge of the espresso machine—a task she never relished because she was always scared her coffee wouldn't meet Brian's standards—and Zelma served food. Whenever the queue died down, one of them would dash around with a cloth, wiping tables and clearing crocks.

Brian arrived just after ten, relief etched on his face. "The doctor examined my moobs and says they're just fat deposits. He said if I lose a few pounds, they'll disappear."

"Told you so," Amy and Zelma chorused.

"So, now you're not turning into a woman," Zelma said, "you could maybe do a little work around here." She grinned and thrust a cloth into his hand. "You can start with wiping the counter. I've got a dishwasher to load."

Amy watched him as he started wiping down the counter. He was actually smiling.

"Tell you what," Brian said, using the cloth to steer cake crumbs into his hand, "I'm feeling generous. For the next few days, why don't we sell Crema Crema Crema at the same price as our normal coffee?"

"Blimey," Zelma said, "hark at John Paul Getty here."

"No, I think it's a good idea," Amy said. "With Bean Machine about to open, we've got to do everything we can to keep people loyal."

Brian decided to put up a pavement placard. This, combined with *The Guardian* running another piece on Crema Crema Crema in its food and drink section, meant that by midweek the queue of commuters reached into the street. Everybody wanted to know more about the coffee: Where did it come from? What gave it that amazing taste? Where could they buy it? How much was it? That much? Was there any way they could get it cheaper? In the end Brian printed out some information leaflets, which he left on the counter and all the tables.

He calculated that coffee sales had almost doubled in three days. He and Amy were allowing themselves to think that when

Bean Machine opened, they might hang on to some customers, after all. On Wednesday things were so busy that they started to run out of milk. Amy said she would nip to the supermarket and pick up three or four liters, which would tide them over until the milkman came the next day.

She was walking past the pet shop, thinking that she might win Charlie over with a pet rabbit, when she felt a tap on her shoulder. Startled, she swung around.

"Sorry. I didn't mean to make you jump." It took her a moment or two to register that the apologetic face in front of her belonged to Sam Draper. "I've been trying to catch up with you." He sounded breathless.

"That's okay," she said, offering him a reassuring smile. "Not your fault. I was miles away." She paused, not quite sure what to say next. She couldn't work out if she should launch straight into her apology for having been so rude to him the other day or wait until they'd exchanged some small talk. "So how are you?" she heard herself say.

"I'm good . . . Actually, I was coming to see you. I reached the café, then I caught sight of you down the street."

"I'm off to pick up some milk. We've run out." He was wearing an expensive-looking, slim-fitting gray suit with a narrow pinkish-purple tie. Very *Mad Men*, she thought.

"Oh, right." He was clearly feeling the awkwardness, too.

"Customers have been going crazy for this posh coffee we're selling."

"Oh, what, Crema Crema Crema? I've been reading about it." For a moment his eyes met hers.

"Actually," she said, "I'm glad I ran into you. You left the other day before I could apologize for being so rude. I was completely out of order. I'm so sorry. I don't know what got into me."

"You don't have to apologize. I understand. You were just sticking up for your boss."

"I know, but when I realized you weren't part of Bean Machine, I should have stopped behaving like an ass, but I didn't. Instead, I just carried on attacking you."

"Oh, come on. I was just as bad. I seem to remember accusing you of being a hypocrite."

"But you're right. People like me do bang on about fair trade while buying cheap products from countries with terrible human rights."

"Maybe, but I didn't have to push it home quite so hard. I'm sorry."

She offered him another smile. "Apology accepted."

"But what you said about me working for Bean Machine hit home. It's just that I only set up my company a few years ago. It's still pretty small, and particularly with the recession, we're in no position to turn down work. All I'd say in our defense is that we do a fair amount of pro bono work."

"Really?" She was impressed.

"Actually, for the last few days, I've been in Africa—in Rwanda, to be precise—checking on the building of a school that we designed."

"Oh, God, now I'm even more embarrassed. I don't know what to say."

"You don't have to say anything. You couldn't know."

"So you're still working on the Bean Machine project?"

"Yes, I've just come from the site."

"Any more news on when it's due to open?"

"A few weeks, a month, maybe. I know that isn't good news for you . . . "

His sentence trailed off.

"Oh, I'm sure something will work out. Actually, our coffee sales are up over a hundred percent since we started selling Crema Crema Crema, so you never know. Customers who appreciate really good coffee might stay loyal."

"That would be fantastic."

She got a sense that he was working up to saying something. She let a few seconds pass before she jumped in to fill the silence. "Nice laptop," she said, nodding toward the ultrathin Apple Mac he was carrying.

"Thanks. It's new. I have to admit that I wasn't sure. I usually plump for titanium, but I thought this time I'd go for the black. Except they don't make the black anymore, so I bought a black rubbery cover thing, which also means I can drop it from time to time."

"Good choice," she said. "Black goes with everything."

"Doesn't show the dirt."

"It's slimming."

He looked down at his stomach.

"God, no . . . not that I'm suggesting you need to slim. Far from it. You're very slim. Well, not too slim. I mean just right. All I meant was that in principle black can be very slimming." She felt her cheeks redden.

"Amy, I was wondering. Are you seeing anybody at the moment?"

"Me? No. Why?"

"I just thought you might like to go out for a drink sometime."

"A drink?"

"Yes."

"With you?"

He was giving her an awkward grin. "Yes."

"Oh, right . . . I'd like that."

"You would? Great."

They decided on Saturday night at the Carpenter's Arms in Chiswick.

WHEN AMY got back to Café Mozart, she went straight into the kitchen to put the milk away. Zelma was standing at the stove, frying bacon.

"I have news," Amy announced, heaving two Tesco carrier bags onto the counter. "Remember that guy Sam who came in last week—you know, the one I had that bit of a set-to with?"

"Of course. Lovely-looking chap. I sold him a slice of ginger cake."

"Well, he just asked me out."

"And naturally you said yes."

"Actually, I did."

"Good for you, darling. Mazel tov."

At this point Brian appeared. "Hey, Zelma, could you make that two bacon sarnies instead of one?"

"Will do." She turned down the light under the frying pan and went to the fridge to get more bacon. Zelma never objected to frying bacon. She adored the smell. Jewish porn, she called it. Her neighbors cooked it all the time. One of her few regrets in life was that her extractor fan couldn't be turned to "suck."

"By the way, Amy," Brian said, eyeing a box of custard tarts, "did I just hear you say you had a fight with a customer?"

By now, Amy was loading the fridge with milk. "Yes, but only because I thought he worked for Bean Machine and was out to destroy the business. I was thinking of you, that's all. Anyway, turns out he doesn't work for the enemy, after all."

Brian picked up a custard tart and bit into it.

Zelma waved her spatula at him. "I thought you were supposed to be on a diet. All that fat and sugar is bad for your heart. Don't you come crying to me in a few years when you drop dead from clogged arteries."

"Deal," Brian said, shoving the second half of the tart into his mouth. He turned back to Amy. "So who is this bloke?"

Amy explained that he was the same chap she had approached outside Bean Machine to ask when it was opening and how, when he came into the café a few days later, they'd ended up clashing. "Turns out he's the architect Bean Machine took on to do the renovation work. He doesn't work for them at all. God, I felt like such an idiot."

"Stop beating yourself up," Zelma said. "You were only thinking of Brian."

"But he does work for Bean Machine," Brian piped up. "He's got a contract with them."

"Come on, Bri, there's a recession on. None of us can afford to be too fussy who we work for. And his firm does a lot of pro bono work. He's building a school in a village in Rwanda."

He shrugged. "Bully for him. It still pisses me off."

"Brian, darling," Zelma said, "tell me, what car do you drive?"

"You know what I drive—a VW."

"Aha, and do you know who designed it? Adolf Hitler, that's who."

"Zelma, Hitler did not design the Golf GTI."

"Maybe not, but that company still has a lot to answer for."

"I'm not sure it does anymore," Brian said. "The war has been over for almost seventy years. The human exploitation I'm talking about is happening all over the world, and it's happening now."

"Huh, you think Hitler didn't leave a legacy of misery that goes on to this day?"

"I know. I know," Brian said. "Of course he did. I didn't mean to be insensitive. This is a different debate, that's all."

"You know what? My Sidney, God rest his soul, would never have a German product in the house. And if we happened to be traveling through Germany in the camper, he always insisted we stop"—she lowered her voice—"but only to do a number two."

Brian, who was smiling and shaking his head, could see he wasn't going to get anywhere. He picked up another custard tart and went back into the café.

By then Zelma was arranging bacon slices on buttered bread. "This Sam, who's just asked you out," she said. "I remember now what struck me most about him—his lovely brown eyes."

"Actually, they're gray."

"You sure?"

Amy started laughing. "Zelma, we've been through this."

ON THURSDAY, when Brian decided his Crema Crema Crema experiment had cost him enough, he decided to put it back to its old price of £5 a cup. Interest immediately dwindled, and trade at Café Mozart went back to normal. "Okay, you don't have to tell me," he said to Amy and Zelma. "It was a daft idea. People enjoy quality, but they don't enjoy paying for it." It was clear that when Bean Machine opened, the only customers who would remain loyal to Brian would be a handful of coffee enthusiasts. By Friday, he was full of the miseries again and there was nothing Amy or Zelma could say to cheer him up.

It didn't help that on Friday morning, Zelma had arrived waving an article she'd clipped from *The Daily Mail* health pages. "Here, Brian. Stop staring into that blinkin' coffee cup and read this. It's all about moobs." That grabbed his attention. He looked up and took the article from Zelma.

"Wassit say?" Amy said when he'd finished reading.

"Seems like there's been a surge in men developing moobs." He explained that in Britain and the United States, doctors were reporting several new cases a week. They were particularly confused because the enlargement didn't seem to be linked to weight. The men going to their doctors tended to be diet-conscious, slim, and fit. Even more perplexing, they were all high earners. "That's hardly a mystery," Brian said. "Everybody knows that the middle classes consult their doctors more often. They're better informed about health issues, and that makes them worry more."

Amy scanned the piece. "Yes, but don't you think it's odd that out of several hundred patients, both sides of the Atlantic, not one is working class? Not a single one. I mean, you'd expect a few. You have to ask yourself why this condition is only affecting middle-class men like . . ." She hesitated.

"You were going to say 'like you.' "

"Yeah, but that's no reason to panic."

Brian downed the last of his Crema Crema Crema and asked if they could manage without him for a few minutes. Then he disappeared into the kitchen.

"Now I've put the cat among the pigeons," Zelma said. "Look how worried he is. I bet he's gone to look it up on the

Internet. I only brought the article in because I thought it would interest him. I'm so stupid."

"Yeah, well, that makes two of us. I should have kept my big mouth shut, too."

When Amy went into the kitchen a few minutes later to get some serving platters, she found Brian sitting at the counter, staring into his laptop. "I've been Googling 'middle-class men, moobs,'" he said without looking up. "There's masses on it. There are chat rooms, scientific forums, dozens of blogs from blokes with these absolutely massive malumbas. You can even click on the images. Look . . . "

Amy winced. "Well, you look nothing like any of them."

"The piece in the *Mail* was right," he said. "None of the doctors or scientists have got the remotest idea what's causing it."

That day's newspapers had just been delivered and were lying on the counter. Amy started going through them and found almost identical articles in *The Times, The Independent,* and *The Guardian.*

Brian glanced at them when she'd finished. "This could be really serious," he said.

"It could, but nobody has actually gotten ill."

"Yet."

"Look, Brian, unlike these men, you are a few pounds overweight. Maybe in your case the doctor was right and there is a simple explanation."

"I'd say with the way my luck's been going recently, the chances of that are practically zero." He closed his laptop and got up. "I need another cup of coffee."

WITH BRIAN'S mind only half on the job, it wasn't the easiest of days. By the time it was over, even Zelma, who wasn't one to admit she was feeling the strain, started making noises about how she "wouldn't need any rocking tonight."

On her way home, Amy popped into the Italian deli and

picked up three portions of ready-made lasagne. She and Charlie were going to her dad's tonight. Phil had just treated himself to a sixty-inch plasma screen TV, and Arsenal was playing Real Madrid in the European Cup semifinal. Phil had agreed to pick them up at the flat and take them home after the game. Amy said she would bring her dad's favorite dinner: lasagne, green salad, and profiteroles.

A few months ago, Phil had taken Charlie to his first match—Arsenal versus Chelsea. He had invited Arthur, too, but Victoria disapproved of soccer on the grounds that its supporters belonged to the lower orders. Phil was quick to make the point that at thirty quid a ticket, very few of the lower orders could afford to go these days, but Victoria was adamant. Arthur's school played rugby and golf, and she considered those sports to be far more suitable.

Phil had supported Arsenal since he was a boy, and the idea of at least one of his grandsons keeping up the tradition rather appealed to him. After that first game Charlie had become a bit of an enthusiast, and Phil had started inviting his daughter and grandson over to watch the big games on TV. Amy loved nothing more than seeing her dad and Charlie bouncing up and down on the sofa, cheering and yelling, with Charlie wearing the Arsenal strip his grandfather had bought him. Sometimes Phil would forget himself and start shouting: "Come on, you arse." Then Charlie would giggle and remind his granddad that "arse" was a rude word.

Amy was always telling Phil how much she appreciated his taking such an interest in Charlie. Phil would tell her that it was his pleasure. "Don't get me wrong, I always adored you two girls, but there were times when I did miss having a lad to take to the football on a Saturday afternoon."

To say that football bored Amy was an understatement. For Charlie's sake, she did her best to show an interest. Nevertheless, she was aware that she had a tendency to keep asking how much longer the game had to go. She could just about control her ennui for ninety minutes. If the game went into extra time or, God forbid, a penalty shoot-out, she became filled with an overwhelming desire to eat her own head.

WHILE SHE waited at the bus stop with her carrier bags of food, she called Bel.

"Hey, you know that guy Sam I told you about? The one I said I didn't think I fancied? Well, he just asked me out and I said yes."

"Brilliant. That's great news. I had a feeling he fancied you. And from what you said about how he handled Charlie and Arthur, he sounds like a nice guy. You never know . . . maybe he'll be the one."

Amy told her not to hold her breath.

"By the way," Bel said, "I dumped Mark."

"You did? Well done."

"Yeah. This afternoon. I've just gotten back from his place. God, I hope I don't live to regret it. There were two things that man was generous with: his tongue and his wallet."

They both started laughing.

"So how did you end it?" Amy said.

"You'd have been proud of me. I pulled myself up to my full five foot eleven and told him precisely what I thought of him."

"No! God, I bet he loved that."

"Actually, he did. He said seeing me angry gave him a hard-on. The next minute he's telling me to take off my clothes."

"What did you do?"

"What do you think I did? I got naked."

"You didn't."

"No, but I was very tempted, particularly when he produced the feather and handcuffs. It was the sexual equivalent of walking away from the Vivienne Westwood sample sale."

"Well, I think you've done brilliantly. So how are things with Ulf?"

"Fabulous. When we got back to his place, he read to me from Strindberg's *Röda Rummet*. It's a nineteenth-century satirical novel that relentlessly attacks the political, academic, religious, and philosophical worlds."

"Wow, sounds like you had a stimulating evening."

"Oh, we did. Ulf is a real thinker. He's into literature and music and theater. He's also a gentleman. He drove me home, and do you know what he did? He helped me out of the car and then kissed my hand. Can you believe that? No man has ever kissed my hand."

"So when are you seeing him again?"

"Saturday night. He's taking me to a reading of Nordic sagas. Okay, I know what you're thinking. I know it sounds monumentally dreary, but the audience dresses up in horns, and whenever the baddies' names are mentioned, you all shout Norse curses. Apparently, one of the worst ones means 'Your mother wears Roman soldiers' shoes.' Sounds like it could be a real hoot, don't you think?"

"Yes, absolutely. Total blast," Amy said.

"DON'T GET me wrong," Amy said to her dad as they sat finishing the profiteroles and waiting for the football to start. "I suppose this relationship with Ulf could work out, but you know Bel. She's always been more *Story of O* than Strindberg."

That made Phil laugh. "Poor Bel. After the upbringing she had with that deadbeat father of hers, she deserves to find a decent chap. Can't you help her find somebody suitable?"

"I've tried," Amy said as she sat rearranging bread crumbs on the dining room table. "Actually, I think she and Brian would be perfect for each other, but neither of them wants to know."

Phil and Val both had a soft spot for Bel. They always said how much they adored her humor and arty eccentricity.

Looking back now, Amy realized that although her parents gave every impression of being committed suburbanites, they'd always had a penchant for quirky, unconventional types.

The Christmas parties they used to throw for their charity-tin-rattling crowd were a perfect example. They always contained a smattering of oddballs. Amy remembered a couple of ecowarriors in dreadlocks and hemp shoes, an outrageously camp Buckingham Palace butler, and a woman with a six o'clock shadow who was apparently the lead singer in a band called Birds with Big Hands. Everybody was welcome, and Amy loved her parents for that, unlike Victoria, whose teenage rebellion took the form of eschewing the unconventional. As a consequence, she would retreat to her bedroom, put on some Vivaldi, and play air violin.

"You know," Amy said, "I sometimes think about Bel getting married and that maybe you could give her away. She's got nobody else."

Phil said that if and when the time came and if he was asked, he would be more than happy to oblige. "But given the choice, I'd rather give you away."

Amy was still busying herself with the crumbs. "I know you would."

"You know your mother and I would like nothing better than to see you happy and settled."

"I am happy and settled."

"You know what I mean. And that boy of yours needs a dad."

Amy shushed him. Charlie, who was on the sofa, eating his profiteroles and watching Nickelodeon, was well within earshot. "He's got you and Brian," she whispered.

"It's not the same—you know that. And I, for one, am not getting any younger."

"Oh, stoppit." She put another profiterole on his plate.

"Or thinner," Phil said. "So is there anybody on the scene?"

"Dunno. There might be, but we haven't even been on a date yet."

"What does he do?"

"Architect."

Phil's eyes widened with approval, as if to say "You could do a lot worse."

The next moment he was looking at his watch. "Hey, Charlie, time to change channels. It's a minute to kickoff."

"Yay." Charlie scrambled for the remote, which was at the other end of the sofa.

Phil came and sat next to Charlie and put his arm around his grandson's shoulders, and the pair of them launched into "Arsenal till I die/I'm Arsenal till I die/I know I am/I'm sure I am/I'm Arsenal till I die." Amy smiled to herself and started gathering up the plates from dinner. At one point she stopped to finish the half profiterole Charlie had left. As she chewed, she found herself looking round the room and thinking, not for the first time, how badly it needed decorating and updating.

The Laura Ashley floral wallpaper was faded and looked so old-fashioned. She had vague memories of it going up sometime in the eighties and how excited Val had been. A few weeks before, her mother had been looking through a copy of *House and Home* and discovered something called a dado rail. This was a three- or four-inch-wide strip of wood—usually pine—that was nailed all the way around a room, approximately three feet off the floor. The dado rail was a Victorian invention that had no particular place in a 1930s semi, but in the mid-1980s it was the height of interior design chic, and Val was determined to have one installed. The idea was to put wallpapers with different patterns above and below the rail. It didn't matter if they clashed designwise so long as the colors matched. Val had mint green stripes below the rail and florals in the same color above it.

The darker green Dralon sofas had to be twenty-five years old. They had kept their color pretty well but were dotted with bald patches. In the eighties, everybody bought Dralon: synthetic velvet that you could scrub with detergent. No matter how it was treated, it refused to wear out. Well, it finally had. Ditto for the carpet. Not only was it badly worn, unlike the sofa it hadn't kept its color. Decades in the light had turned it from gold to pale yellow. If Amy remembered rightly, the carpet was also made of what back then had been some fancy new man-made fabric. Enkalon. She even remembered the song from the TV ad: "Squash it and it just springs back/Wash it and the color stays fast/Give it the treatment, the family treatment—Enkalon is made to last for years and years and years and..."

She carried the plates into the kitchen. The dark mahogany units, never really the epitome of style, were chipped and warped. Upstairs the avocado bathroom suite was clean but dull and covered in lime scale.

When had Val given up on the house and let it go? Amy couldn't come up with a date, but she knew from things her mother had said about the marriage that it coincided with Phil losing interest in everything except the business. "There seemed no point in doing up the house," she'd confided to Amy. "It wasn't a home to him. Just somewhere to eat, sleep, and watch TV."

Just then Phil appeared carrying the salad bowl, with just a few oily green dregs left at the bottom.

"Hasn't the football started?" Amy said.

"Flooding on the pitch has stopped play, at least for the moment. It was already pretty wet from a few days ago. They might have to call it off." He flicked the switch on the electric kettle. "Tea?"

"Lovely...So, Dad. How you doing? You seem to have really cheered up."

Phil took two mugs off the pine mug tree and grinned. "I suppose your mother's told you about my floozy."

"She did say something. So did Victoria."

He dropped a tea bag into each mug.

"Your mother's fine about it, but poor old Victoria has totally got hold of the wrong end of the stick."

"In what way?"

"Joyce is a perfectly respectable woman. She's a doctor's receptionist. She is not some scarlet woman. It's just that she's . . . how can I put this? . . . a very sensual woman who enjoys a full and creative physical . . ."

"Okay, Dad. Enough. I get it."

"She also enjoys writing about it. A year or so ago she started advertising erotic poetry evenings, and to her surprise she discovered that other, very ordinary folks enjoyed coming along to listen to her work. I can understand some people thinking it's a bit odd, but Joyce is a lovely woman, and what she does is completely harmless."

"Don't worry. I'd pretty much worked that out for myself. I'm just glad you're happy, that's all."

"I'm happier than I've been for a very long time. That side of things—you know, the physical side—had been off the menu with your mother for a good few years, you know."

"Yeah, Mum said."

He poured boiling water into the mugs. Just then the doorbell went.

"You expecting somebody?" Amy said.

"Actually, that's probably Joyce. She left her phone here this morning. She said she'd be round to collect it."

While her dad went to answer the door, Amy poured boiling water into the mugs and tried to imagine Joyce. Her fantasy was split between middle-aged ethnic type in a tie-dyed kaftan and big earrings and a brassy barmaid. She wasn't expecting the vision that now appeared before her.

"Amy," Phil said, brimming with pride, "I'd like you to meet Joyce."

The first thing Amy noticed was the embroidered black velvet eye mask edged with gold. Joyce was holding it to her face courtesy of a dainty stick attached to one side. Her full-length black dress was slit to the thigh. The plunging neckline showed off her impressive, if wrinkly, bosom. She was waving a purple fan made of ostrich feathers.

"Gosh," was all Amy could manage.

"I know, the getup is a bit OTT," Joyce said to Amy, her voice full of laughter. "I don't usually go around looking like I'm on my way to one of Elton John's masked balls. I'm doing a reading tonight, and I always like to get into the spirit of the occasion." By then she had put the mask and fan down on the kitchen worktop and was making a beeline for Amy, arms outstretched. Amy took in the faded red curls piled into a messy chignon and the face that must have been beautiful once but was now full of smoker's crevasses plastered in heavy foundation and powder. "So this is Amy. Your dad has told me so much about you."

"Really?"

"Don't panic. It's all highly complimentary." When she had finally finished hugging Amy, she stood back to appraise her. "Well, aren't you just gorgeous. I'd give my right arm, not to mention a few vital organs, for a face and figure like yours. Enjoy it while you're young, that's what I say. Because it won't be long before Father Time and Mr. Gravity enter your life, and no matter how hard you try to show them the door, you won't be able to get rid of them."

"My mum says the same." Amy chuckled.

"Anyway, I'm so sorry I have to fly. I'd love to stay and chat, but I just popped in to collect my phone."

Phil handed Joyce her phone, which had a Hello Kitty charm hanging from it. "Present from my five-year-old niece," Joyce said. "What a doll—such a little cutie."

Just then Charlie appeared to see what was going on. "This is Joyce," Amy said, "She's a friend of Granddad's."

Joyce bent down to Charlie's height and shook his hand. "Hello, young man, and might I say what a pleasure it is to meet you?"

"Are you staying to watch the football?" Charlie asked.

"I'd really like to, sweetheart, but unfortunately I have to be going. Maybe another time?"

Charlie nodded.

Joyce turned to Phil. "I'm reading my new poem tonight: 'Erogenous.' I am soo nervous." She touched Amy's arm. "Now, don't listen to anybody who says that what I do is in bad taste. Your father will tell you that I take a huge amount of my inspiration from the Bible. Check out the Song of Solomon: 'Let him kiss me with the kisses of his mouth: for thy love is better than wine.' Could there be a better opening line to an erotic poem?"

With that she picked up her fan and mask, kissed Amy and Charlie goodbye, and said how lovely it had been to meet them. Then she started toward the door, followed by Phil.

It was only as Joyce had kissed her that Amy had smelled alcohol on her breath. She'd probably had a glass of something to calm her nerves before the show, Amy thought. On the other hand, a person needed to drink more than a glass of wine or spirits for it to smell on her breath. What was more, she was driving. Then again, Amy knew for a fact that many people of her dad's age ignored the drunk driving laws. It probably didn't mean anything.

"Mum," Charlie said.

"Yes, darling."

"Whass erojnus mean?"

"Ooh, I'm not really sure. I'll have to look that one up. Tell you what, why don't you go back into the living room and see if the football's started yet."

Phil was coming into the kitchen as Charlie was going out. He stood back to let his grandson through the doorway. "So what do you think?" he said to Amy. "A lot of people find her a bit overpowering, but she's got a heart of pure gold."

"I'm sure she has," Amy said. "Two minutes in her company and you can see how warm and kind she is. I totally get what you see in her."

By then their tea had gone cold, so Amy made some more.

"So how's the journalism going?" Phil said.

"Not brilliant. The editors who bother to get back to me

all say I write well, but it's a question of getting ahead of the game and coming up with a story or a subject they haven't already covered. I keep racking my brain."

"You know, the locals around here are up in arms about that new flyover the council's planning. It doesn't affect me, but for some people, the noise is going to be terrible. It'll take thousands off property values. Now, wouldn't that make a good article?"

"It would, but only for the local paper."

He said he supposed she was right. He looked thoughtful, as if he were trying to come up with another idea. "I've lost my cleaning lady."

"Brilliant. You can see the headline: 'Man loses home help.' "

Phil laughed. "No. I didn't mean it as a story. I was changing the subject, that's all. Mrs. B left me. I only hired her a few months ago."

Amy asked him what happened.

"You know how all the schools are into this healthy eating lark? Well, the older kids are going crazy about it. Mrs. B found out about this and decided to cash in. Each night, kids from the local schools phone or text her with their orders for pizza, KFC, and burgers. The next day, she collects the orders and passes them through the school railings. They pay her ten percent on top of the meal price. Apparently, she's doing very well and there's nothing the schools can do."

"No. You're kidding. You absolutely sure they can't put a stop to it?"

"Positive. By pure chance, I got to chatting to a couple of the parents, and there's some loophole in the law, apparently."

"But that's a fantastic story . . . the lengths kids will go to avoid healthy eating and the woman who supports them. Is she a devil or a savior?"

"Amy, this is Mrs. B we're talking about. She's not the sharpest tool in the box. She can barely string two sentences together. I'm not sure she'd make the greatest interviewee."

"You let me worry about that. Bright or not, this is a fantastic story. Have you got her phone number?"

Phil reached for his mobile and clicked on his contact list.

Just then Charlie appeared in the doorway. "Granddad, Granddad . . . Come quick, the football's started!"

After Phil had disappeared into the living room, Amy wrote down Mrs. B's number and then texted Victoria: "Just met Dad's lady friend, Joyce. Eccentric, but definitely not hooker."

Amy was in the middle of doing the washing up when Victoria replied to say that she supposed they should be grateful for small mercies.

When she'd finished doing the dishes, she noticed that the sink was covered in tea stains. She got out the bleach and soaked them. When the stains were gone, she gave the sink the once-over with Shiny Sinks. Then she had a go at the kitchen floor, which was looking a bit mucky. Her dad so needed to find a replacement for Mrs. B.

By the time she'd finished, it was after nine. The game still had over half an hour to go, more if it went into extra time. Charlie would be exhausted in the morning. Still, tomorrow wasn't a school day. He could lie in.

It was clear from all the excitement and yelling coming from the living room that her presence wasn't going to be missed, so Amy decided to go upstairs and watch TV. She was settling down with another cup of tea on what had once been her parents' bed when her arm brushed against some sheets of paper on the nightstand. They fell onto the floor. Amy picked them up and almost put them back without giving them a second glance. Then it occurred to her that maybe the papers were in some kind of order and she ought to put them back as she'd found them. It was then that she saw it. The heading was in inch-high red letters: "Penis Extensions for U . . . many styles and finishes to choose from." Her hand shot to her mouth. She found herself staring at a second sheet. Before her was a field of flesh-toned cucumbers with names like B. Cumming, Birth of Girth, and Doc Johnson Cock Master.

Chapter 7

"OKAY, MAYBE THIS works better," Bel said. "'Caution, terrain. Pull up. Pull up'—with no emphasis on any particular word. I figure that way the pilot stays calm and the passengers have the best chance of survival. On the other hand, this is a danger warning. Perhaps I should raise my voice and sound more forceful and animated. I'm thinking: *'Caution!! Terrain!! Pull up!! Pull up!!'* But that could put the fear of God into the pilot. He could panic, crash the plane, and it will be all my fault."

Bel had landed another electronic voice job, delivering warning messages to pilots. As usual, she couldn't make up her mind about the appropriate tone and emphasis and was consulting Brian and Amy.

"I don't understand why you always get so worked up about delivering these lines," Brian said. "Each one is just a sentence."

"I'm a method actor. I need to get it right. That means I have to know what my motivation is."

"Your motivation is banking the check," he said. "Now just stop obsessing."

"That's rich," Bel shot back, "coming from the planet's obsessor in chief."

"Okay," Amy said, spreading clotted cream over her scone, "stop bickering, you two, or I'll have to separate you. Why don't we talk about something else?" She bit into the scone and started chewing. "So what do you guys know about penis extensions?"

While Bel seemed amused, Brian winced. "Excuse me?"

Amy supposed he had every right to pull a face. The aspidistra and bone china elegance of the Kew Gardens tea shop didn't exactly lend itself to talk of male genital enhancement.

"Why?" Bel said, "you thinking of getting one?"

"Fun-nee. No, I'm pretty sure my dad is."

Brian's wince morphed into a grimace. "Omigod! He told you that?"

"I don't get it." Bel said to Brian. "What's your problem?" She reached in front of him and helped herself to the cut-glass bowl of strawberry jam.

"My *problem* is boundaries. It's pretty obvious that when it comes to his daughter, Phil doesn't have any."

"Look," Bel said, spooning jam onto her plate, "if Amy's dad feels he can confide this kind of thing in Amy and she's happy to hear it, then I don't see why it needs to be an issue."

"Of course it's an issue."

"Actually, Dad didn't say a word," Amy said. That shut them up. "I found this stuff he'd printed out from the Internet."

"Aha." Bel grinned. "So you were snooping."

"I was not," Amy protested. "The papers fell on the floor, and as I picked them up, I found myself reading them. I couldn't help it. The words 'penis extension' were in inch-high red letters. You couldn't miss them." She paused. "So what is a penis extension? You get all that spam about them, but I always delete it."

Bel said that as far as she knew, they were nothing more than rubber sleeves that fit over the end of the male member. "It must be odd, though," she said, "discovering that your father has a small penis. I mean, girls in particular look up to their dads. Then you find out he's not the great man you always thought he was."

"Okay, let's get one thing straight. My dad does not have a small penis."

"Maybe you could repeat that," Brian said. "A few people on the Isle of Wight didn't hear."

"So how do you know he hasn't got a small penis?" Bel asked, her mouth full. "God, these scones are good."

"I've seen it."

"What, recently?"

"Duh. Of course not recently."

Brian's head was in his hands. "For the love of all that's holy, please can we end this conversation?" Amy and Bel had invited Brian out for tea to cheer him up, but it clearly wasn't having the desired effect.

"Oh, Brian, stop being such a wuss," Amy said. "Surely your family went around naked when you were a kid. It's perfectly normal to have seen your parents without clothes on."

"If you remember, my parents died when I was thirteen, and those events have pretty much clouded what went on before."

Amy put down her scone. "Oh, Brian, I'm sorry. Sometimes I forget."

"Don't worry," he said, offering her a smile.

"I'm convinced," Amy said, "that this is all about Dad's new girlfriend putting pressure on him." She turned to Brian. "I didn't tell you. My dad is seeing this erotic poetess called Joyce. Anyway, turns out—"

"Whoa, hang on," Brian said. "Can we rewind for a second? An erotic poetess?"

"Yes, she writes erotic verse. Anyway, it turns out, as you might expect, that Joyce is pretty demanding in the bedroom department."

"You mean she writes porn," Brian said.

"No, I mean erotica."

"What's the difference?"

"I guess it's less graphic than porn," Amy said. "A bit more flowery."

"Oh, Araminta," Bel began, giggling, "lead my member to your soft moist center."

Brian's face was giving every impression that he was in physical pain.

"God, Bri," Bel said, "I had no idea you were such a prude. You know, it's really rather cute." She ruffled his hair, which he didn't seem to mind.

"Yeah, well, if you'd been brought up by my gran, you'd be a prude, too. Imagine what it's like growing up in a house where it's considered the height of indecency to refer to chicken breast." He took a mouthful of tea and turned to Amy. "Having said that, your parents are a bit odd. I mean, there's your mother with her shaman, and now your dad's dating an erotic poetess. Don't get me wrong, I think they're brilliantly odd, but you have to admit they are slightly out there."

"Again, I don't get it," Bel said. "Why does 'different' have to equal 'odd' in your book? Difference is something that should be celebrated, not ridiculed."

"I agree, and that's why I'm not ridiculing those sparkly red shoes you're wearing."

"Well, thank you. That makes a change."

"You're welcome." He drained his teacup. "So, how you getting back to Kansas? I take it you've tried clicking your heels three times while repeating 'There's no place like home'?"

Bel threw up her hands. "See, you had to spoil it."

"Or you could always follow the Yellow Brick Road."

"Oh, get a haircut!"

"What's wrong with my hair?"

"Oh, please, you two," Amy groaned. "Just put a sock in it. Look, getting back to Dad for a moment. What worries me is that he might be overdoing it. I mean, he's sixty-five, and if this Joyce, who I've met, by the way, has got him swinging from the chandeliers at his age, anything could happen."

"Has it occurred to you," Bel said, "that maybe Joyce isn't putting the remotest pressure on him and they're just having fun?"

"Maybe. She's a lovely woman. You can't help liking her. But at the same time, she's really loud and overpowering. And she smelled of booze. I'm worried about what he might have gotten himself into."

Bel shrugged. "Phil is a grown-up. It's his life, and Joyce is his problem. I know it can't be great discovering intimate details about a parent, but you cannot possibly interfere."

Amy was aware these were almost the exact words she'd used to Victoria when they'd discussed their father's new relationship. It seemed she was struggling to take her own advice.

"I agree," Brian said.

Bel was blinking at him. "You do?"

"Absolutely."

"I can't remember the last time you agreed with something I said," Bel said, giving the impression that she wasn't so much surprised as flattered.

"Now, please, for the last time," Brian said, "can we change the subject? I have news."

"Please make it be the good kind," Amy said.

It was. Brian had been to a dinner party the previous evening and had met "a goddess" by the name of Rebecca. Such was her ethereal beauty that he hadn't taken his eyes off her all night. As yet she hadn't removed any items of clothing beyond her cashmere cardie. This had revealed several unraised arm moles, which Brian decided didn't constitute a barrier to any future intimacy. Of course he couldn't make a final decision about her suitability as a girlfriend until he had seen her naked, but he felt he had every reason to be optimistic that she didn't possess any significant physical blemishes or imperfections.

"The only problem is me and these bloody moobs," he said, clutching his right chest and wobbling it. "I have to get rid of them. I've decided to go back to the gym. Maybe that'll help me firm up."

"I'm sure it will," Amy said.

Amy would have expected some kind of moob barb from Bel at that point, but none came, which was odd.

"So when are you seeing Rebecca again?" Amy said.

"Tonight. We're going out for sushi. I tell you, I haven't been this excited in ages. I haven't thought about the business all day."

"Wow," Bel said, "so that's all three of us on dates tonight with new people. Amy with Sam. Me with Ulf—"

"What?" Brian said. "Who's Ulf? What happened to Jurassic Mark?"

"I dumped him."

"But he treated you like crap. I thought you loved that."

"Not anymore. Meet the new me. Ulf is a Swedish brain surgeon. He's thoughtful, intelligent, and he respects women."

"A brain surgeon?" Brian said. "You're going out with a brain surgeon?"

"Yes, why? Do you have a problem with that?"

"Me? No. Why would I?"

"Just think," Bel was saying, "these people could turn out to be the ones we decide to spend the rest of our lives with. Hey, we could have a triple wedding."

"Brilliant idea," Amy said, laughing. "You and Ulf can wear your comedy horns."

Brian wasn't listening. He had a teaspoon in his hand and was prodding at a dollop of strawberry jam on his plate.

Amy looked at her watch. She needed to get going. Charlie was being dropped home from a friend's birthday party in just over an hour. Before she went out tonight, she needed to give him supper—not that he would be remotely hungry after having OD'd on party food—and get him bathed and wound down for the baby-sitter. She also had to phone Mrs. B and have a chat with her about her junk food school lunches.

"I'm sorry to break up the party," she said to the others, "but I need to be heading back."

Brian asked her why the hurry, and she explained about Charlie and her possible news story involving Mrs. B. Bel and Brian both agreed it had great potential.

"I just need one decent story to get me noticed. Then I might start getting commissions and I'll be away. I can't tell you how much I want this. It's what I've been building up to for so long."

"Well, if you ask me," Bel said, "it's a cracking good story. I could see all the papers picking it up, plus the TV news running with it."

"I agree," Brian said.

"My God," Bel said, "that's the second time you've agreed with me in almost as many minutes. This is starting to feel weird."

"You know, I haven't said this before," Brian said to Amy, "but I'll really miss you when you finally hit the big time and decide to leave the coffee shop. It's been great having you around."

"Aw, I've loved it, too, but for heaven's sake, don't start planning my leaving party yet. My track record's not exactly brilliant. Remember that so far I haven't had a single thing accepted."

"You will," he said. "You're a great writer. It's just a matter of time and coming up with the right story."

"Absolutely," Bel chipped in. "I've got all my body parts crossed."

Amy felt her cheeks turning pink. "Thanks, guys. I really appreciate you having so much faith in me. I don't know what I'd do without you." She looked at her watch again. "God, I really do have to go. Apart from everything else, I've got my prep to do."

Bel frowned. "Prep?"

"Date prep."

"Come again?"

"Sam's an architect. I know nothing about architecture. Tonight, when we're out, I don't want to come across like some kind of ignorant klutz. When he asks me my opinion on the Taj Mahal, I don't want to hear myself say, 'Oh, it's brilliant. They do a mean chicken tikka masala.'"

Yet again Bel and Brian were united in their opinion. They both agreed that prepping for a date seemed more than a tad over the top. "It's meant to be fun," Bel said, "a chance to get to know each other, not a bloody exam."

"I know," Amy said, "but I just feel it's good manners to have some idea about the other person's world. In my experience, it makes conversation that much easier."

Brian and Bel shrugged and let the subject drop. Then Brian offered Amy a lift home, which she was only too glad to accept.

"I don't get it. What's supposed to be wrong with my hair?" Brian said, easing the VW out of its parking space. He looked in the rearview mirror and began running his fingers through his shaggy locks. "I quite like it the way it is."

"There's nothing wrong with your hair. Bel was just cross. You'd been teasing her. Why do you two do that? It's so childish. And it's so wearing listening to it all the time."

He shrugged. "I dunno. It's just how we are. It's not serious. I mean, we don't hate each other or anything."

Amy smiled. "I know that."

Neither of them spoke for a few moments. It was Amy who broke the silence. "You didn't seem particularly thrilled when you found out about Bel and this brain surgeon."

"How d'you mean?"

"I dunno. You seemed a bit subdued."

"Maybe I was thinking about the problems with the business."

"You said you hadn't thought about Café Mozart all day."

"Okay, maybe I was thinking about something else. I can't remember."

"It occurred to me that you might be jealous."

"What? Why on earth would I be jealous? That's absurd. I've got no interest in Bel. You know that. And I've just met Rebecca, who I am absolutely crazy about. How could you think for one minute that I have feelings for Bel?"

"Just something I thought I'd picked up on, that's all ... Okay, I was wrong. I'm sorry."

Another silence.

"So," Brian said eventually, "do you think I should do something about my hair?"

"You like your hair the way it is."

"Yeah, but Bel thinks it needs cutting."

"Brian, why do you care what Bel thinks? It's never mattered to you before."

"I know, but she's got a certain style, and I respect her opinion, and I've just met this new woman...So what do you think? Do I need a change?"

"Honestly?"

"Why else would I be asking?"

"Okay...Well, if you really want my opinion, I think a sharp, trendy cut would do wonders for you. Your mop's lovely, but it makes you look about seventeen."

He nodded. "Say no more."

"Look, don't take any notice of me or Bel. Do what makes you happy."

"I am," he said. "I'm getting it cut."

CHARLIE CAME home from his classmate's party high on sugar. He spent ten minutes charging around the flat yelling the Spiderman theme song before Amy shooed him into the garden with his football to cool off. Each time she looked out the kitchen window, he would be dribbling the ball and singing: "Spiderman, Spiderman, does whatever a spider can, spins a web, any size. Catches thieves, just like flies...Goal!!!"

These days, children's birthday teas tended to consist of healthy dips and crudités and coarse wholemeal bread sandwiches filled with hummus, or pâté made from brain-boosting oily fish. Judging by Charlie's behavior, this had been an old-fashioned, more traditional affair.

Once Charlie had calmed down, he started planning his evening with Lilly, the baby-sitter. Lilly was Ruby's university student niece. Amy used her a fair amount because she felt guilty always asking Val to baby-sit.

Lilly was gorgeous. She had golden waist-length hair and

eyes the color of the Caribbean. What was more, she adored Charlie and would read to him for as long as he could stay awake. For his part, Charlie behaved like the perfect child when he was with her. She seemed to cast a spell on him. Amy suspected that her son was ever so slightly in love with Lilly.

While Charlie sat in front of his new shelving unit, grabbing puzzles, games, and DVDs, Amy phoned Mrs. B, whose surname she had managed to remember.

"Mrs. Brannigan, it's Amy here, Phil Walker's daughter. We met a couple of times at my dad's house, if you remember."

"Oh, yes."

Amy recognized the smoker's voice and Irish accent.

"Dad happened to mention that you've started fetching pizza and KFC for the local schoolkids at lunchtime."

"Oh, yes."

"And you're happy to carry on doing this for the kids?"

"Oh, yes."

It was all coming back to her now, how Mrs. B (a short, inordinately thin woman who, if the need arose, could have sought refuge behind a bread stick) possessed few words and little emotion. She remembered that Phil, who had just finished reading *Angela's Ashes* when Mrs. B started working for him, suspected she'd experienced extreme poverty and drunken male brutality growing up in the Dublin slums in the years just after the war. This experience, he concluded, had left huge emotional scars. Amy tended to think she was just one of those people who didn't waste words.

If Phil was around when Mrs. B arrived on a Thursday morning, she would greet him with some pithy reference to the weather like "Blowy again, then." If the weather was looking really grim, she might be moved to comment: "Reminds me of the winter of forty-seven. All thirteen of us children were snowed in for near on a fortnight. Oh, yes." Having gotten that initial bit of chitchat out of the way, she would take off her coat, hang it over one of the kitchen chairs, put on her apron, and start filling her bucket. Phil would offer her a cup of tea, which she would accept, along with a chocolate digestive, but conversationwise that was pretty much it until she had finished work. Her traditional parting message to Phil was a downbeat "I've left yer smalls in the linen cupboard to air."

"The reason I'm asking about what you're doing for the schoolkids," Amy pressed on, "is that I am doing some freelance journalism and I thought it might make a rather good newspaper story. After all, you are going against government initiatives to try to get children to eat healthily."

"Oh, yes."

"If it is all right with you, I'd like to come along and interview you about it."

"Oh, yes. When might that be?"

"Say, Monday, early evening? Half past six be okay?"

"Right you are. You'll be wanting my address, then."

Amy wrote down Mrs. B's address, hit "end" on the phone keypad, and prayed that when the time came, she would be able to string together a decent quote.

For a few minutes she allowed herself to imagine what her life might be like as a successful freelancer. Not only would she be able to organize her hours around Charlie, she could earn substantially more money. She could learn to drive and buy a car, take Charlie to Disneyland Paris. Maybe in time she could even do up her flat.

She looked at her bedside table. It was piled high with interior design magazines. At night, instead of reading a book, she would flick through a couple to get herself to sleep. She found herself almost salivating over the kitchens, bathrooms, furniture, and wall coverings she couldn't begin to afford. She got so carried away that she could practically touch the granite worktops, smell the wallpaper. At the moment she had her eye on a spectacular stainless-steel kitchen. She couldn't decide between glass and stainless-steel splash boards or whether the floor should be tiled or covered in industrial-look rubber.

Of course it was all moot. She had no money. Until she started earning a decent salary, she would have to make do with her eighties pine kitchen that had turned orange over the years and her crusty old bathroom.

She found herself reaching under her bed and taking out her shoe box full of swatches of fabric and wallpaper samples. She'd been collecting them since she was in her twenties.

On top was a piece of latte-colored silk damask covered in an elaborate rose design. She picked it up and held the soft fabric to her face. A few years ago, while she was in Paris on an assignment for Dunstan Healey Fogg, she'd stumbled across this über-chic upholstery shop in the back streets somewhere near Montmartre. The roll had been placed at one end of a bottle-green velvet chaise longue. Several yards had been unfurled so that it skimmed the floor. Amy couldn't help noticing how each ruche and fold had been arranged with impeccable elegance and grace. She had fallen in love with the fabric on the spot, but it was something like a hundred euros a meter and she couldn't begin to afford it. The owner—a sixty-something woman with a severe bob and edgy titanium glasses—had taken pity on her and let her take away a headscarf-sized sample. Amy looked at the swatch and smiled. It always amused her because it was so over the top, so very Louis Quatorze. She had a special place for it—or something very like it—in her grand design plan.

She imagined knocking down the wall between her galley kitchen and the living room and creating one large, white minimalist space. She could see the pale wood floor, the stainless-steel kitchen units, the brightly colored abstracts on the walls. So far, so brutalist. Then would come the design clash, the bit that would soften and lift it all—not to mention add some fun—a huge crystal chandelier suspended over the dining table and in one corner a pair of the campiest, most ornate bandy-legged French armoires, covered in silk damask.

Aware that time was getting on, she didn't spend long with

the box. Pretty soon, her thoughts turned to what she was going to wear for her date with Sam. They were going to a pub, so nothing fancy was required. Nevertheless, she wanted to give him the impression that she'd made the effort.

A dress, maybe? All her dresses and tops had either wide-scooped or deep V-necks. They flattered her bust rather than emphasized it and made her feel sexy. High necks and turtles in particular made her breasts look like a shelf.

She started pulling clothes off hangers and laying them on the bed. It reminded her of when she was a teenager preparing to go out on a first date. Back then, though, there was rarely any excitement or anticipation. She often went out with boys just to keep up with the other girls. In her teens she dated a stream of greasy youths with mullet haircuts just to keep up with discussions about French kissing and below-the-waist sexual exploration. It was only as she got older and started going out with men she liked and actually found attractive that those few hours before the date stopped being a chore and turned into something thrilling. Tonight, as she laid out more and more clothes on the bed, she was feeling the same excitement.

In the end she chose a purple sundress with tiny white flowers dotted over the full skirt. It wouldn't be warm enough on its own, so she picked out a three-quarter-sleeve white shrug to go on top. She would finish it off with purple ballet pumps. She was wondering if it was all a bit Joanie from *Happy Days*, when she realized she hadn't done her date prep. *Bluff Your Way in Architecture*, a mercifully slim tome she'd found in Waterstone's, was in her bag. She'd read it through a couple of times on her way to and from work, but she wasn't sure how much of it had stayed in her head. She unzipped her bag, took out the paperback, and sat down on the bed. Flicking through the pages, she realized she had absorbed a reasonable amount. If it came to it, she could hold a short conversation on modernist and postmodernist architecture. She knew the difference between Doric, Ionic, and Corinthian columns. If she was asked, her favorite buildings were the AT&T Building in New York and the Chrysler Building.

She didn't hear Charlie come in.

"Mum, where are you going tonight?" he piped up.

"Oh, just to the pub with a friend. I won't be late."

She had decided not to tell Charlie she was going out with a new man. It still concerned her that Charlie was unhappy about her dating because he feared she might abandon him. This was her first date with Sam. At this stage, she had no intention of fueling her son's anxiety.

"A girl friend or a man friend?"

"What?" She hadn't been expecting that. She hated lying to Charlie. "Well, it's actually a man friend."

"Can he be my daddy?"

"So you don't mind me going out with men, then?"

"No. I like it 'cos you might choose a daddy."

She suspected that his feelings were still confused. He wanted a dad, but at the same time he was frightened of his position being usurped. She took his hand and drew him toward her. "Oh, Charlie . . ."

"I'd like a daddy. I mean, I've got Brian and Granddad and sometimes we see Uncle Simon, but I'd like a proper daddy."

"I know, darling. I know you want to be like the other children. It's rotten being the odd one out."

"If I had a real dad, it would be better."

"It would?"

"Yeah . . . He'd get me a snake."

AMY AND Sam took their drinks outside onto the pub terrace. "I really love this old place," she said, her eyes drawn to the high garden walls, the yellow London brick just visible through a waterfall of wisteria.

The terrace wasn't too packed, and they were able to find a table next to a tub bursting with arum lilies.

"I'm so glad you agreed to come out tonight," he said as they sat down. She noticed the fine lines that fanned out from his eyes as he smiled, making him look ever so sexy.

"I'm glad you asked me," she said, returning his smile. He was wearing dark jeans with a white shirt that looked brand new and a black linen jacket with a pale, narrow pinstripe. On his feet he wore brogues—midbrown lace-ups. There was an easy elegance about this man that appealed to her.

"I was sure you were still angry with me," he continued, "and would tell me to take a hike."

She shook her head. "God, I really am sorry for losing it that day at the café."

"C'mon, let's not have that discussion again," he said.

"Okay, deal."

There was a hiatus as he took a sip of wine. In that couple of seconds, Amy's first-date nerves, combined with her need to fill all conversational gaps, kicked in. "It's funny," she said, "you being an architect, because I'm really into buildings."

"Really?" he said.

"Absolutely."

"What kind?"

"Well, I love postmodern architecture and how it evolved from the modernist movement yet contradicts many of the modernist themes. I like the way it combines new ideas with traditional forms and how postmodernist buildings can sometimes startle you, surprise you, or even make you laugh."

He was clearly taken aback. "Wow. I'm impressed. You know, it's so rare to find anybody who takes an interest in architecture. Most people totally ignore the buildings around them."

"Oh, not me," she continued, feeling like she was on a roll now. "Of course, Philip Johnson's AT&T Headquarters in New York is often cited as a perfect example of postmodernism. I always find myself taken by the sleek classical facade. Then, when you look up, there's this oversized Chippendale pediment. It's the clash of two worlds that makes it so amusing." She considered telling him that she was planning something similar with a crystal chandelier and froufrou armchairs in her fantasy open plan kitchen-dining-living room but decided against it on the grounds that he'd think her vision was pretty pedestrian compared with Philip Johnson's genius.

"That's so true. The frustrating thing is that nobody gets that . . . So what's your favorite building?"

Easy peasy.

"Oh, without doubt the Chrysler Building. Did you know that the gargoyles depict Chrysler car ornaments and the spire is modeled on a radiator grille?"

"Actually, no, I didn't."

"And I just adore the Pompidou Center in Paris. I mean, Richard Rogers has to be one of the greatest architects in the world. He's totally up there with Le Corbusier and Alvar Aalto."

"And even Frank Lloyd Wright. Are you a fan?"

Frank Lloyd Wright. Of course she knew the name. World-famous architect. Simon and Garfunkel wrote a song about him. God, how did it go? "So long, Frank Lloyd Wright . . ." Something about architects coming and going. She spooled through what she could remember of the lyrics for specific architectural references. As far as she could tell, there were none.

"Oh, who couldn't be a fan? The man was a genius."

"So which do you think is his best work?"

She tried to deflect the question. "Oh, there are so many to choose from."

"But if I pinned you down, which would you choose?"

"Which would I choose?" She felt sick. Her heart was racing. The game was up. She was about to make a complete idiot of herself. This date was over before it had even begun. "I guess it has to be a toss-up between the—"

"I know what you're going to say: the Guggenheim and Fallingwater in Pennsylvania."

"What can I say? You took the words out of my mouth."

Oh, thank you, God. Thank you. I will never, ever doubt your existence again.

"You know, it's funny you being a fan of architecture because I'm actually a bit of a coffee nerd."

"Really. You'd get on brilliantly with my boss, Brian, then."

"My favorite comes from a company called Hacienda La Evita."

Amy frowned. "Evita? Don't you mean Esmeralda? It's Hacienda La Esmeralda. Brian ordered some recently. Goes for hundreds of pounds a pound. It's right up there with Crema Crema Crema."

"Of course it's Esmeralda. My mistake. Anyway, I just ordered some from Guatemala."

"But Hacienda La Esmeralda comes from Panama."

"Does it? You sure? I could have sworn . . ."

Her face formed a broad grin. "Okay, correct me if I'm wrong. I'm guessing here, but you don't know very much about coffee, do you?"

"Not as such." He couldn't have looked more embarrassed. "The truth is, I was trying to impress you. You must think I'm a complete twit."

She was fighting to keep a straight face. "No, I don't. Not at all. I just think that you didn't work quite so hard at your pre-date prep as I did."

He burst out laughing. "I don't believe it. You mean you mugged up on architecture?"

"I know as much about architecture as I do about molecular physics. In other words, next to nothing. I spent the last few days boning up on it just so's you wouldn't think I was an idiot."

"Well, it worked. You sounded like you really knew your stuff."

"Why, thank you," she said, smiling.

"So does all this date prep make us two insecure individuals who get overly anxious before a date?"

"No, it makes us nice, considerate people who think it's important to be able to engage in intelligent conversation about the other person's work and interests." She paused. "Okay, *and* it makes us insecure and overly anxious."

"I'm sorry that my effort was so paltry."

"Hey, c'mon," she said, patting the back of his hand. "The thought was there."

"Do you want to know something?" he said.

"What?"

"I'm really not that keen on coffee."

"No? Me, too."

"I always think the aroma promises more than it delivers."

"I couldn't agree more. I'm forever telling Brian that. It really winds him up."

"What I really love," he said, "is hot chocolate."

"Me, too!"

"But it has to be the really good stuff."

"Absolutely."

"At least seventy-five percent cocoa solids."

"At least."

"With whipped cream and minimarshmallows. On a really freezing day, you can't beat it."

"But don't you find it's sometimes difficult to find minimarshmallows? The supermarkets only ever have the big ones."

"Ah," he said. "Have you tried aquarterof.com? They have all that kind of stuff."

"No. I'll take a look. Thanks for the tip. God, we sound like a pair of old codgers. We'll be onto supermarket coupons next."

They were both laughing now. The tension was broken. They were out of the starter's gate and off.

They spent the next couple of hours talking nonstop, unaware of people coming and going around them. Sam got up a couple of times to fetch them more drinks, but apart from that they were engrossed in each other. She told him about her time in PR, how she was desperate to break into journalism but wasn't having much luck. "Editors keep telling me it's not my writing that's the issue and that my instincts about what makes a good story are right, but I'm often too late with it. By the time I come up with an idea, it's already been done. And nobody will commission me to write something because I've got no track record. It's so catch-22."

Sam nodded. He said he had a couple of friends who freelanced for the nationals. "Took them ages to break in. But they did it in the end. You just have to be patient and persistent and develop a very thick skin."

She laughed. "Believe me, I'm developing the rear of a rhinoceros." He asked her if there was anything she was working on right now, and she told him about Mrs. B supplying "illegal" school lunches. His eyes widened. "That's a brilliant story." Like Brian and Bel, he said he could see TV picking it up. "This could really make your name."

"Maybe—if I can persuade Mrs. B to give me a quote longer than three words."

Eventually the conversation returned to architecture. Sam told her how his fascination with buildings had started when he was eight or nine. "I got a copy of the *Guinness Book of World Records*, and I became obsessed with skyscrapers. For the next couple of years I collected pictures of the world's tallest buildings: the Sears Tower, the World Trade Center, 40 Wall Street. Then there were the chimneys and towers: the Eiffel Tower, Battersea Power Station. I had photographs all around my room. All I wanted to do was design the tallest building in the world. I hardly ever stopped drawing. I would fall asleep at night over my sketch pad."

She said he sounded like Charlie.

"He's good at art?"

"Yes. He seems to have a real gift, but I've got no idea where he got it from. I have a bit of a flair for color and interior design, but I can't draw or paint to save my life. And as far as I know, his father had no artistic talent."

"As far as you know?"

She paused. She hadn't intended to discuss how Charlie came into the world, at least not on their first date. Sam picked up on her hesitation.

"I'm sorry. I was prying. This really is none of my business."

She ran her finger over the rim of her wineglass. "Charlie was conceived by an anonymous donor. The only information I received was a list of his physical attributes, interests, and aptitudes."

"Please, you don't have to say any more."

"No, I don't mind."

She explained about her mother's early menopause and how she was frightened of waiting too long to get pregnant. "I could have frozen my eggs, I suppose, but I was frightened of something going wrong. You know, the freezer breaking down . . ."

"And your eggs coddling."

She laughed. "I was going to say 'frying,' but 'coddling' is better."

She was surprised that she was revealing so much, so soon. Sam was a very good listener.

He said he couldn't imagine how she'd coped on her own. "My sister's twins screamed solidly for the first three months. Sometimes, when my brother-in-law was away, I'd go around there to help out with the feeding and burping. I'd stay a few hours, and afterward I was totally knackered. It was such a relief to walk out of the door and into the pub." He paused. "Tom and Jo are four now. They're great little chaps . . . heavily into gorillas."

"Huh. With Charlie it's snakes."

"So, have you gotten him one?"

"What? No. You must be joking. I hate snakes."

"That's a shame. Little corn snakes make great pets, and they're harmless. I used to have one when I was a kid. We used to feed it mice. You buy them frozen. It used to be my job to thaw them out in hot water."

"Oh, God," she said, screwing up her face in disgust. "If I needed another reason not to let my child have a snake, then that is it."

He was chuckling. "Spoilsport."

She found herself asking him about his parents. It turned out that Sam's father had walked out on his mother, leaving her with three children under eight. "She raised us all on her own. He never sent her a penny." He paused. "So are your parents together?"

"They were until a few months ago. Now they're separated and talking about divorce. It's strange. You have this picture of them growing old together, and suddenly your mum's dating a shaman and your dad's hooked up with an erotic poetess and about to get a penis extension." She blinked. She couldn't believe she had just made the penis extension remark. It was the wine. It had gone to her head and caused her to lose all brain-to-mouth coordination.

While her face burned with embarrassment, Sam seemed perfectly comfortable with the subject of penis extensions. "I've often wondered," he said. "Do you think that if you agree to have a penis extension, all those spam e-mails stop?"

Feeling at ease again, she laughed. "Maybe I'll buy one and find out."

Their talk turned to midlife crises. They both agreed that whereas the midlife crisis was now recognized along with the quarter-life crisis, during which twenty-five-year-olds panicked about their lack of professional and personal achievement, nobody had acknowledged the three-tenths life crisis that affected the over-thirties. "It's the time when you first start to realize you're growing old," he said. "One day you hear your favorite tune . . . in a lift . . . You start keeping more food than booze in the fridge."

"You start watching the weather forecast. You refuse to have sex in single beds. You can't drink cheap wine anymore."

"But in case you're forced to drink it, you carry antacids in your pocket." He paused. "Speaking of antacids, how do you fancy getting something to eat?"

She giggled at his segue and said she would love to.

They walked along the riverbank. It was dark now. The reproduction Victorian street lamps—designed to give foreign tourists a fake taste of Ye Olde England—had just come on, giving off a mellow yellow light. Couples were strolling arm in arm, chatting, stopping for a kiss, disappearing into restaurants and bars. A fancy white motor cruiser went by, people laughing and drinking up on deck. A pub had a blackboard sign outside offering Pimm's at half price until eight o'clock. They'd missed that. It was after nine. A mother and father duck led a line of fluffy ducklings up onto the bank and stood quacking for a bit before turning around and waddling back into the water.

All the restaurants along the river were full. In the end they wandered onto the High Street and found an Italian place that Amy had been to before and knew was good.

They ate veal escalopes and sautéed potatoes cooked in garlic and rosemary and talked about movies. He loved the Coen brothers. *Fargo* was one of his top films ever.

"Mine, too. Didn't you just love the wood-chipper scene? It was gross but utterly hysterical."

He said she was the only woman he had ever met who had loved that scene. She could tell he was impressed. "Okay," she said, "so where do you stand on Woody Allen?"

"Old stuff great. Gone off in the last ten years or so."

"I agree. Wow, we are really bonding!" She paused. "Okay, final test. The Harry Potter movies."

"So-so scripts. British kids can't act—"

"—is the correct answer. I think we are done."

This man was funny, intelligent, and sexy, did date prep, and even shared her taste in movies. Surely he was too good to be true.

As he drove her home, she decided there had to be a catch . . . like he had a wife.

"So, Sam, you ever been married?" The wine she'd had earlier was still affecting her and making her direct, but he didn't seem to mind.

"Nah. I came close a couple of years ago, but in the end it didn't work out. She took a job in Australia."

"And you don't have any secret vices?" she persisted.

He shrugged. "Not really . . . Okay, actually there is one."

Aha.

"What?"

"Well, I'm kinda into . . . "

Bondage? Threesomes? S&M? Cocaine? Which was it?

"Yes?"

"Cake."

"Cake? I've not come across that. What do you do? Inject it? Snort it?"

He was laughing. "None of the above. I'm talking about cake as in cake. You eat it. Victoria sponge is my favorite, closely followed by coffee and walnut. I'm addicted."

"Oh, right. Sorry. I wasn't with you."

"So why all the questions?"

"No reason. Just curious, that's all."

Because this was their first date and she didn't want things to get too heavy, she couldn't tell him what was on her mind—that as a single mother, forming lasting relationships hadn't been easy and she didn't want to fall for him only to have him let her down.

By then they had turned onto her street. He pulled up outside her flat and turned off the engine.

"I really have had a great time tonight," he said.

"Me, too."

"So, would you like to do this again?"

"Yes, please. Very much."

"Fantastic. I'll call you tomorrow."

He leaned toward her. Finally, his lips met hers—a sweet, tender first kiss.

Chapter 8

"SO HE DIDN'T assume an automatic right to tongue action?" Bel said, phoning on Monday morning for a full report on Amy's date. She was on her way to the studio to record her pilot warnings. Amy was on the bus, heading to work.

"Nope."

"That is so refreshing. Even on a first date most men make a beeline for your tonsils. Don't you just hate that?"

Amy agreed that she did. Thinking back, it was what Duncan had done.

"So when are you seeing him next?"

"Saturday. We're going to the Tate Modern and out to lunch afterward."

"If you're going to the Tate, make sure you catch the Didier Le Boeuf exhibition. There was a huge piece about it in yesterday's *Sunday Times*. Supposed to be amazing."

Amy had never heard of Didier Le Boeuf. Bel explained that he was famous for his installations. "Some of them are massive. The one everybody's raving about is a chain-link fence. And it's possible you might even bump into him. According to the piece in the *Sunday Times*, the man has an ego the size of the planet and likes to hang around the gallery, hoping to catch snippets of praise. He even gives impromptu lectures, apparently."

Amy thought that neither Didier Le Boeuf nor his installation sounded hugely appealing, but she made a mental note anyway.

The bus pulled in at Amy's stop. She stood up, moved along the gangway, and waited for the hiss of the automatic doors.

"So you really like this Sam?"

"Definitely. He's intelligent, funny, incredibly sexy. He's even into kids. He used to help his sister with her baby twins. I just worry that he's too good to be true."

"Hey, come on—has it occurred to you that maybe he isn't and that this is your time?"

Amy shrugged. "You think?"

"Absolutely. Stop trying to find fault. Enjoy it."

"I know. You're right."

"Okay, I have news: Ulf stayed over—Saturday *and* Sunday."

"No."

"Yep. He only just this minute left."

"So . . . how was it?"

"Nice."

"Nice?"

"Yeah. It was different. Enlightening, educative—a bit like the Norse saga evening."

"You mean boring."

"No. I mean it was very Scandinavian."

Amy giggled. "You mean lots of hot tub action?"

"I don't have a hot tub."

"Ah, there is that. What, then?"

"Well, we were on the couch making out, and suddenly he asks me how I'd feel about us becoming more intimate. I said I'd like that, and he says: 'Can I have permission to touch your breast?'"

"Wow, that's spontaneous."

"Yeah, so anyway we carry on, but he insists on asking permission before he touches a new bit of me. I keep telling him I'm his adventure playground and he can touch any bit he wants, but he seems to have a mental block. I'm thinking it's maybe some PC thing they have in Sweden. But on the upside he is such a sweetie. He's kind and respectful. So different from

Jurassic Mark. He needs to loosen up a bit, but I know we'll get there."

"'Course you will," Amy said, her tone cheery and reassuring. She wouldn't have upset her friend for the world, but she suspected that after the way Jurassic Mark had treated her, Ulf's kindness and gentleness were little more than a novelty. Like all novelties, it would wear off.

Amy rang off as soon as she reached the café. Brian was standing behind the counter, head down, cleaning the coffee machine. He didn't hear her come in.

"Hi, Bri. Wassup? You seem miles away." It was only then, as he looked up, that she noticed. "Omigod. I am loving the hair." It was very short but not cropped. His sideburns had been trimmed and left long. "Really suits you. Puts years on you."

"Gee, thanks."

"No. I mean in a good way. You always look so young. This makes you look more mature."

He shrugged.

"What's the matter? Don't you like it?"

"It's not the hair," he said. "I love the hair."

"What, then?"

By then Zelma had emerged from the kitchen with a bacon sandwich. "A treat for Mr. Grumpy here. Not that he deserves it."

Brian put down his cleaning cloth. "I'm sorry. I don't mean to be in a mood. It's just that nothing in my life seems to be working out right now, and it's really getting me down."

"I'm guessing this has something to do with your date with Rebecca," Amy said.

Brian took a huge bite of sandwich and started chewing. "She's shaving herself."

"I'm not with you."

More chewing. "She's shaving herself for marriage."

What was this? Some trendy prenuptial ritual she hadn't caught up with?

"I think what he's trying to say," Zelma piped up, "is that she's *saving* herself."

"That's what I shed."

"You mean she's into the whole abstinence thing?"

"Yup."

"I can't believe it," he said, swallowing. "I'm crazy about this girl. We met up again on Sunday after I got the haircut. She seemed to be really into it and kept saying how hot I looked. Anyway, we had lunch out, and afterward we went back to her place. She put on some music. I put my arm around her. It was all starting to get smoochy and cozy, and then she came out with it."

"So she's a virgin?"

"No, and that's the bit that really pisses me off. She's been in several relationships. She describes herself as a 'born-again virgin.'"

"How does that work, then?" Zelma said.

Brian took another bite of sandwich. "She's had an operation."

"What?" Amy said. "To sew it back?"

"Yep."

Zelma flinched. "Oy."

"You ought to see her Facebook page. She goes into all the gory details."

"So what is she?" Amy asked, "Some kind of religious nut?"

Brian shook his head. "No, she just wants to experience— let me get this right—'the joy of being deflowered by the love of my life on my wedding night.' I asked her where this left us, and she said for her abstinence was the only choice."

"Look, you've only just met," Amy said. "Maybe she'll change her mind after a few weeks."

"I don't think so. She takes this thing very seriously. I wouldn't mind waiting a few weeks, but I'm mad about her."

"You know, in my day," Zelma piped up, "we waited."

"No, you didn't," Brian said. "You just pretended to. There were thousands of shotgun weddings."

"Well, my Sidney, God rest his soul, never laid a finger on me until our wedding night. I remember it like it was yesterday. Three wonderful performances and a rehearsal."

Amy frowned a question. "A rehearsal?"

"You know," Zelma said, lowering her voice. "Nobody comes." She let out a cackle.

"Zelma!" Amy was snorting with laughter. "I cannot believe you just said that."

"You think my generation never told a risqué joke? You should have lived through the war like I did and heard some of the dirty stories they told . . . and I was only a child."

"My question is this," Brian said, shoving the last of the sandwich into his mouth. "Would it be morally acceptable to stay in the relationship and have sex with other women?"

"You cannot be serious," Amy said.

"I'm perfectly serious."

"You're going to cheat on her from the get-go?"

Zelma was looking heavenward, open-palmed.

"Yes. I don't see an alternative. I cannot survive without sex."

"Then you have to be honest and tell her that," Amy said.

"On the other hand," Zelma said, "you could make do with solo sex. At least you're doing it with somebody you like and there's no performance anxiety. And you don't have to pay for dinner first."

Amy and Brian exchanged wide-eyed looks. Both of them were struggling not to laugh. This was a side of Zelma they had never seen before.

Zelma picked up on this. "Hey, I lived through the sixties. I saw *Hair*—"

"Your Sidney took you to see *Hair*?" Amy said.

"Good God, no. He would have been scandalized. I went with a couple of girlfriends. Sidney never knew." She turned to Brian. "So you're really going to cheat on this poor girl?"

Brian shrugged and said that maybe he would give it a few weeks. Meanwhile, he would brush up on his seduction techniques.

"Ah, now you're talking," Zelma said, a faraway look in her eyes. "Sidney used to buy me a half pound of chocolate liqueurs every Saturday night, regular as clockwork—never missed. Later on, he'd go upstairs for his bath. We could only afford to bathe once a week because of the cost of the electric. Afterward, he'd Brylcreem his hair and I'd be waiting for him in my see-through baby-doll nightie and dripping in Youth Dew. I kept that nightie for years. He loved seeing me in it. Of course, eventually he got his cataracts and it didn't quite have the same effect." With that she picked up Brian's empty plate and disappeared into the kitchen.

"So how are you going to woo Rebecca? Do you remember that dreadful line you used when we were students and you went out on the make?"

Brian grinned. "You may mock, but I had many successes with that line."

"Bri, there is no way any woman is going to fall for 'I'm a meteorologist, and I'd like to study your warm front. Let's go to an isobar and have a drink.'"

"But they did. Back then I could laugh women into bed."

"Well, maybe that's what you have to do now."

"You think? Perhaps I could wow her with my *Seinfeld* impressions. There's that great one I do of George: 'I'm a great quitter. It's one of the few things I do well. I come from a long line of quitters.'"

Amy was forced to admit that the voice, the delivery, the stance were perfect. "'My father was a quitter. My grandfather was a quitter...I was raised to give up.' I could work on that."

Just then there was a knock at the door. It was the delivery-man with that day's bread and pastries. Brian went to the door still reciting lines from *Seinfeld*: "'Hello, Newman...You're an anti-dentite...These pretzels are making me thirsty.'"

Amy was smiling and shaking her head. "Yeah, that'll get her straight into bed," she murmured.

• • •

MRS. B FILLED two large schooners with sweet sherry and insisted that Amy call her Dymphna. In her tiny council flat, surrounded by her china saints and framed prints of the Holy Father suffering unspeakable agonies on the cross, she verged on chatty.

"Now, then, Amy, will you be having some cheese and onion Hula Hoops? Or I've got bacon flavor if you'd prefer. Oh, yes." She held out a plastic bowl that was meant to look like cut glass. It was decorated with an image of the Holy Virgin cradling the bloodied corpse of her deceased son.

Amy put down her notepad and pen and helped herself to some Hula Hoops. "No, cheese and onion is fine," she said. "Actually, they're my favorite."

"Mine, too." Mrs. B was aglow, apparently delighted that the two of them shared a taste for cheese-and-onion-flavor Hula Hoops. "I find the bacon repeats on me, don't you?"

"Er . . . not really . . . So, Mrs. B . . ."

"Dymphna—please."

"Sorry. Dymphna . . . Don't you think it's irresponsible to be buying kids pizza and KFC at lunchtime, when the country is facing a huge obesity problem and the government's spending vast amounts providing healthy school meals and promoting healthy eating programs?"

"The kids like JFK."

"You mean KFC."

"What did I say?"

"JFK."

Mrs. B looked blank.

"JFK was the American president," Amy said. "John Fitzgerald Kennedy."

"Would that be right? And here's me thinking that the K stood for 'Kentucky.' So it's Kennedy Fried Chicken, then?"

Amy scratched her head, not knowing quite how to proceed.

"You see," Mrs. B went on, apparently in no need of an answer to her question, "the kids like the junk food. It's got some taste. You know, a bit of a kick." She took a small, ladylike sip of sherry.

Amy made the point that the so-called taste was produced by high levels of fat, sugar, and chemicals.

"But kids are growing. They need energy. Fat and sugar give them that. Oh, yes. When I was a child, growing up in Dublin after the war, all we had was boiled vegetables. There was barely a scrap of flesh on our bones. And our spirits were crushed. We were dead behind the eyes. Walking corpses we were."

"But these kids aren't starving. Quite the opposite. They have plenty of choice. They choose to binge on food that makes them fat. We live in a country where nearly forty percent of the population is obese, and it's only going to get worse."

"You say obese. I say well covered. There's no shame in a person having some meat on his bones."

Amy noticed that Mrs. B's eyes were filling with tears. "What is it, Dymphna?"

She took another sip of sherry. "You want to know?" she said, her tone verging on tart. "Right, I'll tell you. I clean half a dozen houses locally. None of the women I work for eats a square meal. Turn them sideways and they disappear, but they all think they're fat."

Amy was forced to note the point that Dymphna was extremely slim. Did she diet?

"Heaven help us, no. I got the TB when I was a child. I never could put weight on after that . . . Look, it doesn't bother me what these rich women do to themselves, but I can't abide it when they starve their little ones . . . particularly the girls. Babies they are . . . ."

It turned out that one of the women Dymphna worked for had put her four-year-old daughter on a diet and almost killed her. "No milk. No cheese. No butter. Just vegetables, nuts, and a bit of boiled chicken. The weight fell off the little mite, and all she wanted to do all day was sleep. I couldn't stand by and do nothing, so I phoned the child protection people. The next day that child was in the hospital on a drip."

"So you saved her life?"

"I did, but I got no gratitude from the parents. Not that I was expecting any. They were all for suing me until their lawyer told them they didn't have a hope in hell."

"And this was never reported?"

"Never. It all got hushed up. You asked me why I don't hold with so-called healthy diets. That's why. Oh, yes. Now, then, will you be having some more Hula Hoops?"

INSTEAD OF catching the bus, Amy decided to walk the mile or so home. She needed some time to think about how she was going to approach this piece.

She was in no doubt that she had uncovered a damned good story: A woman whose attitudes toward food were formed by poverty and the modern obsession with thinness fights back by feeding junk food to schoolkids.

Within the next day or so she needed to visit the school at lunchtime and speak to the kids. She had to find out what they thought of Dymphna and why they wouldn't at least try the healthy meals provided by the school. There was only one problem: She worked in a café. She couldn't possibly ask Brian to give her time off at the busiest time of day. Sometimes things got so hectic that the three of them found it hard to cope. What she needed was somebody to cover for her.

As soon as she'd put Charlie to bed, she phoned Bel.

"God, that is so weird," Bel said. "I was about to call you. I need a favor."

"You do? So do I. You go first."

"Okay, I've got my first proper audition tomorrow—the Young Vic is putting on an improv version of *Hamlet*. I'm trying out for Ophelia. I don't know when I'll be finished, so I was wondering if you could pick me up some shopping."

"No problem. Tell me what you need and I'll make a list."

"Don't worry. Everything will be packed and ready for you to pick up."

"Okay, which supermarket."

"Dildo King."

"Excuse me. Dildo King?"

"Yeah, it's that new sex shop on Clapham High Street."

"I know what it is. Bel, I am not going into a sex shop. They're so bloody seedy. I'll get leered at by all the dirty old men in raincoats. I can't. Why don't you order what you want online?"

"They take over a week to deliver, and I really want this stuff ASAP. I'm desperate to try it out on Ulf. I've ordered an edible thong—cherry-flavored—some chocolate body frosting, and handcuffs. What do you think?"

"I think that I'm not going."

"Oh, please. Dildo King is on your way home. It'll take you five minutes."

"But what if somebody sees me?"

"Who's going to see you?"

"The parents from Charlie's school, for a start." It wasn't lost on her that she was starting to sound like her sister.

"Oh, please, Ames. I'll do anything you want in return. Name it."

"Oh, all right, then, but only 'cos I need a favor in return. Are you free Wednesday during the day?"

"No. But I've got a couple of hours free Thursday lunch-time."

"That'll do. I don't suppose you could fill in for me at the café for a couple of hours. I've just done this amazing interview with Mrs. B, and now I need to speak to the schoolkids. I have to go at lunchtime, when she's there delivering the food."

"You want me to be a waitress?"

"Yes. Can you do it? I know you've got no experience . . ."

"Hello. I've done bar work, plus I'm an actress. Of course I can do it. What are we going for? I can do gutsy coffee shop waitress with five kids, on the run from her violent drunk of a husband. I can do sexy wannabe actress. I can do the whole TGI shtick. You name it."

"Could you just take orders, give the right change, and maybe wipe down a few tables?"

"Yep. No problem. I can do that. Don't worry, I can work out my own character and motivation."

"Excellent."

ON HER way home the following evening, Amy got off the bus at Clapham High Street and made her way to Dildo King. The moment she stepped inside the shop, she wished she hadn't made such a fuss about picking up Bel's "shopping." The place exuded trashy, but it was a long way from the sordid pornmonger's she'd been expecting. There were racks of red polyester basques and thongs embroidered with "enter here." One wall was devoted to magazines and cheap plastic sex toys. Tame stuff.

The place was empty apart from the studenty-looking girl at the till wearing a "Peace in the Middle East" badge and reading Plutarch's *The Age of Alexander*.

"You have a package for a friend of mine," Amy said, feeling the need to dissociate herself from the purchase. "The name is Bel Flemming."

"Oh, yes," the girl said, offering Amy an easy smile. She reached under the counter and produced a brown paper bag. "It's all paid for. Tell your friend that because she's spent over twenty pounds, she qualifies for a free clit stick." She opened the bag and popped in a gaudy box labeled "Dildo King Clit Stick Supreme . . . because she comes first!"

Amy thanked the girl and made her way to the door. It couldn't have been simpler.

She stepped off the curb and was about to cross the road when she saw a motorbike speeding toward her. As she stepped back, she tripped on the pavement edge. She managed to right herself, but the brown paper bag fell to the ground close to the gutter, spilling out its contents. In front of her lay one clit stick, an edible thong (cherry-flavored), a can of chocolate-flavored body frosting, and a pair of handcuffs. There was also a copy of the latest Dildo King catalogue. A couple of teenagers, about to cross the road, hovered for a few seconds and sniggered. Amy bent down and reached for the catalogue.

"Can I help you?" Despite the traffic noise, she recognized the voice at once. Red-hot blush shot through her face like squid ink in water. The next moment Sam was squatting beside her, picking up the Dildo King clit stick.

She decided humor might be her best option. "Of all the porn shops in all the towns in all the world . . . "

"I had to stop outside yours." He was looking at her, grinning that sexy grin of his.

"Actually, not mine. My friend Bel's," she said, relieving him of the clit stick, "I just came to collect this stuff for her."

"Hey, whatever. It's your life."

"But it really isn't mine. I don't have a life. No, that came out wrong. Of course I have a life, just not *that* sort of life . . . you know, with cherry-flavored thongs and stuff."

He looked almost disappointed. This made her feel she should clarify her position.

"I mean, that's not to say I'm not liberated in the bedroom department. I am. I'm into stuff. Certain stuff. Not all stuff. I do draw a line."

"So no whips, no rubber, no threesomes?"

"Good God, no."

"Not like me, then."

Her eyes widened in alarm.

"I've got this rubber wet suit I love to wear in bed," he said.

"You have?"

"Yeah. Women go really wild for the flippers."

"What? . . . Oh, behave," she said, her face breaking into a smile.

He was laughing now. "I'm sorry, that was mean, but you should have seen the look of terror on your face when you thought you were dating some weirdo."

"Rotter," she said, scooping up the rest of the items and putting them back in the paper bag. He stood up and helped her to her feet.

"So what are you doing in this neck of the woods?" she said.

"My office is in that house over the road. We rent the basement." He pointed to a pretty white Regency house in the middle of a terrace of identical houses, "We've got clients coming in for a late meeting. I was on my way to do a tea and coffee run."

Amy said she wouldn't hold him up. "I'm in a bit of a rush myself. I've got to collect Charlie from the child minder." She paused. "So I'll see you on Saturday. I'm really looking forward to it."

"Me, too."

She gave him a quick kiss on the cheek.

"Oh, by the way, how did your interview go?"

"Great," she said. "I'll tell you all about it on Saturday."

They agreed to meet at Amy's flat at ten.

"You'll recognize me," he said. "I'll be the one in the wet suit and flippers."

FIRST THING the next morning, Amy had a chat with Brian and explained that having interviewed Mrs. B, she needed to go to the school one lunchtime to speak to the kids. "I know it's the worst possible time of day, but I can't see any way around it. If it helps, Bel said she'd cover for me."

"Fine."

"Really?"

"Yeah. I'm not going to let her loose on the espresso machine, but I'm assuming she can clear tables, slice cake, and stack the dishwasher."

"She's worked in pubs. Of course she can, and I'll be back in a couple of hours. Bri, I promise I'll make it up to you."

"Amy, will you just stop fretting? We'll manage"

"Thanks," she said. "You're a really good mate."

On Thursday morning on the dot of half past eleven, Bel arrived. She was wearing a candy pink polyester waitress dress, very tight, very short, the top buttons undone to her cleavage. A dainty white apron completed her ensemble.

Amy rolled her eyes. "What, no frilly cap, no notepad, no pencil behind the ear?"

"Hi, y'all. My name is Bel"—she strung her name out to three syllables—"and I'll be your waitress for today. Our specials include deep frah-ed chicken, turnip greens, black-eyed peas, fried catfish, and key lime pie."

Zelma burst out laughing. "My God, Blanche DuBois has gone into catering." She kissed and hugged Bel and told her off for being such a stranger . . . "and so thin."

"So what do you think of the outfit?"

"All I can say," Zelma replied, "is that most women wear more when they give birth."

At that point Brian walked in. He'd been in the kitchen, on the phone to one of the suppliers. His eyes went from Bel's cleavage to her legs and back again. Not that she noticed. Her eyes were elsewhere.

"Haircut, haircut," she chanted.

Brian looked self-conscious. His hand darted to his head. "You hate it."

"Hate it? Of course I don't hate it. I think it's great. Very sexy." Bel had called Brian a lot of things in the past. As far as Amy could remember, "sexy" had never been one of them.

"Really?"

"Come on, you know me. When do I ever lie? So how do you like the outfit?" She did a twirl. "If you think it's too much, I've brought ordinary clothes. I can change."

Brian seemed unable to take his eyes off her. He didn't speak.

"Bel to Brian—come in, Brian. I said if it's all too much, I've brought civvies I can change into."

"No," he said. "You're fine. Honest."

Brian said he would take Bel into the kitchen to show her how to work the dishwasher.

"Oh, by the way," Amy said to Bel, "the *shopping* you asked me to pick up is on the top shelf in the cloaks cupboard."

"Thank you so much. You're a doll."

After Brian and Bel had disappeared into the kitchen, Zelma turned to Amy. "Is it my imagination," she said, "or do I detect a spark between those two? In the past, all they've ever done is rub each other the wrong way."

Amy shrugged. "Your guess is as good as mine. They're both seeing new people, so if there is something between them, it's all going to get very messy."

BY TWELVE o'clock, Amy was standing outside the gates of Nelson Mandela High School. Mrs. B was there, too. Beside her was a shopping basket on wheels, filled to the brim with KFC and McDonald's bags. The flat pizza boxes were stacked neatly on top to stop them from getting squashed. Amy didn't dare say anything, but she was forced to admit that the aroma was sublime.

Three or four teachers now hovered in the background. A few minutes earlier they had been only too eager to speak to Amy, saying how they feared for the health of their charges and how the law had to be changed to give schools the power to ban the likes of Dymphna Brannigan. Of course Dymphna had been listening to all this, but being the mild-mannered soul she was, she didn't retaliate. She didn't need to. For the time being at least, she had the law on her side.

A gang of thirteen- or fourteen-year-olds was climbing the school railings, excited young primates yelping for their grub. Mrs. B stood her ground and refused to hand out any food until they had all calmed down. She started with the pizza orders. "Wayne Pyke—one stuffed crust with extra bacon, chicken, ham, and cheese . . . Shelby Lacy—thin 'n crispy pizza, chicken wings, large Coke." She passed the cardboard flat packs sideways through the bars. The kids took their food and handed her the cash. More than once Mrs. B scolded them for not having the exact change. The teachers looked on, angry and helpless. All they could do was keep reminding their pupils not to drop litter.

"So," Amy said, having introduced herself to the kids and explained why she was there, "what do you lot make of Dymphna?"

"Hero!"

"Genius!"

"Legend!"

"But why won't you eat the healthy meals the school provides?"

"Don't taste of nuffink."

"They want us to eat salad an' that. It is disgusting."

"All those vegetables give you ass gravy. Know what I mean?"

"Yeah, really messes wiv yer Donald Trumps. That can't be healthy, can it?"

"But don't you worry about getting fat?"

One of the girls jumped in. "My mum says if I get too big, I can always have one of them gastric band things fitted, so I don't need to worry."

"Oy, Dymph, where's my Coke?"

"Oh, here you are, Wayne, darlin'. It was the two-liter, wasn't it?"

WHILE AMY was on the bus heading back to Café Mozart, she phoned the news desk at *The Daily Post*. There was no doubt in her mind that this was a perfect tabloid story. She chose the *Post* for no other reason than she had something approaching a relationship with the news editor, Boadicea Asquith. Amy had pitched two or three possible pieces to her in the last few months. She had turned them down but had encouraged Amy to call with other ideas.

"Oh, hi, Amy," came the languid, upper-class drawl. "Look, sweetie, I'm just about to go into conference."

"I won't keep you," Amy persisted. "It's just that I've got this amazing story." She pitched it in thirty seconds flat.

"Right. Okay. Yah. Actually, that does sound interesting. I'll put it up in conference and get back to you in an hour or so."

Amy spent the afternoon on what Zelma kept referring to as *shpilkes*. This was Yiddish for "tenterhooks." Bel—who decided to "hang out" at the café for the rest of the day because a meeting she was meant to have with her agent had been canceled—went around practicing the word. "So, how are your *shpiel keys*, Ames? Still on them?"

"It's not *shpiel keys*," Zelma corrected, laughing. "It's *shpilkes*. And you can see she's still on them. Just look at her. That's the third time she's given a customer the wrong change."

It was after six, and Amy was at home, stirring Bolognese sauce, when the phone rang.

"Hi, Amy, it's Boadicea. The editor loves the story. We're running it in the morning. Can you e-mail me a thousand words? And we'll need the woman's details to sort out a picture. I'll be in the office until seven."

Bloody hell. A thousand words? In an hour? "Okay, fine. No problem," Amy said.

She dished up Charlie's spag bol and left a portion of chocolate ice cream on the kitchen counter to thaw. As he started on his supper, she did something she swore she would never do: She bribed her child. "Charlie, if you can amuse yourself and not disturb me for the next hour, I will give you some money to spend this weekend when you go to stay with Grandma."

"Why can't I zisturb you?"

"Because I have something very important to write. It's an article for a newspaper, and they want it very quickly."

He nodded. "How much?"

"How much what?"

"Money."

Although Charlie still didn't get pocket money, he had, in the last few months, started to take an interest in cash.

"I don't know," she said. "Two pounds."

"Five."

"No way."

"Four."

"Three, and that's my last offer." She couldn't believe that she was haggling with a six-year-old.

He thought for a moment. "Okay."

"But you can't spend it on sweets. Deal?"

"Deal."

She left him to eat his supper and went into her bedroom, where her laptop was on charge. She sat on the bed, propped up by pillows and cushions, and began typing.

A 73-year-old London woman is single-handedly taking on the government's healthy eating initiative by organizing mass lunchtime deliveries of junk food to schoolchildren.

Children at Nelson Mandela Comprehensive telephone or text their orders to grandmother Dymphna Brannigan.

For a small fee, she collects their lunches from fast-food outlets, including McDonald's, KFC, and Pizza Hut, and delivers them to the school gates.

Teachers are powerless to act . . .

Fifty-five minutes later, she was pressing "send." She just prayed she had gotten the house style right.

When she went into the living room, Charlie was sprawled out on the living room floor with his crayons. She sat down beside him and ruffled his hair. "Thanks for not disturbing me, poppet. I really appreciate it."

He didn't react other than to swat her hand away from his hair. He was busy finishing a picture and didn't want to be disturbed. It was a street scene. Amy recognized it at once. "Look, there's the deli and the dry cleaner's and Café Mozart. You've done buses and cars and people. And you've even remembered the ice-cream van." She was no expert, but he seemed to be developing a real understanding of perspective and scale. When she looked more closely at the people, she couldn't help laughing. The women in particular were unmistakable. There they were, Richmansworth mummies in their A-line Boden skirts and sandals, pushing their tank-sized strollers. "Oh, Charlie, I don't know what to say. This is wonderful. It's one of the best drawings you've ever done. You really do have a photographic memory."

"What does that mean?"

"Come and get in the bath and I'll explain."

ONCE CHARLIE was in bed, Amy went to check her e-mail. There was one from Boadicea titled "Great piece, will be in touch re fee." There was no actual message. Her fist shot into the air. "Yes! Cracked it." She was on the point of phoning Bel and Brian and her mum and dad to tell them her piece was going to be in the newspaper the next morning, but she thought better of it. Experience had taught her that an editor liking a story and promising to run it was no guarantee that it would appear.

She went to bed and flicked through some of her interiors mags until she felt drowsy. She dreamed that it was the next morning and she was out trying to buy a copy of *The Daily Post.* Everywhere had sold out. She ended up tramping across London, going into hundreds of newsagents, and nobody had a copy. Her frustration turned to desperate panic when she realized she was lost and couldn't find her way back to Charlie. She woke up sweating, her heart pounding, to find Charlie jumping on the bed. "Yay—swimming today. Have you packed my stuff?" He slid under the covers.

"Yes, I've packed your stuff. Come here." She hugged him to her. "Don't I love you."

"Love you, too. So when do I get my five pounds?"

She burst out laughing. "You little so and so. We agreed on three, and you know it."

"Okay, so when do I get it?"

"Saturday morning."

Amy sent him into the bathroom to brush his teeth. She was desperate to see *The Daily Post* and cursed herself for not having the newspapers delivered rather than buying them on the way to work. She could get it online, but it wasn't always reliable. They often missed out on stories. She looked at her clock on the nightstand. The paperboy would be dropping off papers to other residents in the block just about now. She decided to stop him and beg him to let her have a quick look at somebody's *Daily Post*. She tightened the cord of her dressing gown and went out onto the landing. No sign. She hovered for a couple of minutes, but he didn't show. She would have to pick up a paper on her way to work, as usual.

While Charlie ate breakfast, she showered and got ready for work. Afterward she made his lunch and double-checked that he had his swimming gear. All the time her stomach was churning the way it used to before she took an exam.

She stopped at the newsagent by the bus stop. It occurred to her that last night's dream was going to come true and they would have sold out of *The Daily Post*. But they hadn't. She'd just finished paying when her bus pulled up. There was a long queue, so she didn't have to rush. She stood at the back of the slow-moving queue and opened the newspaper. It wasn't easy turning pages with nothing to rest on. To make it worse, there was a strong breeze. She fought with the billowing pages. Page four, five, six . . . twelve. By the time she got to page nineteen, she was pretty sure they hadn't used her piece. By the time she reached the funnies and the horoscope section, she knew they hadn't. She fought the urge to swear out loud. On the other hand, she knew how things worked on the dailies. No doubt a big story had come along late last night and hers had been dropped to make room for it. They probably were holding it over until tomorrow.

Just after ten, Amy rang Boadicea to find out what was happening, but all she got was her voice mail. That went on all day. The woman was either out of the office or—and Amy couldn't help thinking this was the most likely—she had caller ID and was avoiding her.

Brian accused her of being paranoid. "Why would this Boadicea woman ignore you? Surely she understands that you need to know what's going on. And if they've decided not to use the piece, it's only polite to let you know so that you can try placing it elsewhere."

"Yes, but she's scared I'll be pissed off, and she's trying to avoid a confrontation."

Amy knew that Boadicea would be in the office until well after six, so when she got home, she e-mailed her to ask what was happening to the piece. Eight o'clock came and went with no reply.

The next morning, Amy managed to catch the paperboy and plead with him to let her look through a copy of *The Daily Post.*

"But you'll get creases in it and mess it up."

"Please. It's really, really important. I'll be ever so careful. Please?"

He grunted and handed her a folded newspaper. Her story was mentioned on the front page. Yes! Way to go.

"Grandmother encourages pupils to defy Government's healthy eating initiative. Celebrity chef Jamie Oliver reports. See page three." Staring up at her was a picture of the cheeky chappy, all roguish grin and *"easy peasy."* What? No! Wrong way to go.

Amy turned to page three. This was her story, all right, but not the one she had written. Above Oliver's byline was a short introduction: "Jamie Oliver, who has worked tirelessly to revolutionize the quality of food served in British schools, meets the grandmother setting out to single-handedly destroy his good work."

Miserable and pissed off as she was, she supposed it made

perfect sense that the desk editors had changed their minds about using her story. Jamie Oliver was a huge name. *Jamie's School Dinners*, the TV series in which he taught school cooks how to prepare decent, nutritious food on a budget, had been watched by millions. Why wouldn't they send him to cover this story? She couldn't help thinking, though, that it wouldn't have hurt Boadicea to phone or e-mail her to explain what was going on.

She thanked the paperboy and handed him back the newspaper, which she had carefully smoothed and refolded.

Back in the kitchen, Charlie was eating his cereal "It's Saturday. You said I could have my money today to spend with Grandma and Trevor."

"I did indeed," she said, reaching for her bag. She took three pound coins from her purse. As she handed the money to him, she asked him what he was going to spend it on.

"Secret."

Then the penny dropped. "Charlie, you are not buying a snake. Do you hear me?"

"Duh. You can't get a snake for three pounds."

"Yes, but you'll convince Grandma and Trevor to put up the rest. You are absolutely forbidden to do that. Are we clear?"

Charlie's crest couldn't have looked more fallen.

Val and Trevor didn't arrive until after nine. "Sorry we're late," Val said. "We were driving around for ages looking for somewhere to park."

"I chanted for a space," Trevor said. "Never fails. We ended up getting a spot right outside your building."

"Trevor, you chanted for twenty minutes," Val said, hands on hips. "Doesn't it strike you that we might have found a place anyway in that time?"

"What? Right outside Amy's flat? I don't think so. This was the universe providing us with what we needed. You see, the universe is divided into a single dynamic web of energy. It's all part of the Noble Eightfold Path, and when we combine this with our own consciousness, which Buddhists describe as *vinnana*—"

"Trevor, please," Val said. "Not now."

"Okay, no need to get irritable."

"I'm not irritable. It's just that for once I'd like to talk about something other than tantras and mantras and the Noble Eightfold Path."

Trevor shrugged. "Fine."

Amy looked at her mother. She didn't look so much irritable as weary. It seemed that Val wasn't finding Trevor quite as cool and interesting as she once had. If there was tension between them, Amy didn't want Charlie picking up on it and getting upset.

"Mum, could I speak to you for a sec in the kitchen?"

"Of course." Val followed her daughter. Meanwhile, Charlie was asking Trevor if he would teach him to chant. Trevor scooped him up. "Absolutely, young man. We shall practice in the car."

"Oh, perfect," Val murmured. "Now I'll have a duet."

"Mum, I sense a bit of an atmosphere between you and Trevor. Is everything okay?"

"Not entirely, but it's nothing to worry about. I'm sure we'll sort it out."

"Sort what out?"

"Look, don't get me wrong, Trevor is an absolute sweetie, but he's so passionate about shamanism. In the beginning I found it fascinating. It's one of the things that attracted me to him. I loved being with somebody who was so spiritual. So different from your father. Trevor and I would take long romantic walks and talk for hours about life and the universe and what it all meant. But he lives his life with his head in the clouds and never seems to connect with the real world. He doesn't understand that I need an occasional break from talking about astral planes. Sometimes all I want to do is sit in an armchair with a cup of tea and watch the soaps or my *Mamma Mia!* DVD. But I can't concentrate because he spends most evenings chanting upstairs. Some evenings he's got people with him who have come for healing and they're chanting together. It's such a racket."

"Sounds like you need to sit down and have a serious talk about how he needs to take your needs into account."

"I know, but I'm too scared."

"But Trevor's a lovely man," Amy said. "He would do anything for you. Why on earth would you be scared?"

"Whenever I asked your dad to take me to the pictures or even come out from behind his newspaper to talk to me for five minutes, he refused. He rejected me over and over again."

"And you're frightened that Trevor's going to do the same."

"It has occurred to me."

"Mum, speak to him. Tell him how you're feeling. Do not let this thing fester. It will only get worse."

"I know. You're right. I just need to find the right time, that's all."

"You mean that?"

"Cross my heart." She paused. "So, this new chap of yours is an architect? You know, you could do a lot worse."

"That's what Dad said."

"He's right. A woman needs a decent chap in a solid job." She paused. There was a concerned look on her face. "Darling, are you all right? You look a bit pale."

Amy explained about her latest journalistic setback. "I totally get why they decided to go with Jamie Oliver, but it's so frustrating."

Val gave her daughter a hug. "I know, darling, but you just have to hang in there and believe in yourself. You are a talented young woman. Your time will come. I promise."

Amy smiled. "You can't promise stuff like that. Nobody can."

"Well, I can. I'm your mum, and mums know these things."

"I love you," Amy said.

"Love you, too, darling."

As they made their way back to the living room, Amy warned her mother that Charlie might try to get around her to buy a snake.

"He's got some hopes," Val said with a shudder. "I hate the things. Do you remember that python that escaped when you were little? Huge fuss about it in the local paper. Spike, I think it was called."

Amy said she had never forgotten.

"So, Charlie," Val said. "You up for a big surprise?"

Charlie gave a vigorous nod of his head.

"We are all off to Legoland."

"Yay!"

"Mum, you sure? A hot Saturday at Legoland? It's going to be mobbed."

"Amy, I'm sixty-three, not ninety-three. I'm not quite ready for my bath chair and ear trumpet."

Two minutes later, they were out of the door, Charlie with his Spiderman knapsack over one shoulder. "Have fun. See you tomorrow," she called after him. "And remember what I said about that money. Grandma knows all about your plan."

"Whaddever."

Amy smiled. When had he started with the "whaddever" thing? Any minute now he was going to sprout upper lip hair and zits.

Chapter 9

AMY WENT BACK into the kitchen and washed Charlie's cereal bowl and spoon. She'd just finished when she happened to glance at the kitchen clock. It was half past nine. Sam was due to pick her up in half an hour for their Tate Modern date, and here she was, still in her dressing gown. She hated the thought of him having to hang around waiting for her.

On the other hand, she could speed things up if she didn't spend ages on her hair and makeup. After taking a shower, she pasted her upper lip in hair remover cream. This was a habit based not so much on need as on neurosis. She'd inherited it from her mother, who mustachewise wasn't prepared to put her trust in the naked eye.

Afterward, she rough dried her hair with the dryer and set about it with the straighteners. Her hairdresser, Xavier—he of the permed eyelashes and pec implants—had warned her that overstraightening her hair would make it lose volume and hang flat around her face. His instructions were to blow-dry it first with one of those big round brushes and finish it off with the irons.

This morning, she decided to leave out the round brush part. Her timesaving strategy turned out to be a huge mistake. She'd been going for a soft, voluminous Rachel and had ended up with something between Morticia Addams and Sonic the Hedgehog. There was nothing for it but to damp down her hair again and repeat the drying process, only this time she included the round brush stage. She had just finished and was feeling rather pleased with the result when the doorbell rang.

Once she'd buzzed Sam in, she shot to the bedroom to swap her old dressing gown for her embroidered green silk kimono. It was usually hanging on the back of the door, but when she looked, it wasn't there. Neither was it on the bed or under it. She wondered if she'd hung it up in the wardrobe. She hadn't. There was a knock at the door. She cursed herself for her lack of organization, took a few seconds to flick bits of dried cornflake off her toweling dressing gown, and went to answer it.

"HI," SHE said, ushering Sam in. "Sorry I'm not ready. Mum and Trevor arrived late to pick up Sam, and then I got chatting with Mum..."

"Hey, don't worry. There's no rush. Take your time."

By then, she had noticed the charcoal T-shirt he was wearing. This was sufficiently close-fitting to reveal his torso. Well developed without being muscle-bound. She felt her stomach flip with excitement. Unaware of the slight unease on his face, she puckered up and made a beeline for his lips. He kissed her back but without the enthusiasm she had anticipated.

It was only as they pulled away and she saw the blob of white gunk on the end of his nose that the realization dawned. "Omigod, this is *so* embarrassing. I was in a rush, and I totally forgot to rinse it off. Now you've got it on you." She produced an ancient ball of toilet paper from her pocket and wiped the blob off his nose.

"Amy, stop panicking." He was offering her a reassuring smile. "It's not remotely embarrassing. In fact I think it's rather"—he paused, clearly searching for a suitable adjective—"charming."

"Sam, I'm in my old dressing gown, my face plastered in

depilatory cream. Precisely which bit of that do you find charming?" By now she was wiping her top lip with the tissue.

"All of it," he said, grinning. With that he pulled her toward him. Amy resisted, saying she really needed to rinse her face, but he shushed her.

She closed her eyes, allowing herself to sink into his embrace. She felt his lips part, his tongue probing hers. For two pins she would have dragged him off to the bedroom there and then.

When they finally pulled away, he stood back and looked at her, his head tilted to one side. "Something's different about you."

"No more hairy outcrop on my upper lip?"

He laughed. "No, it's not that. It's your actual hair. It looks great—dead sexy. What have you done to it?"

"Oh, I just washed it and gave it a quick blast with the dryer. I'm very lucky. I never have to spend too long on it."

HALF AN hour later they were in the car, heading toward the Tate Modern. "So," Sam said at one point, "what's happening with the school dinners piece?"

She explained.

"And you've heard nothing from this Boadicea woman?"

"Not a word."

"That's just so rude."

Amy shrugged. "In my experience, people in newspapers are all the same—even on the broadsheets."

"And you want to break into this world because ...?"

"I believe I'm a good writer and know I'd get a buzz from breaking stories. It's like being first with the gossip."

He smiled and said he could understand that.

The conversation got around to art, and he asked her if she'd been to the Tate Modern before. She said she hadn't. "Which is a shame, because I love modern art. So are you good at art?" she said. "I always imagine that architects must be pretty talented, particularly at drawing."

"I paint a little."

"You do?"

"Yes. Abstracts mostly."

"So, have you sold any?"

"One or two. Last year, I had an exhibition at a gallery in the East End."

"You had an exhibition? Wow. That's amazing. So you're famous."

He laughed. "Not really. A friend of mine owns the gallery. It was my birthday, and he organized the exhibition as a sort of gift. It was just a bit of fun."

"Really? You sure that's all it was?" She offered him a coy smile. "You should know that I do intend to Google you."

He rolled his eyes in defeat. "Okay, I sold a dozen or so paintings, and Boris Karpenko bought a couple."

"Karpenko? Isn't he that Russian property tycoon?"

"Yeah. He bought them to hang in his dacha on the Black Sea."

"See, you are famous."

"Okay, a bit, maybe. In Odessa."

ONCE THEY got to the Tate Modern, Amy picked up a guide. They studied it for a few moments and agreed that they should start on the top floor and work their way down.

They wandered through rooms full of abstract canvases. Mondrian's black lattices and brightly colored rectangles gave way to Kandinsky's geometric lines, circles, and arcs and Jackson Pollock's drips and spills. Amy spent ages in front of each painting, unable to tear herself away. She didn't begin to understand what they were about, but she knew they affected her, which Sam said was the whole point.

Eventually, they came to the Cubists, Picasso and Georges

Braque. "I love modern art, but it has always baffled me," she said. "I really struggle with Cubism. I can see it's brilliant, but I don't know why." They were standing in front of a head and shoulders portrait by Picasso. Before them was a disjointed woman, her breasts where her chin should be, one eye on the side of her head, her nose where her ears should be. "You're the expert," she said to Sam. "What is he trying to say?"

"Okay, Cubism is all about the artist representing an object or subject by showing all views at once. This is done using cylinders, cubes, or cones. The image is deconstructed and re-assembled in the sum total of its parts."

"So you abandon traditional perspective?"

"Exactly. You catch on fast, grasshopper."

"Big head." She slapped him playfully on the arm.

Amy wasn't quite as bowled over by the art installations as she'd been by the paintings.

The first they came upon was the Didier Le Boeuf exhibit that Bel had been so excited about. It consisted of a five-hundred-foot-long chain-link fence running down the middle of the hangar-sized gallery. It was seven or eight feet high with barbed wire looped around the top.

It was called *Animus*. According to the blurb under the large black-and-white studio photograph of Monsieur Le Boeuf, the fence represented class hatred.

> Major towns and cities in the west are turning into white, middle-class ghettos. Developers in the pay of the rich are building more and more private, gated housing developments, policed by security guards. These areas are built to exclude the poor. Safe behind their high walls, residents can forget the underclass. They can lock them out of their lives and ignore their plight.

An elderly woman with a severe slate-gray bob, her bird frame shrouded in a black silk kimono-style coat and Palazzo pants, stopped to read the blurb. She gazed at the fence and gave a grave nod of understanding and approval. A gaggle of teenage tourists went by, barely giving the fence a second glance. Then a middle-aged couple stopped to look at it. "It's a fence," the husband said. "It's a bloody fence. Who in their right mind gives somebody three hundred grand to put up a fence? They should have asked me. I'd have done it for fifty quid."

"I'm with him," Amy whispered to Sam.

Sam said he was inclined to agree. "If you ask me, no real thought has gone into this. Le Boeuf's having a laugh."

"And yet everybody thinks he's a genius," Amy said. "I know nothing about art, but to me this is like something a bunch of first-year art college students would come up with."

"Maybe, but I think their tutor would have taken one look at the preliminary sketches and sent them away for a rethink."

"If I were arts minister," Amy said, "I'd have a real problem explaining to the struggling masses that I was giving three hundred thousand pounds of taxpayers' money to the Tate Modern so that some poncey, deluded, third-rate creative on a social crusade could erect a chain-link fence and call it art."

She took a step back and felt her body connect with another. She turned around to see a fiery-faced man with beady eyes and Art Garfunkel hair.

"I'm so sorry," Amy said, referring to the collision. "My fault." She found herself staring at the man. "Don't I know you? I'm sure I recognize your face from somewhere."

"Oh, shit," Sam murmured. "Amy, the photograph...over there...on the wall."

Amy's eyes went from the man to the photograph and back again.

She let out an understated "Ah."

"*Oui*," Didier Le Boeuf said. "Zat is me—zee poncey, deluded, third-rate cree-ateef."

What was he doing there? Artists never visited galleries where their work was on show, at least not famous ones. They would be mobbed by fans. Then she remembered what Bel had said about Le Boeuf being addicted to praise and how he would hang out at the gallery, giving visitors informal lectures on his work.

"Omigod. I am so sorry," Amy said. "What can I say? Look, when I accused you of being poncey and third-rate, I didn't really mean it. I should tell you that I know nothing about art, I mean absolutely nothing."

"Ah can see that." Le Boeuf offered her a patronizing smile. "You are a philistine, *n'est ce pas*? You British. You are all ignorant peasants and 'ooligans."

"Hey, that's enough," Sam said. "The lady has apologized. Now let it go."

"Hang on. Who are you calling bloody hooligans?" It was the middle-aged chap who had offered to build the fence for fifty quid.

The artist ignored him. Instead he took a few steps forward and squared up to Sam. "Nobody tells Le Boeuf what to do," he snarled.

The middle-aged man, a burly fellow, wasn't about to be snubbed. He tapped Le Boeuf on the shoulder. "The gentleman told you to let it go. I suggest you do as he says."

Le Boeuf swung around. "What? You are challenging me? Okay, we take this outside, *n'est-ce pas*?"

Amy and the middle-aged man's wife exchanged horrified looks. "Malcolm, leave it. Please. It's not worth it."

"I agree," Amy said to Sam. "Come on, let's go."

Malcolm decided to stand his ground. "The young lady is right," he said to Le Boeuf. "This so-called piece of art is nothing but pretentious, meaningless crap. *Merde*, as you Frenchies say."

"Actually, I didn't go quite that far," Amy whispered to Malcolm.

"Nobody calls my work *merde*," Le Boeuf roared, veins standing out on his forehead. "I am a genius. You hear? A genius." With that he drew back his arm and punched Malcolm in the face. Malcolm collapsed to the ground.

The two women and a handful of onlookers gasped. Malcolm's wife rushed to his side. "Omigod, Mal. Speak to me. What has he done to you?"

Malcolm managed to sit up. His hand was clamped to his right eye. "You bastard," he snarled at Le Boeuf.

By then a security guard had arrived. "Monsieur Le Boeuf, sir. Are you all right?"

"Yes. I am fine. I merely acted to defend myself. Please throw zeez troublemakers onto the street."

The onlookers protested that Malcolm had done nothing and that Le Boeuf had been the aggressor, but the guard refused to listen. Instead, he helped Malcolm to his feet and insisted that he, his wife, and Amy and Sam leave.

"But why? We haven't done anything," Amy protested.

"Madam," the guard said, "I have no intention of arguing with you. You either leave now or I will be forced to call the police."

Didier Le Boeuf smiled a valedictory smile. Meanwhile, the two couples were escorted to the exit. Once outside, the four commiserated briefly before parting. Malcolm and his wife set off to find a pharmacy and get something for his eye. Amy and Sam decided to take a calming walk along the river.

"I'm so sorry," Amy said to Sam. "That was all my fault. Me and my blinkin' big mouth."

"Oh, come on. It's a free country. You're entitled to your opinions. You couldn't know that Le Boeuf was behind you."

"I guess."

"If you ask me, the reason he's so sensitive to criticism is that he knows he's a con merchant. He'll get his comeuppance. You wait."

"I hope so...By the way, thanks for sticking up for me back there."

"You are more than welcome."

A few yards ahead there were a couple of market stalls full of costume jewelry. Amy would have adored nothing more than a quick look, but she wouldn't have dreamed of inflicting her—albeit minor—jewelry habit on Sam, certainly not on their second date. She couldn't believe it when he said, "Hey, come on, let's take a look."

"No. Honestly. We don't have to."

"Oh, come on," he said. "You know you want to. It's written all over your face."

"Well, okay. I wouldn't mind a bit of a rummage, but only for a minute."

"There is, however, a quid pro quo," he said. "If we are out and I find myself overcome by the need to take a look at the latest gadgets for the iPhone, you have to allow me to drag you around the Apple Store. I should warn you that this need is both powerful and frequent."

She laughed. "Deal."

She moved in on the first stall, which was covered in a tatty purple velvet cloth. "These are pretty," she said, picking up a pair of silver filigree earrings.

"Everything's twenty pounds," the woman stallholder chirruped.

Sam looked at the silver earrings and wrinkled his nose. "Nah."

"What do you mean, 'Nah'? They're lovely."

"Reproduction Art Nouveau," the woman said.

"They're all right," Sam said to Amy, "but these are much more you."

He was holding a pair of oval drop earrings.

"Okay, I admit that those are gorgeous." She took them from him and picked up the hand mirror, which was lying in front of her.

"Tell me the emerald green doesn't look great with your auburn hair," he said.

She carried on staring into the mirror. "You're right. It does. I'm taking them." She started to unzip her bag.

Sam covered her hand with his. "My treat. No arguments."

"Oh, Sam . . . no . . . I can't let you."

"Of course you can."

He reached for his wallet and took out a twenty-pound note, which he handed to the stallholder. She asked Amy if she would like them wrapped.

"No, thanks. I'd prefer to wear them." As they walked away, she turned to Sam.

"Thank you so much. They are absolutely perfect. You have great taste."

He thanked her and said he was glad she liked them.

"I love them." She said, leaning in and kissing him.

AFTER A while, they found themselves walking along an almost empty stretch of riverbank. As they passed under a tree, he stopped her. "Come here," he said gently. She felt his arms close around her. She closed her eyes and breathed in his warm smell. As his tongue found hers, she felt her limbs weaken. Her stomach gave its familiar flip. Warm moisture began seeping from inside her.

She wasn't sure how long they remained in each other's arms, oblivious to passersby. When they set off again along the river, they stopped every few paces to kiss again or to hug.

"You know what?" she said at one point. "I know we were supposed to have lunch, but I've sort of lost my appetite for food."

"Me, too."

She kissed him again. "I was thinking that maybe we could spend the afternoon at my place. Charlie's at my mum's until tomorrow."

"You sure?"

"Completely sure. He's not due back until the afternoon."

Sam smiled. "No, I didn't mean that. I meant are you sure you want to do this? After all, we've only been on two dates. But don't get me wrong, I'm ready if you are."

"Oh, I are. I most definitely are."

Amy still hadn't gotten around to fixing the lock on the front door, but today it gave her no trouble. She took his hand and led him to the bedroom. "I changed the linen this morning." She giggled. "I guess I was planning this all along." If she'd been planning it, there was one thing she had forgotten: her diaphragm. "Sam, I hate to spoil the mood, but could you excuse me for just two ticks?"

She left him sitting on the bed, flicking through one of her interiors magazines, and dashed to the bathroom. Her diaphragm was in its box on top of the medicine cabinet, well out of Charlie's reach. She used to keep it in her underwear drawer until Charlie found it one day and appeared with it on his head while she was at the door paying the milkman.

She was grateful that she still needed to use it. At thirty-six, thoughts of early menopause were never far away.

"Sorry about that," she said, returning to the bedroom. "Contraceptive issue."

"Oh . . . actually you needn't—" He stopped himself.

"What?"

"Nothing. It can wait."

He came toward her and started to run his fingers through her hair. His hand went to the tie on her wrap dress. She watched as he tugged on the bow and pulled the dress open. All the nerve endings in her body were tingling as he pulled the dress off her shoulders and slid the sleeves down her arms. The dress fell to the floor, leaving her in her bra and panties. His eyes went to her breasts.

"They are amazing."

She blushed.

"You have no idea," he said, "how hard it's been not to stare at them."

She laughed. "Most men don't have that problem when they meet me. They don't see my face, just my cleavage."

"That's why I resisted. I thought that if you caught me

gawping, you'd think that sex was all I had on my mind. I mean, it wasn't not on my mind. It just wasn't all that was on my mind."

"That's okay," she said, smiling. "I get it."

She unhooked her bra but held the cream lace cups against her breasts. "Show me," he said. He lifted her hands off the bra and let it fall on top of the dress.

"You are so beautiful."

He planted kisses on her shoulders, her collarbone. Finally his lips went to her breasts. He licked and nipped at them, flicked her nipples with his tongue. She heard herself let out a soft moan. He pulled off his T-shirt, and she unbuttoned the fly on his jeans. She ran her finger along the thick hairline that led down under the waistband of his boxers. She watched his stomach quiver. As she eased his boxers down over his buttocks, his penis sprung out, thick and hard. A moment later he was completely naked.

He bent down and trailed his tongue down her abdomen toward her panties. She thought he was about to pull them down, but he didn't. Instead he squatted down and moved to her inner thighs with a gentle, almost imperceptible touch. He pushed his hand between her legs and traced the outline of her labia. Her body trembled.

Sam stood up and guided her back onto the bed. He knelt in front of her. Now he pulled off her panties. "Open your legs." She did, but he didn't move. Instead he just looked at her. He told her to close her eyes.

Nothing happened. She waited, wondering when and where his touch would fall. Half a minute passed, maybe more, before it happened. She gasped as he ran his finger along the outside of her lips. He came in farther, easing her apart. His finger slipped and slid over her vulva, spreading the wetness. The next moment he changed position. She felt his head between her legs. His tongue was everywhere. She arched her back, let out a whimper. His tongue probed, licked, flicked. She felt her body sink into the bed. She was aware of nothing other than this sublime sensation.

When he stopped, she begged him to continue, begged him to concentrate on her clitoris so that she could come. "What's your hurry?" he whispered. With that she felt his fingers hard inside her. It wasn't painful, but she yelped in surprise. He spent time slowly exploring her. Occasionally he would stop to caress her breasts or thighs.

At one point, she helped herself to some of her wetness and spread it over the head of his penis. She moved her hand slowly, rhythmically. He gasped, but at no point did his focus go from her. By now he was concentrating on the spot that mattered. His touch was firm one second, barely there the next. "Please. Please. Don't stop."

"Ssh."

He made her turn onto all fours. His fingers were up inside her again. He spread her juices over her buttocks. She let out another gasp as his penis entered her. "It's okay, just relax." He moved in and out in a slow firm rhythm, kissing the back of her neck. He was still on her clitoris, his finger moving in a firm circular motion now. "There you go. There you go."

Her quivering was growing now, taking her over. There was no stopping it. His thrusts were becoming harder and sharper. He kept up the pressure between her legs. She was all sensation. She held on tight to her breath. Another thrust came hard inside her. Then another. She felt his body go rigid as she let out one final moan. But the shuddering and quaking inside her wouldn't stop. Unaware, he took his fingers away, but she made him put them back, begged him to carry on until the sensation had subsided. When it did, she let her body sink down onto the bed. The two of them rolled over so that he was on top of her. He kissed her gently on the lips and stroked her hair.

"Do you have a thesaurus?" he said. She noticed that he was panting.

"A what?"

"A thesaurus. You know, it's a lexicon, a word list."

"I know what a thesaurus is. What I don't understand is why you want one. A postcoital cigarette is one thing, although I can't say I approve, but a postcoital word search is a new one on me."

"It's just that I'm lost for words. I'm not sure how to describe what just happened," he said. " 'Fantastic' doesn't quite do it justice."

She laughed. "I'll drink to that. Okay, how about incredible . . . unbelievable . . . out of this world?"

"It was all those things, but I think we can come up with something better."

"Extraordinary? Stupendous?"

"More."

"Quintessential? Awesome?"

"Where's your laptop?" he said.

She told him it was on charge under the bed. He reached down and picked it up. A few seconds later, he let out a loud, "Aha. I've got it . . . *thaumaturgical,* that's what it was," he told her. "You and I just had *thaumaturgical* sex."

Things got thaumaturgical twice more that afternoon before they realized it was nearly four and they were both starving.

Amy made them beans on toast, covered in grated cheese, which they ate at the kitchen table. They chatted about his pro bono work in Africa. It turned out it had all started six years ago when he took a gap year from his job to do volunteer work in Rwanda.

"So when I was having Charlie, you were in Africa. God knows I wouldn't not have him for all the world, but I wish I'd taken some time out to do charity work abroad. Sometimes I look back on those years I spent in PR and think what a waste they were. On the other hand, it did give me a chance to save enough money to become a mum."

A moment's silence followed. Sam was looking around the room. "You know, this is a great flat," he said.

"It's certainly got potential. I've got plans, but I can't afford to do anything right now."

"You need to knock this kitchen wall down and open up the living space."

"I know. And I thought I'd lose the French doors into the garden and replace them with a wall of sliding glass." She was warming to her theme now. "I've thought loads about paint color. I was thinking basic white, but with the odd wall covered in paper. I'm mad about all those fifties sciencey space-age designs. And I've thought about fabrics. I've got dozens of samples. Would you like to see?"

"Absolutely."

She went into the bedroom and came back with her box of swatches.

"Wow, how many have you got here?"

"I've been collecting them for years. I love them all. I'd like to use each one someday, but this is such a tiny place, I know I could only choose a couple of accent colors. Look at this one." She produced a heavy cotton print in olive green, yellow, and white. This was more than a swatch. There was enough fabric to make a couple of cushion covers, maybe. It was an original fifties fabric that she'd picked up at Camden Market. They agreed that the design reminded them of the ancient TV aerials that people used to have on their roofs. "I can just imagine curtains like this with a low Scandinavian sideboard and perhaps an Eames chair. Not that I could begin to afford the real thing. They cost a fortune."

Finally she produced the cream damask she'd bought in Paris and told him about her plans for her froufrou French armchairs. "I'm thinking now that they would look terrible if I went for a fifties theme. I'd need to put them in the bedroom."

She got more and more excited, spreading swatches over the floor, asking for his opinion on various color and texture combinations. "Don't you just love fuchsia and orange?" she said. "It's the ultimate clash, but it works so well."

"If design is such a passion and inspires you this much," he said finally, "why on earth don't you try to make a career of it?"

"You mean designing for other people?"

"Why not?"

"I've thought about it, but it just doesn't give me the buzz I get from writing."

He looked thoughtful. "Okay, if you could do one thing to this flat today, what would it be?"

"Oh, I dunno...take up all the old carpets, maybe, and strip the floors. I've been thinking about doing it for ages."

"Let's do it now."

"Yeah, right."

"I'm serious."

"What, now, as in right this very minute?"

"Why not now? If we can hire an electric sander, it really won't take that long. I've done it loads of times. We could do the entire flat in a few hours."

"You're kidding."

"I'm not. What do you say? Let's give it a go."

She laughed. "You're mad."

"No, I'm not. It's called seizing the day. What do you say?"

"Okay, consider it seized."

An hour later, with a floor sander rented until the following evening, they were ripping up carpets. The difficult part was moving the heavy furniture, particularly Amy's double bed, but they managed. While Amy made tea, Sam got started with the sander. "These are lovely pine boards," he said.

"Aren't they? How do you think I should treat them? I'm thinking white floor paint."

"Floor paint. Definitely. And white would work really well with those curtains you have in mind."

"Umm...maybe with a shaggy olive rug."

The sander wasn't too noisy, so Amy wasn't worried about disturbing the neighbors. The problem was the dust. Despite wearing face masks and the sander having a bag attached to collect it all, they still coughed and sneezed. All they could do was drink water and suck sweets. They took turns on the machine, but Sam, having sanded floors before, was a bit of an expert and worked faster than Amy. Despite her being slow and not very skilled, by ten they had done the living room, Amy's bedroom, and the hallway. They fell onto the sofa, sweaty, dusty, and exhausted.

Amy opened a bottle of wine and ordered pizza. While they waited for it to arrive, they went from room to room, admiring their work.

"It looks amazing."

"Fantastic."

"Awesome."

"Out of this world."

"Quintessential."

"Sam, thank you so much. I don't know what to say. You bought me the earrings, now this."

"I enjoyed it, really. I love doing stuff like this."

"You're like Ulf."

"Ulf?"

"He's a Swedish friend. Well, not exactly a friend. I hardly know him." Amy explained how a couple weeks earlier Bel had virtually press-ganged him into assembling Charlie's IKEA furniture and they were now going out. "Lovely chap. Brain surgeon. Bit earnest, though. Into Strindberg and Norse sagas."

As they sat on the sofa, demolishing a seventeen-inch American Hot with extra salami, Amy suggested opening another bottle of wine.

"No. I really mustn't have any more to drink," Sam said. "I'm driving."

"Stay," she whispered. "It's late."

"You sure? I snore, and I'm well known for stealing all the duvet."

"Well, I'll just have to steal it back again."

"Okay, I'll stay."

"Good." She paused. "Sam, can I pick your brain?"

"Sure. Go ahead."

While he opened the wine, she went back into the bedroom to fetch the large folder full of Charlie's artwork that she kept behind the wardrobe.

"These all belong to Charlie," she said, handing Sam the folder. "He forgets what he's done and moves on to the next thing, but I don't have the heart to throw anything away. I'd love to know what you think."

Sam sifted through the drawings and paintings. The more he sifted, the more his eyebrows rose.

"Amy, these are incredible. I can't believe Charlie's only six. There's such maturity here. He's got a grasp of perspective and color. Look at the character in the faces. I'd say you have a prodigy on your hands."

"You think he's that good?"

"I do. Are you having him tutored?"

"I've thought about it; I'm worried it might put too much pressure on him. I don't want his art to turn from a delight to a chore."

"On the other hand, a child like this really needs to be challenged and brought on. I don't know Charlie, but I bet you anything he'll love having one-on-one lessons. And if he starts kicking up and saying it's too much, you stop."

"I guess. Makes sense."

She said she needed a shower before bed. "Care to join me?" she said with a sexy giggle.

"You bet."

There wasn't really room for two in the narrow bath, plus the spray from the ancient overhead shower was more trickle than torrent. They took turns standing under it. Afterward, kissing and laughing, they set to work on each other with the shower gel. His hands slid over her breasts. Hers followed his hairline south from his stomach. She lathered his balls, watched his penis lengthen. She squeezed more gel onto her hand. They watched her hand glide the length of his penis. As she ran her fingers over the tip, he closed his eyes and let his head fall onto his chest. Her pace quickened. His face was contorted with pleasure. He was thrusting himself into her hand now. A tiny pearl of sperm appeared. Fearful that he was about to come too soon, he took her hand away. "Your turn," he whispered. She leaned back against the wall tiles as he slipped a soapy hand between her thighs. As he parted her and moved his fingers over her clitoris, she let out a tiny cry of delight. At one point he turned her around to face the wall. He massaged her buttocks, slid his fingers between them, moved slowly forward until he was back on her clitoris.

"Come in me," she whispered.

She turned around. He grabbed her thigh, pulled her leg onto his hip, and pushed hard inside her. She gripped his shoulders, felt the thrusts getting harder and deeper. She felt him hold his breath. His body shuddered. This time, because it was harder for him to reach her clitoris, she found it harder to come. As his penis slipped out of her, he started working on her again, firm circular movements over her vulva. He didn't let up. The certain rhythm made it easier for her to lose control. As the familiar waves built up inside her, she let out a series of soft moans. "There you go," he whispered. "There you go."

Her nails dug into his shoulders. Her mouth opened. He held her until she was still. Then he kissed her gently on the lips. They stayed, resting in each other's arms, until the hot water started to run out.

"SO DOES Charlie ask why he doesn't have a father?" Sam said a few minutes later as they lay in bed.

"Sometimes. They're not easy conversations to have. He can't understand why his father can't at least come and visit. It breaks my heart having to tell him that will never happen."

"I can imagine."

"And I know that when he gets older, he might get angry with me for not giving him a proper father. I mean, even divorced kids get to see their dads. He never does. He wants to be part of a family that's more than just me and him."

"Maybe, but at the same time he knows that you wanted him so much that you were prepared to raise him alone. That will always mean a great deal to him."

"I like to think so." Neither of them spoke for a moment or two.

"You know," he said eventually, "I used to be a sperm donor."

"No. Really?"

"It was years ago, when I was a student in Manchester. I'd just lost my part-time job, and I was really hard up."

"Omigod, was it excruciating? You know, being shut in a little room with a load of dirty mags."

He laughed. "I have to say it wasn't easy. First, the clinic was a converted church. Saint Bernadette's, it was called. As a well-brought-up Catholic boy, it wasn't easy jerking off in church, I can tell you."

This made her laugh.

"Then one day I forgot to lock the door, and a nurse came barging in. There was me with my jeans around my ankles and... well, you can imagine the scene. I never went back again. I was too humiliated." He stopped laughing. There was a pause. "Actually, there was another reason I never went back."

"What was that?"

She watched as he gathered his thoughts. "Okay, there is something I need to tell you. I know we've only just started dating, so what I'm about to say is going to seem premature and a bit forward, but I couldn't bear the thought of us getting serious and this being a deal breaker."

"Go on."

"I never got any money from the clinic, and when I asked why, they said I was sterile."

"Oh, Sam, that's awful. But isn't there anything that can be done? I mean, you got that diagnosis years ago. There are operations. Or maybe your body's changed."

He shook his head. "If you've got a negligible sperm count, that's pretty much it. I've done a fair bit of reading."

"So how do you feel about never becoming a father?"

"As a student, fatherhood wasn't something I'd given a moment's thought to. You don't at twenty. Over the years, I think I've just grown to accept it." He paused. "The thing is, if my being sterile is going to be a problem for you, I'd rather you told me sooner rather than later."

"I'm not going to lie. Part of me would love to have another baby, but with my family history, I know I'm extremely fortunate to have Charlie. I could try some more IVF by donor, but I'm not sure I want to bring another fatherless child into the world. A second child has never really been on my agenda. I think that like you, I've just come to accept it. So, to answer your question: The sterility issue wouldn't be a deal breaker."

"You sure?"

"Positive."

"Wow, that is a weight off. I'd geared myself up to getting dumped."

She kissed him on the cheek. "*You're* not getting dumped."

"Don't be ridiculous. Why would any man in his right mind dump you?"

She let out a soft laugh. "Because they don't want a child in their life, particularly one who isn't theirs. The last guy I dated suggested farming Charlie out on the weekends so that he wouldn't get in the way."

Sam was shaking his head. "That's appalling."

"Men often don't understand that I'm a mother and Charlie will always be my top priority."

"Amy, I get it. I have a sister with small kids. I would always expect you to put Charlie first. In fact, I'd find it strange if you didn't."

"Thank you," she said. "I can't tell you how much hearing you say that means to me."

"So we're okay?" he said.

"We're absolutely okay," she said, stroking the side of his face. He wrapped her in his arms, and they both drifted off to sleep.

THEY WERE woken about nine by frantic buzzing at the door.

"Whassat?" Sam mumbled.

"Paperboy can't get into the building."

Amy pulled the duvet over her head, hoping one of the other residents would come to his rescue. When the buzzing carried on, it occurred to her that it might not be the paperboy.

She sat up and swung her feet onto the floor. "Okay, I'm coming." She reached for her dressing gown, which was at the end of the bed, and padded to the front door. She lifted up the handset on the intercom.

"Hello?"

"Amy, it's me."

"Who me?"

"Me...Victoria."

"Victoria?"

"I've left Simon," she wailed through the intercom. "He said I'm a monster. Amy, please tell me I'm not a monster."

"Sweetie, of course you're not a monster," Amy said, buzzing her sister in. A few moments later, Victoria was weeping into Amy's shoulder.

Victoria never cried—at least not in public—and she never left the house unless her hair, makeup, clothes, and accessories were in perfect order. Now here she was, sobbing for all she was worth, wearing not a scrap of makeup, and looking like she'd slept in her clothes. A bewildered Arthur was at her side.

"I am so sorry." Amy said.

"You and Mum were right. Things haven't been good between Simon and me for ages. I just never thought it would
come to this. I just don't know what to do. Suppose he wants a
divorce? How would I cope?"

Panic was something else that rarely figured in Victoria's
emotional repertoire.

"It's okay," Amy soothed. "It won't come to that. It will all
get sorted out. Don't worry."

At that point, Amy turned her attention to Arthur. "Hi,
poppet," she said, bending down and giving him a kiss. "How
you doing?"

He shrugged.

"Where's Lila?" Amy asked Victoria.

"School trip. Left yesterday for ten days."

"I guess that makes things a bit simpler."

Victoria put a piece of crumpled tissue to her nose and
nodded.

"Mummy and Daddy got cross with each other," Arthur
piped up. "It was in the night, and I was frightened."

Big as he was, Amy scooped him up and gave him a kiss.
"Oh, darling, that must have been awful. The thing to under-
stand, though, is that they weren't cross with you. Mummy and
Daddy absolutely adore you."

He looked at Victoria. "Of course we do, darling," she said
between sniffs. "None of this is your fault. You mustn't think
that. And I'm sorry we frightened you."

"Okay," Amy said, putting her nephew down again. "Why
don't you go into the living room and watch TV or put on a
DVD. I'll bring you some juice. I might even have some chocolate cake somewhere."

Under normal circumstances Victoria would have demanded
a comprehensive list of the ingredients in the chocolate cake with
particular reference to sugar, saturated fats, and gluten. Right
now she couldn't have seemed less bothered. Arthur was about
to head off when Sam appeared wearing Amy's green silk kimono, the one she hadn't been able to find.

"You're that man who told me off," Arthur said, pointing at Sam. "Why are you wearing that? It's for a girl, not a boy. You look stupid."

Victoria told him to be quiet and said it was bad manners to point and make rude comments.

"But he does look stupid," Arthur persisted.

"I know," Sam said, offering Arthur a smile. "But I've been staying, and I seem to have mislaid my clothes."

"Sam," Amy broke in, "you remember my sister, Victoria."

He checked that the ill-fitting kimono was protecting his modesty before moving toward her, hand outstretched. "Of course. Hello again."

She did him the courtesy of taking his hand.

"Look," he said, "I'm really sorry we got off to a bad start the other day in the café. I can be a bit heavy-handed sometimes. Maybe we could start again."

"I don't see why not." Victoria offered him the thinnest of smiles.

He bent down. "And if I remember rightly, this is Arthur. How you doing? Hope you haven't been getting into any more stick fights."

Arthur gave an enthusiastic shake of his head.

"Good boy." Sam ruffled his hair.

"Look, I'd best be getting off," Sam said to Amy. "Don't suppose you know what happened to my clothes."

Amy said she'd put them in the washer-dryer last night because they'd gotten so dusty. "They should be dry." He headed into the kitchen while Arthur wandered into the living room to watch TV.

Amy and Victoria were alone in the hall. "How could you?" Victoria said in a whispered hiss. "I mean, after the way that man insulted me. How could you be so disloyal?"

"Look, I have gotten to know Sam. He is a great guy. He's apologized for upsetting you. Now, please let that be an end to it."

Victoria grunted. "What happened to the floor?"

"Sam helped me sand the boards. I'm going to paint them white."

"That'll look good," Victoria said.

"You mean you actually approve?"

"Yes, why wouldn't I?"

"You never approve of anything I do."

"Amy, please don't confuse a genuine desire to stop you from making mistakes with disapproval."

Just then Sam reappeared fully clothed, if a little rumpled. Victoria was clearly feeling better because she took one look at him and found the strength to observe that Amy clearly hadn't used the dryer's anticrease setting.

"Right, I'll be off," Sam said, kissing Amy on the cheek. "I'll call you later. We'll get together during the week."

Amy nodded. "Great."

He picked up the electric sander, which was standing by the front door, and said he would get it back to the rental shop.

"You sure you don't mind?"

"Positive...Bye, Victoria. Nice seeing you again."

"You, too," she said in a tone that verged on amicable.

THE TWO women went into the kitchen. Amy put the kettle on and filled a glass with orange juice for Arthur.

"By the way, don't you think Sam looks a bit like Charlie?" Victoria said, sitting herself down at the kitchen table.

"You think? Mmm. They've got similar coloring, I suppose."

"No, there's something about the eyes."

Amy said that now she came to mention it, maybe there was a similarity.

"Oh, by the way," Victoria said, "I need to get my stuff from the lobby."

"Stuff? You're staying?"

"Yes, if that's all right. Just for a few days until I get myself sorted out."

"No. Yes. I mean, of course it's all right. Stay as long as you want. Look, why don't I go and fetch your case?"

"Would you?" Victoria said. "I'm so exhausted. Simon and I were up all night arguing. I'm not sure I could manage it."

Victoria took Arthur his orange juice and chocolate cake while Amy went outside into the lobby. There she was confronted by three Louis Vuitton suitcases, a yoga mat, a giant exercise ball, and copies of *Juicing for Life* and *The Caring Parent's Guide to Child Nutrition*.

"You off on your holidays?" Amy heard a voice say. It was her neighbor old Mr. Fletcher coming out of his flat, he of the British Gas altercation, which had by now been settled to his satisfaction. He was in his "going out" attire: navy blazer with gold buttons and nautical pocket motif.

Amy explained that her sister was staying for a few days.

"Really?" old Mr. Fletcher said with a chuckle. "You sure she's not moving in?"

"Oh, no, just a short visit," Amy said with a nervous laugh.

Mr. Fletcher opened the main door to leave. A chap in green overalls was standing outside. "I was just about to ring the bell," he said. "Delivery for Amy Walker."

"This is Miss Walker," Mr. Fletcher said.

Amy frowned. "But I wasn't expecting anything."

"No groceries from Planet Organic?"

"What? Oh, God. My sister must have ordered them. All right, you'd better bring them in."

"Do me a favor, love," the deliveryman said, "and prop the door open. It's gonna take me forever to get this lot off the van."

Old Mr. Fletcher turned to Amy and let out another chuckle. "What was that you said about a short visit?"

Chapter 10

VAL AND TREVOR brought Charlie home just after five. They'd spent the day at the Natural History Museum.

The moment her mother appeared, Victoria turned on the waterworks afresh. "Simon's thrown me out," she wailed.

"I knew it. I knew things weren't right," Val said. She put her arms around her daughter and patted her back while offering soothing there-theres.

Arthur, upset and frightened at seeing his mother in tears again, took out his anxiety on Charlie by snatching the model stegosaurus Val had bought him. Charlie responded by snatching it back and lashing out with a splendid right hook, which caught Arthur on the nose. It immediately started to bleed. Arthur started screaming in pain. Amy panicked and found herself shouting at Charlie, who took fright and fled to his bedroom. Val scooped Arthur up and tried to calm him. Trevor handed her a clean handkerchief, which she held under Arthur's nose. Victoria said she would get some paper towels. "I'll damp it down to make a cold compress." She turned to Arthur. "Darling, lean your head back. It stops the bleeding."

"That's not right," Val butted in. "You tilt the head forward for a nosebleed."

"No, back."

"That makes the blood run down the throat and might make him gag."

"That's rubbish. I know I'm right."

"It is not rubbish," Val insisted. "I took the Inland Revenue first aid course, and I am now my department's designated first aider. So for once in your life will you stop being such a know-it-all and accept that somebody might just know better than you."

"Right. Fine. Tilt his head forward, then." Forced to abandon her high horse, Victoria disappeared into the kitchen.

"My God," Val said with a chuckle. "My elder daughter just listened to something I said."

"Way to go." Trevor grinned.

"I'll say," Amy said.

They could hear Charlie crying in his bedroom. Amy decided to go talk to him, but he didn't want to hear. He lay on his bed kicking and thrashing around and telling her to go away. She had little doubt that he was furious with himself for having hurt Arthur and with Amy for shouting at him. In the end she decided to leave him to calm down.

When she got back to the living room, Arthur was sitting on Val's lap while Victoria pressed a compress to her son's nose. She immediately turned on Amy and said it was clear that Charlie had anger issues and needed to learn how to curb his emotions. Amy accused Victoria of raising a spoiled, undisciplined bully. Victoria announced she was leaving. Amy said that was fine by her.

For a second time, Val took charge. "Nobody is going anywhere. Now, will you two just behave? Whatever issues you have between you can wait. We need to work out if Arthur needs to go to the hospital."

Trevor suggested they hang on for a few minutes to see if the bleeding stopped. He crouched down in front of Arthur, assuring him he was going to be fine.

"Trevor," Val whispered. "Don't you dare go into one of your trances and start praying for spiritual healing. It'll scare the living daylights out of the poor child."

"I wasn't going to," Trevor said. He looked back at Arthur. "I could tell you a story to cheer you up."

"Not if it involves Inuit spirit guides and wolves," Val hissed.

"It doesn't," Trevor said, shooting Val a sharp, get-off-my-back look. "You want to hear a funny story, Arthur?"

He nodded.

Trevor started telling Arthur how when he was a boy he was always getting into fights at school with a boy called Hilary.

Arthur laughed. "Hilary's a girl's name."

"It can be a boy's name. But it gets worse. He had a twin brother called Lesley."

"No! That's a joke."

"It's not. Honest. Hilary and Lesley Smelley, they were called."

Arthur burst out laughing.

"Anyway, one day for a joke, I decided to phone Hilary and Lesley's mum. When she answered the phone, I pretended not to know her and I said, 'Are you Smelley?' She said 'yes,' and I said, 'So what are you going to do about it?'"

This made everybody laugh, even Victoria. By now the color had returned to Arthur's cheeks.

"Darling, I need to feel your nose," Val said to Arthur. Victoria, continuing to defer to her mother's superior knowledge of first aid, removed the compress and let her examine Arthur's nose.

"I think it could be broken," Val said.

Amy felt sick with guilt. Even though she felt sorry for Charlie and understood why he had thumped his cousin, she was furious with him.

By now Val was starting to panic and insisted that Trevor take Arthur to the accident and emergency room. Trevor said no problem, but they would have to leave right away as he had the annual Shaman Soul Retrieval Forgathering in Streatham. It started at eight, and he needed get home to shower and change.

"Fine," Val said, "if you think your shaman shindig is more important than a child with a broken nose."

"This isn't a 'shindig,'" Trevor said, looking wounded. "It's an important meeting. They're even planning a vision quest. Look, I'm more than happy to take Arthur to the hospital. I'll even leave you lot with the car, but I can't stay, that's all."

Val grunted.

Amy decided it was time for her to step in and attempt to bring down the emotional temperature.

"Mum, take it easy. Victoria has her car. If we decide Arthur needs to go to the hospital, we'll take him." She paused and turned to her sister. "That's assuming you're staying."

Victoria looked sullen and didn't say anything.

"I'm sorry," Amy said to her. "I was angry, and I lashed out at you. Charlie had no right to hit Arthur. He'll be punished, and I'll make sure he apologizes. Please stay."

Victoria offered a shrug, which Amy took as a yes. Only Amy caught Arthur's weak but nonetheless victorious smile.

By now the bleeding was easing off. Once Val was satisfied it had stopped, she and Trevor said their goodbyes. As the pair disappeared into the hall, the sisters could hear them bickering.

Once the front door had closed, Victoria turned to Amy. "Well, well, well, it seems that Mum has finally had enough of chanting Trevor. If you ask me, it's only a matter of time before she gives him his marching orders."

Amy took no pleasure in saying that she could well be right.

The sisters examined Arthur's nose and decided their mother's diagnosis that it was broken had been born of panic. It looked a bit red, but there was no swelling, and according to Arthur, the pain had gone.

When Charlie finally allowed his mother into his room, she found him sitting on the bed, drawing a purple monster. "I hate Arfur," he declared. "I don't want him here. He steals my stuff."

Amy explained that Arthur was upset because Victoria and Simon had been fighting.

"Whaddabout?"

"Well, you know how you sometimes get cross with friends at school and you don't like them for a bit? Well, adults do the same. Occasionally they get angry. But when children see adults shouting at each other, they often get scared and upset. That's what happened to Arthur. He saw Auntie Victoria and Uncle Simon fighting, and he got really upset. He got even more upset when he saw his mummy crying, and I think he took it out on you by taking your stegosaurus."

Charlie nodded.

"It was an unkind thing to do, but it didn't give you the right to lash out and punch Arthur on the nose. You really hurt him, and that deserves a punishment. Tomorrow there will be no drawing for you. I'm taking away your paper and pencils."

He glared at his mother, arms folded in defiance. "Don't care." He kicked his sketch pad and pencils onto the floor. Amy walked over to the door. "I want you to pick everything up and bring it to me. Then you must apologize to Arthur."

Half an hour later, Victoria had popped out to buy a bottle of wine and Amy was in the kitchen stirring Bolognese sauce. She was just about to put the pasta on when Charlie appeared. He was holding his sketch pad and pencils, which he handed to his mother. She thanked him. Judging by his sullen expression, it was the smell of supper cooking rather than a sense of contrition that had brought her son to the kitchen, but she wasn't about to question his motives. "Now, then, what do you say to Arthur?" Charlie looked up at his mother as if to say: "He started it. You know he did. Please don't humiliate me by making me apologize."

"What do you say?" Amy repeated.

Charlie turned to his cousin, who was standing by the sink drinking a glass of water. "Sorry I punched your nose."

"That's all right," Arthur said with an amiable shrug. "You wanna build a Lego tower?"

"K."

By then Victoria had returned with a bottle of Barolo. She

turned to Charlie. "Well done, you, for saying sorry," she cooed, bending down to give him a kiss. Charlie looked a bit embarrassed and then charged into the living room with Arthur. Amy called after them to say supper would be ready in ten minutes.

"Of course," Victoria said to Amy, "you are going to have to come down hard on Charlie's behavior from now on. I mean, with his anger issues, which clearly stem from him not having a father and you raising him in such a rough neighborhood, you could have an out-of-control yob on your hands before you know it."

Amy's instinct was to get hold of her sister's fabulous blond highlights and pull them out at the roots. She didn't because hard as it was to hear, she found herself thinking that Victoria might have a point.

That night, Amy put both boys in Charlie's bed, arranging them end to end. She read them Roald Dahl's *The Twits*, which had them in hysterics, particularly the bit about when Mr. and Mrs. Twit get their heads glued to the floor. She'd just finished when Victoria appeared. Both women kissed the boys good night and made them promise to go straight to sleep. The moment Amy and Victoria left the room, the boys started jumping on the bed and horsing around. It wasn't long before it turned nasty and they were kicking and fighting.

Victoria said she didn't feel up to playing referee, so it was Amy who got up from the sofa every five minutes to remonstrate with the boys. It did no good, so in the end Amy put Charlie in her bed. Half an hour later, both boys were sound asleep.

"God," Victoria said, draining her second glass of wine. "Do you think Simon and I have traumatized Arthur for life by letting him see us fight?"

Amy decided it was the wine that had induced this rare demonstration of self-doubt. "Don't be daft. Of course you haven't. He's upset and a bit scared right now, but so long as you and Simon resolve things, he'll get over it."

"Well, that certainly isn't going to happen in a hurry."

The two women stayed up late, talking.

"I just don't understand why Simon hates me so much," Victoria said at one point. "What have I done that is so dreadful? I've given him two beautiful children. I've made a wonderful home for him. I cook. I look after myself. I keep up with current affairs. I'm more than accommodating in the bedroom department."

Amy made no attempt to challenge Victoria or suggest that she had a part to play in the breakdown of her relationship with Simon. Her sister wasn't ready to hear that, at least not yet. For the time being, Amy simply listened and helped dry her sister's tears.

ON MONDAY morning, when Amy got to work, she found Brian in the kitchen in what was now his usual miserablist mood. It turned out that he hadn't managed to woo the reluctant Rebecca with his *Seinfeld* impersonations. What was more, his man boobs were sprouting like brassicas in muck.

The only chink of light was that, as of this morning, the builders working on the Bean Machine had walked off the job. According to the postman, with whom Brian was fairly matey, the builders had turned up at the site and immediately started ranting at the project manager over late payments. Brian had no idea how long the strike would go on or to what extent it would delay the Bean Machine's opening, but the postman said things had looked pretty heavy. Brian was praying the strike would last for weeks rather than days. "Not that it's going to make much difference," he said. "It's only delaying the inevitable." He paused. "Unless, of course, Bean Machine is suddenly in some kind of financial trouble and that's why they're not paying their bills." He decided the idea was daft. The whole world knew about the billions Bean Machine made in profits each year.

Just after eleven, Bel popped into the café to drown her sorrows in a full-fat, half-caff latte. She hadn't gotten the part of

Ophelia, nor had the Dildo King paraphernalia done much to improve her sex life with Ulf. Not that she wasn't grateful to Amy for going out of her way to get it. Much to Bel's dismay, Ulf was stuck on the notion that nature had placed the human mouth at the head end rather than the "toilet" end for a very good reason.

"Don't let anybody try to convince you that Scandinavians are sexually liberated," she said, shaking chocolate over her coffee. "It's a myth."

"This Ulf reminds me of my Sidney," Zelma chimed in. "Don't get me wrong. He loved me to bits, but he was very repressed sexually. The moment I suggested doing something more adventurous in bed, he'd say he could hear his dead mother screaming: 'Sidney, take that out of your mouth; you don't know where it's been.'"

"So are you going to dump him?" Brian said, once they'd all stopped laughing. Amy wondered if she was the only one to pick up on the anticipation in his voice.

Bel said she still liked Ulf and wasn't prepared to throw in the clit stick just yet.

Brian didn't say anything.

Just as everybody was commiserating with Amy about *The Daily Post* piece and having Victoria come to stay, she got a call on her mobile from Boadicea. "Look, Amy," she said, sounding less like she was dragging on a joint than usual, "I'm really sorry about what happened. The editor wanted Jamie. There wasn't a lot I could do." Amy was about to have a moan at her for not having let her know what was going on when Boadicea added, "Of course there is a kill fee. Is eight-fifty okay?"

"Excuse me? How much?"

"All right, since we did treat you rather badly and you're not going to be able to place the piece elsewhere since we've covered it, I'll see if I can push it up to a grand. But don't tell anybody. We're supposed to be cutting back, you know—the recession and all that."

"No. No. A thousand's fine. I'll invoice you, shall I?"

"Brill."

Still in shock, Amy flipped down the lid on her phone. She turned to Brian, Zelma, and Bel: "Okay, lemon drizzle cake all around. I'm buying."

JUST AFTER two, as usual, things went quiet in the café. Zelma popped out to do some shopping while Amy sat down at one of the window tables with a cup of tea, a smoked salmon bagel, and yesterday's *Sunday Times*.

She read a boring but important piece on why the prime minister's cabinet reshuffle was a disaster. Afterward she grappled with an analysis of the recession written by an Oxford professor of economics but got lost after the first paragraph. As she turned the page, a headline caught her eye: "Moobs Men Shown to Have High Levels of Estrogen." The article was based on a Harvard Medical School study. Doctors and scientists investigating why slim middle-class men were developing breasts had carried out more than five thousand blood tests. The results, which had just been published, showed that nearly all the men had higher than normal estrogen levels.

Amy went into the kitchen and showed the piece to Brian. "It says tests have also been carried out on men in Britain and Europe. At first they thought it could be something to do with the water supply—you know, women on the pill peeing out estrogen—but it's not. In every country, the estrogen levels in water turned out to be insignificant. They're calling it a 'moob pandemic,' and nobody has any idea what's causing it and why it only affects rich or middle-class men."

Brian read through the article. When he got to the bit about high levels of estrogen in men being linked to male breast cancer, he said he was making an appointment for a blood test. "This has to be what's going on with me. Somehow I'm absorbing estrogen."

"Maybe its all that Crema Crema Crema you've been drinking," Amy said with a chuckle. "Only rich people can afford to buy that."

"Don't be daft. There's no estrogen in coffee. Here, I'll check it out."

He opened his laptop, which was sitting on the worktop next to him, and Googled "coffee estrogen."

"There you are," he said, inviting her to look at the screen. "Top hit. Coffee reduces breast cancer risk."

"Okay," Amy said. "I wasn't really being serious."

For the rest of the day, Amy and Zelma did their best to calm Brian and assure him that somebody would come up with an answer, but they could see he was scared. "This isn't just about my looks anymore," he said at one point. "I could die from this."

Zelma got cross with Brian and insisted that nobody was going to die, but later on, when she and Amy discussed the issue in private, they couldn't hide their fears.

"God, Zelma, suppose they don't discover what's causing this rise in estrogen levels? It doesn't bear thinking about."

By the following day, all the newspapers, plus the radio and TV news, had the story. The tabloids in particular had gone to town printing beach photographs of male celebs and postulating whether their moobs were due to raised estrogen levels.

Radio 5 even devoted its morning phone-in to the moob question. Brian had it on in the kitchen. It didn't do much to reassure him. A breast cancer specialist was insisting that only long exposure to estrogen caused cancer. He urged men not to overreact and to keep calm. "The moment people in authority tell you to keep calm," Brian said, "you can be certain there's something to worry about."

It was only when Brian went to see his own private specialist, who was, according to Brian, "the best tit man in the country," that he started to relax. Best Tit Man did a blood test, the results of which Brian was still waiting on, and reiterated what the doctor on the radio had said.

If Brian was starting to lighten up, Victoria wasn't. She would burst into tears at odd times, such as in the middle of *Battlestar Galactica*, and start raging and railing against Simon. Seeing her sister so miserable and vulnerable, Amy continued to take pity on her and let her sound off. She ran her baths, gave her foot massages, cooked, and got the boys off to bed each night.

Amy wasn't looking for thanks. On the other hand, she wasn't looking for constant criticism, either.

Victoria's faultfinding and self-promotion rarely let up: Amy was feeding Charlie too much salt and sugar and not enough omega 3 and 6, which had been proved to boost brainpower in children. Why was she using soap on Charlie? Didn't she know how bad all the antibacterial agents were for children's skin? Of course she had been using Yucca Root soap substitute on Arthur since day one.

Amy wasn't sure how long she could keep her temper. She had held out until now only because she felt sorry for Victoria, plus Brian, Bel, and Sam all said that challenging her wasn't worth it because she was incapable of handling criticism and would only fly into a rage.

Then, on Friday, Amy returned home to discover that Victoria had been spring cleaning. The flat wasn't merely spotless, it was sterile. It had been purged, pasteurized, bleached, and boraxed to within an inch of its life. A human appendix could have been removed on Amy's kitchen table without fear of patient infection.

The cooktop and oven had been degreased. The hard water buildup around the kitchen tap was gone, ditto the gunk that had collected under the range hood. She had even gotten rid of the goo from around the nozzle on the washing-up-liquid bottle. The food cupboards had been scrubbed and their contents meticulously rearranged. Jars and cans were on one shelf, packets of flour, sugar, and other dry products on another. Herbs and flavorings had their own shelf. The cutlery container, instead of overflowing with knives, forks, and spoons, had been put to its proper use. In the bathroom, the toilet, sink, and bathtub shone. The dirty laundry, clean laundry, and ironing piles had disappeared.

Everywhere there was the smell of Pledge and condescension.

Amy had just put the kettle on, when Victoria appeared with the boys. She had taken them to get low-fat frozen yogurt cones and was now shooing them into the garden because they were dripping on the floor. "So, what do you think?" Victoria said, beaming at Amy. "I have to admit that I'm totally exhausted, but I think you'll agree I've done a pretty good job." Amy had no trouble picturing Victoria in her pinnie, singing "Whistle While You Work," a bluebird perched on her shoulder.

"It's amazing. Thank you," Amy said, her gratitude less than fulsome. "But it really wasn't necessary."

"Well, you may not think so, but we both know that you've been letting things slide houseworkwise. Now I've got you back up to speed, all you need to do is spend a few minutes each day cleaning and tidying, and that way you'll stay on top of things. I've drawn you up a daily job roster, so that should help." She handed Amy a densely typed sheet of A4. "Of course the place still isn't quite up to my standard. The outsides of the windows still need cleaning and you're hoarding way too much clutter, but I'll sort through that tomorrow and have a good chuck-out."

"What?" Amy blurted. "No, you won't. My clutter belongs to me. If anybody's going to sort it out, I will." By now the electric kettle was boiling. Amy watched it switch itself off but made no attempt to reach for mugs and tea bags. Instead she sat down at the kitchen table. She folded her arms. Then, realizing this looked too confrontational, she unfolded them.

"Victoria, why have you done this? I mean, why have you *really* done it?"

"What do you mean? I did it to help you. I know you don't get much time for housework, and I thought the place could do with a thorough spring clean."

Amy thought carefully. She wasn't sure whether to risk her sister's wrath by saying what was on her mind.

"The problem with you," Victoria continued, "is that you've never been able to stick to a routine. You're so scatty and all over the place."

Amy hesitated, but only for a second. "And the problem with you is that you are a control freak."

"Excuse me?"

"You're a control freak. You cleaned my flat because it makes you feel superior and in control."

Victoria seemed genuinely aghast. "I don't know what you're talking about."

"Yes, you do." Amy was fighting to remain composed. "You think everybody should live their lives to your standards. This spring cleaning is all about you proving how wonderful you are and how crap I am. And it's not just me. You do it to everybody."

"You're mad. I like to help, that's all."

"You don't help. You boss and scold."

"I do not!"

"Yes, you do." Amy paused to calm herself and gather her thoughts. "Victoria, has it occurred to you that Simon wants a soul mate?"

"I am his soul mate."

"You may think you are, but you're not. You're his boss. You communicate with him by barking orders and issuing commands. You always think you know best."

"No, I don't."

"Oh, Victoria. How can you say that? You're always telling people how to run their lives. Me, Mum, Claire in the café the other day. You seem to take pleasure in making people feel small."

Victoria flinched. She went to the fridge, took out an open bottle of white wine, and poured herself a glass. She didn't offer to pour one for Amy.

"Why does queening it over everybody give you so much pleasure?"

Victoria gave a thin laugh. "What's this, you Freud, me Jane?" She tipped back her head and downed some wine.

"You know, sooner or later you will have to confront this."

"Confront what? I don't know what you're talking about."

"Yes, you do."

"I don't have to stay here listening to this," Victoria said, but made no attempt to leave. Her eyes were glassy with tears. After a few moments she came and sat down opposite Amy. "Okay." She cleared her throat. "Maybe it's because deep down I feel small." She downed some more wine.

"But how could you possibly feel small after all you've achieved?"

"I haven't achieved that much. I went to Oxford, got a good job. So what?"

"In most people's books, that's pretty amazing. Plus you were and are very beautiful. When we were young, I was so jealous of you."

Victoria shrugged. "Okay, I was pretty, but so were you. And you had all the charm. You had so many friends. I was never as popular as you. I suppose I compensated by becoming a smart-ass."

"But don't you see that you hurt people when you put them down?"

Victoria shrugged. "Part of me thinks they deserve it because they're such fools."

"Do you think Simon's a fool?"

"No, of course not. He's much smarter than me. I've always known that."

"So why do you put him down?"

"I don't know." Victoria's elbows were on the table, her head in her hands. "Actually, yes, I do...I have to compete with him. I daren't let him win. I'm like that with everybody."

"And if you don't win?"

"I never let that happen."

"But just suppose for a moment that it did."

Victoria looked up, genuine fear and confusion on her face. She hesitated. "I think that if I didn't win, people would see how inadequate I really am and I would disappear. Not my body, but the inner me. It would vanish into thin air...Poof... I'd be nothing. I wouldn't exist...Amy, you have no idea how frightening that is."

Victoria was shaking and crying. Amy took her hand and held it tight.

"Mum and Dad had so much invested in you," Amy said. "All that pressure can't have been easy. I was jealous of you, but I'm just starting to realize that I was the lucky one. I was let off the hook." She paused. "You know you have to get some professional help—for your sake and for the sake of your marriage."

"What? See a shrink?"

"I think it might help."

"You think I'm mad, don't you?"

"Don't be daft. You're not remotely mad. You're just struggling with some very difficult issues, that's all, and you need a bit of help to deal with them."

"There's no way I'm discussing personal stuff with a stranger. I'll talk to you."

"That won't work. I'm your sister. I'm involved. I have my own agenda. Honestly, a therapist is the only answer."

Victoria bit her bottom lip. "Seeing a shrink feels so weak. All my life I've tried to be strong."

"Getting therapy isn't weak. It takes great strength to reach out and admit you need some help. Think about it."

"Okay, but I'm not making any promises."

"Fine. That's all I'm asking."

"Amy, I just want to say thank you."

"What for?"

"For being so wise."

"I'm not sure I'm so wise, but I'm glad to have helped. And

thank you, too, for everything you did today. The place looks fabulous."

"I'm glad you like it."

"I love you," Amy said.

"I love you, too."

They were still holding hands.

"I was wondering," Victoria said, gently pulling away, "if I could ask a favor. Sorry I seem to be asking so much of you lately."

"Not a problem. Ask away."

"Okay, well, you know it's Arthur's birthday on Sunday. Simon said we can have it at home as arranged, but I've been thinking maybe that's not such a good idea. I've just had a new lawn put down in the back garden, and I'd rather not have kids tramping over it. So I was wondering if we could have it here. After all, your garden's a complete mess; it wouldn't make much difference."

"SO, WHAT did you say to her?" Sam asked Amy a few hours later over dinner at his place.

"I agreed to having the party in the garden, but only because I thought I'd challenged her enough for one day and because it's naive to think she'll change overnight. It'll take loads of therapy—that's if she's willing to go." Amy scooped up another forkful of Sam's sublime Thai green curry. "God, this is good, but I wish you had let me take you out to dinner. I wanted to say thank you for all your hard work stripping the floorboards, which, by the way, even Victoria thinks look great."

"Praise indeed," he said, topping up her glass. "And as far as cooking goes, I enjoy it. It helps me unwind, so stop feeling guilty. You brought champagne and that fantastic homemade Victoria sponge."

"I remembered you said it was your favorite. I had to make it after Charlie went to bed and then hide it. He'd have demolished the lot if I'd let him. But next time we'll go out. My treat. Agreed?"

"Okay, if you insist. Agreed."

They clinked glasses.

"So did Victoria mind baby-sitting tonight?"

Amy shook her head. "She's got me on party food detail tomorrow. I'm doing the guacamole dip, the snapper and ginger wontons, and the tabbouleh."

"God, do kids actually eat that stuff? What happened to sausages on sticks and fondant fancies?"

"Too much sugar, too much fat, too much gluten…Anyway, the quid pro quo is I have an overnight pass tonight if I want."

"And do you want?"

"Oh, yes. I want very much."

"Good."

Sam's flat above his office in Clapham wasn't quite what she'd been expecting. He had led her not into a chic minimalist, high-tech space but a vast, paint-spattered artist's studio. There were trestle tables covered in dirty rags, dried-up brushes, and palettes. Dozens of canvases—brightly colored abstracts, some half-finished—were propped up against the walls. One of the first things she'd noticed was the smell of oil paint and turpentine competing with the delicious Thai curry smell coming from the kitchen.

The kitchen wasn't so much a room as an area at one end of the studio given over to a few ancient kitchen units and a fridge and a stove, which had to be fifteen years old. The glass dining table, where they were sitting now, was new but nothing fancy.

At the opposite end was the bedroom area. It contained a low double bed with a wooden headboard, a desk and computer, and one of those portable hanging rails on wheels, full of clothes. In the middle of the studio, things got smarter. There were two brown leather sofas, a giant plasma TV on a stand, and a couple of black monolithic speakers that looked like they had been nicked from the set of *2001*.

"I like this place," she said as he served her another helping of green curry. "It's nice. Sort of boho."

"But I could tell by your face when you walked in that it wasn't what you were expecting."

She smiled. "I have to admit I did have something rather different in mind. You being an architect, I was thinking more white walls, marble floor tiles, glass walkways, swanky science lab kitchen full of gadgets. And it turns out your kitchen's older than mine and one of your bathroom taps won't turn off."

"Oh, God, I meant to tell you about that. There's a knack to it."

"Don't worry. I worked it out." She paused. "So, why no edgy, designered space."

"I'm working on it," he said.

"You're planning to renovate this place?"

He shook his head. "No. What I really want to do is build a house that I've designed. That's if I can get the money together. I've been saving, rather than spending money doing up the flat."

"That is such a wonderful idea. Where are you going to build it?"

"*If* I build it. It's still only a pipe dream."

"Okay, where are you dreaming of building it?"

"Dunno. I was thinking maybe somewhere close to the sea. I'd love to wake up every morning to hear waves crashing on the beach."

"And gulls. I love the sound of gulls." She felt herself blush. Idiot. Now he was going to think she was planning their future and had ideas about living there, too. Okay, the thought may have crossed her mind, but only for a nanosecond, and there was no way she wanted Sam picking up on it.

"I thought maybe Cornwall," he said. If he had any thoughts about the gulls remark, he was keeping them to himself. "Until she died, my gran lived in a cottage in a tiny seaside village called Trescothick Strand. After Dad left us, we couldn't afford posh holidays, so my mum used to take us to stay with my gran. I still love it down there."

"Omigod, that's amazing. I can't believe you know Trescothick Strand. It's my all-time favorite place."

"You're kidding."

"Uh-uh." Amy told him how most summers she rented a place just a short walk from there. "Only for a week and it's usually freezing or chucking it down, but Charlie and I fly kites, collect shells, or go fishing in rock pools. I get fat gorging on too many cream teas."

Sam said he could still remember his first box kite. "Then one day it got attacked by a particularly vindictive seagull. I remember crying until my mum bought me a new one."

"Tell me about it." Amy laughed. "I must have bought Charlie dozens of kites...Sometimes Brian and Bel come down, too. In the evenings, if the weather's good, we make a fire on the beach and cook fish. Of course Charlie refuses to eat it because of the bones, but I can't tell you how much I love those times. I never ever want to come home."

Sam said he was the same way.

She took a sip of champagne. "It can't have been easy having your dad walk out when you were so young."

Sam said it was particularly hard on his mother. Because she never received any child maintenance, she ended up doing two jobs to support him and his siblings. "But it wasn't easy for us kids. I think we all grew up thinking we'd done something wrong, that we deserved to be abandoned."

Amy said she could see that. "So have you had any contact with your dad since he left?"

"Not until a few years ago. I'd gotten to the stage where I wanted to hear his side of the story. We always knew where he was, so I phoned him. He and I went out for a pub lunch. He talked about his new wife and family. He wasn't really interested in discussing the past. When I asked him why he'd left us, he said he and Mum weren't getting along; he'd found somebody else and thought it was for the best to make a clean break."

"What sort of a human being thinks it's for the best to walk out on three kids and leave their mother penniless?"

"Oh, he's a real piece of work, my dad. We got to the end of our lunch, and I realized he hadn't once said sorry or expressed even slight regret. By the time we said goodbye I had decided that I never wanted to see him again. My brother and sister met him separately and came to the same conclusion, so we're all agreed, which is something, at least. I think there could have been friction if one of us had wanted a relationship with him."

"It must be awful not having a male role model. There's no-body to show you how to be a good father."

Sam fell silent. He sat running his finger over the rim of his glass.

"You okay?" Amy asked. "Did I say something to upset you?"

"No. Not at all." He had cheered up now. "How about we make a start on your cake?"

"I'd rather see your paintings."

They got up from the table. Sam had dozens of canvases stacked up against one wall. He worked in oils and acrylics. His abstracts were linear and geometric. Then there were the semiabstracts—industrialscapes, mostly. A particularly brutal-ist image of Battersea Power Station really appealed to her, not that she would have wanted it on her living room wall. The paintings she liked most were of house interiors. They didn't depict smart, designered rooms, just run-of-the-mill bath-rooms, kitchens, and living rooms. One kitchen was very like her own, pre–Victoria's purge. There were open food packets left out on the counters, dishes piling up in the sink, a garbage can overflowing. Another showed a woman's bedroom, the bed unmade, stockings and underwear strewn over the floor as if they'd been removed in a hurry. These paintings were about real-life muck and mess and sex. She adored them and told him so.

"I can see why these are selling," she said, standing back to admire a painting of an open cupboard overflowing with coats and shoes. "They are just so original. You are so talented, but I don't need to tell you that."

"You're very kind," he said, a tad ill at ease with her praise. "Now, let's have cake."

They took their peppermint tea and Amy's Victoria sponge to the sofa.

"So, have you done any sketches for this house of yours?"

"A few, but they're incredibly rough."

Despite his protests, she insisted he show her.

He went to his desk at the bedroom end of the room and returned with a folder full of architect's drawings. He spread them out on the floor. Amy knelt down beside him.

"Like I said, these are very rough," he said. "There's still a long way to go."

They didn't look remotely rough to Amy. They looked meticulous. The house was a simple, unpretentious glass construction with a flat roof.

"Most of the glass walls slide back in the summer."

She was examining the stairs. "I don't get these. They seem to be hanging in midair."

Sam explained that in a way they were. They were floating stairs, essentially platforms with space between them and a slender support in the middle that made them appear to float. "And upstairs you've got glass walkways. All the bedrooms have their own bathrooms, and like the living room, they have a glass wall that looks out over the garden."

Amy carried on studying the drawings. "Umm, I'm not sure this bit is right."

"Really? Why?"

"Well, to get from the living room to this smaller room

next to the kitchen, you have to walk right around the house. You need to put in a connecting door."

He studied the drawing for a few moments. "You are not wrong." He grinned. "I have totally forgotten the door. I did tell you it was a rough draft."

"And how's about upstairs in the master bedroom, keeping the en suite loo and shower but putting the bath in the bedroom? I've seen these amazing stone resin baths."

"That's very sexy."

"What, stone resin?"

"No." He laughed. "Having the bath in the bedroom."

"Of course you'd have to have one-way glass so that passersby couldn't see in."

"Of course."

"And have you thought about self-cleaning glass? It's expensive, but in the long run it has to work out cheaper than employing a window cleaner."

"I'll make a note."

"And insulation. You have to think about insulation. And solar panels for heating."

He was leaning back, smiling at her.

"What?"

"Nothing. I was just thinking how much I enjoy being with you."

"Me, too," she said.

He stood up, pulled her to her feet, and kissed her. The next thing she knew, she was unbuttoning his fly and he was doing the same to her shirt. In a few seconds they were standing naked in front of each other. She rested her head on his shoulder and ran her hand over his buttocks. He forced his hand between her legs and pushed his fingers hard inside her.

"You are so wet."

"Please. Can we go to the bed?"

"Sure."

Once they were on the bed, he made her bend her knees and

spread her legs. The next moment, she felt him pushing something hard and cold inside her. It took her breath away. Her body gave a jolt.

"What the——?"

"You said you did stuff," he whispered.

"I said I did *some* stuff."

"No, if I remember rightly, you said you did stuff."

"Yes, but I qualified it by saying 'not all stuff.'"

"Do you like it?"

"I'm not sure."

"Okay. Check this out."

The dildo, which she assumed was metal, since it was so cold, started to vibrate hard inside her. "That is amazing."

"And I've got this little tiny one that goes . . ."

"Omigod. Where?"

A second dildo was starting to vibrate.

"Here."

As it touched her clitoris, she cried out in delight. "Omigod, you went to Dildo King and bought a clit stick."

"I did. I thought it might be fun."

"It is. It so is. Don't stop. Please don't stop."

"You forget. You're not the one in control here."

He carried on like that for a minute or so, working on her with both dildos, and then, without warning, he removed them.

"No!"

"It's okay, just wait."

The next moment his tongue was circling her vulva. Then she experienced a sensation she had never experienced before. The tiny vibrator was pressing against her back passage. For a second, her eyes shot open and her body froze.

"Tell me if you want me to stop," he said.

"I don't know. I've never . . ."

"Try it for a bit."

"K."

She had no idea there were nerve endings there that could

produce the sensation she was feeling. He probed gently, not too hard or deep, letting the vibrator do its work. "I'm not going to hurt you. I promise."

She gasped.

"Just relax. Feel the sensation."

And she did. He kept her relaxed by concentrating on her clitoris.

Another millimeter. Nerve endings were firing all over the place. She was gasping, fists clenched at her sides.

"Just let go," he urged.

And when she did finally relax her pelvis and her arms and hands, it started to happen—a slow gentle buildup that ended in her entire body shaking and shuddering. Afterward she took his penis, which was still rod-hard, and guided it into her vagina, moving her hips toward him. His thrusts came hard and fast and then began to slow down and get deeper. When it was over, he lay beside her, trying to catch his breath.

"Sam, that was amazing."

"You sure you didn't mind? I wasn't sure."

"With anybody else it wouldn't have been right, but with you it was just exploring something new together, and it *so* worked."

DESPITE THE amount they'd eaten at dinner, they both had the munchies.

A few minutes later, they were sitting at the dining table, drinking tea and eating sponge cake, discussing how Amy might dispose of her thousand-pound kill fee from *The Daily Post*. In the end she decided to spend it on having the floorboards professionally painted. She would also get a new lock for the front door. Whatever was left would go toward this summer's Cornwall trip.

By eleven they decided they still weren't sleepy, so they watched *Armageddon* on Sky, which Sam insisted was the best action movie of all time. "You've got romance, action, adventure, humor, drama, a ticking clock. Plus there is one of the greatest comedy lines ever: 'Get off of the nuclear warhead. Now.'"

Amy kept insisting it wasn't as good as the *When Harry Met Sally* line "I'll have what she's having." They were still arguing as they fell asleep.

"You know, you really are perfect," Sam said, giving her a final kiss.

Amy was barely awake. "You're perfect, too."

Chapter 11

"UURRGH, THAT GREEN stuff looks like boogers in cat puke! I'm not eating it."

Amy, who was removing a tray of tofu nuggets from the oven, gave her son a weary look. "Charlie, stop playing around; you've had guacamole at Arthur's house, and if I remember, you rather liked it." She glanced up at the kitchen clock. It was just past two. Arthur's party was due to start in under an hour, and she and Victoria still had the sandwiches and going-home bags to do.

"No, I didn't. And I don't like that stuff, either."

He was referring to the celery boats, hummus, and crudités his mother had just put into serving dishes and laid out on the table.

"Charlie, why are you being such an old grump?" She suspected he was jealous of all the attention Arthur had been getting today. On top of that, Charlie's birthday present to his cousin hadn't gone down well. He still hadn't spent the three pounds of bribe money his mother had given him, so when he saw a rubber stegosaurus almost identical to the one Arthur had tried to grab from him the other day, he insisted on buying it.

It cost five pounds, so Amy added the extra two pounds. He was convinced his cousin would be delighted. Instead, Arthur had taken one look at the stegosaurus and discarded it with barely a thank you. Amy got him three Captain Underpants books, which most boys his age adored because they were full of gross stuff. When she saw them, Victoria gave a disapproving sniff. Arthur mumbled his thanks. Amy didn't take offense. She was wise enough to understand that his apathy toward his presents wasn't due to his being spoiled and ungrateful. He was simply miserable because his parents weren't together and his dad hadn't been there when he woke up to wish him a happy eighth birthday.

"I'm not being a grump," Charlie said. "I just want to know why we can't have pizza. We had pizza at my party."

"I know, but this is Arthur's party, and he's having different food. Here, taste one of these. You might like it." She blew on a crispy tofu nugget and handed it to Charlie. He squirmed, but Amy urged him to try it. His trepidation bordering on the theatrical, he took a bite out of the nugget. A second later he was spitting it into his hand. "That's disgusting."

"You didn't even taste it," Amy said, wiping his hand with a paper towel. "Listen, Charlie, I need you to behave today. I know you don't like this kind of food, but at least give it a try. And do not start spitting it out."

"What am I supposed to do?"

"Okay, you can spit it into your napkin, but try to be discreet."

"What does 'discreet' mean?"

"It means don't make a big fuss."

Charlie shrugged. He was just about to head into the garden, when Victoria appeared.

"Charlie, darling, take off your Arsenal shirt, there's a good boy. I think maybe you should wear something a bit smarter for the party."

Charlie looked wounded. As far as he was concerned, his Arsenal shirt was the smartest garment he owned.

"Oh, come on, Victoria," Amy pleaded. "Don't make a fuss."

"I'm sorry, Amy, but I find football shirts so unspeakably

common. And if Charlie wears his, Arthur will insist on doing the same. Please..."

Amy rolled her eyes. She put the tofu nuggets back in the oven to brown a bit more and took a protesting Charlie into his bedroom to find a clean T-shirt.

WHEN AMY got back, Victoria was arranging candles on Arthur's sugar-free, egg-free Hogwarts Express cake. She always created magnificent birthday cakes for her children. She would spend days on them. This year, though, she hadn't been up to it, and the masterpiece had come courtesy of one of her girl-friends, who ran a business making novelty cakes.

Victoria, as the self-appointed *capo di capi* among her group of mothers superior, was always scrupulous about providing healthy food on these occasions. Conscious of childhood aller-gies, she made certain that there was nothing that contained nuts, although Amy was convinced that Victoria kept a couple of EpiPens about her person just in case the odd peanut slipped by her and a child collapsed and went into anaphylactic shock.

Today Victoria was providing soya milk shakes for the lactose-intolerant and cow's milk shakes for the soya-intolerant. There were no eggs, strawberries, or shellfish. Everything had been checked and double-checked for additives, food colorings, and nitrate levels. The piñata had been especially commis-sioned and filled with boxes of organic raisins.

Everything was sugar-free, gluten-free, fat-free, fun-free.

At Arthur's last birthday party, Victoria had decided not to hire a clown. Instead, a Japanese chef came and taught the chil-dren to roll vegetarian sushi. That was followed by a Japanese tea ceremony. Worst of all, Victoria insisted on no presents. In-stead, a goat was donated in Arthur's name to a village in Africa. When the children arrived empty-handed, Arthur burst into tears. Then one child, whose mother hadn't gotten the message about the goat, arrived with a plastic remote-controlled truck, which Victoria confiscated and returned to her on the grounds that it wasn't recyclable and would only end up in a landfill site.

This year there was to be a clown and presents. According to Val, it was Arthur's father who had come to his rescue. She had been speaking to Simon in an attempt to broker a truce between him and Victoria. During their conversation, Simon had let it slip that he had told his wife "in no uncertain terms" that he would pay for the party only if there were presents and a proper entertainer.

What Val didn't know but Amy did was that Simon had also set Victoria an ultimatum: She had to get a shrink or the marriage was over. "What choice do I have?" Victoria had said to Amy. "I still love him, so I agreed."

"So you're going home?" Amy had asked. "Not that it hasn't been great having you. And if you're not ready to go, don't. Feel free to stay as long as you like."

"That's kind of you, but we'll be leaving after the party. Lila will be home in a few days. I've upset one child by moving him out of his home; I'm not about to do the same to his sister."

Amy assured her she was doing the right thing by agreeing to see a therapist, but she could tell her sister felt threatened by the idea. Being a patient would undermine her sense of power and superiority.

Simon arrived at half past two. Amy opened the front door. "Hi, Si. How you doing?" He was carrying a large box covered in Spiderman paper.

"A lot better, thanks. And apparently it's you I've got to thank. How on earth did you manage to get through to Victoria? She never listens to me."

"It's you who got her to agree to see a shrink."

"Yes, but you did all the groundwork."

"Maybe it was easier for me," Amy said, "because I'm not married to her. There isn't that inevitability that it's all going to end in a fight or one of you walking out."

"I guess."

"You know, Victoria's got a lot of issues to sort out, and that's going to take time. You're going to need to be patient."

"I know. That's what worries me. I've put up with her behavior for so long. I'm just not sure how much more I can take."

Amy urged him to hang on.

"I'll do my best. Thanks again, Amy. You don't know how much I appreciate what you've done." With that he gave his sister-in-law an affectionate squeeze. "So I hear from your mum that you're stepping out with a rather eligible architect slash artist. Is it serious?"

Amy paused and allowed her face to break into a smile. "Dunno...could be."

"Good for you."

No sooner had Simon walked into the kitchen than Victoria started berating him. "Simon, I told you specifically to wear chinos and a shirt, and here you are in jeans."

"What difference?" he said, putting Arthur's present down on the table.

"And for God's sake, mind the food," Victoria scolded.

Amy could sense an altercation developing. It was nipped in the bud by Arthur appearing and launching himself at his father. Simon picked him up and hugged him so tight that Arthur screamed that he couldn't breathe. Simon put him down. "Here you are," he said, handing Arthur his present. "This is from me and Mum."

Arthur ripped into the paper and began tugging at the box. His mother warned him to take it easy or he would break what was inside. "Yay!" Before him was a radio-controlled yacht. "Let's take it to the pond and try it out."

Simon promised they would go with Charlie after the party.

Just then the door buzzer sounded. Amy looked at the kitchen clock. It was too early for Arthur's friends to be arriving. "Oh, God, this is either Mum or Dad," Amy said to Victoria. "I hope we didn't make a mistake inviting both of them. What if they start fighting?"

"It'll be fine," Victoria insisted. "They're grown-ups.

They'll behave. And I wanted them here. Now that Simon's mother and father are gone, they're Arthur's only grandparents."

"I think you just want to get Mum and Dad back together again," Amy said with a good-humored chuckle.

"Hey, don't pretend you wouldn't like it."

Amy couldn't.

When Amy opened the door, it wasn't just her parents standing on the mat. With them were Trevor and Joyce. Phil and Val were carrying presents for Arthur.

"Surprise!" Joyce cried. "Now, don't panic, Amy. Your dad and I discussed with Val and Trevor whether we should all come today, and we decided it was the most civilized thing to do. We even drove over in the same car, and we all got along like a house on fire."

Well, aren't we the very picture of a modern and postnuclear family, Amy thought, but she didn't say anything. Instead she greeted the group with delighted astonishment. "Right. Yes. Absolutely," she said. She looked at the four of them. Her dad and Trevor were standing behind the women. Phil was jingling the change in his pocket. Trevor was rocking back and forth on the balls of his feet. Amy suspected the men had discussed the recession and cricket and had discovered they had absolutely nothing left to talk about. Val was putting on a brave face, without doubt because it was Arthur's birthday. The only person who seemed totally relaxed and at ease was Joyce.

Amy greeted her with a double kiss. Once again she smelled alcohol on her breath. This clearly went some way toward explaining her demeanor.

Having ushered them all in and welcomed them with more kisses, Amy suggested they go into the living room.

"So where's the birthday boy?" Joyce said, clapping her hands.

Amy said she would see if she could find him. Instead she headed into the kitchen.

"What? The porn poetess is here?" Victoria hissed. "In my house?"

"My house," Amy said.

"Whatever. Get rid of her. If the other mothers find out what she does, I'll never live it down."

"Victoria, calm down. I've told you, Joyce is lovely. Now come into the living room and say hello."

By then Arthur and Charlie were already there, whooping and cheering and tearing into presents. Val had bought "a little something" for Charlie so that he wouldn't feel left out.

Victoria took one look at Joyce and winced. "What does she look like?" she muttered to Amy as she took in the bright blue eye shadow, the gash of red lipstick, and the low-cut top that exposed several inches of crepey cleavage.

"Now, this must be Victoria," Joyce cooed. "I've heard so much about you from your dad." She turned to Phil. "These girls of yours are such beauties. Of course they take after their mother." She winked at Val, who seemed pleasantly taken aback by the remark.

Victoria extended her hand to Joyce. "How do you do."

"Oh, not so bad, thanks. Now, then, no need to stand on formality with me. Come here and give me a kiss." Joyce grabbed hold of Victoria and pulled her toward her so forcefully that Victoria collided with the woman's shelf of a bosom. As Joyce's arms engulfed her, Victoria went boss-eyed and looked like she might choke.

At that moment, Simon appeared. Victoria introduced him to Joyce.

"Now, then, aren't you a handsome fella. I bet you've broken a few hearts in your time."

Amy shepherded everybody, including the boys, out to the garden and said she would be along shortly with glasses of wine. Joyce stopped off on the way to use the "little girls' room."

Amy and Victoria went back to the kitchen.

"My God, that woman is so loud and over the top. And she stank of booze. Couldn't you smell it?"

"As it happens, I did."

"So she's not only a pervert, she's a lush. Fan-bloody-tastic." Victoria pulled the Saran Wrap off the guacamole. Amy had considered telling her sister about Phil's penis extension and decided against it. Right now, she was glad she had. Straws and camels' backs suddenly came to mind.

Victoria's anguish was relieved by the arrival of the clown. Lulu, a bulky lass, ambled into the kitchen, followed by Amy, who once again had been dispatched to answer the door. Lulu was in full costume: clown face, bowler hat, jacket covered in sparkly stars, stripped leggings, and a pair of purple Doc Martens. Her assemblage was completed by a pair of outsized heart-shaped sunglasses.

It was a moment or two before Victoria looked up. She was using pastry cutters to create space-rocket-shaped sandwiches and cursing the tuna mayo for daring to ooze out at the edges.

"Nightmare," Lulu said to Victoria by way of greeting.

Victoria shook the clown's hand, took in her getup, and smiled with approval. "I know," she said. "I think I put in too much filling."

"No, I meant the traffic. The traffic was a nightmare." Lulu put down her ghetto blaster and bag of magic tricks and took off her sunglasses. Apparently the A3 had been chockablock from Guildford to Clapham. She was gagging for a cuppa—two sugars, thanks. Ooh, and a biscuit would be nice. Digestive if you've got it. Amy invited her to sit down and said that she happened to be in luck with the digestives. Lulu explained that she hadn't eaten since breakfast on account of Jessica having developed an anal fissure.

"And Jessica would be your partner?" Victoria said, attempting to be right on for once.

"What? No. She's my pet rabbit. You know, Jessica Rabbit. I spent the morning with her at the vet."

"Of course. I just assumed...I'm sorry."

A mug of tea and half a packet of chocolate digestives later, Lulu said she was desperate for a cigarette, which she was more than happy to smoke in the street. Victoria said she couldn't possibly do that because the children were arriving and would see her. Amy suggested she go into the bathroom and lean out of the open window.

The open window did not stop the smell of marijuana escaping from the bathroom and into the kitchen. Victoria's nose was soon twitching.

"What's that strange smell?"

If Amy told her it was weed, Victoria would throw Lulu out and the party would be over. She couldn't do that to Arthur.

"Oh, it's old Mr. Fletcher brewing coffee."

"It doesn't smell like coffee."

"It's one of Brian's posh blends. I gave the old boy some beans as a present last Christmas."

At that point, Lulu emerged from the bathroom and announced that she had her shit sufficiently together to start the party. This was just as well, as it was past three and most of the children had arrived. Much to Victoria's embarrassment, not to mention Charlie and Arthur's fury, most of the boys were in football shirts. Simon was herding them into the garden, where they were running riot. The idea was that parents deposited their offspring and returned half an hour before the end of the party for a glass of wine.

Lulu went into the garden and put the ghetto blaster on the lumpy, scruffy patch of grass that passed for a lawn. The next moment the kids' noise was being drowned out by "Monster Mash." "Okay, everybodee...It's...party time. And we're starting with...balloon bending."

"Yay!"

For the next couple of hours Lulu segued from magic tricks to sing-alongs, from puppets to face painting. The adults all said they were exhausted just watching her. To give Lulu a break, Amy and Victoria supervised tea time, which went down better than expected because Val had come bearing fondant fancies with Day-Glo icing, chocolate fingers, and salt and vinegar Hula Hoops. Victoria tried to stop her from dishing out the fatty sugary contraband to the children, but Amy guilt-tripped her into allowing it by saying, "Aw, just look at all those excited little faces. How could you possibly refuse them?"

As Lulu departed to wild cheers and applause from the children, their parents started to arrive—mothers mostly, some with babies and toddlers.

Amy overheard a few quizzing their offspring about how much sugar they'd consumed. One woman caught sight of a leftover fondant fancy and picked it up as if it were a dead rat and showed it to her friend. They both eyed Victoria and started muttering. Amy heard the word "hypocrite" uttered more than once.

While Simon and Trevor supervised an impromptu kids' disco in the living room, other mothers and a few fathers stood around in groups discussing house prices, loft extension night-mares, or the *gîtes* in Périgord that they'd picked up for a song, thanks to the recession. Education was the other biggie. Moth-ers who had been showing their children flash cards from the moment they emerged from the birth canal and had started them at Mini Maestros, Little Hawkings, and Smarty Artists soon after were now concerned that their five-year-olds weren't being sufficiently challenged at school. Most of the mothers admitted to visiting their child's teacher regularly to point out that little Inigo or Tamsin was gifted and to demand that the school ramp up its act. They seemed at a loss to understand why the teachers were so unhelpful.

By then Amy and Victoria were wrapping up slices of birthday cake and adding them to the going-home bags. Phil and Val were loading the dishwasher, reminiscing about their daughters' childhood birthday parties. Victoria nudged her sister and jerked her head in their parents' direction as if to say, "Look how well they're getting on."

Victoria was wrapping another slice of cake in kitchen paper when Arthur appeared.

"Mum, what's a member?"

"A member is somebody who belongs to a group. For instance, you are a member of the school chess club. Why do you ask?"

Arthur looked confused. "Do members go to hot, moist centers?"

"Activities sometimes happen at sports centers, but I'm not sure they're hot and—" She broke off. The penny had dropped with the most almighty clang. "Omigod! Where's Joyce?"

Arthur said that she was in the garden, "doing poems for the mummies and daddies."

"What?"

By now all the adults were exchanging glances. Phil went to the kitchen window, which looked out onto the garden.

"Joyce says that Volvos are soft, red, and wet," Arthur continued, "but that's wrong. Granddad drives a Volvo, and it's green and made of metal and it only gets wet in the rain or when he takes it to the car wash."

Amy let out an involuntary snort of laughter. Victoria glared at her and shot off into the garden. "I cannot believe that bloody woman!" Fearing things might get violent, Amy followed, but Phil overtook them both. He grabbed hold of Victoria's arm. "Leave this to me." His tone brooked no argument.

He began trotting toward the far end of the garden, where a group of parents were hovering around Joyce, who seemed to be holding a spontaneous poetry recital. It was clear that the parents didn't quite know where to put themselves, but they were too polite to walk away. As she spoke, an empty wineglass in her hand, Joyce was wobbling and swaying so much that she could barely stay upright.

"His manhood arose," she proclaimed, arm outstretched like a Greek tragedian who had downed one too many Chardonnays. "A tower of vermilion, penetrating a forest of curls/Her swollen mound aglow/He gave her his pearls."

Chapter 12

WHILE PHIL WAS bringing a precipitate end to the poetry recital, Amy did her best to convince her sister that Arthur was far too young to decipher Joyce's erotic metaphors and that his childhood innocence remained untarnished.

"How can you be so sure?" Victoria snapped. "You have no idea what this has done to Arthur's moral compass."

By now Simon was on the scene, having been brought up to speed by his mother-in-law. "Victoria, stop being so bloody neurotic. Believe me, our son's moral compass—such as it is— has come to no harm."

Victoria grunted and then started ranting about how Phil had brought shame on the family name by consorting with Joyce. Simon told her not to worry, since the Walkers weren't quite up there with the Montagues or the Capulets. Victoria demanded to know how he could make jokes at a time like this and raced off to speak to the parents. She passed Joyce and Phil on the way. Phil was half guiding, half frog-marching an un-steady Joyce toward the back door.

"How dare you humiliate me like this?" Victoria spit. "How dare you?"

Phil raised a hand as if to let his daughter know that she should back off and he had the situation under control. He and Joyce were only a few feet from the door now. Everybody could hear what they were saying. "Haven't you got any bloody sense?" Phil barked at her. "How could you do that here? At a child's birthday party? What were you thinking? Victoria is mortified. How much have you had to drink?"

"Pop Tart, I had two glasses of wine. No more. I promise."

"Rubbish. You were pissed as a pudding before we got here. You know it and I know it."

Amy heard Victoria offering the parents "my most profound and heartfelt apologies." None of them claimed to be angry or offended by the recital, which, it transpired, had come from Joyce's self-published collection, *Pudenda.* In fact, most of them said they'd found the whole thing highly amusing. Their only concern was for Arthur, who had gotten bored with the kids' disco and had decided to hang around with the adults. Everybody felt guilty for not noticing him.

Victoria was convinced that they were just being polite in claiming to find Joyce's display funny. "I'll never live it down," she said to Amy on the phone late on Sunday night. "I've told Simon we're going to have to emigrate. It's the only thing for it."

Amy burst out laughing. "Behave. Nobody's emigrating."

"Okay, maybe not emigrate, but we'll have to move to Surrey. I hate Surrey. It's full of orange women with boob jobs and big lips."

Victoria decided that her only hope was to send hand-tied calla lily bouquets to all the mothers who had been forced to witness Joyce's obscene display.

When Amy's phone rang on Monday evening, the last person she was expecting to be on the other end was Joyce.

"Amy, I just don't know what to say about what happened yesterday. I am mortified. I came into your home and behaved in a way that is unforgivable. Your dad was furious with me, and quite rightly. He and I had a long talk last night, and I told him he had every right to walk away, but he refused. Instead he wants me to join AA, and he's said he'll support me. I can't begin to tell you what a wonderful, caring man he is. I really don't deserve him."

It was true, Amy thought. In so many ways, Phil was a wonderful man. He'd worked for charity all his life. He doted on his daughters. Yet during the last few years of his marriage to Val, he had neglected her so badly. What was it he had found in the troubled, alcoholic Joyce that he hadn't been able to find in Val? The answer was pretty obvious. Joyce was a damaged soul who needed him in a way that Val never had. Maybe Amy had never understood just how much her father needed to be needed.

"AA sounds like a good idea," Amy said.

"It's time. I've been in denial about my drinking for so long. My mother was an alcoholic. She spent most of my childhood smashed or in bars getting smashed, and in the end it killed her. I don't want that to happen to me." She paused. "Amy, I really am so sorry about yesterday. If there were just some way I could make it up to you…"

"Look, it was embarrassing, but no harm was done. I think it's Victoria you should be apologizing to."

"I've tried phoning, but she refuses to speak to me. Simon was surprisingly understanding and said he'd get her to call me, but I'm not holding my breath. I was wondering if you could talk to your sister and try to impress upon her how awful I feel about what happened."

Amy said she would do her best. "And Joyce, good luck with AA. I hope it works out."

"So do I. You have no idea how much my relationship with your dad means to me."

As soon as she got off the phone, Amy phoned her dad to tell him about her conversation with Joyce.

"I knew she would phone," Phil said. "Joyce has her problems and yesterday's display wasn't good, but deep down she's a good woman. She's loving, caring, funny. She's got a heart of pure gold."

"I know. I can see that," Amy said. "And most important, she needs you to be her rock."

"Ah, there is that."

"But Mum needed you, too."

"Oh, she did when we first married. Back then she wasn't much more than a girl, but as she got older, her self-confidence grew. She got a job, had her own money. Like I've said before, I felt superfluous to requirements."

"So you couldn't deal with her independence."

"It's the old male ego thing, I guess. I'm not proud of it, but I'm too old to change now and I know that even after Joyce has kicked the booze, she will always need me." He paused. "You know, with me and your mum, it wasn't all my fault. For years she'd been telling me how dull I was and how I'd gotten old before my time. She used to tell people that she was married to a farting sofa. None of that did my self-confidence much good, you know. The problem was that we married too young, before we really knew ourselves and what we wanted."

"It's okay, Dad, I'm not accusing you. I know it takes two for a relationship to break down. I just get sad sometimes, that's all."

"I know, love," Phil soothed. "I know."

WHEN AMY told Brian and Bel about Joyce's erotic poetry recital, they hooted and demanded to know why they hadn't been invited to the party.

Bel said she was going to order a copy of *Pudenda* to read in bed with Ulf. On Tuesday night, when she spoke to Sam on the phone, he couldn't stop laughing either, especially when Amy got to the bit about Arthur coming into the kitchen asking about members and Volvos.

"So when shall we get together this week?" Sam said.

Amy suggested Friday. "Charlie has a birthday sleepover. You could come here."

"Great."

She didn't say anything.

"Amy, you there?"

"Yeah. I was just thinking. Charlie's feeling a bit iffy about going to this thing on Friday. Although this kid's in his year group, he's in another class and Charlie doesn't know him that well...I could suggest he give it a miss, and then you could come and meet him."

"Amy, this has to be your call. If you're ready for Charlie to meet me, then I'm ready, but you have to decide."

She didn't skip a beat. "I'm ready."

"Okay." Sam laughed. "Looks like we're both ready."

IN THE end, Amy thought it would be a good idea to kill two birds with one invite. She spoke to Sam again, and they agreed that on Friday he would arrive about six. The three of them would hang out for a couple of hours so that he could get to know Charlie. Then, after Charlie had gone to bed, Bel and Ulf and Brian and Rebecca would come for dinner. "I've only met Ulf once," Amy said. "I've never met Rebecca. Oh, and FYI, she's a born-again virgin. So if Brian seems a bit irritable and tense, you'll know why." She giggled, and Sam said it was the first time he'd been in a relationship with a woman who could list shamans, erotic poetesses, and born-again virgins among her friends.

"By the way," Sam said, "you sure Brian's not going to punch my lights out because of my tenuous connection with Bean Machine?"

Amy laughed. "Of course not. He knows it's nothing personal."

AMY DECIDED that if she was going to have a dinner party, she wanted her floorboards finished. It seemed ridiculous even to think she could get a decorator at such short notice, but she managed it. The last chap she phoned, after having called a dozen or more, said he'd just had a cancellation.

He turned up at seven on Wednesday morning and painted the floorboards while Amy was at work. By the evening the rubberized paint was dry. Amy couldn't get over how magnificent her floors looked. The white walls and matching boards looked so stylish. Her flat had gone from shabby to shabby chic in a couple of coats of paint. Now she wanted to buy a new dining room table and chairs and have the kitchen and bathroom refitted. Like that was going to happen. Instead she made do with treating herself to some new orange velvet cushions from the Habitat sale, which, although she said so herself, looked stunning on her acid green sofa. In the same sale, she also found some giant orange silk tulips. Usually Amy hated artificial flowers and silk ones worst of all, but these were so big and over the top that they didn't pretend to be real. She put them on the coffee table in a tall metallic vase. They looked magnificent. Charlie said they got in the way of the TV screen and insisted on moving them while he was watching cartoons. When Amy asked him what he thought of the floors, he said they were all right and could he have some crisps.

She cooked for Friday's dinner party the night before. She made a Spanish chicken casserole with orange and chorizo. It all went into one pot, along with the rice, so all she had to do was heat it up an hour before they were ready to eat. For dessert she made chocolate mousse, which she decanted into six pink cocktail glasses and left in the fridge to set.

That evening, while she and Charlie were having supper, she dropped into the conversation that her new friend was coming over the following day, a couple of hours before the dinner party, and that he was the man who had sorted out Charlie's fight with Arthur at Café Mozart.

"I remember him. He was nice," Charlie said, nodding. "So is he going to be your husband?"

"Oh, sweetie, it's far too early to start talking about things like that. At the moment we're just friends. Okay?"

"K."

•   •   •

SAM TURNED up at six on the dot with a very large bouquet of white roses.

"Oh, Sam, you shouldn't have," she said, taking them from him. "But I'm glad you did. They are gorgeous."

"I've done my Charlie prep, by the way."

"What?"

"I worked out my conversation strategy while I was driving over," he said. "I thought I'd start with Arsenal and move on to Nintendo via popular cartoons, superheroes, and his art, of course."

"Sam, please tell me you're joking."

His face broke into a grin. "Of course I am, but it did cross my mind."

It was only as they walked into the living room where Charlie was watching *Shrek* that Sam noticed that the floorboards had been painted. He said how great they looked and how he couldn't believe she had gotten them done at such short notice.

"Pure luck," Amy said. She turned to Charlie. "Sweetie, could you switch that off now. I'd like you to say hello to Sam. Do you remember him from Café Mozart?"

Charlie looked up. "You told Arfur off."

"I did indeed," Sam said.

"I'm watching *Shrek*. Do you like *Shrek*?"

"Actually, it's one of my favorite films."

"Guess what my favorite bit is."

"When the dragon chases them?"

"Uh-uh . . . Come here. I'll whisper. It's a secret. You can't tell my mum."

"Oh, thanks," Amy said, chuckling. "You boys just gang up and leave me out, why don't you."

By now Charlie was cupping his hand over Sam's ear. They both burst out laughing. "I agree, that is a brilliant bit," Sam said.

Amy suggested letting Charlie finish the film, which had

only a few minutes left to run. "Then, as it's such a lovely evening, we could all go for a walk in the park." She explained to Sam that there was an Italian café there with a pretty sundeck. "Charlie can have spag bol and ice cream, and we can sit with a couple of Peronis."

Amy couldn't help thinking that Sam played the next couple of hours pretty much to perfection. He didn't make too much of a fuss of Charlie, nor did he attempt to become his new best friend. He chatted with him about school and drawing, and the two of them played knockabout with Charlie's football. When they got back, Charlie asked Sam if he'd like to see his magic tricks. Amy took Sam to one side to warn him that these "needed some work" and tended to go on a bit, but Sam didn't seem remotely bothered. "I've lost count of the number of magic shows my nephews have subjected me to," he said. Amy left them to it and went into the kitchen to put the casserole in the oven and make the salad.

Twenty minutes later, when she came back with two glasses of wine, Charlie was still performing his terrible tricks, but Sam was hanging in there and giving every impression of being transfixed.

"You know what, Charlie," Amy said, "I think it's time for a bath and bed."

"Aw."

"Come on. It's almost half past eight. Brian and Bel will be here any second."

Charlie agreed to get in the bath as long as he could stay up to say hello to Brian and Bel.

"Okay. Deal. Now scat. I've run your bath and put bubbles in. Don't forget your ears."

Amy and Sam sat on the sofa. Sam told her how sexy she looked in the clingy black dress she was wearing and kissed her on the lips.

"Charlie's a great kid," he said. "Lively, polite, funny—and very smart."

"That's not to say he can't be a handful sometimes."

"Aren't all kids?"

"So, go on," Amy said. "What's Charlie's favorite bit of *Shrek*, the bit you couldn't tell me?"

"You can't ask me that," Sam said in mock horror. "I took a solemn oath. A chap doesn't give up another chap's secrets. It's simply not cricket."

"Don't tell her," Charlie's little voice cried. "Don't tell her."

Amy and Sam swung around.

"I wouldn't have dreamed of it," Sam said. "It's our secret."

"Good," Charlie said. He turned to his mother. "No soap."

Amy told him to get in the bath and she'd come in with a fresh bar.

A minute or two later she was in the bathroom, handing him the soap and reminding him again to do his ears.

"I like Sam," Charlie declared. "He kept my secret." He began soaping his face. "Do you think he likes snakes?"

"As it happens, I think he does."

"If he became your husband, he would make you buy me one."

"Why?"

"Because when children get new daddies, the daddies want to be their friend."

"Blimey, there are no flies on you, Charlie Walker."

"There was one tiny one a second ago, but I drowned it."

Amy laughed. "No...if somebody tells you there are no flies on you, it means you are very smart."

Amy watched her son basking in parental approval.

"Now, then, get washed. There are clean PJs on your bed."

As she left the bathroom, she closed the door behind her. From inside came a muffled, high-pitched imitation of Eddie Murphy, straight from *Shrek*: "And then one time I ate some rotten berries. Man! There were some gases leaking outta my butt that day!"

· · ·

BRIAN ARRIVED first, minus Rebecca. She had phoned him to say she had an emergency at work and would be along as soon as she could.

Brian and Sam shook hands, but it was clear that they weren't entirely comfortable in each other's company.

When Amy had invited Brian to dinner and told him that Sam would be there, he hadn't look too pleased. "I just can't get over the fact that Sam is helping to close down my business."

"Come on, Brian, we've been over this. Sam's a good guy. He does pro bono work in Africa, but he also has to make a living. He didn't accept the Bean Machine job to spite you."

"Duh. I do get that."

"Well, it doesn't feel like you get it. Now promise you'll behave."

"Hey, I'm a grown-up. Of course I'll behave. I seem to remember that it was you who lost your temper with Sam the first time you met."

Amy grunted.

When Bel and Ulf arrived, the tension eased. "Omigod," Bel cried. "Don't these floorboards look fab? You know what would look great in here? Some distressed old pine furniture."

"What, you mean like a panic-stricken sideboard?" Brian piped up.

"Yeah, yeah. Very funny," Bel came back. "It means you paint it and then treat it with chemicals so that it looks old and beaten up."

Amy said she wasn't sure that was the look she was going for, but Bel wasn't listening because by now she had noticed that her green tunic and leggings were a perfect accessory to Amy's sofa and cushions.

Amy just about managed to interrupt her to make the relevant introductions. Then she was off again. First she mouthed to Amy that she thought Sam was gorgeous, and then she proceeded to tackle him on the subject of Prince Charles's influence on British architecture. "I mean, the man is a total dinosaur. All he's interested in is neo-Georgian suburban eye-sores, and people in the architectural establishment kowtow to him. If you ask me, he has set British architecture back twenty years."

Sam was in the middle of explaining why the Prince of Wales didn't have quite the influence people thought he did, when Charlie appeared, insisting on performing another magic show. Amy protested and said it was well past his bedtime, but Bel and Brian said they would love to see some of Charlie's tricks.

After ten minutes of Charlie asking people to "pick a card" or "say the magic word," Amy put her foot down and insisted it was bedtime. "Okay, but only if Bel and Brian read me stories."

By nine o'clock, stories duly read and Charlie silent, if not asleep, they were still waiting on Rebecca. The last of the nibbles had been finished ten minutes earlier, and everybody was starving.

"I don't get it," Bel said to Brian. "Rebecca teaches night school French. What's the emergency? Somebody get tangled up in a reflexive verb?"

"Very droll," Brian came back. "As it happens, she had to teach a later class as well as her own because one of the other tutors is ill."

Rebecca arrived five minutes later, full of apologies and bearing a bunch of freesias. Rebecca was every bit the doe-eyed beauty Brian had made out. She was tall and willowy, with dark curls that cascaded down her back. She was wearing a short vest top over skinny cropped jeans with turnups. Her belly button contained a pretty sapphire piercing.

Brian stood up as she came into the room and immediately offered her some wine, which she turned down in favor of sparkling water. "You sit down," he said. "It's coming right up." He couldn't have been more attentive or looked more smitten if he'd tried.

Amy couldn't help noticing that she wasn't wearing a bra. Because she had no bust to speak of, this made her look girlish and vulnerable rather than sexy.

It was only when Amy started serving the food that she realized how Rebecca played on this. She couldn't have the chorizo because the fat upset her lipid balance. Chicken was fine, but rice wasn't. She didn't do carbs after six. Amy was about to serve her a chicken breast when Rebecca stopped her. "It is organic, isn't it?"

Amy said it was free range, which was pretty much the same deal.

"Actually, I won't have any if you don't mind."

Brian didn't seem remotely irked by her behavior and even offered to make her an egg white omelet. She refused it on account of her egg allergy.

"Oh, dear," Amy said, "so I guess that means you won't be wanting any chocolate mousse for dessert."

Rebecca said she wouldn't. "And even if I weren't allergic, I would never eat raw eggs."

"Of course you wouldn't," Bel muttered.

Amy was aware of Brian kicking Bel under the table.

In the end Rebecca accepted some cottage cheese. She ate this with Amy's salad, using chopsticks, which she produced from her bag.

"And you use chopsticks because…" Bel said, irritation seeping from every pore.

"Oh, they force you to eat smaller amounts, so it's so much kinder on the digestion."

"Makes sense," Brian said. "Maybe we'd all be healthier if we ate with chopsticks."

At that point Rebecca announced that she just happened to have a spare set. She handed them to Brian. Looking more than a tad awkward, he took them and dutifully attempted to finish his Spanish casserole. Unable to cut into his chicken breast, he stabbed the thing and tried to eat it as it hung off a single chopstick. In the end, his T-shirt covered in gravy, he apologized and went back to his knife and fork.

Toward the end of the meal, Sam finally raised the Bean Machine issue with Brian and said how bad he felt about it. Brian said that these things happen and that he shouldn't give it a second thought. "Plus, we've had a stay of execution because the builders are still trying to get money out of Bean Machine."

Sam said that he knew about this and that they seemed no closer to resolving it. "The word on the street is that Bean Machine is in financial difficulty, but the company is denying it."

This cheered Brian up no end. From then on, the two of them started to hit it off. They both got to chatting with Ulf about his job, and Brian said how he'd watched this operation to cure Parkinson's disease. "Ah, it isn't actually a cure, but it can really help the symptoms," Ulf singsonged. Twenty minutes later he was still regaling everybody with the minutiae of the procedure. Once he had finished, there was silence. It seemed that nobody wanted to ask him any questions in case this set him off again.

In the end Bel broke the tension—only to create more.

"So, Rebecca, Brian tells me you're a born-again virgin."

Brian glared at her. For a second time Amy was aware of his foot lashing out in Bel's direction.

"Ouch!"

Ulf asked her if she was all right.

"Fine," she said, looking daggers at Brian.

If Rebecca was angry with Brian for revealing that she had reclaimed her virginity, she wasn't about to show it, at least not in public.

"Yes," she said, "that's true. Last year I took a vow of chastity."

Bel asked her why.

"Don't you find that you've indulged in far too many meaningless sex acts in your life?"

Bel grimaced, clearly assuming this was a barb aimed at her, but she let it go.

"Yeah, but as meaningless sex acts go, some of them were pretty amazing."

"Well, when I find the man I want to marry, I want the love-making to be really special. I decided the only way to make that happen was to give up on sex until I get married."

"So you've had the hymenoplasty operation, then?" Ulf inquired.

"Excuse me?" Sam said, eyes wide.

"Yes, I've had my hymen restored," she said as if she were discussing her new highlights.

"I've read about the procedure," Ulf said. "The surgeon takes the residual tissues of the hymen and stitches them back together. It's very successful, apparently."

"That's right," Rebecca said. "In fact, some wives do it every year as a present to their husbands. That really appeals to me. It's sort of an annual cleansing and rededication, if you will."

"Actually, I won't if you don't mind," Bel said, reaching for the wine bottle.

They were having mint tea or coffee—or in Rebecca's case, white tea that she carried with her in a tiny Chinese enamel tin—when Bel's mobile went. After a couple of seconds, the color drained from her face. "Okay, I'll be there in a few minutes." She flipped the lid on her phone. "I gotta go. That was my next-door neighbor. She found my back door swinging open. I've been burgled."

It turned out that Ulf couldn't take Bel home because he was getting the sleeper to Edinburgh, where he was speaking at a conference the next day. They'd already planned for her to take a cab home.

"I've got my car," Brian said to Bel. "I'll take you. No arguments."

"But what about Rebecca?"

Rebecca said she could call a cab, but Sam said he would drop her home. He and Amy had agreed earlier on that Charlie-wise it was far too soon for him to spend the night.

Thank yous and goodbyes were hurried, and in less than five minutes everybody was gone. Afterward Amy did the dishes and tidied up. It was funny that since Victoria's marathon clean she was experiencing a newly acquired urge to keep the place tidy. She fell into bed around midnight, wondering if she ought to phone Bel. She imagined she would still be up waiting for the police. She dialed her number. It rang out for a few seconds and then went to voice mail. Amy decided that the police—with uncustomary efficiency—had come and gone and that Bel had hit the sack.

Just after nine the next morning, the phone rang.

"Hi, it's me."

It was Bel.

"Hon, is everything okay?" Amy said. "Was much taken?"

"Oh, you know, the usual: laptop, the Nikon Jurassic Mark bought me. Of course the police weren't remotely interested. Oh, and by the way, I slept with Brian."

"What?"

"I know. I can still hardly believe it. He insisted on staying over because the burglars had broken the lock on the back door and the place wasn't secure. Anyway, then we had this huge fight."

"What about?"

"He had a go at me for bringing up the chastity thing at dinner and said I only did it because I wanted to get him in trouble with Rebecca and split them up. I said if I wanted to split them up it was only because I thought Rebecca was a self-obsessed princess and totally wrong for him. He said that was none of my business and I had no right sticking my nose into his relationships, which I guess is true. Anyway, then he accused Ulf of being a bore and said he'd had more interesting conversations with his coffee blender. I started shouting, defending Ulf. He shouted back, swearing and calling me names, and before we knew what was happening, we were tearing each other's clothes off."

"About blinkin' time! How long have I been saying that the

two of you were meant for each other? So have you finished it with Ulf?"

"Whoa. Hang on. Brian and I slept together. That does not make us an item."

"What are you saying? Of course it does. You and Brian are like Bacall and Bogie, Ben and Jerry. You're made for each other."

"No. The way I see it, I was upset and vulnerable. There were masses of sexual tension in the air because neither of us is getting laid—Okay, I'm getting laid, but not satisfactorily. I think that in a sense we just used each other."

" 'Used each other'? I can't believe I'm hearing this."

"Amy, I've told you before, I can't be in a relationship with somebody who presses my buttons all the time. Can you imagine how wearing that would be? The constant sniping and fighting would get us both down."

"So what are you going to do about Ulf?"

"I really don't want to hurt him, but I guess I'll have to end it. Sleeping with Brian made me realize that I can't be in a relationship where the sex is lousy."

"So apart from the sex, you've got no feelings at all for Brian?"

"Even if I did, they're irrelevant. He's crazy about Rebecca."

"Oh, yeah—so crazy that he slept with you."

"Amy, I'm telling you, this was a one-off. It was a stupid mistake, and it won't happen again. Now let it go."

FIVE MINUTES later Brian was on the phone to say he had slept with Bel.

"It was truly amazing, but the thing is, I can't work out if I did it because I have feelings for Bel or because I'm so sexually frustrated. To be honest, if I'd been at Miss Piggy's house last night, I would have come on to her."

"God, you two are impossible. Bel said almost the same."

"What, that she would have slept with Miss Piggy?"

"No. She said you used each other."

"She's right."

"I don't get it...How can two people be so blind? Brian, listen to me. Of course you have feelings for Bel, the same way that she does for you. If the pair of you weren't so insecure and would just stop competing for five minutes, you'd be able to see it."

"But all we ever do is compete with each other. Isn't that the point?"

"All I know is that I saw how jealous you were when Bel started going out with Ulf. You're mad about her."

"No, I got over that. It's Rebecca I'm mad about now."

"But the woman refuses to sleep with you!"

"Okay, I don't deny that the point may come when we split up over that, but it doesn't alter the fact that what Bel and I did was a huge mistake. We both know that. I think the best thing is for me to call her and suggest we just put it behind us and move on."

"Perfect," Amy said. "Just perfect."

THAT AFTERNOON Sam came over. Amy found an old car rug, which they took into the garden and spread out over the balding lawn. They sat in the sun drinking tea while Charlie played in the tent he had made by covering his climbing frame with old sheets.

"I just can't believe how complicated some people's lives get," Amy said, plucking at some grass. "My dad's trying to rescue poor Joyce. My mum's seeing a man who is sweet and kind but can't see beyond his own narrow world. Bel loves Brian and Brian loves Bel, but for some reason they're both too scared to admit it. Oh, and then there's Victoria and Simon, but at least they're trying to sort themselves out. It's exhausting just thinking about it all."

"We don't realize how lucky we are," Sam said.

"I know. Our relationship may have gotten off to a rocky start, but now it feels so easy and straightforward."

He nodded and smiled, but at the same time she got the sense that something was bothering him. She was about to remark on it, but he got in first.

"You know, Amy, I'm really falling for you in a big way."

"Ditto," she said.

He stroked the end of her nose with a buttercup. Then he kissed her.

Chapter 13

"HEY, AMES," BRIAN said as she walked into the café on Monday morning. "You still on the lookout for possible newspaper stories?"

"You bet."

"Well, I may have a something. It's nothing huge, but I thought it might make a piece for one of the newspaper food and drink pages. CremCo, the company that produces Crema Crema Crema, has developed this fancy new espresso machine. I don't know much about it, but it's meant to be pretty revolutionary. The launch party is on Wednesday night, and I've been invited. Apparently I am one of their 'valued customers.' The ticket admits two, so I thought you might fancy coming along. Only problem is, it's in bloody Luton. They have their roasting plant there and want to show it off."

Amy wrinkled her nose. "I dunno. All the newspaper and magazine food journalists will have been invited. I'm not sure there'll be anything in it for me."

"When I phoned to RSVP, they did mention there would be some pretty fancy freebies. Free bags of Crema Crema Crema, plus a fifteen percent discount on new orders, which is why I'm going."

"Bearing in mind I don't like coffee, you're not selling it to me so far."

"Oh, and the name Prada did come up. They've something

to do with the design of the coffee machine. We *could* be talking handbags, especially when they've dragged the media thirty miles out of London."

"Seriously? Wow. I have to say I'm tempted, but I'm not sure I can justify it. I've been leaving Charlie quite a lot lately. It's not fair to abandon him again just so's I can pick up a Prada bag. Why don't you bring it back for me?"

"Amy, you're not abandoning Charlie. You'd be leaving him with a baby-sitter. You're always saying how much he loves Lilly. Please come. It's a schlep up there. The do is bound to be deadly dull. I'd really appreciate the company."

"Why don't you ask Rebecca? Or Bel?"

"Rebecca's working, and I can't ask Bel."

"Why?"

"It'll look like I'm asking her on a date."

"What's wrong with that? You just slept with her."

"Yes, but we've agreed that was a huge mistake and that the best thing is to pretend it never happened. If I start asking her out, it'll look like I've got a thing for her."

"Which you have."

"No, I haven't."

"Have."

"Amy, can we please get back to Wednesday? You're right, the food journalists will all be there to cover the espresso machine story, but you never know, you might get chatting to somebody and stumble across something else."

"It's not very likely, but I suppose I shouldn't be turning down opportunities."

"So you'll come?"

"Okay, so long as I can get a baby-sitter."

"Great." He paused. "By the way, what happened between me and Bel can never get back to Rebecca, right?"

"Oh, come on. What do you take me for?"

"If she finds out, she'll never forgive me. She's already furious with me for telling everybody about her reclaiming her virginity."

Amy said she wasn't surprised.

"I'm going to have to make it up to her in some way. God knows how."

"I guess you could always take her out to dinner. Oh, no, I forgot, she doesn't eat anything." Amy immediately regretted the comment, but she felt frustrated that Brian had let Bel go.

"You don't like Rebecca, do you?"

"I'm sorry. I didn't mean to be bitchy. I'm sure when I get to know her . . . "

"Well, just for the record, I really like Sam."

"Yeah, the two of you seemed to be getting along really well. I'm glad. I would have hated for there to be any ill feeling between you."

"There's none. Believe me."

They were interrupted by Zelma bustling in, humming "I Feel Pretty."

"You've got a spring in your step," Amy said.

She winked. "I got some action yesterday."

"No kidding? Good for you, Zelma."

"Yes, all that dreadful bloating has gone, and I didn't need to take any fiber today."

AMY WAS in the middle of eating lunch—a slice of tarte provençale—when Bel rang, full of excitement.

"You'll never guess what."

"What?"

"No, you have to guess."

"But you just said I'd never guess."

"Okay, get this: They're making a new Bond film . . . and I am up for a part."

"Bel, you are kidding! That is amazing. So what's the part?"

"The voice of the Aston Martin's satnav."

"Wow . . . that's amazing," Amy said, trying not to sound too underwhelmed.

"No, you don't get it. If I was to get the part, my voice would become really famous and the likelihood is that one of the satnav companies would use me. And other big stuff would be bound to follow. I could be the voice of TomTom. Kerching!"

"Okay, now I'm with you. That really is fantastic news."

"I know. I'm so excited. The audition is in a few days. I'm going for purring, sexy dominatrix. What do you think?"

"Purrfect!"

Amy asked her if the police had been back in touch re the burglary.

"Some hopes. Once they know all the stuff's insured, they're not bothered. Hey, I'm really sorry I broke up the party on Friday, particularly after all that effort you went to. And I meant to say how fabulous Sam is. He's great-looking, intelligent, funny. Do you think he could be, you know . . . a contender?"

Amy laughed. "It's early days yet, but just between you and me, I think he could. And it really helps that he and Charlie like each other."

"You know, he really looks like Charlie."

"It's funny, Victoria said that. I guess they do both have the same coloring."

"No, it's more than that. They have the same eyes."

"She said that, too."

"I can't believe you haven't noticed. Take a look the next time they're together."

Amy said she would. "So, are you okay with the whole Brian thing?"

"Fine. The other night was just something that happened. It's all forgotten."

Amy let out a sigh of frustration.

"Sweetie, I don't know how to put this," Bel said, "but has it occurred to you that maybe it's you who has the problem with this?"

· · ·

THAT EVENING she had only just gotten Charlie to bed when Sam turned up unannounced. "I thought I'd surprise you," he said, kissing her.

"I'm glad you did. Come into the kitchen. I'll make tea."

"I'd rather go into the living room and make out."

"No way." She giggled. "Charlie's barely asleep. I've got cake, though."

"Ah, even better."

Sam sat at the kitchen table, and she filled the kettle. "You know, it's the weirdest thing: People keep telling me that you and Charlie look alike. I was looking at him tonight as I put him to bed, and I think they're right."

Sam shrugged. "Really? Not sure I've noticed, but I'm not very good at seeing resemblances. Maybe it's a bloke thing."

"Well, Bel and Victoria can see it. Don't you think it's odd?" she persisted. "I mean, you look alike, you're both talented artists."

He was laughing. "Amy, you are joking, right? I'm sterile, and even if I weren't, I donated sperm fifteen years ago."

"I know that. I just think it's a strange coincidence, that's all."

WEDNESDAY NIGHT'S Crema Crema Crema launch was due to start at seven. Brian said that since they would be driving in the rush hour, they should allow extra time. They got changed at the café and set off exactly at half past five. They were walking to Brian's car when his cell started ringing. "Yes . . . okay . . . I see . . . I'll phone and make another appointment. Thank you for letting me know."

He turned to Amy. "The clinic just got the results of my blood test. Turns out my estrogen level is above normal. Shit. What do I do now?"

Amy took his arm. "Come on, take it easy," she soothed. "The doctor already told you it could take years before the estrogen causes any real harm. I know it's worrying, but there will be an answer to this thing. It's just a matter of time."

"I hope you're right. Meanwhile, I'm going back to the doctor to talk about having some liposuction to reduce the size of my moobs."

"Hey, maybe he'd give us a twofer and do my hips and thighs while he's at it."

As soon as they got in the car, Amy phoned Ruby to make sure Charlie was okay. She had arranged for her to give him supper. Afterward, Lilly would collect him, put him to bed, and wait for Amy to get home. Ruby said that everything was fine and that Lilly had phoned to say she was on her way. "Fab," Amy said. "Give him a kiss from me and tell him I won't be too late."

The traffic was by no means light, but there were no actual holdups and they managed to keep moving.

At one point Bel phoned Brian to say she was filling out her insurance claim form and how much had he paid for his Mac-Book Pro, as she'd lost the receipt and she knew they'd both bought them around the same time.

"Look, I'm driving. I'm with Amy; we're on our way to Luton to this CremCo gig I told you about. I'd have to check what I paid. Why don't you take a look online . . . okay, sorry, yes, of course . . . you don't have your laptop . . . What? No, Amy didn't tell me you were auditioning for a part in the new Bond film. That's amazing . . . " Then he said he had to hang up because there was a police car behind them and he didn't want to get a fine for being on the phone.

Amy brought him up to speed re Bel's latest audition and the moneymaking possibilities if she got the part. Brian said he often worried about Bel.

Amy asked him why.

"She's had a rough time of it over the years, what with that

scumbag father of hers. I really hope she makes it. I'd love nothing more than to see her do well."

Oh, he so had feelings for Bel, but Amy wasn't about to
tackle Brian on the subject again. He'd made his position clear.
Plus, they were just pulling into the CremCo car park.

AS THEY got out of the car, they were greeted by the powerful aroma of roasted coffee. Brian inhaled deeply. "Wow,
don't you just love that smell?" Amy said what she always said
about coffee aroma promising more than it delivered, and Brian
called her a philistine. As they made their way over to the
CremCo building, they continued to exchange good-humored
insults.

A jolly, hair-flicking PR girl named Sophie welcomed them
at the reception area. She referred to her guest list, crossed off
their names, and directed them to a large conference room on
the ground floor. Inside, waiters were hovering with trays of
champagne and canapés.

Amy and Brian helped themselves to champagne and
miniature portions of piping hot fish and chips.

About forty people had shown up. Judging by the snippets
of conversation Amy was picking up, most of them were food
writers. Others ran Internet businesses or shops selling upmarket tea and coffee. A few, like Brian, owned cafés and restaurants. As they waited for a few latecomers, Brian spotted a face
he recognized. He nudged Amy. "See that bloke over there,
working the room? That's Hugh Cavendish. He's the head of
CremCo UK."

An excessively tall, forty-something chap with slicked-back
hair that was a particularly unnatural shade of chestnut was
chatting earnestly to a group of journalists. Amy took in the
chalk-stripe suit, the pink shirt and white collar, the gold signet
ring on his little finger. Had she been asked what the CEO of
CremCo might look like, she would probably have said über-

trendy, thirty to forty-something, with an edgy haircut and slightly weird German specs.

"He looks like one of those upper-class types you read about in the papers," Amy whispered to Brian. "You know, the ones that claim to be a lord and then con unsuspecting women out of their life savings."

Brian laughed. "It's the hair. My gran always used to say you could never trust a man with dyed hair." He broke off. Hugh Cavendish was coming their way.

"Good evening to you," he brayed like an off-duty master of the hunt. "I am Hugh Cavendish from CremCo. Welcome to our little soiree."

"Thank you for inviting us," Brian said. He went on to introduce himself and Amy.

"And I'm assuming that you and the delightful Ms. Walker are members of the press."

"I'm a freelance," Amy said. "Brian owns a coffee shop called Café Mozart. It's on Richmansworth Common."

"Fascinating," he said. Cavendish, who couldn't have looked less fascinated if he'd tried, took Amy's hand in his and didn't so much kiss it as slobber over it. Amy shot a look at Brian to let him know that she thought the man was a complete sleazeball.

"We're all looking forward to seeing the new espresso machine," Brian ventured.

"Ah, yes. It's been several years in development, and I have to say that all of us at CremCo are immensely excited. We're confident it's going to claim the majority of the market share over the next couple of years. And of course sales of Crema Crema Crema coffee are continuing to soar. We are struggling to keep up with demand."

"I'm not surprised," Brian said. "It is quite exceptional . . . that smoky top note with a hint of caramel. Then there's that citrusy insouciance and a really complex finish that is quite—"

"Yes . . . well, if you'll excuse me." With that Hugh

Cavendish took his leave, but not before he had patted Amy's rear.

"Did you see that?" Amy hissed at Brian. "The jerk patted my bum. I've a good mind——"

"Amy, calm down. It's not worth it. The man is an idiot."

"I know. So why were you brownnosing like your life depended on it?"

"What was I supposed to do? I was just trying to be polite."

"You didn't have to be quite so obsequious."

They were interrupted by Sophie the PR girl clapping her hands for attention. She gave a flick of her shoulder-length hair and explained that before the unveiling of the new coffee machine, there was to be a guided tour of the coffee-roasting plant. Apparently, huge demand for Crema Crema Crema meant that the staff now worked through the night.

Amy could almost hear the silent groan from the hacks. From experience she knew that all they wanted to do was get as much champagne and food as they could, grab their information packs and goody bags, and head off home.

Sophie led the reluctant group down the hall and through several sets of double doors. The smell of roasting coffee grew even stronger, to the point of being overpowering.

The final set of doors was guarded by two uniformed security guards carrying walkie-talkies. Sophie presented her ID card to one of them. He and his partner held the double doors open to let everybody through. Somebody asked about the guards.

"Oh, we've had a couple of break-ins over the last few months," Sophie explained cheerfully. "Crema Crema Crema has become a hot commodity on the black market. So we've had to beef up our security."

They found themselves in an echoey tiled space with a high corrugated ceiling. Machinery buzzed and whirred in the background. Along one wall there were a dozen cast-iron roasting drums. They were painted dark green and looked like old-fashioned steam engines. Instead of a chimney, there was a wide funnel-shaped hopper where the beans were loaded. Amy looked at the mostly young male workers—recent immigrants from Eastern Europe at a guess—loading the hoppers and checking the temperature of the drums. A dozen or more, dressed in white coats and hairnets, sat at tables sorting the roasted beans and packing them by hand.

"Okay, ladies and gentlemen," Sophie said, clapping her hands again. "It's now my pleasure to hand you over to Gordon Pettifer, our chief coffee roaster at CremCo."

The applause from the group was distinctly halfhearted.

Gordon Pettifer, a short, stocky chap with a particularly bad comb-over, exuded the life and enthusiasm of an anally retentive librarian. "Hello . . . my name is Gordon Pettifer, and I am the chief coffee roaster at CremCo. I have been chief coffee roaster for twenty-five years, taking up my post in October 1984."

"Oh, for the love of God," somebody murmured.

Amy found herself watching the workers going about their routine and thought what tedious menial work this was. She wondered how much they were paid. It occurred to her that a sleazeball like Hugh Cavendish might well be paying below the minimum wage. Maybe she should try to speak to them and find out.

Gordon Pettifer droned on in the background.

"By the time the beans get to the roasting stage, they have been cleaned and cleared of debris. They are then poured into the hoppers and roasted. The roasters you see here typically operate at temperatures between 370 and 540 degrees Fahrenheit; that's 188 and 282 degrees Celsius . . . "

Very slowly Amy backed away from the group and dipped behind one of the roasting drums. She headed toward the sorting table, shielded by more drums.

It was then that she noticed Hugh Cavendish walk in. She

could hear him raging into his cell. "I don't give a fuck about your workers' rights . . . This is Indo-fucking-nesia. They don't have any rights. I need this consignment yester-fucking-day. Just make it happen . . . Do whatever you have to do. I don't care if things get violent. Just deal with it."

Amy watched him stab his phone off. His expression suitably rearranged, he ambled over to join the tour. It seemed pretty clear that Cavendish had been on the phone to one of his plantation managers in Indonesia. By the sound of things, the workers were up in arms, most likely about pay and conditions. It seemed likely that CremCo was abusing both its domestic and its foreign staff. She could have a good story here.

She waited a minute or so and then made her way back to the group. She decided that with Hugh Cavendish there, it would be far too risky to confront the workers.

". . . and the beans are roasted for a period of time ranging from three to thirty minutes."

"Omigod," Brian said. "Somebody shoot me."

Amy laughed. "By the way, I may have found a story."

"Really?"

"Yeah. Tell you later."

"Roasters are typically horizontal rotating drums that are heated from below and tumble the green coffee beans in a current of hot gases . . . "

Twenty minutes later, Gordon Pettifer's talk was over and everybody was given bags of freshly roasted Crema Crema Crema to take home.

"Right, if we could all reassemble back in the conference room," Sophie said, "because we have reached the high spot of the evening, the unveiling of the CremCo Caffeineissimo espresso machine."

Back in the conference room Hugh Cavendish assumed center stage. "Ladies and gentlemen, I give you the Crema Crema Crema Caffeineissimo." With that Cavendish pulled a velvet cloth off what Amy would have described as a perfectly

ordinary-looking espresso machine. He delivered a dry technical speech about the machine being a revamped piston espresso
machine based on the models that had been popular in the
sixties. There was limp applause. Cavendish introduced the
two engineers who had worked on developing the Caffeineissimo, and the journalists began scribbling halfheartedly in their
notebooks.

Amy turned to Brian and said she was off to find the loo.
Brian said he wanted to take a brief look at the Caffeineissimo
and then they might as well go. He said he would meet her back
at the car park.

She had no idea where the loo was and there was nobody
to ask, so she walked down the corridor toward the roasting
room. One of the guards would be able to direct her.

When she got there, the doors were open and unguarded. As
she stepped inside, she noticed that the workers were dressed
differently. Previously they had been wearing hairnets and white
coats over their normal clothes. Now they were in zip-up overalls with hoods, face masks, and surgical gloves. They were also
wearing white rubber boots. They looked as if they were in the
middle of a lethal biohazard rather than a few coffee beans.

"Ah, Ms. Walker, we meet again." The familiar oily upper-
class voice came from behind. Amy spun around to see Hugh
Cavendish. He offered her a thin-lipped smile that she couldn't
help finding rather threatening. "Come back for a second look,
I see. Or is it more of a journalistic snoop?"

"I wasn't snooping," Amy said, keeping her cool. "I couldn't
find the ladies and was looking for somebody to ask."

"I see. Well, you turned the wrong way out of the conference room. Go back down the corridor and it's on your left." He
opened one of the double doors, inviting her to leave. "After
you," he said. Another slimy smile.

She stepped back into the corridor, and Cavendish followed. "I don't understand," Amy said, deciding that since he
already had her down as a snooping journalist, she had nothing

to lose by asking a few questions. "Nobody was wearing protective gear when we did our tour of the roasting plant."

"That's true. We find that visitors tend to get anxious when they see the staff in their usual uniform. They assume there's some sort of biohazard, which there isn't. So now we always get them to change."

"So if the staff aren't coming into contact with dangerous chemicals, why do they need to wear protective clothing?"

"Microfibers."

"Microfibers?"

"Yes. Billions are produced during the roasting process. They irritate the lungs. It's called coffee roaster's lung. Very common in South America."

"Is that so?" Amy said, her voice heavy with sarcasm. "I never knew that. You learn something new every day."

"Don't you? Now, if you would excuse me, I have some urgent business to attend to in the roasting room."

"Of course."

Cavendish went back inside. Amy stood staring at the door, which had just closed in front of her. "Coffee roaster's lung . . . yeah, right."

She headed back down the corridor. There was a reason those people were wearing protective clothing, and it had nothing to do with coffee roaster's lung.

Eventually she found the ladies. She was just about to open the door to one of the stalls when the main door opened. A young woman walked in. She was wearing overalls, but she had removed her hood and face mask.

"Are you journalist?" she said. Amy picked up on the East European accent.

"Yes."

"You tell in newspaper that coffee beans no good. They are bad poison. Very bad poison. People here know. Everybody knows, but peoples too scared to speak. We lose jobs if we speak."

Amy frowned. "What do you mean poison? What sort of poison?"

The woman shrugged. "Bad poison. I go now."

"Okay, but maybe I could meet you somewhere. I'd like to discuss this some more. Have you got a mobile number?"

"No. I go. You tell in newspaper. Please. Very, very important. These bad mens. Cavendish very bad man."

"Before you go, can you tell me what the poison does?"

But the woman was gone. It didn't matter. Amy was pretty sure she knew the answer.

"IF YOU ask me," Brian said, pulling out of the car park, "there's some pay dispute going on between CremCo management and the coffee roasters and this woman is simply trying to discredit the company."

"Maybe. But she seemed really genuine. Plus Hugh Cavendish is an oily creep who exploits his workers." She recounted the conversation she'd overheard between Cavendish and somebody she took to be one of his plantation managers. "I don't trust him farther than I can throw him. Look, I could be barking totally up the wrong tree, but something has occurred to me."

"What?"

"Do you remember me joking about how it was only rich people who could afford Crema Crema Crema and that the coffee could be the reason men are growing breasts? What if I was right?"

"Amy, we Googled coffee and estrogen. There's no link."

"Yes, but what if CremCo was adding the estrogen for some reason?"

"What reason?"

"I have no idea."

"But it's meant to be organic."

Amy laughed. "The hell it is." She paused. "Look, it all

makes sense. Who buys Crema Crema Crema? Rich or middle-class people like you. What sort of men are growing moobs? Men like you. When did they first appear?"

"Soon after I started drinking Crema Crema Crema ... Shit."

"My nuts in a thoughtshell ... You know what you said about me possibly uncovering a story tonight? Well, I think I may have done just that. I would put money on Crema Crema Crema containing estrogen. God, Brian, if we have discovered the cause of the moob outbreak, this is huge. Every newspaper in the Western world will cover it. Can you imagine?"

"It's just like that episode of *Seinfeld*."

"You're telling me there's an episode where they all become reporters and get a world exclusive that launches them as journalists?"

"Not exactly. What happens is they get addicted to this supposedly no-fat yogurt. Only they start putting on weight. In the end they get it tested at a lab and discover it contains fat, after all."

"So the health of thousands of men is never at stake?"

"Look, I never said the two scenarios were precisely identical."

Amy laughed and said she was just teasing. "We do have to get the beans analyzed, though, and not just here. To make our case really watertight, we should get them tested in the United States as well."

"Okay, I've got this friend Melissa in New York who is a big Crema Crema Crema fan. She also happens to be a doctor. She'll know exactly how to get the analysis done over there. But suppose it all turns out to be rubbish and this woman of yours is nothing but a fantasist?"

"So I've wasted a few hundred quid getting the coffee tested."

"Hang on, shouldn't you be selling this story to a newspaper and getting them to pay for the testing?"

"Ideally, but I'm just not established enough. No newspaper

would be prepared to spend money based on some apparently wild fantasy from a reporter they don't know. No, the only way I can approach an editor is with the lab results."

"Okay, then I'm paying," Brian said. "I am not about to let you lay out for this. You can't afford it."

"Brian, I can manage a few hundred quid. Thanks for the offer, but this is my story, my responsibility. I want to do it."

"Okay, if you insist," he said. "You know, if you're right and it is the Crema Crema Crema that has been causing men to grow moobs, this will make your journalistic career. God, you could find yourself up for a Pulitzer."

"Let's just take it one step at a time." Amy laughed. "Right now, this is nothing but conjecture. We will know nothing until we've had the beans analyzed."

"I know, but just imagine . . . "

"I am, but I'm scared I'll jinx it. All we can do is wait." She paused as a thought occurred to her. "Hey, I left without getting my Prada bag."

"Don't worry," Brian said. "I got you one."

"You did? Fantastic. Where is it?"

He reached into his jacket pocket and pulled out a six-inch-long pouch made of light brown suede. He handed it to Amy.

"A comb sleeve?" She pulled out a cheap tortoiseshell comb. "That's what they were making all the fuss about?" She started searching for the Prada logo.

"I've looked," Brian said. "There's no logo. It's just a bit of old junk."

"Why am I not surprised?"

AMY GOT home just after ten. Lilly said Charlie had been as good as gold. He'd gone to bed exactly at eight and hadn't stirred. "Oh, by the way," Lilly said, "some flowers came for you. I took them into the kitchen and stood them in a bucket of water."

Amy went into the kitchen and found a bunch of the most glorious white orchids. There was a card attached: "Thank you so much for having us and for being so wise. Love, Victoria." There were two kisses.

"My pleasure," Amy murmured, smiling.

She called a taxi for Lilly, checked on Charlie, and wondered if it was too late to call Victoria. Deciding her sister would probably be up watching *Newsnight*, Amy dialed her number.

"Hey, thank you so much for the orchids," Amy said. "They're beautiful."

"I just wanted to let you know how much I appreciated you letting us stay ... not to mention our little talk. I don't know what I'd have done without you."

"You know, I'm always here if you need me," Amy said.

"Thank you. And vice versa. By the way, I've made an appointment with a shrink."

"You have? Well done. I know it couldn't have been easy."

"It wasn't, but as you know, Simon gave me no choice."

"So how are things with you two?"

"He's pretty distant. Every time I open my mouth, he just seems to get so angry."

"You've both got a long way to go," Amy said. "But I'm sure the therapy will help."

"Maybe." Victoria didn't sound too confident.

"So," Amy said. "Have you spoken to Dad?"

"I have, and he's adamant that he is going to carry on seeing that woman. He's completely infatuated. I'm convinced he's losing his mind. Do you think we should have him tested?"

"Tested? For what?"

"I don't know. Maybe he's going senile."

"Now you're being ridiculous. Our father is no more senile than you or me. He is in love. I had a long talk with him, and he explained that he has this thing about needing to be needed, and Joyce needs him."

"What about Mum? Didn't she need him?"

"According to Dad, not in the same way. He sees Mum as

confident and independent and making her own way. He admits he's a bit of a chauvinist and that he's probably too old to change."

"Well, I refuse to speak to Joyce. Simon said she phoned and wants to talk, but I'm having nothing to do with her."

Amy told Victoria about Joyce going to AA. "She's so ashamed about what happened. Why don't you try giving her another chance?"

"No way. Drunk or sober, she's still a pornmonger, and I will have nothing to do with her."

"Oh, come on, Victoria."

"No. Dad can do what he likes, but she ruined Arthur's party and she ruined my reputation. I can feel everybody laughing behind my back. Look, it's late. I need to get to bed."

After everything that had happened that evening, Amy wasn't surprised she couldn't sleep. She lay in bed looking up at the ceiling, hands under her head. Suppose, just suppose, Crema Crema Crema coffee beans tested positive for estrogen or for some chemical that mutated into estrogen in the body. She would have a world exclusive on her hands. She would make a name for herself virtually overnight. Editors would be clamoring for her to write for them. She had dreamed of breaking into journalism and becoming successful, but it had never occurred to her that her career would be launched by a story this big. She was reminding herself not to get too carried away, because so far she had proved nothing, when she heard Charlie calling for her.

"All right, sweetie, I'm coming." She threw back the duvet and reached for her dressing gown.

"What is it?" she said, sitting on the edge of his bed. "Bad dream?"

He gave a vigorous nod of his head. "This huge monster was trying to steal my stuff."

She assumed that the monster was a metaphor for Arthur.

"That must have been scary. Tell you what, why don't I read you a few pages of *The Twits*."

"K."

She turned on his bedside light and picked up the book from the nightstand.

He sat up. "Read, read," he said. It was a refrain left over from when he was a toddler. She looked at his expectant little face. There it was again, the resemblance to Sam.

She read half a dozen pages and then insisted Charlie lie down and try to sleep. He asked her to leave his light on, which she did.

"Night, night, poppet. Sleep tight."

She went into the kitchen, filled a glass with water, and stood sipping it, her back resting against the sink. She stared into the distance, thinking about nothing much: what to cook for tomorrow's supper, how she ought to get a laundry load going before bed.

After a few moments, an image of Charlie popped into her head, apparently from nowhere. His smiley face was looking up at her. The resemblance to Sam—that something around the eyes—was obvious. She put the glass down on the drainer. What's more, they were both talented artists. What if . . . ? The idea was ludicrous. She let out a soft laugh, but the thought persisted. She attempted to drag and drop it into her mental trash, but it refused to budge. She was being forced to consider that the similarities between Charlie and Sam weren't mere coincidence or a fluke.

By now her thoughts were picking up speed. Her brain was making what had to be crazy, illogical leaps and connections, but since she was the only person around to point this out, she didn't much care. She had a feeling in her gut, and she needed to test it.

She went into the living room, picked her laptop up off the coffee table, and took it to the sofa. Aware that this could turn out to be quite a day for revelations, she Googled "frozen sperm life span."

Chapter 14

BY NOW AMY'S heart was racing. It had taken her roughly ten seconds to discover that sperm, properly frozen, could live indefinitely.

But Sam had donated his sperm in Manchester. She had been inseminated in London at the Abbotswood Clinic. She Googled it. No website came up, just links to newspaper articles, all several years old. She clicked on one from *The Guardian*. It seemed that the company that owned the clinic had gone into liquidation six months or so after Charlie was born. Amy knew nothing about this. Not that her ignorance came as a surprise. In that first year after Charlie was born, what little spare time she had was spent catching up on her sleep. She certainly didn't spend it reading the newspaper.

Nor had she had any idea that the clinic—which, when she was trying to conceive Charlie, still had an excellent reputation—had been run by an incompetent, bungling medical staff and managers who lost patients' notes and confused sperm batches. The clinic's downfall came when, on one notorious occasion, a doctor implanted a "white" embryo into a black mother. After the birth, she successfully sued the parent company and it went down, taking with it two other clinics that had been under its control. One was in Newcastle. The other, St. Bernadette's, was in Manchester. Amy had no doubt that this was where Sam had donated sperm. She remembered him telling her how weird it had felt jerking off in a converted Catholic church.

One more piece of information caught Amy's eye. All three clinics had been caught scamming sperm donors by telling them they were infertile when they weren't. That way the clinic held on to the perfectly healthy sperm but didn't have to pay the donors. Why didn't Sam know any of this? The article said that the directors of the parent company went to prison for fraud. There would have been a court case. Then the penny dropped. The scandal became public knowledge around the time Sam was working in Africa. Lawyers or officials trying to let him know that he might not be sterile, after all, wouldn't have been able to find him.

She took a deep breath. The St. Bernadette's and Abbotswood clinics had been owned by the same company. Was it possible that as the need arose, sperm was transferred from one clinic to the other? Was it possible that through a mixture of blunders and dishonesty, Charlie's father—instead of being a six-foot, blond-haired, blue-eyed athlete—was in fact Sam?

She got no more than three or four hours of sleep that night. The next morning Charlie had to wake her. She went through her early-morning routine with him, doing her best not to let him see how preoccupied and troubled she was.

On her way to work, she thought about pouring everything out to Brian, but when she arrived, she could see he was consumed with the Crema Crema Crema story, which by rights she should have been, too. After all, if something in Crema Crema Crema was causing his moobs, then—assuming no permanent harm had been done to the men who had ingested it—the panic was over.

"Okay, I'm not drinking any more Crema Crema Crema," Brian said by way of greeting, "or selling it in the café until we have the test results. So, have you found a lab yet?"

"Bri, I didn't get home until after ten last night."

He shooed her into the kitchen and told her to start Googling labs on his laptop. She protested, saying that there were cakes to be sliced and ciabatta rolls to be filled, but he insisted that he and Zelma could manage on their own for a bit. "When you've found a lab, I'll deliver the beans in my car." He paused. "You look knackered. You okay?"

"Fine. I just didn't sleep very well."

"Me neither. I guess we've let all this excitement get to us."

"What excitement? Nobody's told me about any excitement." It was Zelma. She had just walked in and was heading toward the counter where Brian and Amy were standing.

"I'll explain in a sec," Brian said. He turned to Amy. "Now off you go. I'll bring you a cuppa and a croissant to wake you up."

It took over an hour of phone calls before Amy found a food-testing laboratory prepared to analyze the coffee beans. Most of them didn't take on work from private individuals. The one lab prepared to help said they were snowed under with work. There had been an *E. coli* outbreak in half a dozen schools and several hospitals in South London—which Amy had read about in the papers—and it would be weeks rather than days before they could get around to testing the coffee. Brian said the waiting was going to drive him crazy. Amy said it wasn't going to do much for her blood pressure, either, but they had no choice other than to go with these people, not least of all because they appeared to have an excellent reputation.

Brian said he would drop a bag of coffee beans off at the lab, which was only a few miles away in Wimbledon, as soon as the morning rush was over.

"Great," Amy said. "But I haven't given the lab any idea what this is about. I haven't mentioned moobs or estrogen. If we alert people there, somebody might tip off the press and we could end up losing the story."

At that point Zelma came into the kitchen to collect a carrot cake and said that it was like Watergate all over again and that when they made the film, she wanted her part to be played by Barbra or Bette.

Amy said she would bear that in mind.

THAT EVENING, Amy and Charlie went to Bel's for an early supper. Bel loved to cook and kept going on about how Amy hadn't been around for ages, but what with Bel dumping Jurassic Mark and getting into a new relationship, not to mention all the anxiety and effort she put into her voice-over auditions, it hadn't happened.

On top of all that, Bel's life had become even more complicated. She hadn't gotten up the courage to dump Ulf. "How can I possibly chuck him?" she kept asking Amy. "He's so sweet and kind. What's more, he adores me. It would break his heart."

Amy made the point that if Bel carried on like this, she would end up marrying a man simply because she felt sorry for him and then it would be her heart, not to mention her spirit, that would be broken.

"I know. I will do it. I just don't know when." The words had become Bel's mantra, but she did nothing.

Tonight Ulf was in Dublin, giving a lecture on nonmalignant brain tumors, and for once Bel was feeling relatively calm, as her James Bond audition was still a couple of weeks away.

Bel lived in Southfields, a short bus ride from Amy, in what had once been a railway worker's cottage. It was a bit shabby, but the rent was low and the landlord had no problem with her decorating the place.

Bel had taken that as her cue to put her own stamp on it. Nearly all the walls were painted bright pink, and she had orange sofas, green cushions, and strings of brightly colored beads instead of doors. Charlie said that going to Bel's made him feel happy. What made him happier still was the TV she had in the bedroom. Charlie's special treat was being allowed onto the high cast-iron bed, where, propped up against Bel's fancy brocade cushions, he would watch cartoons and eat junk.

This evening, now that they'd finished their spaghetti and meatballs, he was doing just that. Amy and Bel were still at the table, finishing their wine and munching on salad remains.

"I don't think I ever mentioned," Amy said, breaking a brief silence, "that when Sam was a student at Manchester Uni, he donated sperm at a local clinic."

"Really? Huh . . . Actually, I knew several guys who did it when they were hard up. Must be odd to think that you've got kids running around that you don't know. And what if two of them met years later and fell in love? . . . God, there's a film in that."

Amy decided to come straight out with it. "If it's a rom-com plot you're after, I've got a better one than that."

Bel frowned a question.

"Call me mad, but I think Sam could be Charlie's father."

"You're mad."

"Maybe."

"What are you basing this on? The fact that the two of them look a bit alike and Sam was once a sperm donor? Come on."

"Actually, the clinic said he was sterile."

"Omigod. Now I'm starting to think you really are mad."

"Just hear me out."

"Okay," Bel said when Amy had finished presenting her case, "but even if there has been some huge cock-up—pardon the pun—and Sam is Charlie's father, why would the clinic hang on to Sam's sperm for eight years before using it?"

"The staff was incompetent. Why wouldn't they?"

Bel shrugged. "Maybe you're right." She didn't say anything for a moment or two. "Amy, don't take this the wrong way, but do you think it's possible that this is all wishful thinking and you actually just want Sam to be Charlie's father?"

"Maybe that's part of it. I can't think of anything I'd love more than to discover that Sam is Charlie's father. If I had to nominate a dad for him, it would be Sam, but at the same time, I really don't think my heart is ruling my head. You have to admit that there is a genuine possibility that Sam is Charlie's father."

Bel gave a shrug. "The whole thing sounds totally crazy, but I guess it's possible. So, have you told Sam?"

"No."

"Why ever not? This is about him. He has a right to know."

"I know, but on the other hand, if we do a DNA test and it turns out that he is Charlie's dad, he might feel he has to propose or suggest we start living together as a family. The last thing I want him to feel is obligated."

"But Sam has already said he's in love with you."

"No, he said he thinks he is falling for me. There's a difference. It's like he hasn't quite reached the point of no return."

"But you have reached that point? You love him?"

"Yes. I think I do."

"Amy, he has the right to know all of this—how you feel about him and that you think he could be Charlie's father."

"I know, but I can't do it. I have to wait and see if he comes out and says the L word. That way, I know that if he decides to stay, it will be because he loves me as well as Charlie."

JUNE TURNED into July. Amy was still waiting to hear from the food lab.

The last time she phoned to hurry them up, they apologized profusely for taking so long and promised that the coffee beans were next on their list. By now Brian had lost his patience and was all for finding another lab. Amy, who was finding it only marginally easier to contain her frustration, was determined to stay with the one she had chosen, purely because it had such a good reputation.

By now Brian as well as Bel knew about the possibility that Sam could be Charlie's father. Her friends kept on at her to tell him, but Amy was holding out, waiting for Sam to tell her he loved her. By now he was spending more time with Amy and Charlie. On the weekends, when the weather was fine, they went on picnics. They flew kites on Primrose Hill, took trips to the zoo and Legoland.

At night before bed, Charlie and Sam would have play fights on the floor. Sam, who always lost, would "die" with such long, drawn-out death throes and general melodramatics that they would all be in stitches. These days it was often Sam rather than Amy who Charlie called upon to read his bedtime story. More than once, Amy dared herself to imagine the three of them as a family.

She knew she owed it to Sam to tell him that he could be Charlie's father, but guilty as she felt, she kept holding back, hoping that tomorrow he might tell her that he loved her. When he didn't, she convinced herself that he needed more time.

Once or twice, he picked up on her preoccupation and asked her what was bothering her. She always managed to persuade him that there was nothing wrong and that she was fine.

By now, Amy had told Sam that she was happy for him to sleep over in her bed, but he said he would rather not. When she asked him why, he said he was still worried about how Charlie might take it. Amy assured him that Charlie would be fine, but Sam insisted they give it a bit longer.

It was around this time that she noticed Sam starting to change. It was subtle at first. Sometimes, when they met up, he seemed not quite as sunny as usual. Then he started to find excuses not to come on outings with her and Charlie. If he did come, he seemed distant and self-absorbed. When she asked him if he was okay, he always apologized for being a misery. "It's just that I wish we could spend more time alone together. I miss spending hours in bed, making love, laughing, and talking about nothing."

"I do, too, you know that. But we always knew that this

relationship would involve compromises. I'm not sure what I can do. The last thing I want is to lose you, but this is starting to feel like history repeating itself. If our relationship is getting too much for you, I'd rather know now."

Then he would tell her to stop being so daft. "I'm having a moan, that's all. It doesn't mean I want to end it." This would be followed by a kiss or a reassuring squeeze. "Come on, I've cheered up now. Why don't the three of us go out for pizza?"

When Val rang to say that she and Trevor had arranged to rent a trailer in Dorset for the weekend and would like to take Charlie and Arthur away with them, Amy decided that her mother had to be telepathic or have second sight. She assured her mother that Charlie would love to come.

Of course, they got to chatting about Joyce. "She may be a drunk, but by all accounts they're swinging from the chandeliers. Why couldn't I do that with your dad?"

Amy told her what Phil had said about her not needing him.

"All I did was get a few qualifications and get a job. That was no excuse for him to neglect our marriage. Of course I needed him."

"So how are things with you and Trevor?"

Val explained that things had come to a head after a "sweat lodge" incident.

"Trevor said he had arranged for us to spend a Saturday at a sweat lodge in Gloucestershire. I assumed it was a kind of spa and that he was treating me to a day of pampering. I was so excited, and then it turned out to be this ceremonial sauna in a giant tepee in the middle of nowhere, filled with chanting half-naked hippies."

"Oh, Mum."

"I left him to it and took the car to the nearest village. I treated myself to a pub lunch, and he rang me when he wanted picking up. Of course on the way home we had the most almighty row."

"And?"

"I told him that I felt the shamanism thing was dominating our lives and that in order for us to have a future, it had to stop being his entire focus. I said he had to become more involved in the things that I enjoy, like eating out and going to see plays and films."

"How did he take it?"

"Really well. You could have knocked me down with a feather. He said he didn't realize how selfish he was being, but we've still got a long way to go. If Trevor and I are going to make it as a couple, it's going to take a lot of give-and-take from both of us. So far, I've given him an ultimatum about cutting down on the chanting and not seeing patients in the house and he's taken me to see *Oliver*. So I'd say we've made a start."

Val, Trevor, and Arthur collected Charlie on that Friday evening. An hour or so after she had waved Charlie off, Sam arrived, straight from work, bearing a bottle of vintage Chablis. They stood in the kitchen drinking the wine while she began preparing Gordon Ramsay's roast lamb stuffed with apricots, which she planned to serve with new potatoes and green beans.

"By the way," he said at one point, "I'm off to Rwanda again in a week."

"Wow, that's sudden."

"I know. I got an e-mail today from the head of the construction team working on the new school. A problem has cropped up with the flat roof. It's collecting rainwater, which is seeping into the building. Since I was mainly responsible for the design, they need me to look at it and see if it needs to be replaced with a pitched roof. I'm sorry I have to go. I'm going to miss you." He came over to where she was chopping apricots and gave her a squeeze.

"Hey, it's not your fault," she said. She asked him how long he would be away. He said a couple of weeks at least. Maybe longer.

"I'd love to come with you. It's getting on about fifteen

years since the genocide. There's probably a great story to be done on how the country has come on since." She said she would add it to her list of feature ideas.

"By the way," he said, going over to his briefcase, "you had any news from that food testing lab yet?"

Amy shook her head. "They warned me it could be weeks, but I need to hurry them up."

"I thought you might like to see these," he said, producing a wallet of photographs. She stopped chopping apricots and wiped her hands on a clean dish cloth.

"THIS IS a photograph of the school we're replacing." Sam handed her a picture of a building that was little more than a dilapidated concrete box with a tin roof.

"God, look at all the bullet holes in the walls. I assume they're left over from the genocide."

He nodded.

He explained that the school was in a village about fifty miles south of the Rwandan capital, Kigali. "The people are Tutsis. Half a million of them were butchered by the Hutus in ninety-four. They have seen so much violence. Some of them have been left badly maimed. Others saw their entire families wiped out. And yet they are the kindest, most welcoming people you could hope to meet. I don't know how they manage to keep going after what they have been through. It says so much for the human spirit."

He showed her a picture of a young African couple. They were wearing rubber flip-flops and shabby, ill-fitting clothes, but they were both beaming. In front of them were four equally smiley children.

"The man is Jean Baptiste. That's his wife, Delphine. He was sixteen when his parents and his five siblings were killed. And here he is nearly two decades on with his wife and kids. He is one of the most special people I have ever met. With the help of foreign aid, he went to college, became a teacher, and got married. Somehow he found the determination to make a life for himself. I wish I had a fraction of his courage." He looked preoccupied, as if he was gearing up to say something.

Amy, too, had become thoughtful. Maybe it was the wine, maybe it was the talk of Jean Baptiste's bravery, but she was suddenly overcome with the feeling that the time had come. Sam was leaving for Africa in a few days and wouldn't be back for weeks. She had already left it too long. She had to tell him that he could be Charlie's father.

"Sam, there's something I need to tell you."

"Actually, there's something I need to talk to you about, too," he said, sounding anxious now. "Would you mind if I went first?"

"I guess not. Go ahead." She was curious more than alarmed.

"Amy, I don't have the words to describe how much I am in love with you."

Her face broke into a smile. "You do? I love you, too," she said. Her voice was soft and gentle.

"I think I've known that for a while. You are the first person I think about when I wake up and the last one I think about before I got to sleep."

"Ditto."

"But . . ."

Amy frowned. Despite the letdowns she'd had in the past, she wasn't expecting a "but."

"You know, I've really come to hate that word," she said.

"I'm sorry, but I owe it to you to tell you how I feel. I adore Charlie. He's a wonderful, brilliant little boy. I think the absolute world of him . . ."

"Sam, what's going on? I don't understand. For weeks you have been reassuring me that you are okay about Charlie."

"I thought I was."

"So I guess you're about to tell me that you're very sorry, but you're not ready to parent a child that isn't yours."

"It's not as simple as that. Please, just hear me out. When my father left us, I was five."

"I know."

"That left me pretty damaged emotionally."

"I'm sure it did, but when I tried to get you to talk about it, you refused. Why?"

"I couldn't risk telling you how much parenting frightens me. After all you've been through with these other losers you dated, you would have walked away, and the last thing I wanted was to lose you."

"Maybe. Or maybe I would have listened and tried to help you."

"That didn't occur to me. Instead, I've done my best to enjoy the moment and not think about the future."

"You mean a future with you as Charlie's stepdad?"

He nodded.

"But now you've started thinking about it and you're petrified."

"Of course I am. From the day my father left, I had no male role model. I have absolutely no idea how to be a father. He left me with nothing other than the certainty that all fathers are bastards who have affairs and abandon their children."

She was shaking her head. "Is that it?"

"Isn't it enough?"

"Sam, look at me." She placed her hands on either side of his arms. "When we first become parents, none of us really knows how to do it. We go on instinct and make it up as we go along. All parents get it wrong one way or another, and often all we remember is our mistakes. We try not to repeat those, but guess what, we make new ones. That's just how it is."

"It's more than that with me. When Dad left us, I felt so abandoned. I still do. I'm thirty-seven, and I haven't gotten over that feeling. I'm still a kid looking for a parent. I'm needy and selfish, just like kids are. I know how pathetic and feeble this must sound and I'm not proud of it, but I'm not sure I have anything to give a child."

"Of course you do. You've been doing it. Surely you can see that. You know, Brian has some of these issues. His parents died in a car crash when he was thirteen. Talk to him. He's been there."

"He can't help me. I'm not going to change. This is who I am. You don't know me. The me you have been seeing since we started dating isn't real. I've just been putting on an act."

"No you haven't. Nobody could fake the way you are with Charlie. And I bet you're equally fantastic with your nephews."

"Yes, but I will never have to raise them. I spend time with them and get to go home. I'm running scared about us because I've realized that parenting isn't just for a few weeks. It's forever. It feels like I would have to sacrifice myself and my needs, and I'm not sure I can do that."

"So that's it? We're finished?"

"Amy, from the bottom of my heart, I don't want us to split up. I love you, but I'm just so confused. I can't see a way forward."

She took a deep breath. "Right. Well, what I have to say is going to confuse you even more."

"What?"

She blurted it all out.

"Amy, you brought this up the other day. I thought it was just a joke."

"It was, but now I've got more information to go on. The clinics were linked. You might not be sterile. They told men they were sterile to get out of paying them."

"Okay, but why would they hang on to it for so long?"

"Sam, the clinics were in chaos. They often had no idea what sperm they were storing or who it belonged to."

"Sorry, I don't buy any of this. You're just letting your imagination run away with itself. And you're wrong; Charlie and I don't look alike."

"You do. You just can't bear to see it."

"Rubbish."

"It's not just me. I told you how other people can see the

likeness. Look, this could be nothing or it could be something. We have to do a DNA test."

"What! No. Charlie is not my son."

"You're probably right, but we need to know for certain."

"I can't handle this—not on top of all the other stuff I was feeling." He was running his hand through his hair and starting to pace up and down the kitchen.

"Sam, I know that I've sprung this on you and it's hard to take. Plus I'm probably barking completely up the wrong tree, but will you at least agree to a DNA test? We have to know the truth. And so does Charlie."

"I know the truth." More pacing.

"You can't be certain."

He stopped and looked at her. "This is total madness. I am not Charlie's father."

She didn't say anything.

"Okay . . . Just tell me where I have to be and when." He picked up the wallet of photographs and his briefcase. "I'm going. I need time to think. I can't discuss this anymore tonight."

"Sam, please don't walk out. We need to keep talking."

But he was out of the door.

THE NEXT morning, Bel popped around unannounced to see Amy.

"I brought croissants," she said, putting a paper bag down on the kitchen counter. She paused. "By the way, you heard from this lab place yet?"

Amy shook her head.

"You must be on *shpilkes*." Bel was using the word regularly now and pronouncing it to perfection. Zelma would have been delighted. "You know this Crema Crema Crema thing story is going to go global. You are so going to become a star."

Amy laughed.

"Oh, major headline—I dumped Ulf. Turns out he's been shagging some nurse at the hospital. Can you believe it? There I was, petrified of ending it with him, and all the time he's been shagging somebody else. What a slimeball."

Amy said the words "pot," "kettle," and "black" were coming to mind.

"Ah, there is that," Bel said. "I suppose I was the first to stray."

She paused. "Amy, you look awful. You okay? . . . Oh, no. Crap! Sam's here. I've burst in on your weekend. Amy, forgive me, I totally forgot."

"It's okay. Sam's not here. He left after I told him he might be Charlie's dad."

"Oh, Amy. I'm so sorry." Bel came over to Amy and hugged her.

"He says he's not up to becoming a parent because being abandoned by his father left him feeling needy and without anything to give a child."

"So is it over?"

"I don't know," Amy said, shrugging. "He said he needed time to think."

ON MONDAY morning, Amy phoned Sam from the café to say she had contacted her doctor's office about the DNA test. "The practitioner nurse will do it. All you need to do is call and make an appointment."

"Fine." He sounded less than enthusiastic.

"So maybe," she ventured, "we could get together sometime and talk about things some more."

"I guess, but my head is still all over the place. I'm not sure I'm going to be able to tell you what you want to hear."

She flipped her phone shut. She wasn't sure what she'd been expecting him to say, but disappointed didn't begin to describe her emotions. She must have been standing staring into space for a while, because eventually Brian came over to ask if she was all right. By then he and Zelma were up to speed on the state of play between Amy and Sam.

"I'm assuming that was Sam on the phone," Brian said.

She nodded. "He says he's still confused and can't tell me what I want to hear."

"Amy, would you like me to speak to him? Our backgrounds aren't dissimilar. If it would help, I'd be more than happy to."

She shook her head. "Thanks for the offer, but he's so mixed up. I'm not sure he'd be very receptive just now."

"You want to take the rest of the day off?"

"Nah . . . it's better if I'm working. Gives me something to think about . . . Oh, by the way, did Bel tell you she dumped Ulf? Been cheating on her with a nurse, apparently."

Brian managed to look shocked and thoughtful at the same time. "No . . . no, she didn't," he said.

Zelma made Amy a mug of tea with two spoons of sugar. "You and Sam are going to sort this out, you know."

"I doubt it, Zelma."

"Oh, you will, and you know why? From what you've told me, this Sam of yours is a good man. I admit that he's got some growing up to do, but if he's got anything going for him, he won't let a beautiful intelligent woman like you slip through his fingers. He'll come around. You just see if he doesn't."

Amy gave Zelma a hug and said she wished she had her faith.

AMY HATED herself for lying to Charlie, but she could hardly tell him the truth about why the nurse needed to take a sample of his blood. Amy thanked God that he didn't have a fear of needles. If he had, she would have felt even worse. She told him he was going to the doctor's for a routine blood test that people often had to check that they were healthy. He didn't question this and beyond a slight wince and sharp intake of breath made no fuss when the nurse inserted the needle into his arm. To Amy's surprise, he even insisted on watching the blood being drawn into the syringe. Afterward, he accepted his strawberry lollypop and smiley sticker and jumped out of the chair. Amy said he had been such a good boy that he could have anything he wanted for supper. "Burger King," he announced. Amy and the nurse exchanged amused "What do you do with them?" glances. "You're on," Amy said.

Friday was parent-teacher evening at Charlie's school. Amy was due there at half past eight. Lilly was baby-sitting. At five she called to say she couldn't make it because she had a temperature and was throwing up. Amy told her not to worry and wished her better. Then she started phoning around to find a replacement. It being Friday night, none of Lilly's baby-sitter friends could make it. Val was away again, this time at a health farm with a couple of girlfriends. Bel wasn't answering her mobile. Phil had a Rotary meeting, and Brian had a date with Rebecca. She didn't try Victoria because she knew she would be busy with her kids. Ruby wouldn't be able to help, either, because she and her husband were due at the parent-teacher evening, too.

Amy realized she had two choices. She could phone the school and make another appointment to see Charlie's teacher—which she knew wouldn't go down well because it would make her look like one of those selfish mothers who didn't put their children's education first—or she could call Sam, assuming he hadn't left for Rwanda. She dialed his number. He picked up on the first ring.

"I wasn't sure you were still in the country," she said.

"Actually, I'm leaving in the morning."

"Oh, God, you must have so much to do. I needed a favor, but it doesn't matter."

"What is it?"

She explained. "And Charlie will be in bed by the time you get here."

Sam told her it was no trouble. He would be there by eight.

CHARLIE'S TEACHER, Mrs. Ogilvy, made no bones about it: Charlie was "an absolute joy to teach." Moreover, he was polite and helpful, and popular with his classmates. Overall he'd had an excellent academic year, although he did struggle with arithmetic. On the other hand, his verbal and writing skills were well above average, and as for his art, she had to admit that she was at a loss for words. She called over another teacher, who was an art specialist, and the three of them sat discussing what might be best for Charlie. They all agreed that one-on-one tuition was the way forward. The art teacher said she had some contacts and would phone Amy to let her know if any of them could take him on.

Despite all the upset she was going through with Sam, as she made her way home, Amy felt like she was walking on air.

She smelled the burning the second she walked in. "What the—"

As she ran toward the kitchen, there was a terrified scream. Amy charged in. A frying pan was on fire on the stove. The flames were licking the range hood. "Omigod!" Amy grabbed her son and pulled him out of harm's way. Sam, who could have gotten there only a moment or two before her, was turning the heat off under the pan. Looking frantic and pale as veal, he ran to the sink and wetted a tea towel. He threw it over the frying pan. The flames spit and sizzled before dying. The kitchen was full of acrid smoke. The top of the stove and the range hood were black with soot.

"Charlie, what the bloody hell has been going on?" Amy said.

"I was hungry," Charlie replied meekly.

"He woke up," Sam broke in, looking stricken, "and said he fancied a snack. I told him to go into the kitchen and help himself to something." He took the tea towel off the frying pan and looked inside. "I didn't say he could come in here and start frying stuff . . . What were these? Eggs?"

"You let a six-year-old fry his own eggs? What sort of an idiot are you? He could have killed himself!"

"I just told you. I thought he was getting potato chips or some cookies. I had no idea he was messing about with the stove."

"I knew what to do," Charlie said to his mother. "I've seen you do it. I cracked the eggs into a cup and everything. The oil just got too hot, that's all."

She checked his face and arms for burns. There was nothing.

"Charlie, you have been extremely naughty. How many times have I told you not to go near the stove? Now get back to bed. I'll be in to speak to you in a minute."

"But Mum, it was an accident . . ."

"Don't 'but mum' me. Go."

Charlie loped off.

"I am so sorry," Sam said. "I was watching the football. It didn't occur to me for a second that he would start lighting the stove."

"He's six, for crying out loud. He needs to be watched. He must have been in the kitchen for ages. Why didn't you check on him? And how come you didn't smell burning?"

"I don't know. I was concentrating on the game."

"I don't believe this." She could feel the fury rising. Then something snapped inside her. "You know what? You really are a manipulative bastard."

Sam blinked. "Excuse me?"

"You allowed this to happen to prove what a useless father you'd be. Now you're standing there waiting for me to dump you. If anybody asks, you can say that I ended it. You can tell them that it was me who forced you out of Charlie's life and that it had nothing to do with you. That way you get not to hate yourself. Very clever."

"You're suggesting I put Charlie's well-being at risk to stop myself from feeling guilty?"

"At some level I think you did. Well, you've done what you set out to do. Now get out."

After he'd gone, she threw herself onto her bed and sobbed.

"Mum, I'm sorry for touching the stove," Charlie called out from his bedroom. "I'm really sorry."

Chapter 15

THE NEXT MORNING, Amy had a long talk with Charlie about how dangerous it was to light the stove and made him promise faithfully not to go near it again. She decided not to punish him on the grounds that he'd had a severe fright, which was probably punishment enough.

"You and Sam had a fight because of me," Charlie said. He was sprawled out on the living room rug, penciling over the same spot on his drawing pad. He finally made a hole in the paper. "Now you're not friends anymore, and it's all my fault."

Amy sat down beside him and pulled him onto her lap. "Now, then, look at me."

He looked.

"It is absolutely not your fault that Sam and I are cross with each other. I know it's hard for you to understand, but the fight we had was only partly about him not watching you. We were also arguing about other grown-up stuff."

"K. So will you ever be friends again?"

"I don't know."

"You look sad."

"I am sad right now, but I'll get better."

He hugged her and said he would look after her and stop her from being sad. "I could make us some hot chocolate with marshmallows," he said. "That always stops me from being sad."

That made her smile. "Charlie, you just promised me you

wouldn't go near the stove again." She ruffled his hair. "Tell you what, why don't I go and make us some hot chocolate?"

While she was waiting for the chocolate to melt, she found herself thinking, not for the first time that morning, how cruel she had been to Sam. He had neglected Charlie, no doubt about that, and she had every right to be furious with him, but only a mad psycho would have manipulated last night's events to suit his own agenda. She loathed herself for having suggested it. All that she could come up with in her defense was that there must have been so much adrenaline pumping through her body that she wasn't thinking straight.

She had to call him to apologize. After everything that had gone on between them—not just last night—she had precious little hope for their relationship, but she couldn't let it end with him thinking she was a first-class bitch.

She added some milk to the melted chocolate. As she stirred the mixture, she dialed his number. She thought she might catch him at the airport, but the call went straight to voice mail. Leaving a message—however heartfelt—seemed cowardly. It meant he had no chance to say his piece. She owed him that. She guessed he would be flying for twelve hours or so. She would phone again tomorrow.

Her instinct was to spend the weekend in bed, curled up in a fetal ball, crying her heart out, but she couldn't because she had Charlie to think about. When Victoria rang to say that she was going to Wimbledon Common with Arthur and two yellow Labrador puppies they had just bought and would Amy and Charlie like to join them, she jumped at the chance.

"Bloody hell, you look rough," Victoria said by way of greeting.

"Huge fight with Sam," Amy said.

She strapped Charlie in next to his cousin in the back of the car and climbed in beside Victoria. Bert and Ernie, the Hallmark-cute puppies, yelped from behind the dog guard. The boys knelt on the backseat to watch the animals.

"Hey, boys," Victoria said, looking at them in the driver's mirror. "Put your seat belts back on. We're going now." She turned to Amy. "So, what happened?"

Amy whispered that she didn't want Charlie to hear and said she'd explain when they got to the park.

The boys ran ahead with Bert and Ernie. "Don't go where we can't see you," Victoria called out. "And be gentle with those poor animals. They're only babies."

"You know, a dog would be so good for Charlie," Amy said. "It would be a companion for him. And maybe it would stop him banging on about wanting a snake."

"I'd rather have a snake any day," Victoria said. "These things poop all over the carpets and scratch the furniture."

"So why did you get them?"

"My shrink says I have to stop being so controlling and demanding of the children and have more fun with them."

"Is it working?"

"Well, I hate clearing up after the dogs, but on the upside, I don't think I have ever been more popular with Arthur and Lila."

Amy asked Victoria how the therapy was going.

"The sessions have gone up to two a week. Simon now comes to one, and we have couples counseling. I think we're making progress. Slowly. So what's going on with you and Sam?"

Amy brought her sister up to speed. "So we've done the DNA test. The results should be back in a couple of weeks."

Victoria didn't say a word. Instead she stopped walking and closed her eyes.

"What?" Amy said.

"I'm reciting my mantra."

"Your mantra? You sound like Trevor."

"I know it sounds a bit hippie-dippy, but my therapist says I have to work on my need to be so judgmental. Instead of saying 'I told you so,' I have to recite this mantra: 'Mistakes are human. I am human. I must not judge myself or others.' And don't ask if it's made me think about picking up the phone to Joyce. It hasn't. I am nowhere near doing that yet."

"That's okay. You might feel different in time. But the mantra helps?"

"The words make me feel like I'm just one of the herd. I hate that. I've spent my entire life trying to rise above the herd."

"I know." Amy smiled. "It was never going to be easy."

"I was going to tell you how I always knew your relationship with Sam would end in tears and that men rarely take on women with children. What I actually want to say is that I understand why you decided to have Charlie. You were very brave, braver than I would have been. And I'm so sorry you have struggled with relationships and that it didn't work out with Sam."

Amy's eyes were wide with delight. "Good God. I cannot believe you just said all that."

"Hey, meet the new nonjudgmental me."

"Thanks," Amy said, putting an arm around her sister's shoulders. "Hearing you say that means so much to me."

In the distance they could see the boys dressing Bert, or it might have been Ernie, in Arthur's fleece and Charlie's baseball cap.

"Hey, boys," Amy called out, "stop that. You're upsetting that poor animal."

"You know," Victoria said to her sister, "you really shouldn't let Charlie wear baseball caps. It's so common."

ON SUNDAY, Amy kept trying Sam's number, but each time his phone went to voice mail. Then she remembered that the village where he was building the school was in the middle of nowhere and unlikely to have a mobile phone signal. She decided to call his office the next morning. His colleagues were bound to have a number for him.

She had just decided to have an early night when Bel rang.

She was kvetching about her James Bond satnav audition, which was first thing on Monday morning.

"Okay, this is the deep sexy, purr: 'At the roundabout, darling, take the third exit.'"

"Bel, a satnav wouldn't call its owner 'darling.' Not even if its owner was James Bond."

"I know, but I thought it might be fun to make the satnav a real character. Nobody else will have thought of it."

"I guess not."

"Amy, you okay? You sound a bit down."

She told Bel about the kitchen fire.

"Omigod, is Charlie all right?"

Amy assured her that he was. "Oh, then I called Sam a manipulative bastard."

"That must have gone down well. And you called him that because . . . ?

Amy explained her thinking. "I didn't mean it. I was just high on adrenaline. I know I've blown it with him, but to tell you the truth, I'm pretty certain it was blown already. I just want to apologize, that's all, but I can't reach him 'cos he's in Rwanda."

Bel offered to come over and keep her company.

"Thanks, hon, but I think I'll just have an early night."

"AMY, YOU okay?" Brian said the moment she arrived at the café. "Bel called me last night and told me what happened."

"Oh . . . you know . . . licking my wounds. Feeling like a complete bitch."

"Hey, c'mon. You didn't mean to call him that."

"I know. It's just so frustrating not being able to reach him."

"Listen, if there's anything you need . . . time off . . ."

"Thanks, Bri, but I'll be fine. Honest. Thanks for being there. I don't know what I'd do without you."

"Hey, my pleasure."

She left it until ten o'clock before phoning Sam's office. Once she'd explained who she was, one of his colleagues gave her the number of the school. Rwanda was only an hour ahead, so she dialed the number right away. She must have tried half a dozen times, but all she got was a continuous bleak tone. She was about to try again when her phone rang. It was a very apologetic technician from the food lab calling to say they finally had the results of the coffee bean analysis. Amy's heart started to race. While the technician broke off to deal with a call that had just come in on his mobile, Amy dashed over to the counter, where Brian was grinding beans. "Quick, turn off the grinder. The results are in."

He flicked the switch.

"Okay," the technician said, back on the line now. "The bottom line is, your coffee beans contain a chemical called Texapene."

"What's that?"

"It's used in fertilizer. Or it was, years ago."

"Go on."

"Just after the war, scientists were anxious to boost food production. Early research indicated that Texapene added to fertilizer made crops sprout like heck. And according to reports from the time, it did wonders for the taste, particularly of fruit and veg. But there was a problem with Texapene. Once ingested, it acts like the female hormone estrogen. Test subjects of the scientists experimenting with it started to grow breasts, and the chemical was banned."

"They did? It was? Omigod." Amy was giving Brian the thumbs-up. He started doing a dance and punching the air.

"I'm just wondering," the technician continued, "if these coffee beans of yours could be connected to this outbreak of men growing breasts. If some unscrupulous coffee grower has gotten hold of this chemical, it could be very dangerous. I don't even know where you would find it these days. So if you would let me have the name of the coffee, I can inform the appropriate authorities."

"Of course," Amy said, knowing that if the technician informed the Department of Health, it would be weeks or months before the civil servants got their act together and issued an alert. Her newspaper story, on the other hand, could be out in days.

"The coffee is Crema Crema Crema. It's imported from Indonesia."

"I've heard of that. It's very expensive. Isn't it the one all the Hollywood stars are supposed to be drinking?"

"I think it is," Amy said. She thanked the technician for all his help and asked if he would mind sending an e-mail summarizing everything he had just said.

"No problem. I'll do it right now."

Amy turned to Brian

"The lab is on to the story. The bloke there is going to report this to the Department of Health, which isn't a problem because they move so slowly. On the other hand, I'm totally screwed if he gets to the newspapers before me." She asked Brian if he could phone Melissa, his doctor friend in New York, to see if there was any news from the American food lab. They had been dragging their feet, too, owing to an outbreak of toxic pretzels among street vendors in Manhattan.

Meanwhile Amy kept trying the school in Rwanda. Mostly she got the continuous tone, but once or twice it rang, so she knew she didn't have the wrong number. She gave up at around four, assuming that by then the school had closed for the day.

The next morning Brian got an e-mail from Melissa in New York. The American lab had discovered Texapene in the coffee beans. What was more, the technicians had put two and two together and she didn't think it would be long before one of them went to the newspapers.

Amy knew she had to move fast if she wanted to get the story out before anybody else. She thought about which newspaper to contact. *The Daily Post* was the obvious choice, simply because she had a relationship with it. Boadicea had treated her pretty shabbily over the school lunches story, but she had come across in the end by getting her such a generous kill fee. She could be wrong, but Amy felt she could trust her.

"Features," Boadicea answered in that jaded, pass-the-joint voice of hers.

"Hi, Boadicea, Amy Walker here."

"Amy who?"

"Walker. You remember my school lunches story . . . the one you got Jamie Oliver to do instead of me."

"Oh, yeah. Hi . . ."

"Look, I've uncovered an amazing story, but I'd rather not discuss it on the phone."

"Okay, but I've got some lunch thing with Kylie Minogue, would you believe, at one." She made it sound like she was being forced to attend a local council refuse committee meeting.

"I'll be there at twelve."

AMY ARRIVED ten minutes early. One of the news desk interns, a pretty, studious-looking girl called Ellie, was dispatched to collect her from reception. She took her up to the third floor and led her into the newsroom. This was a large, noisy open-plan office with journalists on the phone scribbling notes while others sat drinking coffee with their feet up. Two or three, no more, were sitting in front of their computer screens, bashing away at their keyboards as if their careers depended on it.

Ellie pointed out Boadicea, and the two said their good-byes.

Boadicea, a tall, rather lumpy twenty-something in a baggy beige shift that looked like it had been left over from the Peasants' Revolt but probably cost five hundred quid at Harvey Nichols, was on the phone. From time to time she drew on a dummy cigarette. A couple of nicotine patches were hanging off her upper arm.

Not wishing to eavesdrop, Amy kept her distance. Boadicea caught sight of her and beckoned her over.

"Amy?" she said, covering the phone mouthpiece with her hand.

Amy nodded.

"Be with you in a sec. I'm hanging for somebody at Kabbalah Centre. There's a rumor that Madonna's been trying to recruit Sarah Palin." She suggested that Amy go over to the coffee machine and help herself to "some of our lousy office cappuccino."

When she returned, Boadicea was putting down the phone. "Ten minutes they kept me waiting, all for a 'no comment.'" She invited Amy to sit down. "Right," she said, taking a drag on her dummy cigarette. "Tell me what you've got."

"I've found out why men are growing breasts."

SHE WAS prepared to bet that Boadicea had never moved so fast in her life. Five minutes later, she was ushering Amy into the editor's office. Roy Hargreaves, a short balding man in shirtsleeves, his pink silk tie at half-mast, was dwarfed by his giant walnut desk and black leather chair. The boss of *The Daily Post*, who had started out in life selling fruit and veg off a barrow in the East End before becoming a messenger boy at *The Daily Express*, was renowned for his lack of charm.

"This is Amy Walker," Boadicea said. "She's a freelancer."

"Successful?" Roy Hargreaves demanded. "Do you make a living at it?"

Amy swallowed. "Not so far. I earn a living as a waitress . . . but I did work in PR for some years."

Her afterthought didn't manage to impress Hargreaves. He rolled his eyes and looked at Boadicea, as if to say, "Why are you wasting my time with this woman?"

"Roy, this really is a fantastic story. I think you need to hear what Amy has to say."

"You'd better sit down," he harrumphed, pointing at Amy with a Biro. He left Boadicea standing.

Finally he sat back in his chair and perused her over his specs. "So, what is this fantastic story of yours?"

"Okay, as you know, over the last few months thousands of men all over the world have started growing breasts. I know why." She handed Hargreaves the lab report. He started reading. After a few moments, his face lit up. As he carried on studying the report, he started rubbing his hand over his chin. "Fuck me," he said, chuckling. "This is fucking brilliant." He looked at Amy. "What's your name again?"

"Amy Walker."

"Right, Amy Walker, this is what you do: First you get a quote from this Cavendish bloke. And we need a picture, so take a snapper with you. Your best bet is to wait outside the CremCo offices until he leaves. That way you catch him unaware. If you phone to make an appointment, you give him time to prepare a statement. Get back here when you've got something. We can hold the front page until ten for something this big. Okay, what are you waiting for?"

It was all she could do to stop herself from saluting and saying aye-aye.

The moment she left Roy Hargreaves's office, Amy phoned Ruby to ask if she could hang on to Charlie until she got home. Ruby knew that she was trying to break into journalism, so when Amy told her she was working on a potentially huge story for *The Daily Post*, she didn't hesitate to say that if it looked like Amy was going to be very late, Charlie could stay the night. "Ruby, I don't know what to say. Thank you so much."

THE CREMCO head office was in Manchester Square, off Oxford Street. The cab dropped Amy and Derek, the photographer, outside a white stucco villa that, judging by the brass plate, housed three or four different companies.

Derek—built like a bouncer, ancient blouson leather jacket—said there was no way he was hanging around outside for hours on the off chance that "this Cavendish geezer" might appear. West Ham was playing Real Madrid tonight, and he had booked a front-row seat in front of the telly.

"Somehow," he said, "you need to get into this bloke's office. How's about I create a diversion at reception while you get in the lift?"

"But if I confront Cavendish inside the building, you won't get your picture."

"Maybe you could work out some way to lure him into the street."

Amy laughed. "Right. How on earth am I going to do that?"

"I dunno. Look, I can get you into the office. The rest is up to you. If we don't get the snap, so be it."

It couldn't have been easier. Derek hid his camera in a plastic carrier and ambled into the CremCo reception area. He took up a position in front of the desk and started ranting and raving about how Michael Jackson was living with Elvis and Marilyn in a cellar in Graceland and that they would all reveal themselves once the human race gave up eating protein. While the doorman and the chap at reception manhandled him off the premises, Amy slipped into the lift.

CremCo's offices were on the second floor. Double doors led in from the hallway.

Inside there was a second reception desk. Another barrier to get through. A young woman looked up at Amy and smiled a greeting. Amy couldn't think of anything to say other than: "Hello, Amy Walker for Mr. Cavendish."

The woman consulted her clipboard. "I'm afraid you're not on the list."

"Really? Well, reception downstairs had me on their list."

"Okay, just let me check with Mr. Cavendish's secretary." She picked up the phone. "I have a Ms. Walker here for Mr. C...No, she's not on my list either." The receptionist turned back to Amy. "I'm sorry. We have no record of an appointment. What was it regarding?"

"Look, don't worry. If I'm not on the list, I'm not. I'll make another appointment." There was nothing she could do. She'd messed up because it hadn't occurred to her that there would be another reception desk. She would have to go back onto the street and wait for Cavendish to leave the building. Derek was not going to be happy.

She realized she needed to pee. "Excuse me," she said to the receptionist, "is there a ladies on this floor?"

"Round the corner, first door on the left."

As Amy stood washing her hands in the ladies, one of the ceiling spotlights started to fizz. She turned her head toward the flickering bulb. It was then that she noticed the smoke detector.

The thought came to her in an instant. If anything was guaranteed to get Hugh Cavendish out of his office and into the street, it was a fire, or at least the threat of one. Her eyes went to the paper towel dispenser. She would set a load of towels alight in one of the waste bins. But what if it all went wrong and she started a real fire? She thought back to Charlie and the kitchen and how little it had taken to start a blaze. What if she hurt herself, killed herself even, and left Charlie without a mother? No, she couldn't risk it. It was far too dangerous.

On the other hand . . . She found herself rooting around in her bag. She knew she had some matches. She'd bought them to light Arthur's birthday candles in case Victoria forgot, which of course she didn't.

Hands shaking, she pulled a load of paper towels out of the dispenser and placed them in the metal waste bin. She put it down on the floor and struck a match. She broke the first one without it lighting. The same thing happened the second time. The third lit up. She dropped the match into the waste bin. One of the towels caught fire. Then the rest burst into flames. She picked up the bin and held it under the smoke detector. Nothing happened. "Come on. Come on." Still nothing. Seconds went by. Then . . . Bingo. The earsplitting whistling sound began. She carried on holding the waste bin. If she pulled it away, the alarm would stop. The metal was starting to get hot now, but she had to give it a minute or two. Once the building's main fire alarm began and people started leaving their offices, she could put the bin down and extinguish the flames. She prayed that nobody would come into the ladies and find her. A minute or so went by. The ringing of the main fire alarm began. Yes. She could hear shouting and activity outside. People were being told to make their way to the exits.

She doused the fire with soaking-wet paper towels. Then she put her foot inside the bin and stamped on the black sodden mush. She looked for the faintest sign of a spark. There was none. Now she could leave.

She opened the door and slipped out. A line of people went by, presumably making their way to the stairs. Then she spotted Hugh Cavendish. He was carrying his briefcase and some files. He didn't seem remotely concerned by what was going on and was talking animatedly to some male colleagues. If she had been asked to describe his behavior, she would have said he looked rather merry, as if he had just returned from a boozy lunch.

She fell in behind some of the CremCo staff and followed them to the stairs. All the time she had Cavendish and his friends in her sights. The stairway was packed, but everybody was moving quickly. There wasn't the remotest panic. People were chatting away, clearly assuming it was a drill or false alarm.

Finally they reached the reception area. The uniformed guard was directing everybody onto the street. Amy beckoned to Derek. He came lumbering toward her.

"That's him," she whispered, jerking her head in Cavendish's direction.

"Clever girl—you set off the fire alarm. I knew you'd think of something." He reached for his Nikon.

"No, wait," Amy said. "Maybe you shouldn't start taking photographs until I've got a quote out of Cavendish. If he sees you, he might get scared and make a run for it."

Derek nodded his agreement.

Amy made her way toward her prey, who was still chatting to his friends.

"Hello, Mr. Cavendish."

Cavendish turned toward her and blinked. "I'm afraid you have me at a disadvantage." His speech was slurred. She was in no doubt that he had downed a few too many over lunch.

"Amy Walker. We met at the Caffeineissimo launch party."

He thought for a moment. Then he raised an eyebrow. "Ah, yes. Amy Walker. I remember you. Did you manage to find the ladies?"

"Yes." It was quicker to lie.

"Jolly good. And I hope you enjoyed your goody bag. I know how you hacks love your freebies."

"Yes, the comb holder was very nice. Most appreciated."

"Excellent. Excellent."

Cavendish's drunken associates roared at this. "Bloody hell, Huge," one of them said, "you cheap bastard. Did you really send them packing with comb holders?"

"They were real suede," Cavendish retorted. "What's wrong with that? Everybody's having to cut back these days." He turned to Amy. "Now, what can I do for you, young lady?"

"Mr. Cavendish, it may surprise you to know that I have had Crema Crema Crema coffee beans analyzed at food laboratories in London and New York. Were you aware that the beans contain high levels of a chemical called Texapene?"

"Nope. Never heard of it."

"In that case, let me tell you a bit about it."

She told him what the lab technician had told her. "When the test subjects started to grow breasts, Texapene was banned and never used again . . . until now, it would seem. Would you care to comment?"

"No, I bloody wouldn't," Cavendish barked. "Other than to say you print one bloody word in whichever scumbag tabloid you work for and you'll be hearing from my lawyers."

One of Cavendish's friends seemed particularly drunk. He was swaying back and forth, barely able to keep upright. "Aha, she's got you banged to rights now, hasn't she, Huge? How you going to get out of this one? Bloody hilarious, if you ask me.

They're going to lock you in the slammer, old man, and throw away the key."

"Austin, shut the fuck up!"

"Donchew tell me whadado. I'm not one of your lackeys, you know."

"And your full name is?" Amy asked Austin.

"Austin Heathcote-Nugent, old school friend of Hugh's. Run a petrochemical company in Venezuela."

"Really?"

"Austin. What is this? You're not just ruining me, you're ruining yourself."

Austin was swaying now. "Stop telling me what to do," he bellowed at Cavendish. "You were always doing it at school. Well, you can fuck off." He turned back to Amy. "I was the one who told old Huge about Texapene, you know. Read about it. Thought it couldn't harm anything to give it another go. And the coffee growers agreed because they would sell more and make more money. Total win-win situation."

"Not quite win-win for the consumer, though, is it?" Amy said.

By then Cavendish was hitting Austin Heathcote-Nugent over the head with a cardboard folder. Despite his hand moving up and down at some speed, she could see it was clearly marked: Bean Machine.

All this time, Derek had been snapping away in the background.

"Thank you, squire," he said. "I've got some great shots there."

"And I appear to have all I need," Amy said. "I think we're done."

When Amy got back to *The Daily Post*'s office, Boadicea gave her a wave and pointed to an empty desk next to hers. "Hanging for Madge's people again," she said. "Such an effing bore." She dragged on her dummy cigarette. "So, did you get a quote?"

"Oh, yes," Amy said, smiling. "Actually, I got several."

She sat down and turned on the computer and Googled

"CremCo." There was loads about Crema Crema Crema but very little came up about the company itself. On a whim she tried "Bean Machine parent company." Bingo. CremCo turned out to be a subsidiary of *Bean Machine!*

"Now, then," she muttered. "Why isn't Bean Machine paying its bills?"

She spent half an hour trawling through LexisNexis and Factiva, the newspaper archive services, trying to find articles on CremCo and Bean Machine. She suspected that one or both were in financial difficulties, but she needed to make sure. She found a small piece from *The Financial Times*, which had appeared in February, saying that Bean Machine shares had been dipping in value. It had been expanding too fast into China and the Far East. Though expats there could afford three dollars for a cup of coffee, the locals couldn't. What was more, they didn't much care for coffee.

According to the article, the company now saw CremCo and Crema Crema Crema as its life raft. But the directors had ignored advice to turn it into a mass-market brand and sell it at an affordable price. The article predicted that sales to the rich and wealthy wouldn't be enough to keep CremCo going and, as a result, the future of both companies was in the balance.

She e-mailed Brian, sending him the relevant links:

PRETTY SURE THAT IF WE BRING CREMCO DOWN, BEAN MACHINE GOES, TOO. THEY'RE RELATED! PS—COULD YOU DO ME A FAVOR? WOULD YOU PHONE AROUND AND TELL EVERYBODY, ESP MY MUM AND DAD, TO BUY *DAILY POST* TOMORROW?!

Then she created a new document, called it *"CremCo moobs,"* and started writing:

An exclusive coffee brand has been identified by scientists as the cause of a worldwide epidemic of potentially life-threatening breast growth in men, *The Daily Post* can reveal.

Researchers at food laboratories in Britain and the United States have discovered that the £50-a-pound Crema Crema Crema contains Texapene, a chemical that acts like the female hormone estrogen.

Crema Crema Crema is sold by a subsidiary of troubled coffee giant Bean Machine and drunk by hundreds of thousands of coffee lovers, including leading celebrities.

After half an hour or so, Roy Hargreaves appeared and began reading over her shoulder. "Not bad. Not . . . bad. But that para would work better higher up . . . and okay, down here, why don't we say . . ."

Amy started to cut and paste and make the changes. Meanwhile, Roy Hargreaves strolled up and down, drinking coffee out of a mug that said "Drink caffeine: You can sleep when you're dead." After a while he was reading over her shoulder again. He started to chuckle. "Fan-fucking-tastic. We have so nailed those bastards."

In the middle of it all, Boadicea, her manner verging on animated, came over to say she had managed to get quotes from the Department of Health, and the FDA in America, to indicate that if CCC was proved to contain Texapene, they would ban it immediately.

By nine o'clock, the piece was finished. Amy and Boadicea were having a cup of coffee before calling it a night, when Roy Hargreaves called Amy into his office. As soon as she walked in, he offered her a smile and invited her to sit down.

"I just want to congratulate you. You just wrote a fucking brilliant piece on an extremely tight deadline. You should be proud of yourself."

Amy felt herself color as she thanked him.

"Okay, I'm not going to beat about the bush. I want to offer you a staff job. I have a team of two shit-hot roving investigative reporters, and I need a third—"

Amy stopped him. "Look, before you go on, don't think for

a second that I'm not grateful for the offer, but I couldn't possibly take a staff job. I'm a single parent with a six-year-old child, and I need to be around for him. My plan was always to freelance."

Roy Hargreaves leaned back in his chair. "Amy, let me tell you something about freelancers that you may not know. The best of them—I mean the very best—have all had staff jobs at one time or another. They didn't leave those jobs until they had years of experience under their belts and had built up dozens of contacts. You are a clever, talented young woman, but don't overestimate yourself. You are a beginner who has had some beginner's luck. Come to work for me and you will learn your craft. Then, when you have done that, you can think about going solo. But believe you me, if you turn out to be as good as I think you are, I will fight like stink to keep you here. For now, I will be paying you a six-figure salary and you will get the chance to travel all over the country—the world even."

"That's the trouble," she said.

"Plenty of women with kids manage, but it's your choice. I am offering you the chance to establish yourself as a serious investigative journalist. As an inexperienced freelancer you will always struggle to find the big stories. On the other hand, hardly a day goes by when we don't get a tip-off from some whistle-blower. Think about it, Amy. You'd be throwing away a massive opportunity."

"I will, but I really don't think I'm going to change my mind."

"Okay, but why don't you go home and sleep on it. Let's speak again in a few days." He paused. "Oh, and by the way, be prepared for a bit of a media circus tomorrow."

Amy frowned. "Meaning what, exactly?"

"You'll see," he said, smiling.

While she waited for the cab in reception, she phoned Ruby, who said she shouldn't worry about Charlie. He'd eaten a huge supper, had a bath, and was fast asleep on an air mattress in the twins' room. Amy must have said sorry half a dozen times, but Ruby kept telling her to stop apologizing. She seemed far more interested in finding out about the story.

When she got home, Amy stuck a Marks & Spencer lasagne in the oven. While she waited for it to cook, she lay on the sofa drinking a glass of wine. She hadn't stopped thinking about Roy Hargreaves's job offer. He was right, of course. Despite her experience in PR, she was a beginner. By taking a staff job she would learn everything she needed to know about newspapers, but how could she possibly leave Charlie to go gallivanting all over the place? It would be different if he had a father . . . if things had worked out with Sam . . . but she was all he had. She hadn't brought her son into the world to abandon him.

At the same time, she craved the challenges this job would provide. A few hours ago, she'd been bashing out a story against the clock, adrenaline pumping through her. Wasn't that what she'd always wanted? What was more, even if she did say so herself, she had done some good in the world. Despite the tabloid obsession with celebrity, newspapers like *The Daily Post* still had the power to bring down the bad guys and change lives—or even save them. Amy wanted to play a part in that.

She never thought she would be forced to make the choice that so many mothers had to make. She'd been so smug, thinking she had her future as a freelancer all worked out. What was it Trevor always said? "You make plans, and the universe laughs."

That night, she couldn't sleep. If she wasn't fretting about the job offer, she was thinking about Sam.

Eventually she turned on the bedside light and picked up a copy of *Homes and Gardens*. Half a dozen magazines later, she was still awake. It was getting light when she finally drifted off. The alarm woke her at seven.

Realizing it was already eight o'clock in Rwanda, she decided to try calling the school again. For once the phone started ringing. Then, to her surprise and delight, somebody picked up.

"Hello? Can you hear me?" Amy said in reply to the male voice.

"Yes. I can hear you loud and clear." The chap spoke with a heavy accent.

"Who's that?" she said.

"Olivier, the caretaker."

"Hi, Olivier. My name is Amy Walker. I'm phoning from London. I'm a friend of Sam's—you know, the architect from England who is helping build the new school? I was told I could reach him at this number."

"Ah, yes. He's gone up-country with Jean Baptiste, one of our teachers. Sam's agreed to start on plans for a new hospital. They've gone to look at some land."

"I see. Do you know when they'll be back?"

"Few days, maybe."

"Okay. Could I leave a message for Sam?"

"Sure."

"Could you say that Amy phoned? Tell him I said sorry and maybe he could give me a call?"

"Ah, you his girlfriend? You had fight?"

"Something like that."

"Okay, I tell him you're a very nice lady and he shouldn't fight with you."

Amy managed to laugh. "I'm not sure that's going to do much good, but if you could tell him I phoned, I'd really appreciate that."

"No problem."

AT HALF past seven, BBC Radio 4 rang to ask if she would come in and do an interview about Crema Crema Crema for *The World at One*. Radio 5 wanted her at ten, as did *Breakfast Time* and *Sky News*. No sooner had she put the phone down with one researcher than it started ringing again.

At one point Bel rang, squealing with excitement and congratulations. "I've just got the paper, and the piece looks fantastic."

Amy said that was a relief because she hadn't seen it yet.

"Of course," Bel said, "you do realize that you are now the most famous person I know. So any invites you get to premiers or celebrity dos, please, please, can I come, too?"

At one point Amy managed to phone Charlie to say how sorry she was about not being able to get home yesterday; she would tell him all about it after school. He didn't seem remotely put out by having to sleep at Ruby's and said he had to go because he was in the middle of eating his boiled egg and Marmite soldiers and then Ruby was taking him and the twins to school. She asked Charlie to put Ruby on the phone. Once again, Amy said how grateful she was to her for having Charlie and made a mental note to take around some posh chocs to say thank you.

Afterward she called Brian to say she wasn't going to make it into work. "I'm so sorry. I hate letting you down like this."

"Amy, the last thing in the world you could possibly do is let me down. Don't even think about coming back to work. I just don't know how to thank you. I feel like I've got my life back. I'm not going to get cancer. This whole scare had an upside, though. I've realized I've got to make the most of everything. You know, carpe diem and all that. That's why I'm going to end it with Rebecca. Life's too bloody short to wait for some ditzy woman to come to her senses."

"But you were crazy about her."

"I was in lust. That's all. I can see that now."

Amy couldn't help wondering if Bel dumping Ulf had played a part in his decision.

"Well, I have to say I think you're doing the right thing."

"I think so, too. Oh, another major headline: Pundits on the radio and TV are already talking about the imminent collapse of CremCo and Bean Machine. Plus, a police spokesman said they are considering an investigation. The likelihood is that Cavendish and Co. will end up facing criminal charges."

"Omigod. That's fantastic. This story's only been news for a few hours and already we've got a result."

"So with Bean Machine gone, I can keep the business

running. For the first time in weeks I'm thinking about the future. The Soho coffeehouse idea is a possibility again, and I've decided to go hell for leather to make it happen. You saved my health and you saved my business, Amy. I don't know what to say. I'm just so grateful."

"I aim to please," she said, laughing.

When Val phoned to congratulate her, she wanted to know why Amy had been such a dark horse and hadn't let on that she was working on the story. Amy explained that it had all happened so fast that she didn't have time. "There's been some other stuff going on, too." She explained what had happened between her and Sam.

"Oh, darling, I am so sorry. What can I say? I had such high hopes for this one." When Amy said she had to go because all the radio and TV stations had been phoning and she had interviews booked from ten o'clock on, Val didn't hesitate. "Right. No arguments. I'll leave work early today and collect Charlie from school. Later on, I'll take him to that place in the park for spaghetti. He'll like that."

"Oh, Mum, you can't start taking time off work."

"Yes, I can. I've got stacks of holiday time owing. I'll speak to Ruby and tell her she doesn't need to collect Charlie today."

Amy had just put the phone down with Val, when Phil rang, bursting with pride and delight. "See, I told you your time would come, and it has."

"Thanks, Dad. It really made a difference, you and Mum having so much faith in me."

"Maybe, but I suspect what helped you succeed in the end was the faith you put in yourself." He paused. "Oh, and Joyce says well done, too. She's already been on the phone to her friends, bragging about you."

"Aw, that's sweet." Amy chuckled. "How is she?"

"Well, she's started going to AA, and so far, so good. She hasn't had a drink for over a month."

"That's amazing."

"She's got a long way to go, but she's working so hard. I just wish Victoria would give her a call. How's she getting on with this therapist she's seeing?"

"She seems to be making progress, but she's at the start of a long journey. You're going to have to be patient."

Phil said he understood. "Maybe I'll give her a call, just to see how she's doing. I won't mention Joyce."

"I think that would be a great idea," Amy said.

Amy's mobile started to ring. "Sorry, Dad, I've got to go. It'll be the BBC or somebody. Love to Joyce and tell her well done from me, for staying on the wagon."

On the way to her first interview at the BBC, Amy made the cabdriver stop at a newsagent so that she could pick up a copy of *The Daily Post*. She got back in the car and just stared at the piece, which took up the entire front page: "Male Breasts—Toxic Coffee to Blame." The headline was in inch-high letters. Underneath came the line that made Amy blink in disbelief: "world exclusive by Amy Walker." Part of her wanted to tap the cabdriver on the shoulder and say, "Hey, guess what, that's me. I'm Amy Walker. I got that story." But she didn't. Instead, she sat back in her seat and gazed out of the window, a daft smile on her face.

Amy spent the next two days in cabs being ferried from one television or radio studio to the next. Less than keen on coffee as she was, she found herself relying on it to keep her going. All the time people were phoning to congratulate her. One evening she got home to find a bunch of flowers from Zelma. The card read "Mazel tov, bubbeleh," which Amy didn't understand, but she assumed it was good.

Instead of being jealous, as Amy had feared, Victoria was glorying in her sister's success. It seemed that Amy's scoop had so impressed the local neighborhood that Victoria was once more persona grata. Amy was tempted to say that since none of the parents had gotten particularly angry over the Joyce incident, Victoria had never not been persona grata. But she decided to let it go. Victoria was so excited, it seemed a shame to burst her bubble.

Between interviews—usually when she was in a taxi being ferried from one studio to the next—Amy found herself thinking about Sam and how much she loved him. Before her appalling outburst, there had been a glimmer of hope that Sam might come around to the idea of being a father to Charlie. Then she blew it. She wondered if he would call from Rwanda and decided he probably wouldn't. If she wasn't thinking about him, she was thinking about Roy Hargreaves's job offer. She'd discussed it with Bel and Brian and her mum. Eventually she even talked to Victoria about it, even though she knew what her position would be. But Victoria surprised her. Along with everybody else, she said that it had to be her decision and that she wouldn't judge her whatever she chose to do.

It seemed that Victoria's position was based on her rethinking her own role as a stay-at-home mother. "My shrink thinks I need to stop focusing on the children and get a broader perspective."

"That makes sense."

"So I thought I might apply to do a law degree and maybe train as an attorney."

"You want to do a second degree?"

"Why not? Studying has always appealed to me. And just think—if Simon and I get divorced, I won't need to hire a lawyer."

Amy wasn't sure what to say to that.

"I'm joking," Victoria said, laughing. "Actually, Simon and I are getting along heaps better."

ONE NIGHT, Brian arranged a thank-you slash celebration dinner for Amy in Chinatown. Bel, Charlie, and Zelma came. Amy and Charlie arrived a bit late because they had stopped at Ruby's to drop off her thank-you chocolates. Amy had just finished thanking Zelma for the flowers when she noticed that

Brian had had his hair cut again. That wasn't all. For the first time ever he was wearing a shirt and a jacket. All three women told him he looked hot, except Zelma used the word "dapper." "And I swear you've lost a couple of pounds," she said, giving his abdomen a motherly pat.

He said it was just the cut of the jacket making him look slimmer. But he admitted to feeling calmer and said that as a result he was eating a bit less. Zelma said he would look like a matinee idol in no time.

Zelma made a huge fuss over Charlie, rolling his duck pancakes for him and telling him what a nosh he was and how she wished she had a little boy like him.

"What's 'nosh' mean?" Charlie said.

"It means you're so adorable I could eat you." With that she pinched his cheek.

"But if you think somebody is adorable, why would you want to eat them?"

Zelma laughed and piled some more Singapore noodles into his bowl.

They all got a bit tipsy, apart from Zelma, who stuck to sparkling water. Charlie had enormous fun trying to use chopsticks. Even when the waiter came over and fastened them together with an elastic band, he still managed to get more sweet-and-sour pork over himself and the tablecloth than in his mouth. Even though the dinner was in her honor, Amy couldn't help feeling a bit removed from it all. She didn't want to spoil the atmosphere by going on about how much she wished Sam was there and how she was struggling not just with Roy Hargreaves's job offer but with the half dozen or so others that had come in.

As well as doing interviews for the British and European networks, Amy did live links to *The Daily Show*, *Larry King*, and *Oprah*.

On Friday evening, just as she was leaving Capital Radio, Roy Hargreaves rang to ask if she'd made up her mind about his job offer.

"I have."

"And."

"And..." She took a deep breath. "I have decided that I very much want a career as an investigative journalist, but I'm going to take my chances as a freelancer. My professional life has to fit in around my son."

"You are making a big mistake. Have you any idea how hard you are making it for yourself without any contacts?"

"Yes, but I'm willing to take that chance."

He told her she was barking mad, but at least he had the good grace to wish her luck.

She found herself thinking about the other job offers she'd received. So far she hadn't gotten back to any of the editors with a decision. Tonight she would sit down and write polite e-mails turning the offers down and letting the editors know that she was available for freelance work.

WHEN AMY got home, Val was in the kitchen dishing up one of her magnificent roast dinners. She kissed her mum hello.

"Mum, thank you so much for all you've done this week. I don't know how I could have managed without you."

"Oh, don't be daft. What are mums for?"

"I got you this. Just to say thank you."

Val wiped her hands on a tea towel and took the envelope from Amy. "Darling, I don't want anything. You know how much I enjoy looking after Charlie."

"I know, but I just wanted to say how much I appreciate it."

Val took the gift voucher out of the envelope. "Ooh, a massage and pedicure at the Sanctuary. You are naughty. But I will definitely enjoy this."

"Love you, Mum," Amy said, hugging her mother.

"I love you, too, darling."

They were still in midhug when Amy said: "By the way, I've turned down the staff job at *The Daily Post*. Maybe other women in my position would have taken it, but Charlie has to be my first priority. I've decided to take my chances freelancing. It'll be a struggle because I'm starting off without any contacts, but I'll get there."

Val pulled back to look at her daughter. "Of course you will. I didn't want to influence you, darling, but I'm sure you've made the right decision."

After dinner, Amy sat with Charlie while he had his bath and said how sorry she was that she hadn't been around that week apart from when they all went out to dinner.

"It's been tough on you, I know. I've hated not getting back in time to read to you and tuck you in."

"Don't worry. Grandma finished *The Twits*, and we've started on *The BFG*. And Grandma is a really good cooker. She makes spaghetti with chicken sauce. I wish you'd make that."

Amy said she would ask Val for the recipe. "So you've had fun, then?"

He nodded. Amy said she was glad.

Afterward, Charlie got into bed and they chatted and read stories for over an hour. He fell asleep while she was still reading. She kissed him on the forehead. "Love you, poppet," she whispered. She turned out his light and went back into the kitchen. Val had just finished loading the dishwasher.

Amy asked how things were between her and Trevor.

"Well, the other night he actually sat through a couple of episodes of *Sex and the City*. We ate popcorn, drank a bottle of wine. I'm not going to pretend he loved it, but he knows our relationship can't be all about him. Having said that, I've decided to go on a meditation course. I think it might be a way to get a taste of his world. So we're making progress."

"You know," Amy said, "Victoria and I were sort of hoping that you and Dad might get back together. We watched the two of you stacking the dishwasher together at Arthur's party and thought how well you seemed to be getting along."

"These days, we do get on in short bursts. That doesn't mean we could live together again. I will always be angry with your dad for the way he treated me, and like you said, he needs to be with somebody who needs him."

"Well, if you're happy . . ."

"I am, darling. I truly am."

Amy found herself thinking about Sam. Her sadness must have been obvious, because the next moment Val was hugging her. "You will find somebody else, darling. I promise."

Amy looked at her mother. "I don't want anybody else."

Chapter 16

"PLEASE, MUM. CAN I get it, please? It's got pictures of pythons and vipers and everything. And look, here's one of an anaconda. That's the biggest snake in the world, Mrs. Ogilvy said."

Amy and Charlie were in the station bookshop, at the start of their annual trip to Cornwall. They were going to the cottage Amy rented for a week each summer.

Since they had a four-hour journey ahead of them, Amy knew that Charlie would require reading material. He had picked up two or three comics along with *The Scary Book of Snakes*. Amy had no objection to him reading about snakes. What she objected to was the price: fifteen quid for what was little more than a kids' picture book.

"Please. Can I?"

Amy let out a sigh. They were on holiday. "Okay, go on. Take it to the till."

Brian and Bel were supposed to come with them on the trip, but Brian was in bed with stomach flu. Amy had offered to stay and help Zelma at the café, but Brian wouldn't hear of it. He had managed to find a couple of reasonably competent students to fill in, and Bel was lending a hand, too, as she wasn't working.

Amy wasn't feeling great either. It wasn't just that Sam hadn't phoned. She appeared to have caught Brian's bug, albeit in a milder form. She didn't have a fever and was managing to get up each morning, but she was feeling sick and didn't have much energy or appetite.

As usual they were catching an early train so that they could have breakfast on board. Charlie thought it was the best fun to eat bacon, sausages, and eggs as the countryside sped by. Since breakfast was always served in first class on damask tablecloths with waiters pouring tea and coffee from silver pots, it had always been a treat for Amy, too, but today she couldn't face a fry up. Instead she made do with dry toast and orange juice.

After breakfast, they went back into economy and Charlie settled down with his scary snake book. Amy gazed out of the window. Her mind was full of Sam. Despite everything that had happened, she couldn't stop loving and wanting him. What distressed her most was the thought of him turning out to be Charlie's father and refusing to play a role in his son's life. That would break her heart. She was expecting the DNA test result any day.

Every so often Charlie would interrupt her thoughts with a fact about cobras or vipers or because he needed help with a word he couldn't read.

They took a taxi from Bodmin to Trescothick Strand. Charlie called it "our village." After half an hour, the busy highway full of holiday traffic gave way to fields and narrow winding lanes with six-foot-high hedges. Ten minutes more and they hit Trescothick's main—and only—street. They drove past the Saxon church, the Tudor pub, and the general store that had been built just after the First World War and was still considered by some to be a modern eyesore.

Amy rented Trevelyan Cottage from a local farmer. It was perched at the top of a cliff known as Polruan Mount. The only way to reach it was along a lumpy but mercifully short un-made-up road. "We're here. We're here," Charlie cried as the taxi started to bump and roll. It was then that they got a glimpse of the sea. "Look, Mum, there's a tanker. And some sailing boats. Maybe this year we could get me a dinghy."

Amy smiled at him. "We'll see."

As they rounded the next bend, Amy saw the steps that led down to their very own private beach. Technically speaking, it wasn't really private, but since nobody knew it was there except a few locals, it amounted to the same thing.

They climbed out of the cab, and Amy produced a couple of twenty-pound notes from her purse to pay the driver. While she stood filling her lungs with the warm, sweet air, Charlie ran up to the weatherboarded house. It appeared to have received a fresh coat of duck-egg-blue paint since their last visit, unlike the ancient tumbledown barn that stood a few yards away.

Before Charlie had a chance to knock on the cottage door, it swung open. A moment later, Colin, one of the farm laborers, who looked after the place with his wife, was throwing Charlie in the air and telling him how much he had grown. Charlie always referred to Colin as "old Colin" because of his weathered, rawhide face, but Amy would have put money on him not being a day over fifty.

"Me and the missus have got it all ready for you," Colin said, scratching his head under his flat cap. "There's bread, milk, eggs, butter, a nice bit of homegrown ham, and some of our own apples—all the basics to get you going. There's even Internet now."

"Colin, thank you so much. Let me know what I owe you."

Colin said not to worry now, they'd sort it out at the end of the week.

He handed Amy the front door key. "Right, well, I'll leave you to it. I'm on my mobile if you need anything."

"Can I come and see the lambs and the pigs one day?" Charlie piped up.

"'Course you can, young fella. And there's some baby rabbits in the barn, but make sure you put them back in their cage when you've finished petting them."

Charlie nodded.

"Good boy."

With that, Colin climbed into his pickup, and they waved him off.

INSIDE THE house, the ceilings were low and beamed. The downstairs was open plan: a decent-sized living room leading into a farmhouse kitchen. The living room walls were tongue and groove, painted the same pale blue as the exterior. Some were draped in fishermen's nets. Cheesy seascapes painted by local artists hung from others. A shelved alcove contained conch shells, starfish, and stained glass fishing floats. There were two white sofas, an old pine dining table, and a white-washed stone fireplace with a mantel made from a single piece of driftwood.

The kitchen contained "the beast"—an elderly Aga stove that Amy still hadn't gotten the measure of. There was also a ce-ramic farmhouse sink and kitchen units with red check ging-ham curtains instead of doors.

Upstairs there were three bedrooms and an attic box room with painted pine chests of drawers and cast-iron Victorian bedsteads. Each of the rooms looked out onto the garden, which was full of sweet peas, lavender, and honeysuckle.

Charlie ran into the barn to see the baby rabbits, leaving his mother to unpack. Later on she sliced some of the ham Colin had left and made a salad to go with it. Charlie wolfed his down while telling her all about the rabbits, but once again Amy only picked at hers.

That night, they were both asleep before it was dark.

The sound of seagulls woke them the next morning. Char-lie came bouncing into Amy's room, and they snuggled under the duvet, planning their day. They agreed that they would go into the village for more supplies. If the general store sold dinghies—which Amy decided it most probably did since it seemed to stock everything from car batteries to tampons—they would buy one and take it down to the shore.

In between sailing his dinghy—with Amy at his side, shivering in freezing waist-high water—Charlie collected shells and explored rock pools. On Saturday the wind got up, and he was able to fly his kite. That was also the day she read in *The Daily Post* that Bean Machine had gone into liquidation along with its subsidiaries, including CremCo. Hugh Cavendish and several of his colleagues had been charged with endangering public health by food adulteration.

On Sunday morning, Amy rang Brian to see how he was doing.

"'lo." Groggy as the voice sounded, Amy was in little doubt about who had picked up the phone.

"Bel?"

"Yeah. Wassup? What time is it?"

"After ten. I was phoning to see how Brian was."

"I'll pass you over. He can tell you himself."

"Whoa . . . hang on. Are you in bed with Brian?"

Bel started to giggle. "I cannot tell a lie."

"Care to elaborate?"

"I think it was the chicken soup that did it."

"Ah, yes, the aphrodisiac qualities of chicken soup are well known."

"Very funny. No . . . what happened was that Zelma kept sending me round to Brian with her homemade chicken soup. I think she was secretly matchmaking because she refused to take it herself. Anyway, I'd stay for a few hours, we'd get talking, and then, as he started to get better, one thing led to another."

"Hang on. I'm confused. Is this just another casual one-nighter or . . . ?"

"No. We're in love."

"You cannot be serious."

Amy could hear Bel speaking to Brian. "Bri, do you love me?"

"Crazy about you. Always have been, but don't tell Amy; she'll never let me live it down."

"And Bri . . . what's the bit you love most about me?"

"The dark and very irregular birthmark on your left buttock."

"Did you get that?" Bel said to Amy. "The man who has spent years looking for physical perfection in a woman loves my birthmark."

"I got it," Amy said, "but why has it taken you all this time to realize you were both crazy about each other? I could always see it. Even Zelma could see it."

"It's complicated. Long story short: Brian and I had a relationship based on competition and piss taking. Then we started to fancy each other, but despite that one night we had together, neither of us was prepared to let on because it meant becoming vulnerable to each other. So we just carried on pretending nothing had changed. Then, when Brian got ill, he let down his guard and I was able to do the same. Pretty soon we were telling each other how we really felt about our relationship. So there you have it."

"Well, I am really happy. In fact, I couldn't be happier. My two best friends falling in love. What a result."

"That's not the only result."

"How d'you mean?"

"You are listening to the voice of James Bond's satnav."

"Get out of here! That's amazing. You must be over the moon."

"Just a bit." Bel laughed. "I still can't quite believe it. You know what? I've decided I don't care if I never make it as a proper actor. That's not to say if I got the chance to play Lady Macbeth I'd turn it down, but I've reached the pinnacle of the automated announcement tree. It may not be the greatest pinnacle, but as pinnacles go, it's okay."

Amy was aware of some giggling in the background. "No, Brian, stoppit. I'm on the phone. You'll have to wait."

"Sorry," Bel said to Amy. "Brian has woken in a somewhat frolicsome mood ... Gerroff ... So, are you and Charlie having a good time?"

"Actually, I'm not feeling that brilliant. I'm wondering if I should see the local doctor. I've got this constant nausea. At first I thought I had Brian's bug, but my period is late . . ."

"Omigod. Are you serious?"

"What else could it be? I've always assumed that because my mother hit menopause in her thirties, I would do the same. I haven't so far, but for the last few years I've assumed I must be heading that way and that my fertility has to be down. And what with Sam supposedly being sterile, there was this one time when we didn't use any contraception . . ."

"God, Amy, it only takes one time. What a pair of idiots . . . Right, you have to do a test."

"I know, but what if I am pregnant? I'm assuming Sam won't want to know. So worst-case scenario, Sam is not only the father of the child I'm carrying but is Charlie's dad, too, and he refuses to have anything to do with either of them."

"Okay, I admit this isn't looking brilliant, but you're trying to second-guess Sam and getting way ahead of yourself. First find out if you're pregnant. Then take it from there. You're not on your own. You've got me and Brian. We're here if you need us, right?"

"Okay . . . And thanks."

"There's no need for thanks. You'd be there in a heartbeat if either of us needed help."

THE WIDE-RANGING supplies at the general store didn't extend to pregnancy testing kits. This meant taking the bus into Bodmin to buy one.

Charlie wanted to know why he was being dragged around town when he could be sailing in his dinghy. Amy told him she was still feeling poorly and needed to get some stomach tablets from the druggist.

When they got back, Charlie went into the garden to hunt for insects and Amy went into the bathroom to pee on the stick.

By now her mind was filling with what-ifs and her heart was pounding. She left the test to "cook" and went into the living room to check her e-mail.

She had one e-mail. The title was "DNA test result." A stomach lurch now accompanied her racing pulse. "Omigod. Talk about perfect timing." She let out a slightly manic laugh. Here she was waiting to see if she was pregnant with baby number two, and at the same time she was about to find out if her ex-boyfriend, the father of baby number two, was also the father of baby number one. She tried to work out which test result she would rather get first. In the end she decided it didn't matter. She clicked on the e-mail and started reading. "Blah, blah blah..." She stopped and let out a long, slow breath. "Huh ... Whadda you know?"

Just then she heard the crunch of tires on gravel. Who could that be? Jerry Springer?

She looked out of the window to see Sam coming toward the house. What on earth was he doing here? How had he found her? She opened the door. "Sam! Gosh! What a surprise. How did you know where I was?"

"Bel told me." He looked anxious and determined at the same time.

"But I spoke to Bel this morning. She never said you were back."

"Maybe she thought you might try to avoid me ... Can I come in?"

"Sorry. Yes, of course." She led him toward one of the sofas. "What can I get you? Tea? Coffee? Oh, I forgot you don't like coffee. I've got hot chocolate, though. Or some rather nice elderflower cordial." It occurred to her that if he was about to fly into a rage over her behavior after the fire, he was unlikely to be placated by offers of hot and cold beverages.

"So how did you get on in Rwanda?"

"Fine. The school project is back on track, and we're on the point of buying some land to build a new hospital ... Amy, can we discuss this later? We really need to talk. Why don't you sit down."

"Okay," she said, "but first I want to apologize for calling you a manipulative bastard. It was an appalling thing to say, and I didn't mean it. Did that chap Olivier at the school give you my message?"

"He did, and thank you. But you were right to be furious. I let you down. I still can't forgive myself for not checking on Charlie. If you hadn't come back when you did, I dread to think what might have happened. I was an idiot, and I'm sorry."

"You were an idiot, but I know how these things happen. You take your eye off the ball for a second and . . ."

"Please, will you come and sit down."

She sat next to him on the sofa. He took her hand in his. "Okay, here's the thing: I love you more than I have ever loved any woman in my entire life, and I have no intention of letting you go. I want you and I want Charlie. I have behaved like a spoiled child instead of a grown man, and I am deeply ashamed of myself. Can you forgive me?"

Amy didn't speak for a few seconds. "You're serious? You really mean this?"

"With all my heart."

"Okay, then of course I forgive you, but I don't understand. Why the sea change?"

He explained that he and Jean Baptiste had spent five days traveling together in the Rwandan bush, and during that time they had spent hours discussing politics and putting the world to rights. "Eventually we got onto the genocide and his past. When I heard his story again, I felt like such a bloody fool. This man has spent most of his life walking alongside grief and loss. He remembers events so brutal and sadistic that we can't begin to imagine. He made me realize that it's all right to grieve for the father who left me but it isn't all right to carry on behaving like a needy child. He talked about how as adults we have to parent ourselves. I'm not sure quite how to go about that yet, but I'll work it out. What's more, I can see now that just because my father walked out, it doesn't automatically follow that I will do the same. I can choose to be a good father. Amy, I want the three of us to be together."

She sat letting his words sink in and thinking how long she'd waited to hear them. "I want us to be together as well." She paused, wondering how he would react to what she was about to tell him. "You haven't seen the result of the DNA test, have you?"

"No. When did it come?"

"I got an e-mail a couple of minutes ago."

He looked over at her laptop, which was on the dining room table. "So what did it say?"

"You are not Charlie's father."

"Really?" He looked like he'd been punched.

She nodded.

"I wasn't expecting that. I'd rather gotten used to the idea that I was his dad. I was even starting to think that we looked alike."

"For what it's worth," she said, "despite everything that had happened between us, I desperately wanted you to be his father. I also still happen to think that the pair of you look alike."

"So Charlie's artistic talent comes from you."

Her face broke into a smile. "I guess—not that mine amounts to much more than an ability to color-coordinate curtains and cushions." She paused. "So, do you still want to stay?"

"Of course I do. I have absolutely no intention of walking away. I want us to get married. I want to be Charlie's dad. I want us to be a family."

"Sam, look at me. Are you absolutely certain?"

"I have never been more certain of anything in my life."

"That's what you say now, but what if it all gets too much for you and after a few months you decide you want to leave?"

"I'm not naive. I'm not about to pretend I won't have my struggles, but I am committed to us. You have to believe me."

Amy nodded. "Okay," she said slowly. "I do believe you."

"Fantastic. So, now can we please have a make up kiss?"

"Not yet," she said. "There's one other thing."

"What?"

"Today is turning out to be a bit of a day for test results."

"How do you mean?"

"Stay there. Don't move."

She went upstairs to the bathroom. Half a minute later, she returned with the wand from the pregnancy testing kit. "It would appear," she said, "that I am not heading toward early menopause. And the clinic lied. You were never sterile."

"You're kidding," he said, the color draining from his face.

"I'm not. Take a look." She handed him the wand. "See, two pink stripes. I'm pregnant."

By now Amy realized that she needed to sit down. The news that she was pregnant hadn't exactly come as a surprise, but it was still a shock to have it confirmed. Dazed and a little bewildered, she lowered herself onto the sofa.

"Oh, my God. This is fantastic news," Sam said, his eyes darting with excitement.

"You really mean that?"

"Of course I mean it. I'm the happiest I've been in my entire life. Aren't you?"

"It just feels so unreal. I've dreamed about having another baby, but I never really thought it would happen."

"Well, it has."

Her face finally broke into a smile. "Omigod. It has, hasn't it?"

They fell into each other's arms, both of them laughing and crying at the same time. At one point Sam squeezed her so hard, she could hardly breathe. "I love you so much," he said.

"I love you, too."

Just then Charlie came running in. "Look, Mum, I've found a wood license." He always called wood lice "licenses." She probably shouldn't have encouraged him, but hearing it made her laugh. By then Charlie had noticed Sam.

"Hey, Sam."

"Hey, Charlie. How you doing?"

Charlie turned to his mother. "You two friends again?"

"Definitely," Amy said.

"Then why are you both crying?"

"It's okay, Charlie, they're happy tears. We're crying because we've made up." She wasn't about to blurt out to him that she was pregnant. She needed to choose her moment.

"Good. Sam, can you find some leaves for my wood license? I think he's hungry."

Sam suggested it might be kinder to put the creature on a leaf in the garden. "So," he said, "do you guys feel like coming for a drive?"

"Yay. Where to?"

Amy looked a question at Sam.

"It's a surprise," he said.

She threw up her hands. "Well, I guess a third surprise in one day can't hurt."

They set off along the coast road, Charlie listening to short stories on his Nintendo.

"Oh, God," Sam said. "In the midst of everything, I totally forgot to mention the Crema Crema Crema piece. I saw it when I got back. One of the guys at work kept a copy of *The Daily Post*. He said you've been doing all the news programs and talk shows. It's amazing. You must be so proud. To uncover a story like that and bring a nasty company down single-handed—it's quite an achievement."

"I guess, but while I was doing it, I didn't think about the outcome. I just got on with it . . . By the way, the editor of *The Daily Post* offered me a staff job."

"Congratulations. Though I can't say I'm surprised."

"I turned it down. I've decided to freelance instead, which was always my plan. The staff job would have meant leaving

Charlie for long periods while I traveled. I couldn't have done that. And now that I'm pregnant ..."

"But you're not a single parent now. If you want to change your mind about the job, I'm sure the two of us could find a way of making it work."

She reached over and kissed him. "You are such a sweetheart." She paused. "No. This feels right. Working at my own pace means I get to spend time with Charlie and the baby. I know I've made the correct decision."

By then they had been driving for twenty minutes or so. They had left the coast road a while back. As they'd traveled inland and started to climb, the countryside had become more wooded. Charlie took off his headphones and asked why it had suddenly gotten dark outside. Amy told him to look up. She explained that the tree branches on either side of the road had met, blocking some of the light. Satisfied, he went back to his stories. Amy brought up the subject of Bean Machine and asked Sam if they had gone down owing him money.

"I was lucky. Creditors are queuing up, some of them claiming hundreds of thousands. They'd paid me all they owed, save for about eight hundred quid. I won't see it, but it could have been so much worse."

He turned right into a narrow, steeply descending lane. "Two more minutes," he said.

The dense woodland gave way to a stretch of open land that sloped gently down to a sandy beach.

"Gosh, this is glorious," Amy said as they climbed out of the car. Charlie started running toward the beach. Amy told him not to go where she couldn't see him.

"You really like it?" Sam said.

"I love it."

"Brilliant, because the whole of this three-acre site is for sale. It's ours if we want it."

"Seriously?"

"Yep."

"That means you can build your house."

"*Our* house. But now I'm thinking that buying it wouldn't be our best financial move, bearing in mind we'll have to buy a family house in London and the land alone will cost me all my savings."

Amy let out a sigh. "Yeah, it's a mad idea. How can we think about a holiday home when we haven't even got a home-home?"

"I know. Let's just forget it."

"Even with both of us working, we'd be old before the house was finished."

"You're right," he said. "I don't even know why I brought you here."

"On the other hand, if we saved hard . . . and your paintings are selling well."

"Actually, I just got a call from Boris Karpenko—you know, the Russian tycoon. He wants to buy another half dozen."

"And he's sure to tell all his rich friends about you."

"I guess."

"And to save money," she said, "we could even do some of the building work ourselves. Plenty of people do. Although where we'd find the time . . ."

"You make time. And this spot is so beautiful."

"Breathtaking."

"It would be so hard to walk away."

"Almost impossible."

Neither of them spoke. They stood staring out to sea, listening to the gulls cawing and the waves crashing on the beach. Amy called out to Charlie again, reminding him to keep away from the water's edge. She turned to Sam.

"Let's do it."

"What?"

"Let's buy the land and start building a house."

"You sure?"

"Positive."

"But it'll take forever, and with so many outlays, we'll be really hard up. We'll have to cut back on luxuries."

She laughed. "No change there, then."

They were still laughing and hugging when Charlie broke in. "Did you say that you're going to build a house here?"

"One day," Sam said.

Amy turned to Charlie. "Can you imagine coming here for holidays?"

"When?"

"Oh, in a few years, maybe."

"And by then you might have a brother or sister who could come too."

"No, just me."

Amy and Sam exchanged amused glances. Having been an only child for so long, Charlie wasn't going to take kindly to the arrival of a sibling. Amy decided she would need to break the news very gently.

On the way back, Charlie fell asleep. He woke up just as Sam turned the engine off. "I'll only let you have a baby brother or sister if I can have a snake."

Amy laughed. "This child just never gives up."

"I dunno," Sam said. "It seems a reasonable request to me."

Amy's eyes widened. "What?"

They climbed out of the car. Sam led Charlie around to the back and opened the boot.

"Omigod," Amy whispered to Sam. "I cannot believe you did this. Not after me telling you how much I hate snakes."

"Here, Charlie, take this."

By now Amy had covered her face with her hands. "You rotten so and so," she cried out. "I hate you."

She peered out from between her fingers and saw Sam hand Charlie something long and thin and red.

"Mum, look."

Amy looked. Her face broke into a smile. Charlie wasn't holding a snake. He was holding a dog lead.

"Okay, what's going on?" she said to Sam.

"I bet I know," Charlie piped up. "I'm getting a dog."

"Let's go and see," Sam said.

As they walked over to the barn, Colin appeared, carrying a garden fork. It looked like he'd been doing some digging in the vegetable patch behind the barn. "I kept an eye on 'im for you, like you asked," he said to Sam. "He's a right little beauty."

The three of them went inside. Lying in a wicker dog basket on a cushion was the cutest, whitest, fluffiest, biggest-brown-eyed bichon frise puppy.

"Wow, is he for me?" Charlie said to Sam.

"All for you." He turned to Amy. "I got him from my local pet rescue center. I thought becoming adoptive parents would be more socially responsible."

"Quite right." Amy grinned. "So you had this thing planned from the beginning," she said.

"Yes, but when I arrived, I hadn't quite worked out who was going to look after the dog while I took you and Charlie to see the land. Luckily Colin showed up when he did."

Charlie picked up the puppy. It immediately began licking its new owner's face, causing Charlie to burst into fits of giggles.

"What are you going to call him?" Amy said.

"Fang; then he can be a sort of snake dog."

"Figures," Amy said, grinning. "Charlie, what do you say to Sam?"

"Thank you. This is the best present I have ever had. It's even better than when Granddad got me my football kit. Mum, can I phone Arthur later to tell him that I've got a puppy, too?"

"Why not?" Amy said. "And then I think I ought to make a few calls." She reached out and took Sam's hand. "I know you've barely met, but would you mind if I asked Zelma to be the baby's godmother? She'd like that. I think she gets lonely, and a baby would give her something to focus on."

Sam said he still remembered Zelma fussing around him,

persuading him to buy a slice of ginger cake. "She seemed like a lovely lady. I think it's a great idea."

They were walking back to the house, Charlie carrying Fang, when Amy's mobile rang.

"Amy. Roy Hargreaves. Okay. You win."

"Excuse me?"

"Look, you're a talented young woman with a great future ahead of you, and I don't intend to lose you."

"Roy, I'm flattered, but I've explained my position."

"I know. Just hear me out. I'm probably getting soft in my old age, but here's the deal: In return for working exclusively for the *Post*, you get a contract that allows you to work from home, at your own pace. All I ask is that you come in for weekly meetings and give me a minimum of six investigative pieces a year. I can't be fairer than that. What do you say?"

"I'd say fantastic and thank you, but I'll need some maternity leave."

"Why?"

She laughed. "Because I'm pregnant."

He couldn't have been exactly delighted by the news, but to his credit, he didn't let it show. "Okay, fine. Take all the time you need."

"Roy, could you just hang on a minute?"

She put her hand over the phone and explained Hargreaves's offer to Sam. He agreed with her that it sounded perfect.

Amy put the phone back to her ear. "Okay, it's a deal."

"It is? Good girl. You've done the right thing. I'll get the contract sent out this week."

"Perfect . . . and Roy, thanks again."

"Don't thank me, just come up with a few more stories like Crema Crema Crema."

Amy and Sam linked arms as they continued back to the house. "Well done," he said. "You dug in your heels and you got a result. Hargreaves is clearly desperate to get you."

"Seems like it. Now all I need to do is come up with some decent story ideas."

Back at the house, Sam opened the packet of kibble he had bought. Charlie let Fang eat off his hand and had hysterics because it tickled so much. Amy came over with a bowl of water. She placed it beside the puppy, who immediately started lapping at it. Then she sat down on the floor next to Charlie and Sam.

"So, have you got a baby in your tummy right now, this very minute?" Charlie asked.

"Actually, I have. And Sam is the baby's daddy."

Charlie became thoughtful. "I haven't got a daddy."

"Well, if it's all right with you," Sam said, "I could be your daddy as well as the baby's. But only if you want me to."

Charlie's face became a grin. His head was nodding up and down. "I do."

"And I need you to know," Amy said to Charlie, "that I love you very, very much and you will always be my special big boy. Nothing is ever going to change that." She pulled him onto her lap and kissed him.

"K," he said, wriggling off so that he could get back to Fang. "Can we go and see the pigs and the sheep later?"

Amy said they could so long as it was all right with Colin.

"Right," she said. "If there are no other matters arising, I shall make some tea and then we should think about lunch."

As she stood waiting for the kettle to boil, she became aware that she was tapping out a rhythm on the worktop and humming.

Sam came over, picked up the beat, and joined in the tune.

"What *is* the name of that song?" Amy said. "I know it's one of those 'Lady in Red,' 'You Are the Sunshine of My Life' über-cheesy numbers."

She carried on humming.

"It's not 'I Just Called to Say I Love You,' is it?"

Sam was laughing. "Nope, way more cheesy than that."

"What is it, then? Please put me out of my misery."

"It's 'We Are Family.'"

With that, he pulled her gently toward him and kissed her.

"Urgh. Kissing. Yuck," Charlie cried, burying his face in Fang.

PHOTO: JONATHAN MARGOLIS

SUE MARGOLIS was a radio reporter for fifteen years before turning to novel writing. She has also written *Forget Me Knot, Gucci Gucci Coo, Original Cyn, Breakfast at Stephanie's, Apocalipstick, Spin Cycle,* and *Neurotica*. She lives in England.